Promchanted

MORGAN MATSON

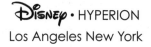
Disney • HYPERION
Los Angeles New York

First Edition, March 2024
10 9 8 7 6 5 4 3 2 1
FAC-004510-23355
Printed in the United States of America

This book is set in Adobe Caslon/Monotype
Designed by Marci Senders

Library of Congress Cataloging-in-Publication Data on file
ISBN 978-1-368-09557-0
Reinforced binding
Visit www.DisneyBooks.com

SUSTAINABLE FORESTRY INITIATIVE
Certified Sourcing
www.forests.org
SFI-01681

Logo Applies to Text Stock Only

For Diya Mishra
You are—and I cannot stress this enough—the best

IN A FARAWAY LAND LONG AGO . . . .

PART

One

One

I don't believe in fairy tales.

Or I should say, I don't believe in fairy tales *anymore*.

Because I used to. When I was younger, I firmly believed in all of it. The insta-love, the immediate connection, the happily ever after. I loved the enchanted forests, the fairies granting wishes, the mice who are somehow also great at sewing dresses, like a tiny rodent version of *Project Runway*. I loved it all—when I was little, all I needed was to hear the words *once upon a time* and I was in. I devoured all the fairy-tale movies and books like they were Skittles (in addition to devouring a lot of actual Skittles).

But in light of certain recent events that I don't have to go into right now, I've come to realize how wrong I was. And how I hadn't even understood how led astray I'd been by the stories that had always been my favorite bedtime tales, how they somehow seeped into my unconscious. And it was a harsh realization to discover that the kind of world I used to watch and read about just doesn't exist.

Because in the real world, there's no such thing as meant to be. There are no true loves riding up on white horses and *definitely* not any happily ever afters.

All of which meant, as I looked around the Harbor Cove High School gym, five hours before the prom was set to begin, I could feel myself getting increasingly irritated. Because the theme this year was *A Fairy-Tale Prom*.

And it had been taken *very* literally.

All around me were decorations showing castles, noble steeds, fairies, spinning wheels, and pumpkin carriages. There were beanstalks, towers, roses with their petals falling. Discarded slippers on palace steps, beauties and beasts, red shoes, princesses and frogs. A FROZEN MOMENT IN TIME! was printed on a banner above the photo booth, adorned with snowflakes and a very wonky-looking Olaf.

I frowned as I looked around me, then I closed my eyes for a moment and drew in a deep, cleansing breath. I was there for a reason—I had a job to do.

Okay, fine, *technically* this wasn't true. As Avery Gallo, head of the prom committee, had reminded me multiple times over the last few months, I wasn't on her committee. But I *was* junior class treasurer (I had also been freshman and sophomore class treasurer), which meant I controlled the prom budget. And good luck putting on a prom without any money. So needless to say, Avery and I had been emailing and texting a *lot* for the past four months, arguing over everything from the streamer budget to the level of DJ we could hire without dipping into the fund for the educational class trip to Sacramento. (She argued that nobody wanted to go to Sacramento. I conceded that maybe she had a point, but I certainly wasn't going to bankrupt the trip just so she could hire some DJ fresh off a Vegas residency.)

And I had fully intended to stay away today. I was planning on showing up at the gym tonight with everyone else, just a participant. I'd spent the morning getting ready—I'd gotten my nails done and my hair blown out. My best friend, Nisha Koorse, and I planned to meet at her house at three, do our last-minute preparations together, and then her girlfriend, Allyson, would meet us there so our pre-prom could begin. I'd been about to head to Nisha's when I made the mistake of looking at Avery's Instagram.

And one glance at the half-decorated gym was enough to let me know I had to get over there ASAP. Because even if I didn't *like* the decorations, I still needed them to be put up correctly.

So I'd texted Nisha and told her I had a logistics emergency. She sent me the eye-roll emoji, but I knew she wasn't really upset. We'd been friends for a long time, and she knew me better than anyone—which meant she especially knew when I wasn't going to be able to let something go. She and Allyson would meet me at the school, and then we could actually get our pre-prom plans started.

I had no doubt that Nisha and Allyson were currently taking their prom pictures together in Nisha's yard, and just the thought of it made my heart squeeze. I couldn't help thinking about the way I'd thought I'd be taking prom pictures, too—the prom night I'd expected to have, the one that didn't involve me being a third wheel with Nisha and Allyson. Until three weeks ago, I'd planned on going to the prom with Cooper Smith, my boyfriend of five months. Until three weeks ago, I'd still believed in things like love. But after a disastrous lunch at the Mermaid Café, he was no longer my boyfriend *or* my prom date. . . .

"Stella?"

I blinked, and focused on the prom committee member that was standing in front of me. Petite, blue hair, head-to-toe BTS merch, freshman . . . "Hi, Lane," I said after a moment of scrolling through my mental Rolodex. I'd always been good at recalling faces and names, which certainly came in handy when I'd been campaigning for treasurer the first two years. (This year, I actually ran unopposed. I'd like to think it was because I did such a good job, but I had a feeling it had more to do with the fact that everyone had actually realized just how much work it was.)

"Um . . ." Lane looked at my dress and then frowned at the wall clock. "Aren't you kind of . . . early?"

I looked down at myself and realized she had a point, since I was wearing my prom dress. It had a slightly off-the-shoulder neckline, a fitted waist, and a long skirt that flared out when I twirled. It hit just above my ankles (well, *now* it did—I was just a shade under five foot three, so it had to be taken up a *lot* to prevent me from tripping over it all night). The whole thing was the most gorgeous shade of light blue, and when I'd tried it on and it had fit like a glove, it felt like a sign. A sign that the prom was going to go perfectly.

Which now seemed ridiculous to have even thought.

But the pre-prom plans I had with Nisha and Allyson meant I'd had to get ready early—which was why I was the only one there currently in a prom dress, while the rest of the prom committee, who were all busy putting up decorations wrong, were in jean shorts and tank tops. I wasn't in my heels—those were in my bag, and I was going to hold off on wearing them until the last possible minute—but even if you're wearing a prom dress with sneakers, you're still wearing a prom dress. So I didn't exactly *blend*.

"Right," I said. "Um—thanks for pointing that out. I'm actually here because there's a problem."

Lane's eyes got wide as she looked around. "There is?"

"We need to rethink the whole layout if we want optimal foot-traffic flow over the course of the event."

Lane just stared at me. "What?"

"Look," I said, as I unlocked my phone to show her the diagram I'd put together in the Uber over here. I could feel my shoulders start to relax and my jaw start to loosen, the way they always did when I had a project to solve. "We need to move the balloon arch by the north doors to designate that as the entrance. We'll establish the south doors"—I pointed with two fingers, military-style, to the rear of the gym—"as the exit, and put the table with the gift bags there. We need to move the photo booth, because it's too close to the DJ's setup and people will be tripping over her cords all night. And the refreshment table is not in a central area—it's going to cause a bottleneck where it is now."

Lane looked down at my diagram, then around at the gym. "Wow. I see what you mean." She looked back at me, her brow furrowed. "How'd you know about this?"

I tried not to smile as I lowered my phone. "It's kind of the family business."

Lane's brow furrowed further. "Decorating . . . for proms?"

"No," I assured her, even though I was secretly thinking we'd actually be great at that. "Logistics."

My parents had a business they ran together, Griffin Logistics. They served as the middlemen (middle-people?) for a number of shipping

9

conglomerates. Our company was the one that figured out how to get goods and objects (and occasionally people) from one side of the world to the other. And we were the ones who got called when a shipping container had gone missing at the port of Los Angeles, or a Met Ball dress was being held up at customs at Newark airport. I'd seen them handle *everything*—and rarely panicking. Always relying on logic, executing their plans, moving smoothly into the next available action, constantly in pursuit of the most effective solution. And above all, we prized efficiency. Which was what it said on all our stationery—GRIFFIN LOGISTICS: WE PRIZE EFFICIENCY.

My parents' work meant I grew up absorbing all of this like a sponge. I was an only child, so it seemed perfectly normal to me to be brought into strategy meetings when I was still crawling around under the table. And naturally, because of this, I was also a total planner. It was in my DNA, after all. I loved a spreadsheet, a bullet-pointed list, a course of action. Which *also* meant I wasn't the best at bouncing back when my carefully laid plans failed to work out.

I flashed back for a moment to the Mermaid Café. Cooper sitting across from me, breaking up with me like it was just no big deal—like our five months together had meant nothing. He'd broken my heart and sent all my carefully constructed plans crashing down in one fell swoop. I could recall it all viscerally, like I was still there: the water beading on the outside of my glass; our waiter, whose name tag had read *Mauricio*, hovering awkwardly next to the table, his presence making my humiliation at being dumped that much worse.

"Can I see that?" Lane asked, nodding to my phone, shaking me out of these thoughts, which I welcomed. It had been one of the worst moments of my life, and I *really* didn't need to keep revisiting it.

I hesitated for just a moment. Normally, I would have had copies of the diagram printed out to give everyone, preferably laminated, but there just hadn't been time. And though I knew she needed to see it, I really didn't like being without my phone. I held on to it for just a second more, then handed it over.

"Thanks," Lane said. She signaled to some of the other prom committee members, who immediately crowded around my phone.

I saw the DJ wander past; she was wearing gigantic headphones and hauling a turntable across the gym. "Hi," I said, seeing my opportunity and deciding to seize it, hurrying to catch up with her. "Jolene?"

She glanced over at me, then frowned at my dress. "The prom doesn't start for a while."

"No, I know. Hi, I'm Stella. I've sent you some emails. . . . Just wanted to make sure you got them?"

Jolene lowered her headphones so that they were around her neck. She was a sophomore at UC Irvine, and a compromise between Avery and me. She wasn't a Vegas DJ like Avery wanted, but she also wasn't a freshman with a Spotify playlist, which I'd been advocating for. "Are you the one who's been emailing me about Band of Brothers?"

I nodded, pretending I didn't hear the judgment in her tone. "Yes!"

Band of Brothers was a boy band made up of the three Powell brothers and also their cousin, Doug, and they'd been huge when Nisha and I were in elementary school. We'd been *very* into them in grades four through six—memorizing the lyrics, writing them on our notebooks and sneakers, going to concerts whenever they were in town. And while we both pretended to be *so* over them as middle school continued, their songs had now taken on a fun nostalgia. My phone case was Band of Brothers–themed, a present from Nisha. I'd usually put one of their songs on the mixes Nisha and I sang along to as we drove around in my car, and I'd been emailing Jolene maybe a little too much to try and get a guarantee of at least two songs tonight. I wanted to see Nisha's face when the opening chords of "HeartPower" kicked in.

Jolene sighed. "I'll play *one* song."

"What if you did two as a medley? Like a mashup?" I took a breath to plead my case. "I really don't think they get their due musically. Do you know they all played their own instruments?"

"Stella?"

I turned around to see Avery, my prom-committee nemesis standing across the gym, sipping on a Trenta iced latte. I'd texted her that I was on my way, but hadn't heard back, which was sadly par for the course for Avery. "Excuse me a moment," I said to Jolene and tried not to be insulted when she visibly brightened as I walked away.

I hurried over to Avery, whose eyes went wide as she took in my outfit—she was in a sundress and flip-flops. "What are you *wearing*?"

"My prom dress," I said, picking a piece of lint off the bodice.

"You know the prom doesn't start for . . ." Avery looked at her watch and smirked at me. "Five hours, right?"

"We're pre-promming," I explained. "At Disney."

Her jaw dropped open and I felt myself smile. Despite the fact that this prom night was not the exact night that I'd planned on—there was the small difference of me not having a date—the one thing that was going to be the same, and the way I'd always dreamed it would be, was the pre-prom at Disneyland.

Harbor Cove was in Orange County, California, which meant Disneyland was only twenty minutes away in light traffic. My parents and I had moved to Harbor Cove when I was in the fourth grade. We'd been up in San Francisco before then, and even though Disneyland was just a short plane ride—or a really long car ride—away, I'd never been until we moved here.

The first time I'd gone to Disneyland had been with Nisha and her mom. Nisha and I had become fast friends, bonding over our shared hatred of dodgeball and our mutual love of the songs of Band of Brothers. That first trip, she showed me all her favorite things about the park, and I had been absolutely dazzled by it all. The rides, the costumed cast members, the feeling that I'd just stepped inside somewhere truly magical. And it was when we were wrapping up our day, and preparing to head back to the Mickey & Friends Parking Structure to find the car, that the most magical thing of all had happened.

Suddenly, I could see that in addition to people wearing their Mickey ears, jeans, and sneakers, there were teenagers who were *really* dressed up. Girls with long dresses. Guys (and some girls) in tuxedos and suits. They were suddenly walking among us, these glamorous teens. It was the coolest thing I'd ever seen, even if I didn't quite understand why it was happening. "What's going on?" I asked as we headed out of Fantasyland and toward Sleeping Beauty's castle.

"It's a tradition around here," Nisha's mom had answered as she smiled at the teenagers, running through to Frontierland in their long gowns, laughing and yelling in groups. "You go to Disneyland all dressed up. You get dinner, ride some rides, and then head to the prom. I did it when I was in high school, too. It was the best." She said it with a kind of wistful sigh, then looked at us. "Not that this isn't fun, too," she amended, glancing at her watch. "We should get going."

I followed Nisha's mother out of the park, but I turned around as often as I could to look at the teens in their formal wear, trying to fix it in my mind. One look at Nisha was enough to let me know she was as enchanted by it as I was. And that night, on the drive back to Harbor Cove in her mom's Jeep, we'd made a pact.

"We'll do that, too," Nisha had told me, looking across the backseat, her face illuminated by the passing streetlights. "When we're in high school. We'll go to Disneyland before we go to the prom."

"Yes," I'd said, nodding fervently. The whole thing—being all dressed up, being in high school, getting to go to Disneyland without a parent—seemed to hint at a much more exciting and grown-up future. And suddenly, there was nothing I wanted more. "It's a promise."

"Promise," Nisha had agreed. She'd held out her pinky, and we'd linked them together and shaken, entering into what every fourth-grader knows is a binding contract.

Over the years, Nisha and I would talk about our Disney prom. Every time we went to Disneyland—which was at least several times a year, if we were lucky—we'd add onto our plans. And then once we entered high school, it all became much more concrete. I was now making spreadsheets of places to have our pre-prom dinner, and keeping a list of the rides where having a long skirt wouldn't be an impediment.

As various crushes and relationships had come and gone, we had never really focused on that part; it was the least important aspect of our planning. Because Nisha and I both knew that the Disney part of the prom wasn't about whatever dates we would bring. It was about *us*—and keeping the promise to the fourth-grade girls we'd once been.

And until three weeks ago, I'd thought everything was going to work out perfectly. Cooper had known about my Disney plans, of course, and had been excited about going. Allyson and Nisha had been together since the end of sophomore year, and even though Allyson got motion sick on most rides (she could do Radiator Springs Racers, but that was about it) she'd promised to be the one holding our bags when we went on rides, and cheering us on from a bench with some popcorn. So I'd bought our tickets and made dinner reservations, secured Genie+ for all of us, and started planning our evening.

And even after Cooper and I broke up, and the thought of going to the prom alone made me more sad than excited, the one thing that hadn't changed was how I felt about the Disney of it all. I might not be as enthused about the prom anymore, but Nisha and I had been planning tonight for nearly a decade. And it was going to be *great*.

"That's so cool," Avery said.

I nodded, feeling myself smile. "I know, I can't wait." I looked around for my phone, then realized Lane still had it. But at least it looked like she was putting it to good use directing the rest of the prom committee members, who were currently moving the refreshment table.

"So did you get the logistics whatever sorted?" Avery asked as she looked around the gym, not making any effort to go and help. It didn't surprise me that Avery had left most of the setup to the underclassmen. She had only cared about the flashy aspects of the prom—the theme, the DJ—and hadn't seemed very interested in doing the work that went along with it.

"Yeah," I said, nodding to Lane. "It looks like it's under control."

"I thought it looked pretty good before," Avery said with a shrug. She gestured to the decorations and raised an eyebrow at me. "So? What do you think?"

I looked around at all the fairy-tale imagery—at all those promised happily ever afters—and tried not to wince. "Well," I finally replied, trying to find something positive to say, "you really leaned into the theme."

Avery threw up her hands. Before I'd gotten to know her, I had thought this was just a figure of speech. But no. Avery did it every time she got even the slightest bit irritated, like she was constantly trying to start a one-woman wave. "You knew what the theme would be, Stella," she said to me, narrowing her eyes. "Don't act surprised that my decorating committee pulled it off flawlessly."

"I just don't know why you couldn't have gone with one of the other themes. I suggested a whole bunch!"

"I know you did." Avery looked like she wanted to throw her hands up again, but maybe realized she'd just done it and that it was starting to get redundant. "I didn't even understand half of them. What was I supposed to do with *Keep Prom and Carry On?*"

I just shook my head, knowing when I was beaten. After all, the prom was in a few hours; there was no way things were going to change now.

"What is your problem with *A Fairy-Tale Prom?*"

"Because it's not real!" I burst out. "Fairy tales don't exist. We're promising all our classmates some fantasy that's never going to happen."

"Who cares if it's not real?" she asked, looking bewildered. "It's a *prom theme.* If we'd gone with *Enchantment Under the Sea*, that also wouldn't have been real. It *would* have been derivative, though."

I frowned. "Why?"

Avery let out a long sigh, like she wanted to let me know I was trying her patience. "It's from *Back to the Future!*"

"Oh," I said, nodding. "Right." I was pretty sure that I'd seen that movie at some point, but I couldn't be sure. Details of stories never seemed to stick with me. It's not that I didn't like movies, or shows, or books. I really did, whenever I was consuming them. But when I was done, the particulars just didn't stay with me, unless it was something I had to know for a class—and even then, it was gone as soon as I turned in my last final.

It was like my brain knew that it needed to save space for actual pertinent information and facts that might prove useful someday. And after all, it's not like knowing the plot of a movie had ever come in handy in a crisis.

"Well, I think you'll change your mind," Avery said. "Tonight, when you come here and it's all done, I think you'll feel differently." She nodded with the confidence of someone who'd never had their heart broken in a fast-casual restaurant.

I resisted the urge to roll my eyes. "Really?"

"Seriously," she insisted. "When the lights are on and the music is playing . . . it's going to be magical. And you'll tell me that I was right all along. You'll see."

"Uh—sorry." I looked over to see Lane standing by my side, holding my phone out. "You're getting texts."

"Thanks," I said. I took it from her just in time to see a text from NISHA 😄💕🦝 disappear off my screen. I could feel myself relax a little bit more now that the phone was back in my possession.

"I took pictures of your diagram," Lane assured me. "So we'll be able to make the changes."

"We'll take care of it," Avery assured me. Lane rolled her eyes at me quickly, and I bit back a smile—clearly, Lane knew that she and the rest of the committee members would do all the work while Avery took all the credit.

"Great," I said, giving them a nod and starting to head over to the corner of the gym where I'd stashed my stuff. "See you tonight!"

"Have fun at Disney," Avery said, the wistfulness coming through in her voice.

I nodded and gave her a wave before she could invite herself along.

Because we *did* have an extra park pass: the one Cooper wouldn't be using. And the last thing I wanted was for Avery to somehow get wind of this.

I picked up my canvas bag, the one that I'd carefully packed this morning. It was from El Arco Iris, my favorite place for tacos, and was decorated with a gigantic rainbow arching over an al pastor taco, garnished with a smiling piece of pineapple. WE'LL GUAC YOUR WORLD! was written in graffiti-style font.

The tote was filled with everything I'd need: heels, toiletry case with essentials and makeup, tiny prom bag that fit almost nothing, snacks both savory and sweet. And because I knew it could get cold once the sun went down, a sweatshirt Nisha had brought me as a souvenir when she went on an Alaskan cruise with her family. The front had a picture of blue forget-me-nots—the state flower of Alaska—and read, helpfully, FORGET ME NOT. And on the back, it just read ALASKA! in a gigantic typeface. It was one of my favorites.

I shouldered my bag and headed out of the gym, scrolling through my messages—all from Nisha, who was getting increasingly worried. Since I always texted back immediately, the fact that I'd gone briefly radio silent seemed to really concern her.

Hi! We're here!

Are you inside?

Stella?

HELLO?!

Is there a prom emergency? A promergency??
Is that why you're not answering?!

Okay, enough. I'm coming in!

Figuring it was fastest, I pulled out my phone and pressed the button to call her. "Hi," I said when Nisha answered on the first ring. "Sorry—I got held up. Heading outside now." I rounded the corner just in time to see Nisha walking toward me.

My best friend was gorgeous, with long dark hair and big eyes with unfairly long lashes. And at five foot nine, she towered over me but never seemed to need to make a big deal of the fact, which I appreciated. Too many people were always resting their elbow on my head and thinking it was *so* hilarious, or calling me pocket-size. In retaliation, I'd already decided on my senior quote for the yearbook next year. We were currently in the middle of a big unit on Shakespeare in English, and as soon as I'd read it, I knew it was the one I wanted: *Though she be but little, she is fierce.*

Nisha's height was the reason that she could pull off her prom jumpsuit: a dark-red, wide-legged number with straps that crossed in the back. Just as I'd known my dress when I'd seen it, Nisha had been stalking this jumpsuit online for months, and when it was finally on sale, she'd pounced.

"Hi!" Nisha yelled, running over to me, closing the distance between us. "You look great!"

"*You* look great!" I said as Nisha pulled me into a hug. "I'm sorry we couldn't get ready together."

"Did you get the logistics emergency fixed?"

"We did," I assured her with a laugh. Nisha always took things a little easier than I did. If I was the planner, she was very go-with-the-flow. We balanced each other out; we had from the beginning. It was one of the million reasons we were best friends. "You'll see it tonight."

Nisha clapped her hands together. "I can't wait! It's going to be so fun."

We started to walk down the hall together, but before we reached the main doors, I stopped. I knew it was my last chance to ask this question, before we were with Allyson for the rest of the night. "Is it really okay?" I asked, hearing my voice come out small and a little bit scared—the way I usually tried hard to make sure it never sounded.

Nisha frowned. She tilted her head to the side, her gold nose stud catching the light. "Is what okay? Your dress? It's fantastic!"

"No," I said, shaking my head. "But thanks for that. I mean . . . me tagging along with you and Allyson tonight. Being your third wheel." I made myself get the words out, expressing the nagging worry I'd been having ever since Nisha had assured me that even though I was no longer going with Cooper, nothing in our prom plans needed to change.

"Hey," she said, shaking her head. "Don't even think that."

"I really don't want to get in the way—"

"We're stopping this line of thought right here," Nisha said firmly. "Tonight is *our* Disney prom. We've been looking forward to it forever. And some jerk named Cooper doesn't get to change that."

I nodded, feeling my heart unclench a little. "You're right."

"And also . . ." I could see Nisha was fidgeting with her bracelets, the way she always did when she was stalling.

"What? What's going on?"

"Okay, fine. But don't get mad."

"How can I promise that if I don't know what I might get mad about?"

"So, Allyson kind of invited someone to take the extra Disney ticket," she said, very fast.

I just stared at her. "Who? *Nisha.* Who?!"

"It's Allyson's new neighbor, Reece," Nisha said glancing toward the doors. "He just moved to town, and he doesn't know many people. He and Allyson got to talking one day, and he got really excited when she mentioned Disneyland. He's been going through kind of a rough time. He just lost his job!"

"Is this a setup?" I asked, feeling my face get hot. "Are you trying to foist someone on me?"

"No," Nisha said firmly. "Nobody's foisting. He's just new in town and wants to come to Disney. And I would have mentioned it before, but it was up in the air about whether he could come or not until this afternoon."

I nodded, feeling myself start to calm down a little bit, now that I no longer had to worry it was some kind of romantic plot. "This wasn't in my plans," I grumbled, and Nisha threw her head back and laughed.

"You'll have to update your spreadsheet."

"I know you think you're joking, but I *will.*"

"Come on," she said, threading her arm through mine. "Let's go have the best night ever."

She pushed the door open and we stepped out into the late-afternoon sunshine. As we walked down the front steps of the high school, I pulled my bag over my shoulder and tried to tell myself that it would be okay. Just because things weren't going exactly according to my plans didn't mean I needed to lose my mind. And Nisha and I would get to be at Disneyland together before the prom just like we'd always planned on. Maybe this would all be okay.

I saw Allyson standing next to her gold Prius, looking beyond chic in a tuxedo with the bowtie untied and draped around her neck. She waved at me, and I waved and smiled back—but then felt my smile freeze on my face as I registered the guy standing next to her.

He was around Nisha's height, wearing jeans, sneakers, and a white T-shirt with a gray Mickey hoodie over it.

He had golden-brown hair, brown eyes, and dark thick eyebrows. He was actually incredibly cute, but I couldn't even really take that in right now.

Because he was, unfortunately, someone I knew all too well.

I could see he recognized me, too, a dawning realization transforming his expression from benign politeness to shock.

We stared at each other for a moment, and then we spoke at the same time. "*You!*"

Two

I stared at the guy across from me, not able to quite believe what was happening.

Because this was *Mauricio*, the waiter at the Mermaid Café who had been witness to my horrible breakup. What was he doing here?

"You two know each other?" Allyson asked brightly, either not picking up on or choosing to ignore the vibes.

"Well—" I started, at the exact same moment that he said flatly, "No. We don't."

I frowned at him, and to my surprise, he frowned right back at me—which I really didn't get. Why was he mad at *me*? I was the one who had the right to be upset with *him*. He, after all, was the one who had made a terrible breakup so much worse. It was the most embarrassed I'd *ever* been. And even though I knew it wasn't logical—much as it pained me to admit that—I couldn't help but somehow feel that if he hadn't been there, with all his interruptions, things might have turned out differently.

It had been a different Saturday, exactly three weeks ago. And as I'd headed to the Mermaid Café, I'd been sure that it was going to be one of the best days of my life. Cooper had asked me a week earlier if I'd wanted to go to lunch, because he had something important to talk to me about. Right away, I'd known what that meant: I was about to be on the receiving end of a promposal. What else could it be?

It wasn't that I really *needed* a promposal—after all, Cooper and I had been together for five months now. It was just understood that we'd be going to the prom together, and I'd already gotten our Disney reservations. But as soon as he asked me to lunch, I realized, all at once, that I *didn't* just want this to be something that was understood. I wouldn't have admitted it to Nisha—she had a theory about how promposals reinforced the gender binary and, also somehow, the wedding industrial complex?—but as soon as it was a possibility, I wanted it. I wanted a grand, sweeping fairy-tale gesture.

And the fact that Cooper had picked the Mermaid Café only seemed to underscore that he was going to ask me. After all, it was the place that we'd had our first date, just the two of us, not in a group with his friends or my friends or our mutual Model UN acquaintances. So I'd known, even without him having to say it explicitly, that something exciting was about to happen.

I'd dressed up for the occasion—a new white dress that I hadn't even worn yet, but that I knew would look perfect in pictures. I wore my favorite white sneakers, and my monogrammed SG (for Stella Griffin) bag. Before I'd left, I'd given myself a last look in the mirror and had been happy with what I'd been able to achieve. I'd blown out my reddish-brown hair so that it hung long over my shoulders. I'd spent longer than usual on my makeup, so I looked a *little* more done up than I usually liked. . . . But I figured it would just help the pictures look good.

Cooper had said we should meet at the restaurant, which I was a little surprised about. I guess I'd just thought that if he was taking me to lunch to prompose to me, he'd want to pick me up? Or I would have been happy to pick him up—we had a carbon footprint to think about, after all. But I decided not to press it, and I figured that there might be something really technical he had to set up and get ready. After all, some of the promposals I'd seen got truly elaborate; when Elliott Franklin proposed to Josh Kang, it had involved fireworks and choreography and a trained falcon who turned out to be not so trained after all.

As soon as we'd taken our seats out on the patio of the Mermaid Café, I could tell that Cooper was nervous. Sweat was beading on his temples, and he kept cracking his knuckles. I wanted to tell him that he didn't need to be nervous—of course I was going to say yes—but I refrained, just smiling at him and picking up my menu.

"So. Stella," Cooper said, taking a big breath. "There's something I wanted to talk to you about."

I'd set my menu down and looked across the table at him, mentally preparing myself for one of my most important moments. "Yes?"

Cooper took a breath, but before he could speak, there was someone at the side of the table, setting down water glasses. "Hi, I'm Mauricio," the waiter said. "What can I get you? Something to drink?"

"Iced tea, please," I said immediately.

Cooper shook his head. "Nothing."

"Really?" I asked, surprised. "You don't want a Dr Pepper?" After all, as he'd told me on our first date, the whole reason we were even at the Mermaid Café was that it was one of the few restaurants in town that had Dr Pepper on tap. Cooper refused to drink any other kind of soda, and always seemed annoyed when places didn't have it, even though I kept pointing out to him that it was not a very normal soda for most restaurants to have. I wasn't going into restaurants and then refusing to eat at them if they didn't have cream soda, or diet Fanta, or whatever. But at any rate, after we'd been together a few months and I'd realized this was going to be a thing, I'd made him a spreadsheet of all the restaurants in town that had it.

"Um—sure," Cooper said. "Dr Pepper."

"Thanks," I'd said, smiling at the waiter. He smiled back, politely, and I noticed that he looked around our age. He was cute, too—not that I was interested. After all, I had a boyfriend and was about to be promposed to. But some things are just objective truths.

And the truth was, he was *very* attractive, with his tawny curls falling over his forehead. He even somehow managed to make the Mermaid Café uniform—jeans and an aqua-colored button-down—look good and not ridiculous. I didn't recognize him, but that didn't mean much. Harbor Cove High was *big*, over a thousand kids, so it was quite possible that we were in school together and had just never met before.

The waiter, Mauricio, disappeared, and I turned back to Cooper. I tried to subtly look around for promposal signs—a hiding videographer or balloons ready to drop or someone to supervise the pyrotechnics, but it seemed like the normal lunchtime crowd. Which was fine.

"You were saying?" I asked Cooper with a smile. My perfect relationship was now going to have a perfect promposal. I hoped there *was* a videographer somewhere, just so we could get the moment captured.

"Right." He nodded a few times, then swallowed hard. "I think we need to . . ."

I closed my eyes, getting ready for the words to wash over me.

". . . break up."

My eyes flew open and I stared at Cooper across the table. I blinked at him, wondering if there was any way I could have misunderstood this, but there didn't seem to be anything to misinterpret. I gripped the side of the table just for something to hold on to; it felt like the world was spinning off its axis. "You . . . What?"

"Bread?" Mauricio was back, hovering by the table holding a napkin-covered basket.

"Thanks," Cooper said, reaching for it and sending a dagger into my heart. He could think about sourdough at a time like this?

"You want to *break up*?" I asked, my voice rising.

"Oh," Mauricio said. He stepped back, taking the bread basket with him. "Um . . . I'll come back." He turned to go.

"I think it's for the best," Cooper said, and I could feel tears start to prick at the underside of my eyelids.

"How can it be for the best?" I asked, my voice shaking slightly. I was suddenly aware that Mauricio was *still there*, hovering with his bread basket.

"Uh . . . sorry," he said. He placed it down on the table between us. "I wasn't sure if . . ."

"Thanks," I snapped, then regretted it a second later. Rationally, I knew this wasn't his fault, and that he was just trying to do his job. But the more he was there, the more I was aware of the fact that someone was observing a very personal—not to mention embarrassing—moment for me.

"Did you guys . . . um . . ." Mauricio looked behind him, where I could see an angry-looking older guy—he was wearing the Mermaid Café uniform, but with a trident-printed tie—frowning at him. Mauricio took a breath and closed his eyes, like he was pained by what he was about to say. "Need more time?"

I just stared at him, incredulous. He expected me to make decisions about burgers versus wraps when my heart had just shattered on the ground?

"We need some more time," Cooper said, and Mauricio nodded, then practically ran away from us.

"This doesn't make any sense," I said, leaning across the table toward the person who, only seconds ago, had been my boyfriend. I was clinging on to logic, and hoping to pull him back with me to a world where things were still rational. "You can't just decide this without me!" A second later, though, I realized that of course he could. That was how breakups worked. I just never thought that *we'd* be having one. I shook my head, feeling increasingly unsteady. "We have to talk about it. Where is this coming from? Everything is great!"

"It's really not," Cooper said, like it was an obvious fact I should be aware of, and not an earth-shattering revelation. "I don't think you really like . . . me. I think you like the idea of us more than the reality."

"That's ridiculous." I tried to push this away, label it as absurd—but suddenly, examples were starting to creep in. The way I'd always tell my good news or complain about my bad days to Nisha, not Cooper. The way that we never seemed to have *that* much to say to each other. But that was just proof our connection went beyond words, right? "We can't just end things. It's not in my—"

"Plan?" Cooper finished for me, sounding irritated. "You always try and control everything, Stella! And that doesn't work with people like it does with suitcases or whatever."

I shook my head, trying not to be annoyed that, after all this time, he still didn't seem to understand what my parents did. "We need to have a discussion," I said, trying to sound calm and rational.

But Cooper shook his head. "I'm sorry," he said, finality in his voice. It was the same way he sounded when he'd told me we'd have to leave yet another restaurant because they didn't have "the Peps."

"But . . ." I felt lost, like I was without a road map—and I *loved* a road map. It was hitting me, all at once, that I'd never prepared for this possibility. I had thought we were living our own version of a fairy tale. And in all those stories, once people were together, they were happy. They didn't get dumped out of the blue at an outdoor restaurant on a random Saturday.

Suddenly, all the plans that I'd made that included Cooper—that assumed there would be an *us*—flashed through my mind, taunting me with everything I'd thought would be happening. And worst of all, there was the spreadsheet I'd been working on the hardest. The one for the event that was basically around the corner. "What about the prom?"

"I'll Venmo you for the Disney pass." Even as he said it, Cooper was pushing back his chair and pulling out his wallet.

He put a twenty in the middle of the table, and I stared at it like I'd never seen currency before. But it kind of felt like that—like I was suddenly adrift, not sure what was happening or which way was up. He was just leaving? Just like that?

"Um, your iced tea is on me. I really think we'll both be happier like this, Stella."

I just looked at him, wondering what the chances were that maybe this was just a really realistic and terrible dream, one that I was going to wake up from at any moment. But deep down, I knew the truth. This was real. This was happening.

"Um . . ." Cooper looked at me, stuck his hands in his pockets and shrugged. "Bye?" he said, then hurried out through the restaurant. I watched him go, then just sat there for a moment.

It felt like I was on the verge of tears, which was something I really didn't want to be in the middle of a restaurant. I took a shaking breath and realized that I didn't have to stay there. The twenty dollars would more than pay for the beverages we wouldn't be drinking. And all at once, I needed to get out of the Mermaid Café. I wanted to go find Nisha, and tell her what happened, preferably over some ice cream.

I pushed my chair back and turned to go—and crashed into someone. A second later, I realized that it was Mauricio. And that he'd been holding our drinks.

I stared down at my white dress—my *new* white dress. It was now covered in iced tea and Dr Pepper, the brown stains already sinking in. And that was it: the last straw. I burst into tears.

And the fact that I was crying in front of this waiter who'd already seen me get dumped was making everything that much worse.

"Oh no," Mauricio was saying. He held out some napkins to me, even though I think it was clear to both of us that this was beyond the help of a napkin. "I'm so sorry. I—"

"Suarez!" the angry-looking guy in the tie barked from across the room, motioning toward him. Mauricio swallowed hard, then turned around and walked across the restaurant.

I ran out, got in my car, and drove straight to Nisha's, and that was the last time I'd seen—or thought I would ever see—Mauricio.

Until right now.

Nisha looked between the two of us and frowned. "Wait—so *do* you know each other? That was super confusing."

"Yeah," Allyson said, looking equally perplexed. "Reece and his dad just moved to town. How did you guys meet?"

"We didn't," Reece said shortly.

"Well, we were never, like, formally introduced," I countered, resisting the urge to glare at him. "But we have *interacted*."

He shook his head at that.

"We met because he was our waiter at the Mermaid Café," I explained. "You know. The last time I went there with Cooper." I widened my eyes at Nisha so that she'd understand what I meant. Then I thought of something and turned back to him, confused. "But Nisha said your name was Reece? At the restaurant, you said it was Mauricio?"

"I go by Reece," he said shortly. "Mauricio's my real name, but nobody who knows me calls me that."

"Oh, so you were the waiter when Stella got dumped?" Allyson asked, then clapped her hand over her mouth. "I mean . . . um . . ."

"Stella here is the reason I got fired," Mauricio—Reece—said, glaring at me as he folded his arms over his Mickey hoodie.

"I— What?" I demanded, now totally lost. "How did I do that?"

"Well, when you ran into me—"

"Excuse me, I think you ran into *me*—"

"And then started crying when the drinks spilled—"

"On me," I said, feeling like something was getting lost here. "The drinks you spilled *on me* and on my new white dress."

"Anyway, when my manager saw how upset you were, he assumed it was my fault and fired me on the spot."

"But I didn't have anything to do with that," I protested, even as I could feel my guilt start to bubble up. "And I'm sorry if I *cried*; I'd just been dumped. I was going through the worst thing that had ever happened to me."

Reece raised a skeptical eyebrow. "That's the worst thing that ever happened to you?" he asked. He let out a short laugh—the kind without any humor in it. *"Seriously?"*

All my feelings of guilt suddenly disappeared, immediately replaced by anger. I narrowed my eyes at him. "Listen—"

"Okay!" Allyson clapped her hands together and we both quieted down. She was a camp counselor during the summers, and whenever Nisha and I were having a giggle fit or acting particularly unruly, Allyson would revert back to counselor mode. We knew we were really far gone if she had to break out the quiet coyote. "We need to get moving if we're going to have enough time in the park. So why don't we continue this"—she looked from me to Reece, like she was trying to find the right word—"discussion in the car?"

"Sure," Reece said. His voice was extra conciliatory, like he was showing just how mature he could be.

"Absolutely," I replied, my tone matching his. We leveled a gaze at each other, then he shook his head. He climbed into the backseat of Allyson's gold Prius, as Allyson got behind the wheel.

Nisha turned to me, looking like she was on the verge of cracking up. "So this is fun!"

"Oh my god," I said, widening my eyes at her.

"I know," she said quickly. "But it'll be fine."

"Reece isn't going to the prom with us, is he?"

Nisha shook her head. "Dressed like that? No way."

"The last thing I wanted was another reminder of Cooper. And now I'm stuck with our waiter."

"Disney isn't about Cooper," Nisha reminded me. "It was our plan long before you even met him. It's about us. Remember?"

I nodded. "You're right."

"And hey," Nisha said, nudging my arm. "At least this way, you don't have to worry about being a third wheel, right?"

"Nisha."

"Sorry. Too soon?"

I laughed at that, and she smiled at me as she got into the shotgun seat. After one more moment to try and get my head around this, I opened the door to the backseat and got in.

Reece was sitting across the seat from me, a black backpack between his feet. I buckled my seat belt and looked pointedly out the window, trying not to notice that we were in much closer proximity than I'd been anticipating.

Backseats always seemed really big until you were in one sitting next to a cute guy. Even if he *was* incredibly annoying.

I took a breath, trying to get my head around just how many of my plans had been upended. But one of the core tenets of being a logistics and efficiency expert is being able to assess a changing situation. You have to salvage what you can of previous plans, and have the flexibility and forti-tude to pivot as necessary.

Which I could also totally do! You know. In theory.

"Okay!" Allyson said as she started the car. At least, I assume she did. It was hard to tell with a hybrid, but at any rate, she shifted the car into drive and looked back at us. I could see that she and Nisha were already holding hands, resting on the console between them. Which was *really* sweet, but I also hoped that they'd stop doing this once we made it to the freeway. I was all for romance, but I preferred a driver have both hands on the wheel for vehicular safety.

"Disneyland!" Nisha enthused, and leaned over to kiss Allyson on the cheek.

"Happiest place on Earth," I agreed, and I could feel myself start to smile. Who cared about Cooper, or terrible prom themes, or cute former waiters bearing grudges? We were off to my favorite place, with my favorite person, and I was wearing the dress of my dreams. We were going to have our Disney prom night, and *nothing* was going to get in the way of that. Nisha turned back to look at me, and I grinned. "Let's do it."

Three

"Okay, we're in Goofy," Allyson said, getting out of the car in the Mickey & Friends Parking Structure. "Who's going to remember that?"

"I'm on it," I said. I climbed out of the car and took my phone out of my canvas bag to snap a picture. Then I dropped it back into my bag, and shook the wrinkles from my long skirt. I saw a little girl, two cars down from us, getting into a minivan. Her eyes widened when she saw us all dressed up, looking as dazzled as I'd been back in fourth grade. I waved at her, then turned back to my bag, making sure that I had everything I needed.

I was leaving my prom heels behind, along with my tiny useless prom bag. What was left were all the things I'd need for a Disney trip: phone, toiletry bag, sweatshirt, snacks.

Reece got out of the car, too, lifting out his black backpack. Needless to say, the ride over had not been filled with easy conversation and sparkling repartee. He answered all of Allyson's questions politely, but wasn't giving out a ton of personal information. All I'd really learned was that he'd moved here from Connecticut last month, and that he did, in fact, go to Harbor Cove High. None of us had classes with him, but he was a junior like Nisha and me, not a senior like Allyson.

"So what's on your list?" I asked as he slung his backpack over his shoulders—but not before I saw he had a paperback in the back pocket of his jeans. I fought against the urge to roll my eyes. Who brings a *book* to Disneyland? It was one thing to have e-books on your phone, but an actual physical book? Where exactly was he planning on reading it, in the Tiki Room?

We started to walk across the parking structure toward the escalators. They would take us down to the ground level, where we'd go through security, then get the tram that would take us to the park. I'd never minded the stages you went through to get into Disneyland—on the contrary, I actually liked them. There was something nice about riding in the tram with a bunch of strangers united by a common purpose: everyone heading to Disney, everyone excited about it. All the steps you took to get there helped build anticipation, so that by the time you were walking into the park, you were practically giddy.

"My list?" Reece echoed, turning back to look up at me—I was one step up from him on the escalator. I couldn't help notice that his tone was noticeably cooler when he spoke to me than when he'd been talking to

Allyson or Nisha. In fairness, neither of them had set in motion a chain of events that had led to him losing his job. But still.

"For Disneyland!" I waved my phone at him, and then realized that it didn't actually explain anything unless you knew me. I unlocked my phone and opened up my spreadsheet app, and felt immediately soothed. An organized plan with everything in columns and rows . . . Was there anything better? "I have our schedule all mapped out," I said, turning the phone so he could see. "This way, we can try and get to as many people's favorite rides as possible, with notes about nearby snack and restroom options."

"Our Stella is nothing if not organized," Nisha said, giving me a smile as she and Allyson stepped off the escalator. We all walked over to the security checkpoint—a bag check and metal detectors—and when we were all cleared, we joined the groups waiting for the tram.

Even though it was after four, there were still lots of people lining up to go to the park. Families in matching shirts, groups of friends with mouse ears, couples taking selfies. I could see a smattering of other people in formal wear, and I exchanged a nod with a girl in a long pink dress. I didn't recognize her, but I knew a bunch of Orange County schools all had their proms tonight. I also saw a couple holding hands; she was wearing Princess Leia mouse ears, and he was wearing Darth Vader. After trying for a minute to figure out just how *that* worked, I gave up and turned back to Reece, realizing I still hadn't gotten an answer to my question.

"So?" I prompted, finger poised over my phone's keyboard. "What is the ride that you absolutely, one hundred percent can't miss?" I wasn't sure we'd be able to get it into the schedule, but I at least wanted to try to get in *some* of his favorites.

"I . . . don't know," Reece said, shifting his weight from foot to foot.

"It can be hard to pick," Allyson agreed sympathetically.

"No, I mean . . ." Reece shook his head. "I've never been to Disneyland before."

I gasped, and so did the crowd around us. Reece's face flushed a dark red. "I'm from Connecticut, okay?" he muttered, a little more quietly. "They don't have a Disney Park there."

Just as he said this, the tram pulled up, discharging the passengers who were leaving the park, heading back to their cars and their regular, non-magic lives. They looked dazed and sunburned and happy, the way you should look when you've just spent a day at Disneyland. Parents carried sleeping children or, alternately, tried to wrangle children who'd clearly had far too much sugar. People were laughing and talking, looking through their pictures, and everyone was laden with souvenirs.

"Well, it's an opportunity," I said to Reece, trying to push past my shock and look on the bright side. I remembered just how dazzled I'd been when, six years ago, I'd seen Disneyland for the first time. Despite the fact that he hadn't exactly endeared himself to me, I did want Reece to have that same experience.

We climbed onto the tram, taking up one row: Allyson, then Nisha, me, and Reece. "Should we try and get him a *first visit* button?" I asked Nisha.

Reece sighed. "I'm right here," he pointed out.

I had the urge to roll my eyes again. "Okay," I said, turning to him. "Should we try and get you a first visit button?"

"No," he said shortly.

I gave Nisha a *Can you believe this guy?!* look, but she just grinned at me. "All right," I said, as I searched back through my Disney spreadsheets.

I selected the one marked *Newbies* and opened it up. "Okay," I said, taking a breath as I looked through it. "Ideally, for your first time at Disney, we should have at least ten hours and a plan for how to use the Lightning Lanes, but let me see what I can do."

Reece waved this off. "I'll be okay. Don't worry about me."

I frowned. "But—"

"I can do my own thing. I don't want to mess up your plans."

And half an hour ago, that would have been just what I would have wanted to hear—that this Disney prom interloper would not be standing in the way of a meticulously crafted schedule. But now that he was turning away my hard-won advice, I was getting increasingly annoyed. "Look," I said, trying to keep what I was feeling from coming out in my voice, "we've been to Disney a lot. I mean, I'm practically an expert. And I can help you get the best experience."

Reece scoffed. "You can't *control* the kind of experience someone has."

"Um, yes you can." My parents' entire business model was predicated on this; it was practically a Griffin family motto. I waved my phone at him again. "That's why there's a spreadsheet!"

"Okay," Allyson said in her best camp counselor voice, "maybe we split the difference. Reece can do his own thing when he wants, but join in when we do some of our favorites. Sound good?"

I looked out the open side of the tram; we were rounding the corner, getting close to the drop-off point by Downtown Disney, with the shops and restaurants. But mostly what it meant was that we were almost there. And I didn't want to walk into Disneyland fighting. "Sounds good," I said, giving Allyson a nod.

"And here we are, folks!" the tram conductor announced. "Please take all your belongings, not to mention your children, with you when you leave. It looks like some of you are pretty dressed up—I think maybe there's a prom tonight?"

A *woo-hoo!* rose up from the other group of dressed-up kids, and I looked at Nisha and laughed. "Well, then, enjoy your prom. And have a magical day!"

We all got off the tram and started walking across the plaza. You didn't have to travel very far before you had a choice of which park to go to—Disneyland or California Adventure. We usually started in California Adventure, but since that was where our dinner reservations were, we'd decided to start with the main park tonight. And as we walked toward the ticket-takers, and I saw that Reece's jaw was hanging open, I was glad that we were doing it in this order. California Adventure was great, but for someone's first Disney experience, you need the real thing. The walk down Main Street, that first glimpse of the castle. It was a necessity.

We had our tickets scanned and our pictures taken, and then we pushed through the turnstiles and there it was.

Disneyland.

As ever, it didn't seem quite real, like it was a place I actually got to go to. The monorail zooming by, the flowers in the shape of mouse ears, the smiling cast members, everyone around you thrilled to be there.

We passed under the bridge that the Monorail ran over, and as ever, I smiled at the plaque there: HERE YOU LEAVE TODAY AND ENTER THE WORLD OF YESTERDAY, TOMORROW AND FANTASY. It had always felt like the best kind of promise—the last sign before you crossed from the regular world into something much more special.

We started our walk down Main Street, and suddenly the fact that I was here, in my prom dress, made me want to twirl. I pulled Nisha into a spontaneous side-hug, and she hugged me back.

"We did it," she said, her eyes sparkling.

"We did."

She held out her pinky to me, and we shook. "Our fourth-grade selves would be so proud."

"And that we're here together." That seemed somehow like the most miraculous thing of all. Because even though I wasn't super excited about the prom anymore, that didn't matter. What mattered was that we'd sustained our friendship over all those years, through the rocky shoals of middle school, and come out the other side, still best friends. Even after that sixth-grade fight about which Band of Brothers song was the best. In the end, we'd done it. "Hold on," I said. I pulled out my phone and Nisha bent down—her cross to bear when her best friend was six inches shorter—so that we could be in the frame together. We grinned, and I snapped the picture.

"Perfect," Nisha declared as she looked at it. "Send it to me?"

"Already sent."

"You're the best."

We started walking again, and I noticed people pointing toward us and smiling. I wasn't sure if they knew about the prom tradition, or if they just thought we wanted to go to Disneyland in formal wear, but either way, I smiled back. "Okay," I said, turning to Reece, who was looking around like he was taking it all in, snapping pictures of everything. "So. The park was founded in 1954—"

"1955," he responded shortly.

I gave him a pitying look. "I'm the Disney expert, remember? I think I know when it was opened."

"It's 1955," he said with an annoying confident tone. "July, to be exact."

"I don't think so," I said, pulling out my phone. "It's . . ." A second later, my Google search revealed that Reece was right. "Oh."

"What was that you were saying about being an expert?" Reece asked. He grinned at me as he tucked his thumbs under his backpack straps.

"Okay, so I got a year wrong," I said, trying not to show just how rattled I was. And how did Reece know? He'd never even been here! "It doesn't matter anyway," I huffed, as I walked away.

"You okay?" Nisha asked as she fell into step with me.

"Why wouldn't I be?" I faked a smile, but then a second later, it turned into a real one as I looked around. "We're at Disneyland."

Main Street was pretty crowded—it looked like people were already staking out their spots for the parade. As we walked, we passed shops and the ice cream parlor and the theater and the Starbucks I always liked to hit before heading home. I could see kids running around waving bubble wands joyfully, clearly living their best lives.

As the castle came into view, I drew in a breath, like I had done from the first time I'd seen it. There was just no other appropriate reaction, really. Because there in front of you, just across a bridge, was a fairy-tale castle.

Its gray bricks gave way to the pink-and-blue turrets of the castle, its one tall tower rising up, and everything edged in gold. In all the time I'd been here, it had never stopped being magical. I may not have been the biggest fan of fairy tales these days, but even I had to admit that walking up to a castle, in the most elegant dress I'd ever worn, felt really special.

I looked over to see Reece and Allyson had caught up with us. Nisha stretched out her hand for Allyson's, and they linked them together. I saw that Reece was looking at Sleeping Beauty's castle, his jaw hanging open. "Wow."

I smiled. "I know."

He lifted his phone and started snapping pictures from every possible angle as we approached. As we walked over the bridge, I could see that there were swans and ducks swimming in the moat. A white swan was ruffling its feathers in a way that could only be described as haughty, like it thought it was swimming in front of an actual castle and not just a reproduction.

We crossed under the gold-painted arch, with the spiked gate, and walked through the passage made of pink, purple, and light-gray stone, with its columns and large, wrought-iron lights. It was darker inside the castle passageway, which meant that when you stepped through to the other side, you were back in the sunshine, and there was the carousel, and you were in Fantasyland.

"Wait," Reece said once we were through. He lowered his phone and looked around, squinting in the fading late-afternoon sunshine. "That's it? We can't go in?"

"You can," I said quickly, glad that I knew something about Disney that he didn't.

"But we don't usually," Nisha said with a shrug. We exchanged a look, and I could tell that she was trying to work out the same thing I was—if we'd actually ever done it.

I was pretty sure I must have, at some point, but a while ago, and nothing about it had really stuck with me. Mostly, what I knew was that Sleeping Beauty Castle wasn't a ride. I was also pretty sure I'd seen the movie at some point, but even that was pretty fuzzy, to be honest. I knew the most basic outline—good fairies, hidden princess, soporific spinning wheels—but that was it.

"Can we do it?" Reece asked, looking up at the castle. His whole face was alight, and expectant, and I was shocked by how different he looked now that he was smiling. He was *really* cute—which I'd known before, of course. But now it was just *so* obvious that I could feel my face get hot. Reece looked directly at me, and I looked away quickly, worried that he'd somehow be able to read these thoughts.

"Sure," Allyson said easily, then glanced over at me. "If it's okay with our schedule?"

"It's fine," I said automatically, secretly glad for the opportunity to unlock my phone and keep my face averted as I looked through our color-coded itinerary. "As long as we do it fast, we should be okay. We have to be at Indiana Jones in fifteen minutes." Nisha gave me a mock salute and headed to the entrance.

I was about to follow, but then I turned my head to the right and a picture caught my eye. It was on the wall underneath a wrought-iron lantern with the bulb inside flickering like it was candlelight. It depicted the very end of the story. The prince—I forgot his name—was leaning over to give Princess Aurora the kiss that would wake her up, as the three good fairies looked on.

I could see Nisha, Allyson, and Reece all disappearing inside, but I stayed just a moment longer and took a step closer to the painting. FROM THIS SLUMBER / SHE SHALL WAKE / WHEN TRUE LOVE'S KISS / THE SPELL SHALL BREAK. was written on it. Those words rattled around in my head for a moment, and I couldn't help but think that it was interesting that *this* had been the picture that had been chosen—not the moment of the kiss itself or the happy ending, but the liminal moment, suspended in the second in between. It was capturing the moment right before everything would change. I looked at it for a second longer, then realized I should probably catch up with my friends, and hurried over to the door that would lead me inside Sleeping Beauty's castle.

It was cooler inside—like you were walking into a real medieval castle, and not just one built to look like it. Inside, the movie's soundtrack played. There were copies of the storybook behind glass, lit up, the pages illuminated as they told the tale of *Sleeping Beauty*. Under flickering "candlelight" from iron chandeliers, as I read, I got reacquainted with the story: the infant princess, Maleficent crashing her christening, the three good fairies who try and do damage control, amending the curse so that if Aurora touches a spinning wheel she'll just fall into a dreamless sleep, but not die, and then can be magically reawakened by true love's kiss. How the king ordered all the spinning wheels in the kingdom burned. This undoubtedly struck a blow to the wool and cloth industry, and probably upended some international trade routes, but the story didn't seem to go into that, much to my dismay.

I climbed the stairs, hoping I hadn't totally lost my friends—but then saw Reece and realized I probably needn't have worried. He was taking pictures of *everything*. Every display and part of the castle. He was spending so much time documenting that I saw Nisha and Allyson already walking ahead, up the stairs to the next display.

"So you're really into *Sleeping Beauty*?" I asked after Reece had taken about a hundred pictures of one of the displays showing Aurora, asleep on the ground after touching the spinning wheel while Maleficent looked on happily, her raven perched on her shoulder.

"Well—kind of?" Reece said, surprising me—I'd mostly meant it as a joke. He put his phone in his non-book back pocket. "It's my little sister's favorite movie. So I've watched it a lot, because it's basically the only thing she ever wants to see. She'd never forgive me if she knew I was here and hadn't taken a ton of pictures for her." He gave me a slightly embarrassed smile.

"Well, you'll have to bring her along next time," I said as we walked up the stone steps into the next display room. "It sounds like she'd love it." I looked back at him with a smile, but then it faltered as I saw his face was no longer open and happy. It was closed off and shut down, his smile totally gone.

"Yeah," he said, his voice flat. "Maybe." He turned away to take in a display, and I just stood there for a moment, wondering what had happened.

I walked through the Corridor of Goons, appreciating how even the EXIT signs were written in a medieval-looking font. There were two little kids in front of the iron door, and one of them reached out to touch the door knocker, then both shrieked happily and jumped back when the door started to bang and rattle.

I turned to point this out to Reece—mostly because I had a feeling it was a Disney secret he didn't know—but saw that a couple was asking him to take their picture. "Sure," I heard him say as he rested his own phone on top of one of the displays with the storybooks in them and turned to the couple.

I made my way down the stairs, all the way through the story's happy ending, and felt more than ready to get out of there. The feelings that had been with me in the gym had started to resurface. *This* was why I had fought so hard against our prom theme—this pull to have everything neatly bundled into a story in which the only ending was a happy one. When I knew from experience that the reality was very different. And that if you expect everything to work out—if you expected a fairy-tale ending—you'd only be disappointed when it didn't happen.

I stepped outside, into the sunshine, and saw Nisha and Allyson were waiting. "Okay," Nisha said, "that was fun, but I want to go on some *actual* rides."

I nodded. "Same."

A moment later, Reece joined us, shouldering his backpack. "Indiana Jones?" Allyson asked.

"Sure," Reece said with a nod. "Sounds great."

"Let's go!" I said, starting to walk toward Adventureland, where our first ride of the night awaited us.

Two hours later, we'd done an abbreviated greatest-hits list in the main park. We'd gone on Indy, Big Thunder Mountain Railroad (Allyson wisely opted out), Rise of the Resistance, and Space Mountain. (We'd skipped Pirates because none of us wanted to risk our prom outfits getting soaked.)

I had decided, as we prepared to board Space Mountain, to put aside the annoyance I was feeling toward Reece. After all, I would probably never see him again after tonight—or it would be just in passing in the halls—so I might as well try and make things pleasant for all of us. I was going to enjoy my Disney prom time with my best friend, and as we rode the rides, wind in our hair, shrieking for the fun of it, I realized that was exactly what I was doing.

And all too soon, my phone was sending me alerts that we were supposed to be at the Wine Country Trattoria in ten minutes. "Okay," I said to the assembled group. "We need to get moving if we're going to make it in time for dinner."

"You guys go," Reece said, slinging his backpack over his shoulder.

"I'll just grab a snack or something. There's still some other rides I want to check out."

I raised an eyebrow at him. "The reservation is for four people." We'd made them back when Cooper was coming with us, but I wasn't sure Reece needed to know about that right now. And it's not like I even really wanted to have dinner with this guy; it was the principle of the thing.

"And yet," he said, his voice overly patient, and immediately rage-inducing, "since there's no such thing as a three-person table, I think everyone will be able to live."

I took a breath to reply, but Nisha put her hand on my arm.

"No worries," she said easily to Reece. "Have a good time."

"You'll have more fun without me," he said, giving Nisha a smile. "But I'll catch up with you later."

"But—" I started, just as Reece raised a hand in a wave and headed off toward Galaxy's Edge. I turned to my friends. "Can you believe that guy?"

I saw Nisha and Allyson exchange a look. "Well—did you really want to have dinner with him?" Allyson asked. "It seemed like he was kind of annoying you."

"He was!" I agreed, then realized a second later I had just undercut my point. "Oh. I mean . . . whatever. We should go."

The three of us headed out, making our way over to California Adventure, where the dinner reservations were. After we passed through the castle, I turned back for a moment just to give it a look.

The flags were flying, the gold bunting was shining, and people were streaming in and out, either starting their Disney experience, finishing it up, or still in the middle of it, like us. The wind picked up, blowing my hair around my face, and I watched two of the ducks in the moat rise up and fly over to dry land.

The sun was just starting to set behind the castle, bathing everything in a golden light. I knew there was a term for this time of day, and after a moment it came to me: *magic hour.*

I looked at it for a moment longer. And maybe it was the setting sun, or the breeze, or a trick of the light, but for just a second, I could have sworn that the castle had started to glow.

Four

An hour later, we'd had our pre-prom dinner, and our very nice waitress—Wendi, from Long Beach—had taken pictures for us, complimented all of us on our prom outfits, and told us to have a great night.

Nisha, Allyson, and I headed out of the restaurant and stepped into the slowly falling twilight. It wasn't fully dark yet, but it would be getting there before too long. All over the park, I could see that lights had started to switch on, and I was seeing more and more sleeping children being carried to the exits by their parents.

"Okay!" I said, turning to my friends. "I think we have time for one last ride. Radiator Springs Racers?" It was, in my opinion, the best ride at California Adventure, hands down.

"Well," Nisha said. She and Allyson exchanged a look. "We were actually thinking we might do the Ferris wheel?"

"The fixed cars," Allyson added hurriedly.

I glanced over toward Pixar Pier, where the Ferris wheel was, and nodded. Half of the gondolas on it were fixed, like a regular Ferris wheel, but the rest had an inner track that let the cars slide back and forth. Allyson had ridden it the first time thinking it was a regular Ferris wheel and had *not* been happy to find out that it wasn't. The people in the car below her weren't thrilled either.

"We can do that," I said with a nod as I made a note in the spreadsheet. It seemed a little boring to me to have the last ride of the night be in a fixed-car Ferris wheel when you could have been doing a car race through the desert, but I was game. "Let me just see what the wait is looking like."

"Um . . ." Nisha glanced at Allyson, then back at me. "We were thinking about going . . . by ourselves."

I just blinked at her for a second, until the penny dropped, and I immediately felt stupid for not getting this sooner. Nisha was with her *girlfriend* on *prom night*. Of course they wanted to spend some time alone together. They wanted to make out on a Ferris wheel!

"Right," I said, nodding hurriedly. "Of course. Sorry about that."

"It's fine," Allyson said.

"I'll just go get some ice cream," I said, tipping my head toward the main park. I glanced at the time: just a little after seven. "But I'll meet you by the Main Street Starbucks at seven thirty? And then we can head to the prom."

"Sounds good," Allyson agreed. "I'll text Reece and let him know the plan."

"Great." I gave them both a wave and started to walk away.

"Stells?" I looked over and saw Nisha had run to catch up with me. "Are you sure you're okay? You can come with us!"

"No," I said, then in a second realized how this sounded. "I mean, yes, I'm fine, and no, I'm not going to go with you. It's your prom night! You two should get some time together. Go enjoy it and I'll see you soon."

Nisha's eyes searched mine, like she was trying to suss out if I was telling the truth. "You're sure?"

"Sure," I said firmly. "I'll see you soon. Have fun!" I gave her a bright smile and a wave and walked away.

But as I got farther away, I felt my smile start to fade. I kept my head down as I made my way toward the California Adventure exit, trying not to notice the couples that were all around me—but they suddenly seemed to be *everywhere*. Maybe more came out as it got dark? Couples who'd now gotten off work and were here to have a date night? I wasn't sure, but I was more aware than ever that I was no longer part of one.

And as I headed down Main Street, toward the ice cream parlor, I was aware that I was surrounded by everything I'd fled the gym to avoid: princess merchandise for sale, cast members in costume, Mickey ears with a crown, a literal castle. All those fairy tales. All those happy endings. And none of it was true.

Because you think you have found what you've been promised from all those stories—you think you've found something real with someone. You make space for them in your life and put them into your plans . . . and then you end up alone at Disneyland, a third wheel with your best friend, about to go to the prom by yourself.

When I reached the Gibson Girl ice cream parlor, I realized I wasn't the only one with this idea; it had a line that spilled out into the street. I glanced across to the Starbucks, contemplating a Frappuccino, but all at once, something salty was more appealing than something sweet. And I knew just where I could find my favorite popcorn in the park.

I went through the castle once more, noticing that the wind seemed to have picked up as I walked, sending my hair flying and probably ruining my blowout. It seemed calmer on the other side of the castle, and I smoothed my hair down as I stepped out. I was heading toward the popcorn cart when I saw Reece. He was sitting on a bench—reading a *book*.

He glanced up from it, and his eyes met mine. Any chance I might have had to sneak past him and get my popcorn in peace was now completely gone. I could feel that I was probably not great company right now—there was a jumpy, unsettled feeling in my chest—but I also didn't think I could just walk away without being completely rude. So I took a breath and headed over to him.

"Hey," I said, as I arrived at Reece's bench. I saw he had a blue plastic Disney bag next to him.

"Hey." He looked around. "Where are Nisha and Allyson?"

"They're riding the Ferris wheel. Allyson said she texted you."

"Oh." Reece shrugged. "I guess I didn't hear it. How was dinner?"

I took a breath, about to say something snarky about how it was good because nobody crashed into me carrying beverages and ruined my dress, but then a moment later, let this impulse go. The night at Disney was winding down, and Reece wouldn't be going with us to the prom. I just needed to get through a little more time, and then I'd probably never have to see him again. "It was great," I said, with a quick smile. Not wanting to prolong this conversation, I started to walk away. "I'm going to get some popcorn."

"Sounds good. I'll come with you." He stood up from the bench and closed his book, then hesitated. "If that's okay?"

"Sure," I said through gritted teeth. The one moment I'd wanted to myself—to try and get my tangled, spiky feelings under control so that I wouldn't be bringing them into the rest of my night with Nisha and Allyson—was apparently vanishing in front of my eyes.

Reece got up, picking up his bag. I nodded down at it. "What'd you get?"

"Nothing."

"Okay," I said, shaking my head. It wasn't like I even cared; I was just trying to be polite.

"Just . . . something for my sister," he muttered after a moment. I nodded, and we walked to the popcorn cart in silence. We got in line behind two dads and their three kids, all five of them wearing matching family Disney shirts.

"So what are you reading?" I asked, just to make conversation, as the family in front of us stepped forward to order. *Why* are you reading might have been the more accurate question, but I bit it back in an attempt to keep things civil.

"Oh," Reece said.

He handed me the paperback and I looked at it. *Dragons & Destiny*, the title read. It showed a guy in a medieval-looking outfit brandishing a sword while a truly gigantic dragon roared down at him. If I was a betting person, I would have put my money on the dragon, not the guy with the sword. I turned it over and saw that the spine was cracked and worn. "I don't know it."

The family in front of us walked away with their popcorn, and we stepped forward. I bought a bucket and grabbed some napkins. I took a handful—careful not to let any kernels fall on my dress—and then held out the popcorn to Reece.

He hesitated a moment, then took a handful. "Thanks."

"Sure. Help yourself."

I crunched down on another handful, then wiped off my hands and looked at my phone. "We should probably start walking over to Main Street. We need to be meeting them before too long."

Reece nodded. He unzipped his backpack and looked through it, then frowned. A second later, he knelt to the ground and started riffling through his bag. "Oh, crap," I heard him mutter.

"Everything okay?"

He straightened up, his expression grave. "No. I think I left my phone up in Sleeping Beauty's castle."

"Are you sure?"

He shot me an annoyed look, but then went through his bag once again. "I'm sure," he said shortly.

"But Sleeping Beauty's castle was a while ago. You didn't *notice*?"

"Of course *you* would have noticed, right?"

"What does that mean?"

"It means I haven't seen you without your phone the whole night."

I just stared at him. Of course I'd had my phone with me. It was *necessary*. It was where our schedule and passes and maps and camera were all located. I was supposed to go without all those things? It was physically impossible. I wasn't commenting that I'd seen him *breathing* this whole night, or anything.

He shook his head and zipped up his bag. "Anyway. I should go try and find it. And hopefully it's still there."

All at once, I remembered Reece setting his phone down when he turned to take the picture of the couple. But I had just assumed he would have picked it up again—who could be without their phone, and for this long? It boggled the mind.

Reece started walking back toward the castle, and I followed, realizing I was still holding his book. "Here," I said, handing it back to him. "So what's it about?"

"It's really great," he said, even though he sounded distracted. "It's the first of a whole series. There's kind of a dip in quality in the middle, but it really finishes strong."

"Wait," I said, feeling like I'd missed something. "You've read that book before?"

"Yeah. Why?"

"I just . . ." I shook my head, trying to understand. "Why would you reread a book you've read before?"

Reece just looked at me like I was asking him something ridiculous. "Are you serious?"

"Yeah. Why?" We were almost at the castle, and I took another handful of popcorn.

"Don't you ever . . . reread your favorite books? Rewatch your favorite movies?"

"No," I said immediately. "Why would you? What's the point, once you know how the story ends?"

"Because then you get to go on living in that world," he said, shaking his head. "You can keep returning to the world of the story. You get to be steeped in all the details."

I waved this off. "Who cares about the details? I never remember them anyway."

"You— What?" Reece was truly looking baffled. It was the same way that Avery had looked at me a few hours earlier, and maybe because of this, I felt myself start to get really irritated.

"Why is that weird?" I took another handful of popcorn in an attempt to calm myself down. "Just earlier tonight, this girl on the prom committee was acting like it was a federal crime that I didn't remember the movie that had the enchanted sea dance or whatever."

"The Enchantment Under the Sea dance?" Reece asked, and I nodded. "You mean *Back to the Future*?"

"That's the one. Why does everyone think it's so weird I don't retain those kinds of things?"

"Because it *is* weird." Reece reached for more popcorn, but I wasn't feeling particularly generous at the moment, and moved it away.

"It's inefficient."

"*Inefficient?*"

"Yes," I said, trying not to bristle at his tone. "It's the same reason I don't reread books. If you think about it, there are only so many books you can read in a lifetime. Why waste time repeating yourself?"

"Because when you love a story, you want to stay in that world. Really live in it."

"Well, *I* don't."

There was a frosty, crackling tension between us. I folded my arms, not sure what would happen next. I didn't want to back down, even though I wasn't quite sure how this had escalated. Reece just looked at me for a moment, then shook his head. "You don't have to help me," he said, his voice now more formal. "I'll deal with it on my own. You go ahead and go to the prom. I'll call an Uber to get home."

"On what? You don't have a phone," I reminded him.

"I'll get it back," he said, even though he didn't sound super confident about it. I was half-tempted to point out that even though I may have been looking at my phone a lot, I never would have *misplaced* it, but decided to be the bigger person and not mention it.

We were nearly at the entrance to the inside of the castle, when I saw a door I hadn't noticed before. It was just a few steps down from the main door, with a sign on it that read, in the Disney font, WHAT'S BEEN LOST.

"Here," I said, pointing toward it with my non-popcorn-holding hand. "Lost and Found."

"That's not where Lost and Found is, Stella," Reece said, and I couldn't help but notice that I really liked the way he said my name. Which was a ridiculous thing to clock at this particular moment in time, from someone I didn't even like that much, but there it was.

I shook my head, more than done with Reece knowing more about Disneyland than me. "Well, maybe they moved it."

I pushed through the open door, and a second later, Reece stepped in behind me, and the heavy door swung shut behind us.

Five

blinked, letting my eyes adjust, since it was darker in here. I looked around, feeling myself frown. I'd expected a regular Lost & Found, but instead was standing inside a small, empty room—more a corridor than a room. Maybe it was being prepared for some kind of exhibit? But there was nothing there now. There also didn't seem to be anyone working there, which was strange.

I looked around, trying to figure out what to do next, when I saw, at the other end of the room, a door with light underneath it. Another sign on this door read FIND WHAT'S MISSING, also in the Disney font. I nodded toward it. "Look."

Reece was looking around—he also seemed a little unsettled by the empty room we were standing in. "What?"

"I guess that's where they're keeping the lost things. Come on." I crossed over to it and pushed through the door, Reece following behind me.

As we stepped through, I felt myself blink. I had been expecting another room like the one we'd left, but hopefully with a cast member manning a table with forgotten or misplaced items on it. But as I looked around, I felt myself frown. We were somehow back in the castle—through a door I just must have never noticed before, or that I had assumed was just decorative, not functional.

"What's going on?" Reece asked, starting to sound a little freaked out. "Why are we back here?"

"I don't know," I said, as much as it pained me to ever say those words. But I tried to look on the bright side; after all, we were looking for Reece's phone, and we'd come back to the spot where he'd misplaced it. And maybe there was a chance it was still where he'd left it. "But now that we're here, let's find your phone. I think you set it down when those people asked you to take a picture."

He narrowed his eyes at me. "You *saw* me leave my phone?"

"I saw you set it down, I just assumed you would have picked it up!"

Reece shook his head, and started to climb the stairs. I followed after him, our way lit by the fake candles in their holders.

"See it?" I asked.

"Yes!" Relief suffused Reece's voice. "You were right." He picked it up from where it had been resting on the top of one of the illuminated manuscripts. "It's where I left it."

"Great." I glanced at my phone. It was 7:24, definitely time to get moving. "Let's get out of here."

We walked across to the stairs on the other side of the room, and as we started to leave, I glanced behind me, taking one last look at the display showing the princess and the prince, the happily ever after, everything working out. I scoffed.

"What?" Reece asked, as he dropped his phone into his back pocket.

"Nothing," I said, taking a handful of popcorn, not wanting to go into it. But a second later, I changed my mind. "Well—just that the display back there is the whole problem." I headed down the stairs, Reece following behind me.

"What is?"

I shook my head. The feelings I'd had as I walked alone through Main Street were bubbling up again. "This fairy-tale nonsense. That everything will work out, and true love is the answer, and everything ends happily. It's not *real*."

As soon as I said this, I felt the ground shake slightly under my feet. I froze, and turned back to see Reece doing the same.

"Did you feel that?" Reece asked.

"Uh-huh." I didn't move, waiting to see if something got worse. All the things I'd learned over the years as a child of California were rushing back to me: stop, assess the situation, get away from things that could fall on you, and, if necessary, get under something heavy, like a table.

It was only after several moments had passed, with no further shaking, that I was able to relax. And it was then I noticed just how close to each other Reece and I were standing. We were less than an arm's length apart, the nearest we'd yet been. At this distance, I could see that he had a smattering of freckles across his nose and cheeks. I could see there were little flecks of green in his brown eyes, and that his dark eyelashes curled up slightly at the ends. . . .

Reece looked down at me, and like he'd also just realized our proximity, took a hasty step back. "Sorry," he whispered, looking around.

"You okay?"

"Was that an *earthquake*?" Reece's voice rose up at the end.

"Why do you sound excited?"

"It's my first one!" I remembered, a second later, that Reece hadn't grown up with earthquake drills and casual discussions of the San Andreas Fault line. He was from Connecticut, where the ground stayed put.

"If it was an earthquake, it was a little one. And I think it's over." You never knew if something was a foreshock, but I was trying not to think about that. Mostly, I wanted to be back out in the open air. "Let's go." I'd just started to walk again when something hot hit my shoulder. "Ow!"

"What?" Reece asked, coming to stand next to me on my step.

"I don't know." Reece took the popcorn from me, and I looked at my shoulder and saw it was a piece of wax that was already starting to harden. We both looked up to see actual candles now flickering in the chandelier.

"The candles are real?" Reece asked, staring at them and at the shadows they were throwing on the stone walls.

I blinked at them, trying to make this make sense. Maybe they were real in this part of the castle? I couldn't help notice just how different the light felt now. Real candles, real flame, just had a different feeling. Like you were actually experiencing something, not just the impression of something.

"Kind of a fire hazard, though, right?" Reece asked. He fell into step with me as I headed down the rest of the stairs. I noticed the corridor felt a little colder—and damper, too. Maybe since we'd been inside, it had started to rain. It was rare in Southern California, especially in May, but it *did* happen.

We were just steps away from the landing—where we could push out of the doors and return to the park, hopefully with nobody the wiser—when I heard the voice. "Attention! You there!"

A man stepped forward. He was wearing a blue tunic, tights, boots, and a hat with a white plumed feather.

"You're not supposed to be here," the man said, frowning at us.

"Oh," I said, looking around. "Sorry—we came here through the Found door? Do you mean we should have left that way, too?"

The man's eyes widened at the sight of my dress. I sighed, about to explain about the prom tradition, when he bowed his head and swept off his hat in one fluid motion. "A thousand apologies, milady. I didn't realize . . . but you shouldn't be here. You should be at the festivities."

I looked over at Reece, who widened his eyes at me. This cast member was clearly *really* committed, which was nice to see.

"Did you get lost?" the man asked.

"Yes!" I said, relieved that he understood and that we weren't in trouble. "We didn't expect the Lost and Found door to lead us back into the castle."

"I'll show you the way," the guy said, bowing again, and putting his hat back on as he did so. I started to say that we'd be fine—after all, the door back to the park was just at the bottom of the staircase. But before I could, Reece spoke up.

"That would be great. Thanks so much."

The cast member turned to look at Reece, taking him in for the first time. I watched the smile fade from the guy's face, replaced with a look of disdain as he took in Reece's jeans and hoodie, the bucket of popcorn. He sniffed derisively. "And I'll point *you* back in the direction of the stables. Where you should return *forthwith*."

"What?" Reece asked with a half laugh, sounding stunned. But the man was already walking on.

"Just ignore him," I said, even though I was pretty shocked that a cast member would behave this way toward a guest. I understood being in character, but wasn't he crossing a line? "We'll just—" I took a step forward, attempting to push through the door ... but there *was* no door. There was just a solid stone wall, and when I pressed my hand against it, it was cool and damp to the touch.

I looked back up the stairs, but in the flickering candlelight, I could see that there were no longer any EXIT signs. I shook my head, trying to make it make sense. "But ..."

"Please hurry, milady," the guy said. He had turned and was now walking down a corridor that I had never seen before. I was pretty sure that castle just ... ended, right? Otherwise, wouldn't we be spilling over into Frontierland?

Not sure what else to do, I followed him, and I heard Reece's footsteps behind me, doing the same. This corridor looked similar to the display room where we'd found Reece's phone ... except that there weren't any illuminated manuscripts telling us the story or displays showing moments from it. It was just a slightly curving stone corridor, our way lit with more actual candles, flickering in their chandeliers. There were also lighted torches in holder things on the stone wall, which definitely gave me pause. Should there really just be open flames out here like this? With kids around?

A door at the end of this corridor was open, and seeing the light streaming through it, I picked up my pace. We'd just gone down some employee-only passage, that was all. And we were just steps away from being back in the park, where we could meet up with Nisha and Allyson at Starbucks, tell them about our weird encounter with the overzealous cast member, shake the whole thing off.

The guy stepped through the door, and I followed—then stopped short.

"What?" Reece said, maneuvering around me. "What are you—" Then he came to stand next to me, his jaw dropping open, as he took in what had literally stopped me in my tracks.

We weren't outside Adventureland, with its ride celebrating the adventures of a professor-archeologist, its souvenir shops, and its Dole Whip. We weren't outside, period.

We were standing at the doorway of a huge . . . room? *Room* seemed like the wrong word for something this large. It seemed like a football field could have comfortably fit inside, or maybe two, and the ceilings were huge and vaulted, like a cathedral.

And it was *filled* with people. But not regular Disney tourists, with their strollers and ice cream and shirts proclaiming how much they loved Kylo Ren. Everyone surrounding us was dressed like the guy who'd directed us here—the men in tunics and tights, the women in gowns and high, pointed hats. It was by far the most cast members I'd ever seen in one place, which was actually a little bit worrying. Should they all be together like this? Who was actually running the park?

"Where . . ." Reece started, shaking his head. He looked the way I felt: incredibly confused and a little freaked out. "Where are we?"

"*We*," the man said, indicating me along with him, "are in the throne room. *You* are returning to the stables posthaste. And take your pig feed with you." He swept away.

I just stared after him, confused, until I realized he must have meant the popcorn. I turned to Reece. "Okay, *what* is happening?"

We were jostled forward by more dressed-up people. I searched in vain for name tags but didn't see a single one.

"I've heard she's a most-sweet little one," one pointy-hatted woman said as she and her similarly dressed friend hurried forward. "With a lovely temperament."

"And that young prince—*such* a little gentleman," the other said. "It's an ideal betrothal."

We were jostled forward in the gently swelling wave of people, and I could see now that at the front of the room, underneath an embroidered canopy thing, there were two thrones—where two people, wearing crowns, were sitting. There was a cradle just next to the thrones. It all looked *really* familiar, I just couldn't put my finger on why.

"It must be some kind of immersive experience, right?" Reece asked, looking around. "Something they're . . . beta testing?"

"I guess?" I looked around, trying to square what I was seeing with logic. I felt like if Disney had been beta testing an immersive experience this complicated—this *big*—I would have heard about it, right? "Or! Maybe it's VR!" The second I said it, I felt myself relax. That was what was happening here. I knew just how real it could seem. After all, everyone at Harbor Cove High—not to mention a *lot* of people on the internet—had seen Chad Wilkinson, headset on, jump into the fountain outside the school, convinced that he was in the middle of some aquatic quest. He then got a really bad infection, which was how we all found out that the water in the fountain was *seriously* gross. But if VR could convince you that you were in an aquatic paradise when you were actually in a fountain filled with poisonous spores, of course it could convince Reece and I that we were . . . well, wherever we were. Right now, it was showing us that we were in a huge, cathedral-like room, filled with hundreds of dressed-up people, but in reality, we were still back in the small display room. "That's the only thing that makes sense."

Reece shook his head. "But VR doesn't work unless you're wearing your headset."

"Oh." I nodded, realizing that he was right. "I guess it's the immersive experience then?"

"I guess," Reece said, but he sounded like I felt: really unsure.

As we walked farther into the room, I noticed that while people didn't seem to think there was anything strange about what I was wearing—their eyes were just sliding over me—everyone seemed to be noticing Reece, whispering and pointing.

"I don't know about this," he murmured to me in an undertone.

"Maybe it's the popcorn? Maybe we're not supposed to have snacks in the immersive experience."

"It's your popcorn," he pointed out, trying to give it back to me. Some kernels flew out and I jumped back, not wanting to get popcorn-grease stains on my dress.

"Hey!"

"Shh!" one of the people next to me hissed. He was carrying a large stick with a banner attached to the top, like we were in *Game of Thrones* or something. "The king is speaking."

"The *king*?" I echoed, but the guy with the banner moved a few steps away, clearly not wanting to be associated with us.

I took a step forward and saw that there was a little boy, standing next to a man with his hand on his shoulder—his dad?—who was talking to the people on the thrones. Using my powers of deduction, I figured these were probably the . . . king and queen? As I watched, the little boy ran his hand forward and backward through his blond hair, rumpling it up in the back.

The baby cradle next to the thrones was swaying slightly, and as I stretched forward to look, I could now see there was a small baby inside, sleeping.

"This isn't . . ." Reece was saying as he looked around. "It can't be . . ."

"What?" I asked, a little louder than I meant to. I saw heads all over the—throne room? Was that where we were?—turn to look at us. I saw the woman who was presumably the queen, her blond hair perfectly coiffed, stand up slightly, eyebrows raised. She looked at us, and the guy next to her—I guess the king?—glanced over as well. He had longish dark hair, a seriously impressive mustache, and was frowning in our general direction.

"It's *Sleeping Beauty*," Reece said. His eyes were wide as he looked around. "It's the opening scene."

"It is?" I shook my head. "Are you *sure*?"

Reece stared at me. "We literally just saw the story all laid out. Like minutes ago."

"Where's the mice, then? Where's Gus-Gus?"

"That's *Cinderella*! How do you not remember this?"

"I told you I don't remember things from stories!"

"Shh!" A woman standing next to me shushed us.

"Okay," I said, taking a step closer to Reece. "So this is some sort of *Sleeping Beauty* . . . ride? Like Star Tours?" Even as I said it, my logic brain was pointing out the problems. I couldn't stop myself from tallying up the costs and time needed to pull it off. A space this large, paying this many employees, all in costume . . . and with so many cast members here, where would the rest of the guests go when it was open to them? How did that make any sense?

"I . . . guess?" Reece said, even though he sounded unsure. "Maybe we should . . ."

But whatever he was about to say was lost as a beam of light opened above our heads and three tiny fairies wearing blue, green, and red floated down it to place themselves in front of the thrones.

"Oh, okay," I said, nodding. "*Now* I remember."

"I think we should go," Reece said, starting to back out toward the door.

"What?" I asked, even as I followed him, weaving through the crowd. Nobody looked particularly happy about it, especially when they spotted his popcorn. "Why?"

"Because unlike you, I know this story. Which means I know what comes next."

"Well, the immersive experience ends at some point, right? Maybe you *don't* know what comes next!"

"Stop saying *immersive experience*," he hissed at me.

"But that's what this has to be, right? It's the only logical explanation."

Reece didn't say anything, just picked up his pace. "Come on." He was hurrying back to the doors we came through, just as a flash of green smoke filled the room, followed by a low, evil-sounding laugh. I turned back in time to see a tall woman with greenish-toned skin, wearing a black, horned headdress emerge from the smoke. Maleficent.

She looked back at us, and I felt a chill as her eyes swept over me, then Reece. She walked forward, and I shivered involuntarily. It was like the temperature in the room had just dropped ten degrees.

"What's going on?" I asked Reece, a nervous wobble in my voice. As I watched in horror, the woman headed right for the cradle.

"Stella," Reece whispered, but my eyes were glued to what was unfolding. Was this awful person going to do something to a *baby*? An actual baby? All at once, this no longer felt like someone pretending, like we were experiencing something with guardrails. This felt real—and terrifying. My heart was pounding in my throat, and I just wanted to get out of there. Fast. The woman opened her mouth to speak just as Reece slipped out the door and I hustled after him.

"What is this?" I asked as Reece started hurrying down the hall the way we'd come in. I knew he didn't have any more answers than I did, but I couldn't stop myself from asking it.

"Let's just . . . get back," he said. He set the bucket of popcorn on the stone floor and started walking again, faster this time.

I followed, picking up my pace to match his. And as we walked away from the throne room—I could hear screaming from inside—I couldn't shake the feeling that something was really wrong.

Reece was practically running now, and I matched his pace, glad once again that I'd left my prom heels in the car and that I was wearing my sneakers. He slipped through the door we'd come in—it was still open—and I followed.

We walked fast down the corridor, falling into step together. We weren't talking about what we were doing, exactly, or if we had a plan, but I somehow had a feeling that Reece had felt in that backward glance the same thing that I had, that we needed to get out *now*. Get back to something that was familiar.

The corridor looked the same as before—torches flickering in their holders on the walls, cold stone—but now, as we reached the staircase we'd come down, I could see that the corridor continued on. I didn't know how, exactly, this was possible, since shouldn't we be running straight into the middle of the castle passage? But I could see a door at the end of it, and under that door, a glint of light.

"There," I said, pointing. Reece had been about to climb the stairs, but

I just shook my head and overtook him, walking faster, my eyes on the light coming through under the door. As we got closer to it, it was like I could hear something, just steps away: music and people talking on the other side. I reached the wooden door first, pulled it open—

And stepped outside, onto grass and almost-gone sunshine as the door slammed shut behind us. A family walked by us with a little girl up on the mom's shoulders, dressed in full Belle regalia. A group of kids ran past, laughing and filming on their phones. Whatever that had been—whatever had just happened—it was over. We were back where we were supposed to be.

"This is weird," Reece said.

I looked around and saw what he'd meant. We'd stepped out of a small freestanding tower with a door in it. It was in a little fenced-off park area. Just to my left was the moat, and the castle. But we'd just been walking *through* the castle—how had we come out this door? And it wasn't like we could go back and check, since the door had swung closed behind us, and there was no handle. And plus, I really didn't want to.

"Huh." I tried to come up with an explanation that would make sense. Maybe the corridor we'd been in had been a tunnel! And there just hadn't been any stairs to come up to ground level because . . . reasons.

Reece looked at me, and it seemed like he was just as baffled as I felt. "Okay," he said, shaking his head. "What was all that?"

I took a breath to answer, then stopped when I realized I didn't *have* an answer. Not one that I felt confident about. My brain was spinning, trying to process something in a logical, methodical way, and failing at every turn, which was *not* a feeling I was familiar with. Or found I liked very much.

So rather than answering Reece, I just lifted my long skirt up to climb over the little white fence that bordered this mini-park. "Well," I said, after

I was over the fence, and Reece was, too, "clearly there must have been a gas leak."

He leveled a stare at me. "A gas leak," he echoed.

"Uh-huh," I said, not meeting his eye. "We saw some things that weren't there—our minds took what we were seeing in the *Sleeping Beauty* exhibit and somehow made it real. But now that we're back in the fresh air, we're back to reality. Mystery solved. Case closed."

"Case opened," he countered. "We both somehow imagined the same thing?"

"Well, maybe we didn't," I demurred, even though this was a very good point—not that I was about to admit that to Reece. "I don't know what you saw. Hey, we should go meet Nisha and Allyson." I headed toward Main Street, shouldering my canvas bag with what I hoped was finality.

"Stella, come *on*," Reece said, catching up with me. "We were there together. We saw the same thing. Throne room, fairies, Maleficent?"

"I don't think—" I started, just as my phone began to buzz in my bag. I saw it was Nisha—and stopped short. I couldn't even focus on her text, because all I could see was the time. 7:26. As in, two minutes after I'd looked at my phone when we'd been in the upstairs chamber. My heart pounded hard, and I was getting increasingly freaked out. My thoughts were buzzing fast, like my mind was in overdrive, trying to find the logic I was *sure* was there somewhere, the one thing that would explain everything.

"What is it?" Reece was looking at me, his brow furrowed.

"How long would you say we were in there?"

"Where? In the gas-leak-induced fantasy that we also somehow shared?"

"Um. Yes?"

"The one in which, for some reason, people thought popcorn was pig feed and they kept telling me to go back to the stables? That one?"

"Right," I said, refusing to take the bait. "How long?"

"I don't know." I could hear the frustration in his voice, like he thought I was asking all the wrong questions. "Ten minutes? Fifteen?"

"Okay." I nodded, like this wasn't making everything worse. Because that's what I would have said, too. Except apparently only *two minutes* had passed. What was happening? I took a breath and held up my phone to him. "Look."

He frowned at it. "Nisha is waiting at . . . bux. What's bux?"

This was Nisha's nickname for Starbucks, the one that she was sure was going to catch on, despite all evidence to the contrary. "It's Starbucks. But I meant the time. All the while we were in there . . . it stayed the same time here? How is that possible?" I started to walk toward Main Street, eyes on the Starbucks, but I couldn't see Nisha or Allyson outside the coffee shop. Maybe they were inside, picking up some treats for the road—Frappuccinos and Rice Krispie Treats to give us a little pre-prom sugar and caffeine buzz.

The *prom*. I shook my head, trying to clear it. But the truth was, with everything that had just happened, I'd almost forgotten about the prom.

But then my eye fell on someone heading toward me. And just like that, I remembered.

Because walking toward me was my ex, Cooper.

He was wearing a tux and had his arm around a pretty, dark-haired girl I didn't recognize. She was wearing a (I had to admit) gorgeous teal prom dress. And I couldn't help noticing that she was practically Cooper's height, unlike me. He was almost a foot taller than me, and toward the end, he was always complaining about getting a crick in his neck when he bent down to kiss me. He'd complain despite not taking any of my suggestions about Pilates or stretching exercises. But it seemed like he wouldn't have a problem now—he and this girl were practically eye to eye.

I stared at them for a second, like I wasn't quite able to process what I was seeing. But a moment later, what it meant hit me.

It meant that though we'd only broken up three weeks ago, Cooper had already moved on. He was bringing someone else to the prom. And he was doing pre-prom at Disneyland after all . . . just not with *me*.

I turned around, my heart pounding. Suddenly, the only thing I wanted was for him *not* to see me, and that would be impossible if I kept walking toward him. Maybe on a regular day I could have blended into the crowd and avoided him recognizing me, but not in my prom dress. And the thought of Cooper and his date seeing me, about to go to the prom alone, was more than I felt I could take right now.

I started to walk back *toward* the castle, the exact opposite direction of where I needed to be going. Allyson and Nisha were already at the Starbucks, waiting for me, but I knew they'd understand.

"Stella?" Reece caught up with me, looking baffled. "Main Street is that way—"

"I know where Main Street is, thank you!" I snapped. "I have been here before."

"But we're walking the wrong way."

I glanced behind me quickly—Cooper's arm was around this girl's shoulders, and he was laughing at something she was saying. Feeling like my heart was being squeezed, I watched as he leaned down, just slightly, and kissed the top of her head.

I looked away and walked faster. My cheeks were burning and angry, unsettled feelings were rising up full force.

"I shouldn't have come here." We were almost back to the castle now. I figured I'd break right, hide behind the rows of strollers in Fantasyland, wait for Cooper to walk through, and then head back to Main Street undetected. It might have been extreme, but it was necessary: I just couldn't handle an awkward conversation with Cooper and the girl he'd replaced me with in record time.

"Shouldn't have come where?" Reece asked, keeping up with me. "Disneyland?"

"This is the worst place for me to be." I felt just how true it was with every step. Pinky swear or no, I should have told Nisha I couldn't make it tonight. We were walking through Sleeping Beauty's castle, yet again, and there they were, the pictures on the walls showing that love always won out. "Because none of it is real," I said. Reece probably didn't know what I was talking about, but at the moment, I didn't really care. My volume was increasing, and I saw a mom with Spider-Man Mickey ears glance over at me.

"None of what?"

"All of it!" We were almost in the middle of the castle now. "There's no true love riding up on a white horse. There's no love at first sight. And there's definitely no happily ever after. Because fairy tales aren't *real*!"

I said this louder than I'd intended, and just as I spoke the last word, the ground shook under my feet again—more powerfully this time. I looked over to see Reece's eyes, wide and fearful, looking back at me.

And then everything went black.

PART

Two

Six

"Stella. Hey. Stella?"

I stirred, trying to get my bearings, then opened my eyes and immediately squinted at the bright sunshine above me.

Wait.

Sunshine?

I pushed myself up to sitting—apparently I'd been lying on the ground for some reason?—and looked around. I was in a . . . field? Meadow? I was on the grass in a clearing, at any rate. There was a dense forest to one side of me, and through the trees on the other side, I was pretty sure I could hear water and see the top of a brick chimney. It was much brighter out than it had been when we were crossing under the castle. This seemed like it was late-afternoon sun—not nearly night, which it had been only a second ago.

I closed my eyes for a moment, ready for this hallucination, or fever dream, or *whatever* it was, to end. I concentrated as hard as I could. I was at Disneyland. Nisha was waiting for me at the Starbucks on Main Street. I had the prom to get to. Any second now, I'd open my eyes, and I'd be back there again. . . .

"*Stella.*"

I opened my eyes to see that nothing had changed. I was still in the meadow/field (what was the difference between them, anyway?) in the sunshine with the sound of birds chirping and no barbershop quartets or people selling bubble wands anywhere. Reece was peering down at me, his expression worried. His brow was furrowed, and his arms were crossed tightly over his Mickey hoodie.

I scrambled to my feet and looked around, shaking the dirt off my prom dress and deciding I was just not going to worry about grass stains right now. At the moment, I had much larger things to focus on.

"Okay," I said, trying to keep my voice calm. Logic had never once deserted me, and logic was how I was going to figure my way through this. After all, I'd helped my parents work out how to get a shipping container from Auckland to the port of Los Angeles on schedule—even though with time zones, the container actually arrived *before* it had been delivered. I could sort *this* out. Whatever . . . this was. I could use my very logical brain to figure out what was happening.

I turned around slowly, trying to take in everything I could see: trees, grass, flowers, brightly colored birds flitting about. I waited for some rational explanation to pop into my head . . . but nothing came. Giving up, I turned to Reece. "What the heck is going on?"

He took a breath. "Stella . . . I don't think we're in Anaheim anymore."

I scoffed at that, and shook my head. "Of *course* we are," I insisted, even as I was secretly trying to calculate how much water this type of grass would require. In California? It seemed pretty irresponsible in a drought-ridden state. I pushed the thought away. "We're still at home," I insisted. "This is just some—"

"I swear, if you say *immersive experience* one more time . . ."

"There has to be some explanation!" I said, even though I couldn't exactly think of what it could be at the moment. "There *has* to be."

"No . . ." Reece said as he looked around. But I had the feeling he wasn't talking to me. I wasn't even sure he'd *heard* me, which, rude. He was walking to the edge of the meadow, turning slowly in a circle. "It can't be . . . but what else . . ."

"What?" I asked, walking over to him, leaving my canvas bag on the grass. "What is it?"

Reece turned to face me, disbelief and joy fighting for control of his expression. "I think . . . I figured out what's happening."

Relief flooded through me. "Oh, thank god." If Reece had the answers, I wouldn't even care that they hadn't come from me. I wouldn't care *that* much, at any rate.

"Okay," he said, taking a deep breath. I noticed that there was a dirt smudge on the sleeve of his Mickey hoodie, and I had the strangest impulse to reach over and brush it off. But a second later, I squashed it immediately. I had much more important things to deal with. Like . . . where exactly we *were*.

"So, here's what I think. When we walked through the castle before, and we ended up in the—"

"Immersive experience—"

"*Throne room*," he finished, talking over me. "We were in *Sleeping Beauty*."

"Right. A re-creation of it—"

"No," Reece said, with enough authority that I stopped talking. "I think we were *there*. There in the story."

"*In?*" I echoed, then shook my head. "We weren't—"

"We *were*. There's no room at Disneyland that big. And they wouldn't, rationally, hire that many cast members. To what, stand around?"

I took a breath to argue this point, but Reece kept going.

"You fit in because you were in your prom dress, but they didn't understand my outfit at all, or what popcorn was. Because we were from the wrong century."

"I don't think that—"

"We were at the start of the story," Reece continued, talking over me. "When Princess Aurora is a baby and Maleficent curses her."

"That's nonsense," I said. "And anyway, we left . . . whatever that was. We went back to Disneyland."

"I know," Reece said, nodding. "But I think we're back *again*."

"Back. In . . . *Sleeping Beauty*?"

Reece nodded, his face serious. "I think we've come to the main part of the story, sixteen years later."

I shook my head. This was truly getting ridiculous. "How can you *possibly* know that?"

He pointed over to where a curl of smoke was rising up from the brick chimney I'd seen earlier. "Because that's the woodcutter's cottage, where Aurora lives with the three good fairies."

I just stared at him for a second, then burst out laughing. "You're serious."

"Yes."

"You think we're *in* a fairy tale. Like . . . actually."

"I've said it like five times. I don't know how to make myself clearer."

"That's impossible."

"And yet." Reece gestured all around us. "If that's not the case, please, enlighten me. Where exactly are we? And how did we get here?" He walked over to a nearby fallen log and sat down at it, looking at me expectantly. "I'll wait."

I felt a wave of irritation, the kind I always seemed to feel when I was around him, rise up sharply. "Fine," I said, as I crossed back to the center of the field/meadow. I don't know why it had taken me this long to remember that I had technology that could answer these questions, but better late than never. I grabbed my canvas bag and rummaged around in it for my phone.

"This will tell us . . ." I pulled it out, then felt all the blood drain from my face. My phone lock screen was, as usual, showing a picture of Nisha and me. We were standing in the surf on a Malibu beach with no idea that we were seconds away from getting clobbered by a wave. That was totally normal. What wasn't normal was that there was nothing else on my screen. *Nothing.* No carrier information, or bars showing service, or the Wi-Fi triangle. But most worrisome of all . . . it wasn't showing me either the date or the time.

I had never seen that before, and it told me what I'd known deep down but hadn't wanted to accept. That we were somewhere without satellites that the phone could connect with. That we weren't anyplace I'd ever been before. "We can't be . . ." I said faintly, dropping my phone back in my bag. I didn't want to look at its blank face any longer; it was freaking me out. "We're *not* . . ."

"Why can't we be?" Reece asked, sounding less combative now.

"Because fairy tales aren't real!" I said, but with a little less conviction this time.

"That's what you said before," he said slowly, like he was putting something together in real time. "Both times we came here."

"Oh, so this is *my* fault?"

He raised an eyebrow at me. "I'm not the one who said it."

"Fine." I was willing to do whatever I had to do to turn this back, even if that thing was making a fool of myself. "I believe in fairy tales," I called, slowly turning in a circle. "I take it back! I believe." I turned to Reece. "Do I need to clap?"

He rolled his eyes like I was asking a ridiculous question. "That's *Peter Pan*."

I waited for a second . . . but nothing changed. I turned back to him, feeling the need to defend myself. "I don't think we're . . . wherever we are . . . just because I was expressing a rational point of view."

"Why did you say it the second time?" he asked, tilting his head to the side, like he was trying to figure something out. "When suddenly you were walking back *through* the castle?"

"Oh." I felt my cheeks get hot as I thought of it. Even though I clearly had much bigger things to worry about at the moment, the memory of Cooper and his prom date still hurt. "I . . . um . . . saw Cooper. My ex. He was with his new prom date."

Reece's face softened slightly, and his expression became gentler. "The guy from the restaurant?"

"Yeah. I didn't realize . . . that he'd moved on already." I swallowed hard after I said it, feeling the sting of it hit me somewhere deep inside.

Reece gave me a sympathetic look. "He seemed like kind of a jerk, if you want my opinion."

"You interacted with him for like two seconds," I said, not wanting to admit I appreciated this.

"You learn to read people when you're a server. It's a helpful quality. At least it was, until you got me fired."

"Okay," I said, feeling my hackles go up again, "so how do we know this isn't *your* fault? You were the one who was saying you wanted to live inside of a story! Maybe we're here because of you."

"So you admit we are in a story?" Reece looked very pleased with himself.

"No!" I shook my head, suddenly feeling exhausted—and hungry. "I don't want to deal with this." I could sense that I was almost on the verge of tears, and the last thing I wanted was for Reece to see that. "I'm going home."

I stomped over to my canvas bag, flung it over my shoulder, then walked across the meadow, toward the woods. I might have gone the other way, in the direction of the clearing and the house with the chimney, but that would have involved walking past Reece, and I didn't want to give him the satisfaction.

"Where are you going?" I heard him call after me, but I didn't turn around. A second later, though, he caught up with me. "Stella, where are you going?"

"I'm going to go home. I don't know how yet," I snapped, anticipating his question. "But this is what I know how to do."

"Which is?" he asked, as we stepped into the forest.

It was cooler in the woods, and darker, and the sound of birdsong was louder. "Logistics. It's what my parents do, and it's what I grew up learning. Getting things from place to place. There's always an answer. Even if the thing is . . . well, us. But I can figure it out, okay? I just need some time."

"It's just that we might be getting lost," Reece pointed out as I took another random turn in the forest. "I think we should retrace our steps. . . ."

"You can retrace all you want!" I said, my voice rising. "It's not like we have to do everything together."

"Fine!" Reece snapped, sounding like he was at the end of his patience. "I don't have time to explain basic facts to you."

"Oh, *facts*? Is that what you're calling your delusions?" I noticed a bush dotted with large blue berries—blueberries, they had to be. As I looked at them, I heard my stomach rumble. I knew I had snacks in my bag—but these berries were *right there*. And plus, they looked really good. I bent down to pick some.

"What are you doing?"

"I'm hungry, if you must know. I didn't get to eat much of my popcorn."

I had just started to lift one of the berries to my mouth when I felt something fly past my ear and then lodge itself in the tree trunk next to me with a *thwack*. I turned slowly and saw that it was a *knife*—just inches from my face. I looked in the direction it had come from and blinked in surprise.

A blond teenage girl was standing in front of me, wearing a black-and-tan dress. She was barefoot with a satchel slung over her shoulder. She nodded down at the berries I was holding, her expression grave. "Do *not* eat those."

Seven

stared at the girl in front of me.

She was tall, more like Nisha's height—definitely taller than me. But honestly, who *wasn't* taller than me? She was strikingly pretty, and with her bright blond hair and red lips and tallness, she had major Taylor Swift vibes. Mostly, though, I was impressed that she was *barefoot*. I mean, we were in the woods. I'd heard of barefoot running before, but never barefoot hiking.

"I'm so sorry," she said, and I could see she was blushing. "Forgive me, I hope I didn't frighten you. I just didn't want you to become ill. Or . . . dead."

I saw I was still holding the berries, and quickly opened my hand to let them fall to the forest floor. "Oh, you mean they're . . ."

"Poisonous," she confirmed. "And nearly always fatal."

"Right. Well." I glanced at Reece, hoping he'd jump in, but one look told me that was not going to happen anytime soon. He was staring at this girl, his eyes wide and his mouth hanging open. Which wasn't that surprising—she *was* gorgeous—but I guess I just didn't expect that of him. And as I saw him looking at her, I felt a twinge of . . . something. Disappointment? Jealousy? Either way, it was ridiculous to be feeling anything about Reece, and I pushed this away. "I guess I didn't . . . um . . ."

The girl's eyes widened as they traveled down my dress. "Oh, I'm so sorry." She dropped into a curtsy, ducking her head. "Milady."

"Oh—no," I said quickly. "Please don't . . . That's not necessary. I swear I'm not a lady or whatever. I don't normally wear this. We were just going to the prom." She raised her head and nodded, but I could tell it didn't mean anything to her. Which made sense—if we really were in a fairy tale, they probably didn't have high school. Or dances. Or high-school dances. "Um, I mean . . . a ball?"

"A ball!" She straightened up, her eyes sparkling. "Truly? That's so exciting! I've always dreamt of going to one."

I took a breath to reply, as Reece, apparently recovering himself, stepped in between us. "We should go," he said, widening his eyes at me, giving the girl a quick nod. "Come on." He took hold of my elbow, and the feel of his hand on my bare skin sent a little *zing* through me. I could see the girl had now crossed over to the tree and was trying to free the knife she'd embedded there like she was John Wick or something.

"What?" I asked, pulling my arm away and turning to face him. We were a little ways away from the girl, and out of earshot, but even so, I lowered my voice. "That was super rude."

"We just got the proof we need," Reece said, tilting his head back toward the girl. "We *are* in a fairy tale. We're in *Sleeping Beauty*. Because that's Princess Aurora."

Oh. So that explained Reece's expression as he looked at her. I know I shouldn't have cared at all, but it did make me feel a little bit better.

I glanced back at her, and tried to think back to the pictures I'd seen in the castle. "She doesn't look like a princess. Wasn't she wearing a pink dress?"

"Blue," Reece corrected. "And she *is* a princess, she just doesn't know it. She's being raised for her own safety in a woodcutter's cottage by the three good fairies, who are pretending to be her aunts."

I shook my head. "This story sounds bonkers."

Reece frowned at that, clearly offended. "It's a classic!"

"Well, why couldn't we have gone into *Moana*? We could be at the beach right now!"

"How is that helpful?"

"You know what I mean!" I closed my eyes for a moment, and took a deep breath. If Reece was right—and I had a sinking feeling that he was—we really were no longer in Anaheim. Or California, or any world that I recognized.

But one of the tenets of logistics was that you had to accept whatever situation you found yourself in, even if it was less than ideal. Like when my parents were responsible for a crate that turned out to have live crickets in it, as well as a substantial hole. It was really not a great situation, but when I'd seen my parents handling it, they hadn't been bellyaching about the fact that the container ship was now overrun with crickets and none of the sailors could sleep. They might have preferred a world where that wasn't happening, but it wasn't the reality that was in front of them. And since time lost is money lost, I'd seen them both get very good at adjusting to changed circumstances quickly, and continuing on.

So even though I was going to need some time to parse this situation later—and I was going to have to reexamine everything I'd thought I understood about physics, and object permanence, and the very nature of reality—for the moment, I had to accept that this was apparently happening, and move forward. Which was when something occurred to me.

"Wait, why are you trying to leave?" I asked Reece. "I thought you'd be in heaven. You're in your favorite movie."

"It's not my favorite movie," he retorted. "I've just seen it a lot. It's my *sister's* favorite movie. And I just think we should get out of here."

"Why?"

"Because I'm not sure that we should be . . . interacting with the story like this."

I frowned, not sure what he meant. I was about to ask, when the girl—Aurora, apparently?—cleared her throat.

"I'm sorry to intrude." She had retrieved her knife from the tree and was currently using it to cut wildflowers; as I watched, she assembled an impressive bouquet in what seemed like seconds. Then she took a shaky breath. "And I apologize if I scared you, or offended you. I didn't mean any harm. I only needed to get your attention, and quickly. But perhaps I went about it all wrong?" She looked down at her bare feet. "I don't usually speak to strangers."

I walked toward her, dodging Reece's fruitless grab for my elbow. "I totally get it. My parents were all about stranger danger when I was little. And when I started to drive, they insisted I take this pepper spray . . ." I suddenly realized that it was in my bag, attached to my keys; it looked just like a flashlight. I pulled my keys out just as Reece grabbed them and dropped them back in my bag.

"You have *pepper spray*?" he hissed.

"I forgot it was on my keys, okay?"

"Pepper what?" the girl asked.

"Hahaha," Reece laughed, much too loudly and unconvincingly. "Haha. So we should go . . ."

Ignoring him, I took a step closer to her. "I'm Stella." I started to hold out my hand, then hesitated. Did people shake hands in fairy tales? I turned it into a wave instead.

"I'm Rose." I shot Reece a look. Clearly, he was getting his fairy-tale details all wrong. "Well, Briar Rose. But my aunts call me Rose."

We both turned to look at Reece, who sighed. "I'm Reece," he said, like every syllable was painful for him to say.

"Is this your stable hand?" Rose asked me.

Reece huffed, throwing his hands in the air in a way that would have made Avery proud. "Why does everyone keep asking me that?"

"No, no," I said, shaking my head. "He's . . . Well, we're . . ."

"Oh!" Rose's face lit up and she gave me a sly smile. "I see."

"No!" Reece and I said at exactly the same time, both of us sounding horrified.

"There's nothing to see," I said hurriedly. "We're . . . that's not what's happening."

"*Definitely* not," Reece agreed, with maybe a little more vehemence than seemed to be strictly necessary.

"We're . . . friends," I finally said, after silently debating how to describe the situation we were in. We weren't, really. But I didn't think the truth—that we were two strangers who didn't get along particularly well but had been thrown together into weird circumstances, potentially into some sort of wormhole, or pocket universe?—would help clear anything up.

"Oh." Rose nodded, looking a little wistful. "Friends. That sounds nice." She gave me a quick smile, but one that I didn't believe at all. She expertly cut off more wildflowers with her knife, then folded it and dropped them both into her satchel. "I should probably leave. My aunts worry about me if I'm gone too long. But here." She opened up her satchel and pulled out a handful of red berries. "These are safe to eat. Just not the blue ones. You'll remember?"

I nodded. "For sure."

"Wait, um, Briar. Miss Rose. Were you out here . . . to pick berries?" Reece had suddenly gone really pale.

"Well . . ." She looked at her bag full of berries, then over at me. I shook my head like I was saying *I know, just go with it*. She gave me a quick smile, then turned back to Reece. "Yes?"

"Oh wow. Okay. So that's where we are?" Reece's breath was coming fast, like he was on the verge of hyperventilating. "This is fine. . . . It's . . ."

"Are you okay?" I asked, even though the answer was very clearly *absolutely not*.

"I'm fine! Hey, I know a fun game! Let's talk about when our birthdays are!"

I just stared at him. I knew that we were in highly unusual circumstances here, but I really needed him to pull it together. He was embarrassing me in front of the princess.

"I'll start!" His voice was too high-pitched, and he was smiling unnaturally, which just made the whole thing worse. "My birthday is December nineteenth." I snorted, and Reece frowned at me. "What?"

"Of *course* you're a Sagittarius. That makes complete sense. I should have known—"

"What about you?" Reece interrupted, turning to Rose.

"I'm actually turning sixteen in a week."

"Oh." Reece smiled happily. He looked incredibly relieved. "Next week? That's great. That's *great* news. So awesome."

"*My* birthday is in September," I said pointedly to Reece, who clearly didn't care about that.

"Why do you want to know?" Rose asked Reece with a smile.

"Oh, um . . ." Reece said, meeting my eye like he was asking for help. Which I was absolutely not going to give him; I had no idea why he was doing this. "I . . . um . . ."

I turned back to Rose, but in that moment noticed that a small gray rabbit was hopping toward us. "Bunny incoming." I suddenly worried there was an evil rabbit I'd forgotten about in the story. "Is that . . . okay?"

"Of course." She smiled at the rabbit, who hopped over to her side. "Why wouldn't it be?"

"Sometimes rabbits are evil."

"Rabbits?" Rose echoed, sounding mystified.

"They are," I insisted, even though Reece was shaking his head at me. But I was pretty sure we needed to get this clarified. If we were in a world where storybook rules existed, we had to be worried about things like bad bunnies. "What am I thinking of? You know."

"He's nice," Rose told me with a smile as she reached out to pet him. "He's a friend." She said this like it was the most normal thing in the world. Which maybe it *was* here.

I reached out my hand, suddenly wanting nothing more than to give his soft gray fur a pat. "May I?" I asked her. He really was a *very* cute rabbit.

With his pink nose! So wiggly! But all at once, I remembered that I was in a *fairy tale*, also known as a place where animals could understand you. "Um . . . may I?" I asked the rabbit. He looked back at me, nose twitching, but then inclined his head with a nod, like he was saying *If you must.*

"Stella, can I talk to you?" Reece asked, already walking away, his expression consternated.

"Sorry. I'll be right back," I said to Rose—and also the bunny, who was looking at me—as I pushed myself to my feet and walked over to join Reece. "Why are you being so rude?"

"Why are you talking about evil bunnies?" He sounded exactly as exasperated with me as I currently felt about him.

"Because they're a thing." I closed my eyes for a second, trying to pull an example up. "What movie am I thinking of?"

"Probably *Holy Grail*," he replied, his tone grudging.

"No . . ." I shook my head, trying to think. It never seemed like much of a liability that I couldn't remember plots of stories until moments like this. Well, not moments like *this*, since this was a brand-new one. But, like, trivia nights.

"*Donnie Darko? Bunnicula?*"

I shook my head. "I'm sure I'll think of it. But the fact that you have so many examples proves my point about rabbits." I glanced back to see Rose sitting on the ground and running her hand over the rabbit's ears. It looked like some birds had also decided to join and were hopping around on the grass nearby. I turned back to Reece. "So can animals talk in this world? Like should I be ready for a rabbit to break into song or something?"

"No," he said, then hesitated. "I think they *can* understand more. But they don't speak."

"So what did you need to talk to me about?" I asked, glancing back over and seeing there were now *two* bunnies who had arrived, flanking Rose like an honor guard.

"We need to leave." Reece was looking at me like this should have been obvious, which I didn't understand. Did he not see there were *two bunnies*? "I think we're okay—we arrived a week before the story begins."

"How do you know that?"

"Because the story starts on her sixteenth birthday. Were you not paying attention *at all* when we were walking through the castle?"

Well, at least that explained why Reece had suddenly been quizzing us about our birthdays. "What does it mean that we're here a week early?"

He shook his head. "I have no idea. I don't understand any of this, and I don't think there's anyone we can ask. But the longer we stay here—the longer we interact with her—the chances that we are going to mess things up will increase. So we should go."

"And do what?" He was making a classic mistake: following emotion and not facts. And admittedly, that was exactly what I had been doing when I'd stomped into the forest, but I could see the error of my ways now. "The first thing we should do is make a plan. I can make a spreadsheet on my phone—"

"We don't need a *spreadsheet*. What we need to do is leave before we cause any more damage."

"What do you mean?" I asked, staring at him. "What *damage* are we doing?"

"It's like in the second Dragons & Destiny book, *Flames of Fate*. Where they discover that dragons can time travel. And every time the characters start to go back to the past, it starts changing things in the present. Think about it. All our choices have *consequences*. Things ripple out based on what we do or don't do."

I shook my head, about to refute this and also call him out on the fact that he was getting these ideas from a time-traveling-dragon book. But all at once, I flashed to the moment that Nisha sat next to me when I was new in school, the first day of fourth grade. And everything that changed because of that one choice.

"We just need to be careful. If we're here, interacting with people, it will alter the story moving forward. We'll mess things up. So let's go."

I bristled at that. "Who made you the president in charge of deciding things? I think we should stay and try and get more information so that we can work out how we ended up here in the first place. Don't I get a vote?"

"Considering that you're the one who got us sent here," Reece said, his voice rising, "I'm not sure you do!"

"We were only in there to start with because *you* forgot your phone!" I was matching him in volume. Rose looked over at us, and two of her birds flew away. "I should have just ignored you and gotten my popcorn and we wouldn't even be here, but I felt sorry for you—"

"You felt sorry for *me*?" he asked, his tone incredulous.

I narrowed my eyes at him. "And just what's that supposed to mean?"

I heard a thundering of hooves and looked over to see that someone else had joined us in the forest. There was a guy who looked around our age—maybe a little older—sitting on top of a white horse. And as I stared at him, I realized that he looked familiar.

"Sorry," he said, glancing around at us. "I heard the commotion. Is everything all right?"

"Who is that?" I whispered to Reece.

He grimaced, and when he answered, his voice was a low, unhappy undertone. "That's Prince Phillip."

Eight

For a moment, I looked around at everyone frozen in place, like maybe there was a photographer hiding behind a nearby tree who'd just yelled, *Hold it!*

Rose had jumped to her feet, her eyes wide. Reece's expression was horrified, like he was watching a nightmare come true in real time. One rabbit had fled, and the other was staying put, but its ears were twitching, like it was on the verge of bolting, too.

And Prince Phillip was sitting on a *literal* white horse. I recognized him now from the pictures in the castle. He was really cute—and not just because I knew he was a prince. He had reddish-brown hair and was wearing a black shirt, pants, and boots. He was also wearing a red hat with a jaunty white feather in it. I was taking in all these details, but I don't think he had any idea; he was looking at Rose like she was the most wonderful thing he'd ever seen.

"Hey," I said a moment later, when it became clear nobody else was going to. The second I said it, I regretted it. My first encounter with royalty and I'd gone with *hey*? Then I remembered that Rose was technically royalty, too—but since she didn't know this, it felt different, somehow.

My *hey*, uncouth though it might have been, did seem to break the spell. The remaining rabbit fled into the woods, Reece seemed to recover himself, and Rose unfroze, pulling her bag over her shoulder and playing with the strap.

"I ... um ..." Prince Phillip said, looking thoroughly dazed, still gazing at Rose from atop his horse. He started to dismount, but his feet got tangled in his stirrups. He tumbled to the ground and landed with a *thump*. His white horse—it really was a very impressive horse, tall and regal, like what you would find in the dictionary if you searched for *noble steed*—looked down at Prince Phillip disdainfully. Then he took a few steps away, clearly trying to distance himself from the whole situation.

"Sorry," Prince Phillip said as he pushed himself to his feet and attempted to brush some of the dirt off his shirt. His hat had fallen, forgotten, onto the ground. "I didn't mean to interrupt. Just wanted to make sure that everything was all right." He ran his hand backward and forward through his hair, leaving it sticking up in the back.

It was a gesture that looked *really* familiar—and a second later, I realized why. This was the kid I'd seen in the throne room! But now he was all grown up. It spun my head a little bit that I was seeing both versions of him in a single day, when in his reality, sixteen years had passed.

"Oh," Rose said. I noticed now that she had basically turned into the heart-eyes emoji and was blushing as she looked at him. "We're fine."

"We're groovy," I called, giving him a thumbs-up. A second later, I realized that this was a lot worse than *hey*. "I mean . . . we're all good."

"No we're *not*," Reece hissed in my ear, pulling me a few steps away.

"What *now*?" I asked, turning to him, keeping my voice low.

He gestured toward Prince Phillip and Rose. "This is not *all good*, Stella. They're not supposed to meet for another week. This is *bad*. We're messing up the story!"

Rose walked over to the white horse and held her hand out flat, letting him snuffle her fingers. Then the horse nudged her with his head and she laughed and patted him on the neck. Prince Phillip watched, looking utterly ensorcelled.

"I don't know." You would have had to be *really* not paying attention to pick up on the major vibes that were currently happening. "Obviously, they like each other. And they end up together, right?"

Reece nodded, even though his expression was pained. "They do."

"Okay. So then why is it bad that they're meeting early? We should just tell them now! And then we can just skip to the end."

Reece stared at me, incredulous. "We can't do that," he hissed, his voice horrified. "They have to fall in love on their own, without two random people hanging around, and we're messing with that. It's not the destination, it's the journey."

"It's *not the destination*?" I echoed, incredulous. "It's all about the destination. The destination is the only thing that matters. Who cares about the journey? None of my parents' clients care about the path their stuff took to get to them, just that it gets there."

"Are you hearing yourself right now?"

"Look, we can save everyone a lot of time and hassle. Let's just tell them!"

"No!"

"Stella?" I looked across the clearing and saw that Rose was giving me an expression that clearly meant *Can you come here, please.* I'd gotten it from Nisha many times. Mostly when she'd first been crushing on Allyson.

I nodded and headed over to them, feeling like I'd let her down. Rose had *told* me that she didn't get to meet that many people, after all. If rabbits had been her primary source of friends up until now, I could imagine that it would be really overwhelming to suddenly encounter a really cute guy who rode up on a white horse.

Well, technically she'd met *two* cute guys today. Because Reece was objectively handsome—right up until the moment he opened his mouth and began to speak.

"Hi, sorry," I said to Prince Phillip. "Everything's good here. You didn't need to pull your horse over."

Prince Phillip gave me a polite, if confused, nod. "Ah. I'm so glad."

"I'm Stella," I said, giving him a wave, still not sure what the proper protocol was when meeting royalty. Even though I thought it might have been a secret that he was a prince? I tried to call up the details of the story, but just couldn't remember. At any rate, he certainly wasn't dressed like a prince—I wasn't sure if princes were allowed to exchange their crowns for jaunty hats.

"I'm Rose," she said, giving him a shy nod. "Briar Rose, but you can call me Rose. If you'd like."

"And I'm Reece," Reece said, his voice resigned.

"This is Samson," the prince said as he gestured to the beautiful horse, who deigned to look over at us and inclined his head a little, as though in greeting. Phillip smiled at each of us in turn. "It's so nice to meet you all."

"It's nice to meet you, too, Phil—" I managed to stop myself before I got the whole word out, realizing too late what I'd done. I glanced over at Reece, who widened his eyes at me, but I knew even without the look that I'd messed up. I wasn't supposed to know Prince Phillip's name. Because I wasn't supposed to know *who he was.*

Which just went to prove my earlier point that this subterfuge wasn't helping anyone. It would have been way better to just get everything out in the open. Tell these two that they'd eventually fall in love, remind Rose to stay the heck away from spinning wheels, and call it a day. Who cared about the journey? In the end, so to speak, the destination was all that mattered.

"Well . . . yes," Prince Phillip said slowly. "Do you . . . know me?" It was like he held his breath after he asked the question, like he was scared to hear the answer.

"No, sure don't. Never seen you before. I'm just really good with names!" I babbled, feeling my heart start to race. "Like, I looked at you and said, *Wow, there's a Phil if I've ever seen one.*"

"Yes," he said, nodding. "You can call me Phil. It's short for . . . er . . . *Philomeno.*"

Reece raised an eyebrow at me, and I looked away quickly. But if Prince Phillip was trying to lay low, and hide his royal lineage, he needed to get better at lying.

"Well—it is lovely to meet you, Phil," Rose said, like she was trying out saying his name, and liking it. I liked it, too. Maybe it was also because he was in his forest outfit, but the fact that we were calling him Phil was letting me forget—just a little bit—that we were dealing with a literal fairy-tale prince.

"And you," Phil replied, looking only at her. "And all of you," he added a moment later, clearly trying to cover.

"I will say," Rose said, "this really is a change for me. I usually don't encounter anyone when I head into the forest, save a rabbit or two."

"I'm so sorry to have intruded," Phil said quickly, taking a step back into a kind of mini-bow. "I just heard the hullabaloo."

"There wasn't any hullabaloo," I said dismissively, even though I wasn't exactly sure what hullabaloo actually *was*. "We were just . . . having a discussion."

Phil nodded, and looked from me to Reece. "With your stable hand?"

"*Okay*," Reece said, sounding like he was at the end of his rope. "I'm not a stable hand. It would be just really great if everyone could stop thinking that I was. I don't know anything about horses, okay? I've even never ridden one."

"You . . . haven't?" Rose asked.

"Oh," Phil said. It was like his royal etiquette training prevented him from saying what he really thought, but they both looked gobsmacked. And looking at their expressions, I wondered if Reece realized he'd just made a huge fairy-tale faux pas. Was not riding a horse here the equivalent of saying that you'd never been in a car?

"I mean, of course I've been on a horse," Reece said quickly, meeting my eye, and I could see he knew that he'd messed up. "I just meant that I hadn't ridden one *well*. So it didn't count. But basically, um, just to circle back, I'm *not* a stable hand. So."

"They're friends," Rose explained. "They were just having a disagreement. They've come from a ball!"

I shook my head. "Well, kind of. We never actually got there—"

"A *ball*?" Phil's eyes lit up like Rose's had earlier. These two really were made for each other. "A ball around here?"

"Not super close," Reece said, shaking his head.

"Bit of a journey," I added.

"Oh. That's too bad. Because I do love to dance. And I'd love to attend a ball. Though I suppose I will before too long. . . ." Rather than these words making Phil happy, they seemed to have the opposite effect. His voice trailed off, and his expression clouded. He sank down onto a nearby tree stump, his whole posture suddenly looking defeated.

"Uh—Phil? Are you okay?" I asked after a moment, even though it seemed very clear that the answer was *No, not really.*

"Very well, thank you," he said, utterly polite. "Lovely weather, isn't it?"

"Okay, dude," I said, and I saw Reece do a double take. Probably you weren't supposed to call princes *dude.* Or *Phil,* for that matter, but here we were. "What's really going on? You can talk about it."

"If the . . . Phil," Reece said, catching himself just in time. "Doesn't want to talk about it, let's not make him."

"I wasn't going to *make* him." *God!* Reece was truly the most annoying guy I'd ever had to be around. If I ever got stuck in a fairy tale again, he was *not* coming with me.

"I really don't want to trouble anyone," Phil said with a stoic smile, but I saw through it right away—because I did this, too. And when I did, it was Nisha who always called me out. She somehow knew just the right moment to come by bearing Froyo or ice cream sandwiches or pizza. She'd show up with treats and badger me into talking about what was bothering me—the thing that, deep down, I always *did* actually want to talk about. I hadn't even realized it until I became friends with Nisha—that I'd internalized my parents' philosophy maybe a bit too much. Because the fact was, I'd been raised in a house where it wasn't productive or efficient to talk about your feelings, or linger on what might have been. You had to find solutions and keep moving forward. And so thank god for Nisha—she'd been the one to call this out as nonsense, and now I was even able to realize when I was doing it and try and change course.

But it seemed like Phil, unfortunately, had not had this kind of friend in his life. Which meant I'd have to be his Nisha. Because I always, *always* felt better after we'd talked through everything and eaten all the snacks. Every time.

So with this in mind, I grabbed my canvas bag from where I'd left it in the clearing and sat on the ground next to Phil's tree stump. I dug in the bag, pushing aside my phone (useless here), my sweatshirt, and hand sanitizer, until I found what I was looking for: the snacks I'd packed for Disney.

I'd been prepared (of course) with options: a bag of salty snacks and a bag of sweet. Sometimes, when we were going to be spending all day in the park, we'd pack actual food, but since we had our dinner reservations, I'd just stuck with snacks. And we'd been busy enough that we hadn't even really dug into them, so it meant there was plenty left over for now. Which was a good thing, because I wasn't sure I'd ever seen someone so in need of chocolate as Phil.

"Here," I said as I took both of the snack bags out. They were gallon Ziplocs, clearly labeled, with smaller bags inside them. There were snack-size Ruffles and Doritos in the salty bag, as well as small packets of almonds and trail mix. The sweet bag had mini bags of M&M's, two full-size Snickers, two Kit Kats, and three bags of Reese's Pieces. I knew when I packed the snack bags that we weren't going to need all of it—after all, we were spending the afternoon at Disneyland, not crossing the Rockies in a wagon—but it just made me feel better to be stocked up. I'd seen low blood sugar meltdowns in line for rides before, and they were *not* pretty. Better to be over-stocked than hangry. That was my basic philosophy.

"Hey," I said, as I held out the sweet bag toward Phil. "Want some chocolate?"

He just blinked at me, ruffling his hair forward and backward. "What is that?"

I stared at him for a moment. Did they not have chocolate . . . back whenever we were? No wonder people were always dying young in the middle ages. What was there to live for?

"Here," I said, when I realized I didn't know how to answer that question, and that in this case, tasting might be believing. I opened the bag of Reese's Pieces and held it out to him.

"Is it all right?" Phil asked Reece.

"With me?" Reece asked, sounding confused.

"Aren't they yours?" Phil asked, squinting at the bag. "Your . . . pieces?"

Reece closed his eyes for a long moment, like he was summoning patience. "It's fine," he finally said, and I tipped a handful into Phil's palm. He regarded the candy warily, but made no move to eat any.

"They're good," I assured him, tossing back a handful of my own and crunching down on them. "See?"

Phil cautiously ate one, and his eyes went big. "Oh *my*," he breathed. "That's delicious!" I smiled and handed him the rest of the bag. "How have I never had this delicacy before?"

"They're pretty common where we come from," I said.

"And . . . where is that?" Phil asked.

I exchanged a quick, panicked glance with Reece, trying to think fast. "The, um, kingdom of . . . Anaheim."

"Ah." Phil shook some more candy into his palm, frowning. I could see that he was about to ask follow-up questions—questions I had no idea how to answer—when Rose came and sat down next to me, clearly curious about these treats we were having. She glanced over at my snack bags, her eyes growing wide at the bright packaging and bold fonts. She had probably never seen neon before, and I was pretty certain she didn't know what *crunchtastic* meant. I couldn't help but notice that, out here in this peaceful meadow, the Doritos font suddenly looked a bit ... garish. Like it was really out of place here, which made sense because it *was*.

She picked up an individual bag of trail mix. "May I?"

"Sure," I said automatically, then a second later, crossed my fingers that she didn't have some kind of undiagnosed peanut allergy.

Reece came a few steps closer but didn't sit down with us. He leaned against a tree instead, like he was trying to show us that he wasn't participating. I rolled my eyes at that but tossed him a mini bag of Ruffles anyway. "Thanks," he said gruffly, before opening them.

Now that we all had our snacks and were eating happily—or just eating, in Reece's case—I remembered the whole reason I'd even broken out the snacks in the first place. Because Phil seemed to be really down about something.

"So?" I asked, turning to Phil. "What's going on with you?"

"Oh—it isn't anything to concern yourselves with," he said, even as he shook out more Reese's Pieces. "It's ... well ..."

"You needn't worry," Rose said, surprising me. She opened up the trail mix bag. "Whatever is going on, we won't tell anyone. Well," she added after a moment, with a laugh, "not ... that I would have anyone *to* tell. Except the rabbits. And everyone knows they can keep a secret." She ate a handful of the trail mix, then looked at me with a surprised smile. I was glad I'd packed the kind with extra chocolate chips.

"Good, right?"

"*So* good. Far superior to berries!"

"I suppose it's . . . my parents," Phil finally said. He shook the Reese's Pieces bag hopefully, but it was empty. He set it down and took a breath. "They're—"

"We don't have to talk about this!" Reece interrupted.

I glared at him, regretting that I'd ever shared my Ruffles. Did he not understand what we were doing here?

"Reece," Rose said, sounding surprised.

"I just mean if it's private, or if, you know, saying it out loud might change things . . . maybe we should just keep it to ourselves! Right?"

"Ignore him," I said firmly, turning back to Phil. "What about your parents?"

"There's . . . something that I'm supposed to do," he said slowly, like he was choosing all his words carefully. "They've planned it out ever since I was little. And I understand they've organized things and put in all this preparation. But they never *asked* me. And I don't see any way around it. It's my duty. And I realize that. But . . ." He sighed, his shoulders slumping. "So that's why I was out riding. I just had to . . . get away." He carefully folded up the empty Reese's bag, and I tossed him a mini bag of M&M's that he caught with one hand. "Thank you."

"It really does suck." This was Reece who spoke, surprising me. "How your parents can just make these unilateral decisions, and you're dragged along with it."

"Yes!" Phil said. "That's it entirely."

I looked at Reece, wondering just what he was talking about. But then, a second later, I remembered that he'd just moved from Connecticut. His parents had moved him across the country and he'd just been pulled along for the ride. I took a breath to ask more about this when Rose frowned up at the sun, then pushed herself to her feet.

"I have to go," she said, slinging her bag over her shoulder, sounding regretful. "I hadn't realized it had gotten so late. My aunts will be wondering where I am."

Phil jumped to his feet. "May I escort you back?"

"No!" Reece yelled, and we all turned to look at him. "I just meant . . ." he stammered. "Rose is fine! She's a modern woman! She knows her way around, and she doesn't need to be escorted anywhere. Right?"

"Uh . . . right," Rose said, even though she looked like she very much *would* have liked Phil to escort her home. "I'll be fine. It's not far."

"And you said you two are traveling?" Phil asked as he looked between Reece and me. "Do you have somewhere to stay for the night?"

I looked at Reece, and the enormity of this—this world we'd just crashed into—hit me all at once. Where were we going to stay? How were we going to survive? I suddenly regretted sharing my snacks so freely. What if this was all the food we'd have access to? Except berries, apparently. But considering some of the berries around here were *deadly*, that didn't seem like a real comfort right now.

"Well . . ." Reece met my eye, and I could tell he was having all the same thoughts. "It's . . ."

"Because you could always stay with me," Phil continued. "It's not my home, it's my father's friend's . . . domain. But I know you'd be welcome. There's more than enough room."

"Oh," I said, raising my eyebrows at Reece. "That sounds . . ."

"Not *so* much room," Phil amended quickly as he glanced at Rose. "Not like a castle or anything! Hahaha!"

"Maybe," Reece said, giving him a smile. "That's a nice offer."

"Reece," I said sharply. I didn't want to blow up Phil's spot but we were being offered a chance to stay in a *castle*. I didn't want to leave this with *maybe*. "I think—"

Just then, I heard someone calling out. The voice sounded far off, and older, a bit quavery. "Rose? Are you there?" Even from this distance, I could hear the worry in it.

"My aunt," Rose said, her brow furrowing. "I don't want to worry her. I should go."

"Yes," Reece said slowly, like he was making a decision, and turned toward her. "Good idea. We'll come, too."

Nine

W hat," I hissed at Reece as we followed Rose out of the woods, "are you *doing*?"

We'd said goodbye to Phil—and Samson—as we left the clearing. Phil looked very confused as to why *we* were walking Rose home, when Reece had made it clear he couldn't, but was obviously much too polite to point this out.

Phil, blushing, had told Rose that he hoped he'd run into her again. And she'd blushed too and told him she also hoped so, and it was all very adorable.

But Reece didn't seem to think so, because he rushed us through our goodbyes and hustled us away from Phil, despite the fact that he was our best hope at getting to stay in a *castle* tonight.

"We need help," Reece said in an undertone to me as we walked. I could see the light brightening ahead of us, the trees thinning—we were almost out of the woods. Literally, that is. Metaphorically, not so much.

"I know we need help," I snapped. Did he think I wasn't *aware* of this? "But we were just offered a perfectly good castle, and you just threw it away—"

"I need to try to understand how we came here. And what it means. So I think we should talk to Rose's aunts."

Rose paused at the edge of the woods and turned back to us. "Is everything all right?"

"Absolutely!" Reece replied.

"So good!" I chimed back. "A hundo p!"

She frowned at that, but then nodded and kept walking.

"*A hundo p?*" Reece echoed, his voice skeptical. "I don't think you should say that even in our normal lives, but *certainly* not here."

"Wait, how do you think Rose's *aunts* are going to help us figure our situation out?"

"Her aunts are the three good fairies!" Reece sounded like he was maybe nearing the edge of his patience.

"Right, right." I frowned, trying to remember. "Flower, Flopsy, and . . . Monique?"

"Where are you getting these? Seriously."

"So you think they can help us?"

"I don't know. But I think they're our best chance to get some answers."

"But what about what you said, how we shouldn't interfere with the story?"

"I think we've gotten too involved now to just disappear without causing issues—or at least raising questions. But maybe you could hold off on giving any more princes Doritos."

"Everyone loves Doritos!"

I thought I saw Reece's mouth twitch in a smile, but then it was gone, like he was trying to flatten it out. I don't know why, but it somehow made me start to smile, too.

We stepped out of the woods, into the fading late-afternoon sunlight, and I gasped.

Right in front of me was the most perfect cottage I'd ever seen.

There was water right next to it, but I wasn't sure if this was a pond, or a lake, or a river (or even an estuary, which was one of those words I'd held on to from elementary school science class but had not managed to retain the definition). At any rate, there was an arched footbridge crossing over the water, and a stone walkway led up to the cottage. And the cottage itself was breathtaking. It had two stories, a thatched roof, and looked like it had been built in and around a giant tree that towered over it. There was a lazy curl of smoke rising from one of the chimneys, brightly colored flowers in the window boxes, and the whole thing just felt *cozy*. You could imagine it was the kind of house where there was always a fire going, there was always something delicious to eat inside, and there always someone waiting for you. The kind of place where nothing bad could ever happen.

"This is where you live?" I blinked in wonder at it.

"Yes." Rose tucked her hair behind her ears and glanced at my dress. "I know it's not so grand . . ."

"It's *wonderful*," I breathed, and I saw Reece glance over at me, surprised.

Rose smiled, her cheeks going pink. "I mean, it's the only place I've ever lived. But I agree."

Reece started to head toward the cottage, but Rose stayed where she was, her bare feet (which, seriously, *how*) planted in the grass.

"So," she said, adjusting the strap of her bag. "I'm not sure if my aunts will be . . . very welcoming. I just don't have friends visit very often. Or, well, ever," she said with a short laugh. "Our landlords come once a year, but that's different." Reece frowned at that, but Rose took a breath and continued. "My aunts have never *said* anything, but I somehow don't think they'd like it. And they are always telling me not to talk to strangers . . ."

"It'll be okay," Reece said confidently.

"Yeah," I echoed a beat later, less confidently. Reece seemed to think that talking to her aunts was the right thing to do, but I still couldn't help but think that we would have been a lot better off in a castle.

"Well . . . all right," Rose said, even though she didn't sound convinced. "I just . . . wanted to give you a warning."

"Rose?" I could hear a voice call from inside the cottage, sounding distinctly worried now.

"I'm here!" Rose yelled in the direction of the cottage.

The front door was the kind that split in two so you could just open half of it. The top part of the door swung open, revealing an older-looking, gray-haired lady, her hair tucked up in a yellow kerchief. She stuck her head out of the door and looked around. "We have been so worried . . . " she started. But her voice trailed off as she looked at Reece and me.

"Hey," I said, raising a hand in a wave.

The top part of the door closed, and a second later the whole thing swung open, and the older lady was hurrying toward us, her expression a combination of scared and worried. "What—what is going on?" she asked. Her eyes widened when she took in my dress, then lowered her head and bobbed a low, awkward curtsy. "My lady."

"I'm really not. So there's no need for all . . . that."

She glanced over at Reece, and her expression got even more confused. "Did something happen to your horse?"

"I'm not a stable hand!" Reece's voice was strangled, like it was taking everything in his power to stop from yelling.

"I met them in the woods, Aunt Fauna," Rose explained hurriedly, twisting her hands together. "They're my . . . friends."

"In the woods?" The lady—Fauna—looked at me, her expression getting more and more concerned, even as it looked like she was struggling to keep a polite expression on her face. The same way I looked whenever Allyson said she was going to cook for us, since every time she tried, it was an unmitigated disaster, involving either the fire department, food poisoning, or in one particularly dark episode, *both*.

"I'm Reece," Reece said, inclining his head, and then giving her a smile. "It's an honor to meet you." I blinked at him, a little taken aback by this smiling, charming version of Reece. He glanced over at me, and I realized a second too late that he was waiting for me to introduce myself, too.

"I'm Stella," I added hurriedly. "What's up?" Reece shot me a look, and I shot him one back that clearly said, *What?*

"Isn't that such a lovely name?" Rose asked with a sigh. "I just love names that have to do with the stars."

Reece let out an involuntary laugh at that, and quickly tried to cover it with a cough. But I saw Flora's eyes widen as she looked at him, her expression changing from confusion to wariness.

"We were hoping to talk to you," Reece said, stepping forward. "To all three of you."

"Is that all right?" Rose asked. "I know I'm not meant to bring people by, but . . ." She shook her head and took a step closer to her aunt and lowered her voice. "I was getting a bit concerned about their survival. When I found them, they were about to eat the thistleberries."

"Were you?" Flora looked more unsettled than ever, her eyebrows knitting together. "I thought everyone knew to avoid them."

"We're not from here," I explained.

"They're from the kingdom of Anaheim," Rose explained. "And so I thought they could use your help. You've always been able to fix anything."

Fauna's concerned expression softened for just a moment as she looked at Rose. "It . . . was a nice impulse, dear," she said, even as her tone said the exact opposite. "But . . ."

"Is there maybe a place," Reece asked, his eyes darting to Rose for a second then back to Fauna, his intent clear, "where we might speak? Privately?"

"Yes," Fauna said, a steely tone coming into her words. She looked at Rose and gave her a smile. "Why don't you run along to your room, dear?" she asked, then turned back to Reece and me. "And your new friends and I will have a chat."

"Oh good," I said, giving Reece a nod, glad this had all worked out so easily. "That's what we wanted."

Ten minutes later, I glared at Reece. "This isn't what I wanted."

We were in the cellar of the cottage, sitting on hard, uncomfortable chairs, our hands tied, while three senior citizens pointed magic wands at us.

And though the cottage had looked cozy from the outside, this did *not* extend to the cellar, which was damp and drafty and heavily spiderwebbed. The only light down here was from three flickering candles, which cast really spooky shadows on the walls all around us.

"Answer the question!" one of them yelled—Flora, I was pretty sure. She was the tallest, and seemed the most serious, the one who had taken charge right away. Fauna was in the middle, height-wise, and seemed the nicest, though that was a pretty low bar to clear at the moment. Merryweather had dark hair and was the shortest. She seemed feisty, like she was throwing elbows maybe a little bit more than was absolutely necessary. But as a fellow short person, I understood it. When you're a whole foot smaller than some people, you have to do whatever you can to make sure you're taken seriously.

"What was the question?" I asked. I was trying to keep my eyes fixed on the wands pointed in my direction. We were *not* in a normal world, after all. Just this afternoon—and also, somehow, sixteen years ago—I'd watched these three float out of the sky on a shaft of light. They seemed like nice old ladies—well, they *had*, before the whole interrogation thing—but I had no doubt they could easily turn me into a toad if they so desired.

"What are you *doing here*?" Flora repeated.

"Look," Reece said. His tone was reasonable, but I noticed that he was also keeping an eye on the wands. "Let's just talk. I know you're not going to use those."

"Reece," I hissed at him. "Shut up." Why was he antagonizing people with the ability to do magic? Did he *want* to be a toad?

"How do you know?" Merryweather demanded, folding her arms.

"Who sent you?" Flora demanded, slamming her hand on the back of my chair, then wincing.

"Oh, that looked like it hurt," Fauna said, tutting. "Are you all right, dear?"

"Fine," Flora said through gritted teeth.

"She sent you, didn't she? Admit it!" This was Merryweather, getting right in my face.

"Who?" I asked blankly, trying to keep my hands still. If I tried to move them too much, I got rope burn, which was honestly the last thing I needed in a land without Neosporin.

"*Maleficent*," she half whispered, like she was afraid to say the name too loudly.

"Oh, right, her. You know, I never saw those prequels. What was her deal, again?"

"We need to get to the truth," Flora said as she turned to Merryweather. "I'll be tough. You be nice."

"*You* be nice," Merryweather retorted, adjusting the kerchief over her black hair.

"I'm nice!" Fauna piped up.

"You're too nice," Merryweather said dismissively. "You'd forget we were trying to get information and give them dinner."

"They *do* look hungry," Fauna said, smiling at Reece and patting his cheek. "Poor dears."

"They might not be poor dears!" Flora snapped. "They might be Maleficent's spies!"

"We're not," Reece assured her.

"Scout's honor," I said. I tried to raise my hand to do the salute and immediately got a rope burn for my trouble. "Gah!"

"That's just what a spy would say," Flora said, shaking her head.

"Um, ladies?" I said. "I'm not sure that good cop, bad cop works when you're telling us who's who." They all just stared at me. "I mean . . . good fairy, bad fairy."

Fauna gasped. "She knows we're fairies!"

"We are holding wands," Flora pointed out, sounding very much like she wanted to roll her eyes.

"Look!" Reece said. "You can untie us, okay? We came here because we need your help. The last thing we want to do is to hurt you, or mess up your plans, or interfere with the way things are supposed to go with . . . Aurora."

Saying the name aloud was like tossing a live grenade into the center of the room. The three women drew in a sharp breath, and I noticed all of them were clutching their wands harder now.

"How . . ." Flora asked, after a moment of strained silence, "how do you know about that?"

"We're not from here," I started to explain.

"But you can tell that, right?" Reece asked, looking at all three of them. And I could see in his expression how much he wanted it to be true—for them to be able to understand, to have someone to help get us through this. "You could tell that the first time you met us."

The women exchanged a look. "There is something different about them," Flora finally said, taking a small step closer to Reece. "I can feel it. Their energy is . . . off. Like a song that's out of tune."

"It's true," Fauna said, leaning a little closer to me. "And I have never even *heard* of the kingdom of Anaheim. And you know how I love cartography."

"We know," Flora said, sounding weary.

"If you untie us," Reece said, "we can explain."

"I promise we're not spies," I said, as they exchanged skeptical looks.

'We're not working for Maleficent. The last thing either of us want is to hurt Rose."

They all looked at me, and for just a second, it felt like I was getting a silent lie detector test—like me, and my words, were being weighed and evaluated. Finally, Merryweather nodded.

"All right," she said. She pointed her wand at me. I closed my eyes and flinched, but a moment later, the ropes, neatly severed, fell to the cellar floor.

"Thanks," I said, very happy I could gesticulate again without pain.

"Yes, thanks," Reece echoed, rubbing his wrists.

"Merryweather!" Flora snapped. "You know we're not supposed to use magic."

Merryweather shook her head. "I didn't want to go through the trouble of untying them. You make the knots impossible; it would have taken all day." She raised an eyebrow at Flora. "And you're one to talk. You used your wand last week."

Flora flushed bright red and crossed her arms. "I did not."

"You did so."

"I did *not*."

"Okay," Reece interrupted. He looked at me and took a breath. "So . . . we're from pretty far away."

"Anaheim," Merryweather piped up, looking proud of herself.

"Well, yes," Reece said. "Technically, that's true."

"It's in a place called California," I said, trying to think of how to explain that I was from a different time, and possibly a different reality entirely. It was not something that, understandably, I'd had a ton of experience with. "But we're also from another . . . time. Like . . . the future."

"Where we come from," Reece jumped in, "your story has already happened. And we know it. The christening and the gifts and Maleficent's curse. And how you raised Aurora here for her own protection. We know all about that. And also . . . what happens next."

"You know . . . the future?" Fauna asked, her eyes going wide. "Oh my."

"Ooh, what happens to me?" Merryweather asked eagerly.

"They can't tell us," Flora said sharply. "Otherwise, it might alter the outcome of events. We might start behaving differently, because we'd be aiming for something, and that changes all our fates."

"Yes, yes, of course," Merryweather said, nodding. Then she leaned closer to me and spoke in an undertone. "But what *does* happen to me?"

"Merryweather!" Flora admonished sharply.

"The story we know actually starts a week from now," Reece explained. "So we're in a bit of uncharted territory. We want to make sure our presence here—even this conversation we're now having—doesn't wreck the way the story is supposed to go." They just stared at him and he took a big breath. "So, in this story called *Back to the Future,* this guy named Marty gets sent back in time—"

"So we were hoping you could help," I interrupted before Reece explained the whole plot of a movie to people who'd never seen a movie. But saying it out loud, explaining our situation, did make me feel better about things. Not that anything had been solved or fixed—far from it. But just to tell someone else what was happening, so this all wasn't just on the two of us to figure out ourselves, was a relief. "Maybe you could get us home again?"

"We don't even really know how we ended up here," Reece said, glancing at me. "Or why."

A second later, I realized that was true. The shock of appearing in this world, and then suddenly having to deal with Rose and Phil (and Samson), had meant that Reece and I hadn't been able to talk about the biggest questions of all—*why* we were here to begin with, and how it had happened.

"I'm not sure we'll be able to tell you the answer to that," Flora said, shaking her head. "Magic has its own mysterious ways. If you were sent here, it was for a reason."

"What kind of reason?" Reece asked.

Fauna shook her head. "I couldn't tell you, dear. It's a journey that you'll have to figure out on your own."

I stifled a sigh. I was honestly sick of hearing about journeys today. Why couldn't anyone be talking about destinations? "But you do think you'll be able to get us home again?" This was, after all, the most important thing. As charming as the cottage was—well, minus this room—and as much as I'd liked meeting Rose and Phil, I really didn't want to stay here forever.

"That will take some thinking," Flora said slowly. "We've never even tried to achieve anything like that. It might be . . . beyond us."

"Not to mention the fact that every time we use magic, we run the risk of being discovered by Maleficent and the spies she has out searching for us."

"Oh." I looked over at Reece, wondering if he was feeling the same stomach-plunging disappointment that I was. We might be stuck here . . . in perpetuity?

"But I'm sure we can figure it out," Merryweather said, giving me a smile. "It might take us some time. But we'll put our heads together and come up with something."

"We always do," Fauna said encouragingly.

"In the meantime," Flora said, her expression grave, "we need to make sure you're safe."

All three of the women looked at me, and I felt my eyes widen. "Me? I'll be fine. I know about the berries now."

"No," Reece said. Understanding and—was I imagining it?—concern was dawning on his face. "It's Maleficent."

"Why would I be in danger from her?" I tried to repress a shiver. Even the tiny glimpse I'd seen of her earlier this afternoon had been enough to see just how scary and formidable she was. And the thought that I might somehow be in her crosshairs was *not* particularly comforting right now.

"If she finds out you know anything about the princess, or what happens to her, you could be in danger," Flora said. "She could try and get information from you about Rose's whereabouts."

"She's desperate to find Rose," Merryweather piped up. "You can feel it—well, we can—emanating from that monstrosity where she's chosen to live. And the closer it gets to Rose's birthday, when her spell will be broken, the more frustrated she's getting."

"I actually don't think she's very happy," Fauna said with a sigh as she shook her head.

"You've mentioned that," Flora said.

"Wait! We haven't explained," Merryweather said, her eyes brightening. She cleared her throat, and when she spoke again, her voice was lower and more sonorous. "It was nigh these sixteen years ago, and everyone had arrived at the christening of Princess Aurora—"

"They know, dear," Flora said. "Remember?"

"I don't get to tell the story?" Merryweather looked very put out. She huffed out a sigh. "*Fine.* Never mind."

"We do know the story," Reece said, sounding apologetic. He glanced at me and sighed. "Well . . . I do, at any rate."

"And also," I added, "we were there."

All three of the women seemed to blink at us in unison. "You . . . were?" Flora asked.

"Just for a little bit," Reece explained. "We stepped through a doorway into the christening, then returned back to our, um, kingdom. And then we were sent back here, but to . . . now."

"A doorway," Merryweather said slowly. "Fascinating."

"Very," Flora agreed. "Well, that's all good information to have. We'll take it into consideration."

"At any rate," Fauna said, "the closer it gets to Rose's birthday, the more desperate Maleficent is going to become. Which means we can't take any chances or let our guard down at all. It was," she added, her cheeks going pink, "possibly the reason I reacted so strongly when I met you."

"So, she'd try and get information out of me?" I asked. I could feel my heart start to race. I hadn't loved being interrogated by three *good* fairies; I was pretty sure I didn't want to face down one of the most famous fairy-tale villains to ever exist.

"Both of you, potentially," Merryweather said, looking at Reece.

"So why don't you stay here? That way, we can protect you," Fauna said, clapping her hands together. "Oh, this will be such fun."

"Stella, you can stay with Rose," Flora said, nodding. "And Reece . . . hmm." All the fairies looked at him, heads tilted to the side like they were all trying to figure this out.

"You know, the cellar is a *wonderful* place to stay," Merryweather said, sounding like an overly optimistic Realtor as she gestured around the damp, spiderwebby room we were in. "Wouldn't you like that, Reece?"

"That's so kind of you," Reece said, even as he looked around skeptically. "But . . . I think I might just stay with my friend. And Stella can stay here with you three ladies. I know you can keep her safe. You're the heroes of the story, after all."

All three of the fairies smiled at this, and all seemed to stand up a little taller (not that you could really tell, in Merryweather's case).

"Wait just a minute," I said, shaking my head. Reece got to stay in the castle? How was that fair?

"We can talk about it outside," Reece said in an undertone to me.

"Do you not want to stay with us, dear?" Fauna asked me, her eyes going wide and hurt.

"Oh, no, of course," I said, suddenly remembering my manners, feeling my cheeks get hot. "I mean—I'd love to. Thank you so much for the invitation." She smiled at me, her hurt expression vanishing instantly, and I suddenly wondered if I'd just had the sweet-old-lady card pulled on me. If so . . . it really was well done. Props to Fauna. "But . . . will it be okay with Rose?"

"We'll ask her," Flora said. "And we should head upstairs anyway; I'm not sure we need to spend any more time in the cellar."

The three women headed up the steps to the main floor of the cottage, and Reece started to climb up after them, but I grabbed the back of his sweatshirt, causing him to stumble back a step. "Ow. What?"

"That didn't hurt," I said, rolling my eyes. "We need to talk about this."

Reece nodded and glanced up the stairs to where I could still hear three voices. "We do," he said. "Meet me outside."

"Because this is not okay. You just castle-blocked me."

Reece shook his head and started climbing the steps. "That's not a thing!"

"Um, it totally is, and I know because you just did it. Meet me outside."

"You mean, what I just said to do? Yes, great idea."

"Fine," I snapped, starting to climb the steps behind him.

"Fine," he replied.

I was tempted to say *fine* again, to have the last word—something I always enjoyed. But I didn't want to sink to his level of childishness, even if he had maneuvered the situation so that he would get to stay in a castle and I wouldn't. So I just contented myself with muttering it under my breath. "*Fine.*"

Ten

I waited until we had walked away from the cottage and were halfway back to the woods before I turned to Reece. "What the heck, dude?"

We'd headed outside when the fairies had gone up to talk to Rose about the idea of me staying, and that she was about to get a new roommate for a while.

The fact that none of us knew exactly how long this would be—not to mention that we still didn't have any concrete ideas for how we were going to get home again—was making my anxiety flare. It was a kind of low-level hum of incipient panic that was just *there*, like a TV on in the next room. I knew if I really let myself think about this whole situation and the enormity of it, I'd start to spiral.

So, instead, I decided to focus on Reece and the fact that he was denying me a stay in a castle.

"I know," Reece said as he headed into the woods, and I followed. I pulled the skirt of my dress closer to me, trying to keep it from getting snagged on branches. If today had taught me anything, it was that there was a reason formal hiking wasn't a thing. "I get that you're mad."

"This is so *like you*," I fumed, as we walked deeper into the woods. It was darker in there, the shadows stretching out.

"What's so like me?" Reece sounded like he was torn between being annoyed and being amused.

"Keeping a castle away from me and taking it for yourself!"

"Oh right," he said, one side of his mouth quirking up in a smile. "You got me. I'm *always* doing that. Just denying people castles left and right. That's what *everyone* says."

I laughed, almost against my will. And to my surprise, Reece laughed, too—a surprisingly nice laugh, low-pitched and musical. The kind that made you want to work harder to be funny, just so you could hear it again.

"You know what I mean," I said. "I'm . . . Where are you going?" I had just followed Reece into the woods, assuming he wanted some privacy where we could discuss this without being overheard, but now we were just walking in the woods, getting deeper in.

"Back to the meadow," he said, like it should have been obvious. I was about to ask *why* when he continued. "I'm sorry about the castle thing." Something in his tone made me believe that he meant it. "But you'll be the safest here, under the protection of the fairies. I wasn't kidding when I called them the heroes of the story. I know you don't remember, but they're pretty badass. They're the ones who really save the day. In the end, it's basically a showdown with Maleficent. They figure out this really ingenious way to subvert her evil magic with good. If the fairies aren't there, helping everything along, the story has a much less happy ending."

"But if the safest place to be is with them, why aren't you staying, too? I'm sure the cellar isn't *that* bad."

"I want to stay with Phil."

"In a castle."

"It's because we're *in* the story now," he continued, like I hadn't said anything. "We're a part of it, for better or worse. So we have to do what we can from either side to try and guide the story where it needs to go . . . to Phil and Rose's happily ever after." I couldn't help rolling my eyes at that. "Which I know you don't believe in," Reece said, and I swore I heard a smile somewhere in his voice. He stopped walking and looked around. "Hmm."

"It's a right at that tree," I supplied immediately.

"You've got a good sense of direction," he said, sounding surprised.

"It's the family business. You can't be in logistics and not keep track of where you've been and where you're going."

"It's still impressive."

We walked in silence for a moment, then something occurred to me. "Wait, how are you going to get into the palace? You're just going to walk in and say, 'Hey there, I'm a friend of the prince'?"

"I might skip the *hey there*. But he *did* invite us. It's not like I'm castle-crashing."

We approached the clearing and Reece stopped. He looked around, then half jogged across it, bending down for a second, then straightening up with Phil's jaunty red hat in his hand. "This might help me get in."

"Good idea."

"Come on, I'll walk you back to the cottage."

"I'm okay on my own. I'm the one with the good sense of direction, remember?"

"No," Reece said flatly. "There's an evil, horned fairy who has spies out looking for teenage girls. The least I can do is make sure you get back okay."

I glanced around; it was getting dark fast, and the leaves rustling and the sound of animals in the underbrush suddenly seemed less charming and more ominous, now that I couldn't see as clearly. "Well—thank you."

"But I am sorry about the castle," he said, after we'd turned back and walked in silence for a few moments, the only sound the crunch of leaves and twigs beneath our sneakers on the forest floor. "Will you be okay?"

I thought about the cozy cottage, and how Rose and I had gotten along right from the outset—the way you sometimes meet someone and immediately feel that potential friendship spark. The cottage might not have been a castle, but it could have been a lot worse. And I was really grateful that we'd both found places to stay. (Well, *potentially* we'd both found places to stay. But if Reece couldn't get into the castle, the fairies had made it clear he'd be welcome with us, even if he did have to sleep in the cellar.) "I'll be great," I assured him. "Don't worry about me."

"Well, I can't promise that. You did call a prince *dude*."

I laughed as we stepped out of the woods. "I think it was good for him." Reece shook his head, but even in the rapidly fading light, I could see he was smiling.

"Oh." Reece stopped and turned to me, like he'd just thought of something. "Maybe don't mention to the fairies that I'm staying with Phil. And if you can ask Rose not to mention him either, I think it would be best."

"Why? If they do end up together, they're going to know about him at some point, right?"

"Yes. But we've accidentally moved everything up. Phil and Rose aren't supposed to meet until a week from now. We've already started messing with the timeline. It's like in *Back to the Future*—"

"Enough with *Back to the Future*!"

"Well, I would have said *Flames of Fate*, but you said you hadn't read it. What example would you like? *Looper? Avengers: Endgame? Hot Tub Time Machine?*"

"I get it," I said before he could give me more examples of why messing with timelines was bad. "Fine. I won't say anything to them, and I'll tell Rose not to tell them either. Can she know he's actually a prince?"

"No! *We're* not even supposed to know he's a prince."

"I think he'll figure out you know when you come looking for him at a *castle*," I pointed out.

"Let's just keep it to ourselves for the moment," Reece said. "I mean, it's not fair to these people that we showed up knowing way more about them than they know about us."

I nodded; this made sense. It was like we'd just done a years-long deep dive on their Instagram profiles without them knowing it. I started to make a joke about this but stopped when I saw Reece's expression. His eyes were serious, worried. "You okay?"

"It's just . . ." He let out a breath and looked over toward the cottage, running his hand through his thick, dark hair and causing a lock of it to fall down over his forehead. "I believe the fairies will figure something out. But I also think that the best hope we have for getting home again is to stick as closely to the original story as possible. If we take it in too many new directions, we'll be flying without a compass. So . . ." He raised an eyebrow at me. "You'll keep the truth about Phil from Rose? And everything from the fairies?"

I nodded. "I will."

"Promise?"

I smiled at that. And thinking about Nisha and our most sacred, binding agreement, I held out my hand to him. "*Pinky* promise."

He laughed at that, but held his hand out, too, and a second later, tucked his little finger around my own.

I felt a jolt go through me when we touched. His skin was warm against mine, and it suddenly felt like every nerve ending in my body was wide-awake and paying attention.

Reece blinked at me, like he'd just felt the same thing. Slowly, centimeter by centimeter, he slid his finger down the length of my pinky and then back up again. It felt like my small finger—which I had spent very little time in my life paying attention to—was suddenly the most important. Had it always been this sensitive and I'd just never realized it before? We stayed like that for a moment longer, then dropped our hands at the same moment, like we'd agreed on it ahead of time.

I went to go put my hands in my pockets before I remembered that I was still in my prom dress, which was sadly pocket-free. I glanced back at the cottage, the curl of chimney smoke rising up to the darkening sky, then back at Reece. And it hit me that there was probably nothing else to do except say goodbye. I knew it wasn't forever, but still, the realization was jarring. It had felt like, for most of the day, all I'd wanted was to be free of Reece. But now that the moment had arrived, I really didn't want to leave. I was just supposed to say goodbye to him and do all this alone?

"Well . . . I guess I should start moving before it gets too dark," Reece said, zipping Phil's hat up in his backpack.

"Yeah," I agreed, feeling myself shiver. As it was getting darker, it was getting colder, and suddenly I didn't love the idea of Reece walking alone on the roads. What if there were bandits? Or dragons? "Are you going to be okay to get to the castle?"

Reece nodded. "I'll be fine."

"Well . . . um . . ." It hit me that I wasn't sure when I'd see him or talk to him again. And how were we supposed to stay in touch? It's not like I could call or text or email or DM him. In addition to being in a fairy tale, it was like we'd been cast back into the olden days in terms of technology, like we were in the '90s or something. "I guess . . . I'll see you soon?"

"Of course. I don't think I'll be able to keep Phil away." I nodded, wondering why I felt a stab of disappointment at this. "And obviously," he added, "we need to make sure we're keeping things on track."

"Right. Well—good luck?"

"You too. Not that you'll need it," he added quickly. "You'll be great."

I felt heat come into my cheeks, and just hoped that it was dark enough out to hide it. "And I hope you can talk your way into a castle."

Reece gave me a smile. "No big deal. Just a regular Saturday night."

We looked at each other for a moment more, and I felt like there was nothing left to do . . . but go. I started toward the cottage, but Reece stayed put.

"I'll just wait here to make sure you get in okay."

"To the cottage?" I pointed at it. "It's right there. Literally."

"I know. But still."

I turned and walked across the footbridge and up the stone steps to the front door. When I reached it, I looked back and saw, sure enough, Reece hadn't moved from his spot. And for just a second, standing there, so tall on the edge of the woods, he looked like he could have stepped from the pages of a storybook himself. Despite the hoodie and the sneakers and the jeans, in the fading light there was something unquestioningly heroic about him.

A second later, I shook it off, blaming this on hunger and the fact that I was trapped in a fairy tale; it was clearly starting to affect my rational thought. From the threshold, I raised my hand in a wave, and Reece gave me a nod in reply.

Then I opened the door and stepped into the cottage.

I hadn't had much time to take it in before, when we'd been hustled down to the cellar by a trio of suspicious fairies.

But now, as I looked around, I was trying to take in every detail. From the inside, you could really see that the cottage had been built in and around a tree; the trunk seemed to be a *part* of the house, creating archways and doorways and even serving as one of the walls.

The downstairs seemed to be one open-plan room—honestly, very forward-looking architecturally—a large, cozy kitchen with a wood-planked table dominating the space. There was an oven built into the wall that looked just like a pizza oven, even though I was pretty sure they didn't have pizza here. Between no pizza and no chocolate, I was really going to have to put pressure on the fairies to find us a way out of here. I didn't even want to think about what the iced latte situation was going to be here. Did they have coffee? Did they even have *ice*?

I decided this wasn't worth spiraling out about—I'd cross that potentially un-caffeinated bridge when I came to it—and cautiously walked around the space, taking it all in. It was getting darker outside, but the lamps lit by candles all around the space were glowing brightly and letting me see the tiny details everywhere. There were small designs, flowers and flourishes, that looked like they'd been painted or stenciled onto every wall and doorway.

But after I'd taken in these details, I started to see more. All at once, I realized it wasn't some museum piece or an exhibit I could have walked through back at the park. It was a *home*.

There were plates drying on the kitchen counter, and a small bouquet of flowers sat in a vase that looked hand-painted. There was a stray sweater draped over the back of one of the kitchen chairs and a stack of books piled haphazardly by the door, a dried flower in the middle of one serving as a bookmark. And climbing up one wall by the door was a series of hand-prints. *Briar Rose* was written at the bottom in beautiful script, and then they climbed up, year by year, the handprints getting bigger and bigger. All of it was evidence of the life that had been lived in this cottage—and the family that had been built here.

"Hello!" I looked over and saw Rose standing on the stairs. She was still in her same dress, but her hair had been pulled back.

"Hi," I said, quickly straightening up, hoping she didn't think I'd seen anything too personal.

"Aunt Merryweather said you're going to stay for a bit?"

"Yes." I twisted my hands together, feeling my pulse start to pick up a little. It seemed like Flora, Fauna, and Merryweather would want me to stay no matter what, for my own safety—but what if Rose didn't want me there? This had the potential to get *really* awkward. "Um . . . is that okay?"

"Of course!" she said with a big grin. "It's going to be such fun!"

I felt my anxiety melt away, and my pulse went back to normal. Maybe this would be okay after all.

"Come on," she said, running up the stairs. I followed, taking just a moment to marvel at the giant tree trunk that had been carved to make the staircase. I'd honestly never be able to think of anything else when I heard *tree house,* because this was one in the most literal sense. "This is my room," Rose said, stopping just inside the bedroom at the top of the stairs.

I stepped inside as well and looked around. There was a large cano-pied bed along the back wall, tucked in under the tree trunk. The canopy was made of a rich purple fabric, and the quilt on the bed was a matching purple, checkered in a diamond pattern of deep green.

Across the room from that bed was a smaller version of it with a mini-canopy, pillow, and pink-diamond quilt.

"Will this be comfortable enough?" Rose asked, nodding toward the smaller bed. "My aunts brought it up for you. I suppose it's been in the cellar the whole time? I'd never seen it before, but I'm glad they had something. We've never had overnight visitors before." She shot me a quick smile and I realized all at once that I wasn't the only one who'd been nervous about this whole situation.

And for just a moment, I was struck by what this meant. I understood why it had to happen—why Rose had to be kept safe. But to have gotten to be our age without a best friend, or a sleepover, to say nothing of chocolate . . . it just made me sad.

"It's perfect," I told her with a smile. It was almost *too* perfect, I realized a moment later as I looked more closely at the bed. They'd just *happened* to have a pristine bed down in the spider-filled cellar? Wouldn't I have noticed it? A moment later, I realized that this was absolutely the product of magic. Not that I was complaining—however it had gotten here, I was happy to see it.

She smiled back and opened her wardrobe. From it, she pulled out two dresses, one in gray, one in yellow, and laid them on the smaller bed. They looked similar in style to Rose's dress, with a full, swirling skirt, cinched waist, and long sleeves. "My aunts thought you might want these, too. They said they had some spare ones. But I've never seen these before. . . ." She frowned for a second, then shook her head. "They do things like that sometimes," she continued slowly. "It's almost like . . ."

Her words trailed off and I felt myself tense up. What was I supposed to do now? Was Rose on the cusp of discovering the truth? Why wasn't Reece here to help me navigate this?

I forced myself to continue breathing, and fought to keep a neutral expression on my face, telling myself it would all be okay. After all, it's a big leap from *my three aunts act strange sometimes* to *my three aunts are magical fairies in disguise.*

Finally, Rose shook her head. "Never mind."

"These are great," I said, picking up one of the dresses, hoping to change the subject. "Thank you." They really were, I could see now. They even looked like they'd fit me perfectly.

"Not that your dress isn't lovely." She sighed as she looked at it. "It *really* is. I'd love to wear something so nice someday. They just thought that you'd be more comfortable in these."

"Girls!" one of the aunts—Flora, maybe?—called up to us. "Come down and help with dinner! Are you hungry?"

"Coming!" Rose yelled down.

"Don't worry," someone else—Fauna, I was pretty sure—added. "I'm not cooking!"

Rose laughed at that, then turned to me, her expression growing serious. "She truly is an awful cook. She tries, but . . ." She shook her head, her face grim.

"Good to know."

"Would you like to change?" she asked, as she gestured to the dresses—mine, at least for the moment—and headed toward the door. "And I'll see you downstairs?"

Suddenly, nothing sounded better than finally changing out of my prom dress and getting real food to eat. And as if on cue, my stomach growled. "You know," I said, giving Rose a smile, "that sounds great."

Eleven

"Want to see something amazing?" Rose asked.

It was after dinner, which had been delicious—roast chicken and vegetables and a fantastic dessert. It was kind of like a cross between a cake and a pie and had been garnished with the berries from the forest (the non-lethal ones).

The meal had been awkward at first, the conversation a little stilted. I could tell the fairies were watching me closely, like they were worried I might let something slip to Rose. And I, in turn, was watching her, ready to jump in and try and cover, or change the subject if she mentioned the nice stranger she'd met out in the woods today, the one named Phil.

But as the dinner progressed, we were all able to relax and enjoy ourselves. And I was happy when the conversation turned to something that didn't involve either what I knew about the story, or anything to do with Phil: the upcoming visit of the cottage's landlords. It was apparently an annual thing, and this year's visit was coming up soon. It sounded like there was a lot of preparation that was going to go into it. I hadn't remembered that from the original story, but honestly, that really wasn't saying much. And since Reece and I had parachuted into the story a week early, it was very plausible that this had been a part of it all along, and we just hadn't known about it.

Rose and I had headed back up to her room after dinner, where I found all the contents of my canvas bag neatly laid out on the bed, along with a white nightgown trimmed with lace, folded and resting near my pillow. The quilt was blue, but I could have *sworn* it was pink when I saw it earlier. Though after just staring at it for a few minutes, I dismissed this, figuring that maybe my eyes were playing tricks on me.

"Stella?" Rose prompted.

I gave up on trying to figure out what was happening with my bedding and tried to focus. "Something amazing?" I echoed. She was standing by the window, a smile on her face. "Sure." I joined Rose, enjoying the *swish* of my new dress as I walked. I was thrilled at how well it fit; it didn't even have a spare yard of fabric pooling around my feet, which was what usually happened when I tried to wear long dresses. Which was just more proof it had been achieved by magic.

I looked to see what Rose was talking about and saw two birds nestled together on the ledge. "Oh, that is cool."

She laughed. "Not them. Go to bed," she chided the birds. Seeming to understand her, the birds got up, ruffled their feathers, and flew away to a nearby tree. I thought back to what Reece had said about this world: The animals might not talk, but they understood more. It was going to take a little bit of time before I got used to it, though. "Look, you can see it if you just lean a little to the right."

I stepped forward and followed her instructions—and then, through the trees, I saw it. The castle in the distance, rising up against the moonlight, the tallest thing around as far as you could see. The same one that was so familiar to me from all my Disneyland visits back home.

But here it was: the real thing, huge and majestic and sparkling under the stars that were just starting to emerge.

"Wow," I breathed.

"I know," Rose said, leaning against the window frame as she looked at it, too. "Isn't it beautiful?"

"Have you ever been?"

"*Me?*" she laughed. "No. Never. I just hope that maybe someday I can at least go a little nearer to it. Maybe even as far as the courtyard? Just to see it a little closer up would be . . . like a dream."

Rose's eyes were full of wonder as she gazed at the castle, and I took a breath, about to tell her that actually, she *had* been inside before. She'd probably been born there, and had certainly lived there when she was a baby. That it was *her house* and the place that (if everything went okay this week) she'd be returning to in the not-so-distant future.

But I stopped myself before I actually said any of this. Just in time, I remembered my pinky promise to Reece. "I'm sure that'll happen someday," I assured her. "I bet you'll even get inside."

Rose smiled at me and then flopped down across her bed. But I stayed where I was for a moment longer, eyes fixed on the castle.

It didn't look that far from here, but without a map's accurate measurements, and data on how fast Reece walked, to say nothing of the terrain he'd be crossing, I couldn't calculate how long it would have taken him to get there.

Was Reece there now? Had he managed to get to Phil? Or had he been sent off to the stables, since that seemed to be where everyone wanted him to go? Or even worse, had he been seen as some sort of spy and tossed into a dungeon? I remembered the way he'd gotten turned around in the woods—was he even headed in the right direction?

I gave it one more look, then pulled the window closed. I couldn't help hoping that it had all worked out—that Reece had gotten something to eat and had somewhere to stay. That he hadn't gotten lost without me to navigate for him. That he was all right.

"Stella?"

I started when I realized I'd been staring silently out the window, which wasn't weird at *all*, and that Rose was talking to me. "What? Sorry," I said, latching the window shut. "I didn't hear you."

"I was just asking about the ball." I couldn't help but notice she said *ball* the way I said *oat milk latte*. Or the way, until three weeks ago, I would have said *prom*. "The one you were meant to attend." She frowned, leaning back against her pillow, like she'd just thought of something. "Remind me—why did you not go?"

"Oh." My mind was suddenly a blank. What would be a plausible excuse back in . . . whenever we were? It's not like I could blame it on a power outage or a burst pipe or the DJ's equipment malfunctioning. Rose was looking at me, expectant, and my mind raced as I scrambled to come up with something. "There was a . . . um . . . plague."

"*What?*"

"I wasn't anywhere near it," I said quickly. "So I'm okay over here.

Plague-free and feeling fine. But when we heard about it we said, *You know what, let's get out of here.* And so we . . . did."

"Oh. Well, that's good," she said, even though she still looked discomfited.

I nodded as I flashed back to the Harbor Cove High School auditorium, with its crepe paper streamers, and the argument I'd had with Avery about the decorations. Had it just been that morning? "We have that, um, ball once a year," I said, choosing my words carefully. "And I'd been dreaming about going to it forever. My best friend and I—that's Nisha, you'd really like her—we'd been talking about it since we were little."

She gave me a sympathetic smile. "I'm so sorry you didn't get to go. After you'd been looking forward to it for so long."

"It's really okay," I assured her. "I actually hadn't even wanted to go that much in the end."

Rose sat up straight, a disbelieving expression on her face. "*Not* want to *go* to a *ball*?" she sputtered, her voice rising with every word. I laughed and flopped across the foot of her bed as she shook her head emphatically. "I don't believe you."

"It's true," I insisted. "I *had* been really excited about going, but then the date I thought I was going with . . ."

"Plague?" she asked, her eyes wide.

"No," I said, trying not to laugh as I shook my head. "He . . ." All at once, my mind was flooded with images. Cooper, telling me it was over at the Mermaid Café. At Disneyland, wearing a tux and walking toward me, his arm around someone else.

"What?" Rose asked, her brow furrowed. "What's wrong?"

I took a breath, trying to figure out where to start. I'd never really had to go through this before; Nisha, of course, had been there from the beginning and hadn't exactly needed a refresher. "Okay. So there was this guy . . ." Off Rose's confused look, I clarified. "I mean—um, a suitor."

"Reece," she supplied immediately.

"No—what?" I looked at her in surprise, then sat up, leaning back against one of the wooden posts of her bedframe. "Not *Reece*. I can't even stand him half the time." But even as I said this, I thought about the way I'd felt when he'd touched my hand—like every inch of my skin was suddenly alive in a way it hadn't been seconds before. I thought about the way he'd looked as he stood at the edge of the forest, strong and steady and true, watching to make sure I got to the cottage safely.

"Very well." Rose looked like she wanted to say a lot more, but instead just gave me a knowing look I didn't like one bit. "If that's what you say."

"It *is* what I say. That's why I'm saying it," I insisted. I pulled my knees up and drew my long skirt over them. "But no, it was another boy. He ended things right before the, um, ball. His name's Cooper Smith."

She frowned and sat up straighter. "That doesn't make any sense."

"I know!" I said, grateful to have someone new to discuss this with. "Like, it came out of the blue, and—"

"No, I mean his *name* doesn't make any sense. Is he a cooper or a smith? I don't see how you can be both."

"He's neither." I realized I didn't know what a cooper actually *did*. Something with chickens? "He's a water-polo player."

"Water polo?" she sounded baffled.

"I know," I said, nodding. "I don't get it either. It's an incredibly stupid sport you play in the water, trying to score goals while swimming." I had gone to more of Cooper's water-polo games than I wanted to admit, considering I found it incredibly boring. And suddenly, I was annoyed at myself for giving up all those Saturdays to watch my boyfriend play a sport

I didn't like and he wasn't particularly good at. "Anyway, we were supposed to go to this ball together. And I thought it was going to be . . . magical. But then he ended things."

Rose's eyes were big. "Why?"

I shrugged one shoulder, trying to act like it didn't bother me, like Cooper's words hadn't cut deep. "He said I liked the *idea* of us more than I actually liked him. And that I was always trying to control things."

"Oh." She tilted her head to the side, like she was contemplating something. "Well—is that true?"

"No," I said automatically. "Of course I liked him. I wouldn't be so upset if I didn't. And as for controlling things . . ." I let out a huffy breath. Why was this a bad thing? To have a vision for something and then try and see it through? Someone had to have a plan, after all. Someone had to be steering the ship. You couldn't just let life *happen* to you. It was practically the unofficial motto of Griffin Logistics: *Hoping for the best is a recipe for disaster.* "It doesn't matter, anyway." I took a breath and made myself say it, even though it stung. "I saw him earlier today, and he was going to the ball with someone else."

Rose gasped, and I realized how good it felt to get that reaction from a friend. I'd seen Cooper and his date right before we'd come here, so obviously I hadn't been able to go through it with Nisha.

"That's awful," she said, her eyes wide. "I just can't believe that." She thought for a moment. "Maybe they'll get the plague!" A second after saying it, she clapped her hand over her mouth. "No! No, wait, I don't mean that."

"Well, now if they do get the plague, it will be your fault," I said, deadpan. I shrugged. "I don't make the rules." I laughed at her horrified expression, and then she laughed, too.

"But I am sorry. About . . . Cooper."

"Thanks." I glanced out the window, at the stars shining against the spring sky. "You know the worst part of it?" I took a breath, finding my words one by one. "It's made me feel like the whole thing is a lie." I'd never even really talked to Nisha about this. It's hard to tell one of your friends who's blissfully happy and in love that you think it's a total scam.

"What whole thing?"

"You know. Love." I shrugged. "Happily ever afters, the whole thing. I don't believe in it."

Rose sat up straighter and stared at me. "How can you not believe in it?"

"Because I don't! I'm allowed to not believe in love. It's not gravity."

She frowned. "What's gravity?"

"Never mind," I said quickly. I remembered what happened to Galileo, after all. "I just mean that it's not some immutable law."

"But it *is*," she insisted. "Love exists whether you believe in it or not."

"Oh?" I shot her a look. "Is this confidence coming from . . . any experience in particular?"

She looked down at her quilt. "No," she said, even as I could see her cheeks getting pink. "I've just *read* a lot."

"You know," I said casually, like the two thoughts weren't linked at all, "Phil seems like a really nice guy." She glanced up at me, and I added quickly, "For you. He's not my type at all. Too . . . um, handsome. And muscled. And nice. Yuck. But he seems great."

Rose raised an eyebrow at me. "So does Reece."

I waved this off. "He's fine. But I'm sure we'll get to see Phil again."

"You think so?"

"We can bet on it."

She grinned at me and flopped back on her bed again, looking up at the ceiling, her expression faraway and dreamy.

And just like that, I could see it in her face: the hope and trust that was there. It was the look of someone who'd never had her heart broken, never had a crush go unrequited, never had a text left on read.

I felt a fierce wave of protectiveness rise in me and resolved to talk to Reece about this ASAP. I knew Rose and Phil—or, I suppose, Princess Aurora and Prince Phillip—got their happily ever after in the end, so I was sure that it all would be okay. But I still thought it couldn't hurt to make it clear to Reece that I wasn't going to stand for anybody breaking her heart, not even the prince on the white horse.

"But maybe," I said in a voice that was trying hard to be casual, "we *don't* mention Phil to your aunts right away?"

She glanced over at me. "Why not?"

"Just . . . until you know what something *is*, it's best not to rush these things, you know? Otherwise, there's always these questions and it puts too much pressure on things. Better to get to know someone first, right?"

She nodded slowly. "I suppose that makes sense. And," she added with a small smile, "it's not like I haven't kept secrets from them before." I took a breath to ask what, when she yawned hugely and shot me an apologetic smile. "Sorry about that."

"It's probably pretty late," I said, looking around for verification and then realizing that there was no clock in this room. "Um . . . is there a way to . . . tell the time?"

Rose nodded and tipped her head toward the window. "We can hear the bells that chime the hour."

I was about to ask what you were supposed to do about the minutes, but maybe minutes weren't a thing yet? Also, I realized a moment later, it wasn't like I had anywhere to be.

I walked over to the smaller bed, where everything that had been in my canvas bag had been laid out. I couldn't see the bag anywhere, but I figured I'd look around for it tomorrow. I set the snack bags aside; I'd bring those down to the kitchen in the morning. And now that I no longer had to worry about where my next meal was coming from, I could freely share. I had a feeling that Merryweather might really be into the Flamin' Hot Cheetos.

Out of habit, I reached for my phone—then remembered a second later that it was useless here and hadn't even been able to show me the time. And as I tapped the screen, I could see that it had died. Normally, I never even let my phone get close to running out of charge. (This was in contrast to Nisha, who seemed to get some perverse pleasure from seeing how low she could run her phone's battery down. I was always grabbing it away from her to charge it up, since this drove me bananas.) But as I looked at it now, I realized that hours of searching for a network or Wi-Fi signal had drained it.

"What's that?" Rose asked.

I turned around, phone in my hand, suddenly worried that maybe I shouldn't introduce the concept of cell phones into a world that was several centuries away from them. What if this wrecked something? But a second later, I thought about the fact that Reece and I had already introduced sneakers and Ruffles and the word *dude* to this world, and it seemed to be doing okay.

"It's my . . . device," I finally said.

"Can I see?"

"Sure," I said, holding it out after only a moment's hesitation. All it would show her, after all, was just a blank screen.

"What's it for?" she asked as she turned it over in her hands.

"Well—everyone in our, um, kingdom has one, pretty much. We use it to . . . communicate."

Rose raised an eyebrow at me. "How does it work?"

"I don't really know," I said honestly. Something with satellites, I was pretty sure? And cell towers. Having a phone had just been baked into my life from the start, so I'd never really felt the need to investigate the *how*.

Rose handed the phone back to me, just as her mouth twisted into a another yawn. She tried to fight against it and then just descended into laughter.

"Oh my god, you just had the best face," I laughed. Automatically, I raised my phone to capture it before remembering, yet again, that it was dead. "I wish you could have seen it." Normally, this was when I would have taken a picture. It hit me a second later, though, that for most of history, this had just been what happened. You didn't have photographic proof of everything. Something happened, and you just had to remember.

"I'd better get to bed," she said with a laugh.

"Yeah." I looked at the small canopy bed that was mine, apparently, and felt all at once just how long today had been. "That sounds great."

Ten minutes later, I'd washed off my prom makeup and changed into the nightgown that had been left for me; it was buttery soft, with a velvet ribbon threaded through the hem, and made me retroactively ashamed of the oversized Griffin Logistics T-shirt I usually slept in. I got into my bed across the room from Rose's. When we were both settled in, she leaned over and blew out her candle, and moonlight filled the room, filtering in through the window.

I settled down into the pillow with a sigh. For just a second, I thought about Reece. I hoped that he was also getting to sleep somewhere. And that he was safe and protected. And maybe also shirtless . . .

I shook my head quickly to stop that train of thought. I was just over-tired, that was all.

"Stella?"

"Yes!" I said a little too quickly, as though Rose could have somehow guessed my thoughts.

"I think you might be wrong," she said, a yawn in her voice.

"I mean, probably. But about what, specifically?"

"About *love*." I looked over. She had rolled on her side, facing me. "I don't think you can let one single person convince you that there's no point to it all. You *have* to believe in it. It's the most important thing of all."

"Maybe," I said, even though I could hear the skepticism in my voice.

"It's like the berries," she said, talking faster now. "What if you'd eaten one of the bad ones? You'd be saying that berries are terrible, and that you'd never eat them again, not knowing that there were these great, delicious berries that you were ignoring."

"These were the berries that would have killed me, right?"

"Maybe just a *little*."

"So if I'm dead, I'm probably not really concerned with my opinions about things like berries."

She burst into giggles, and I did, too, and then I heard the sound of footsteps in the hall.

"Girls," Fauna's gentle voice said. "Time for bed now, hm?"

"Yes, Aunt Fauna."

"Our bad," I added. "I mean, sorry."

We both waited, breath half-held, until we heard the footsteps walk down the hall. "Just think about it, all right?" Rose said, but more quietly now. "You can't let one bad berry ruin the whole patch."

"Okay," I promised, since this seemed like the easiest thing to say. "I'll think about it."

"Sleep as late as you want in the morning," she said, fluffing her pillow a few times and then sinking down more deeply into it. "I wake early."

"You do?"

"I always have. I've never wanted to waste time sleeping. There's too much to do!"

I took a moment before I spoke to make sure I wasn't going to say the wrong thing. "Well, I'll see you in the morning, then. Good night."

"Stella?" Rose's voice was a little hesitant and shy. "I'm really glad you came to stay."

"Me too," I replied, realizing as I said it that it was true. "Thanks so much."

I heard her breath grow slow and even, and after a few minutes, I was sure that she had fallen asleep. I rolled onto my back and looked up at the ceiling. I was absolutely positive I wasn't going to be able to sleep at all. At home, I had the white-noise app on my phone going, ear plugs and an eye mask nearby if needed, and melatonin gummies in my nightstand in case of emergency. Usually, my thoughts were racing much too fast for me to just fall asleep. Whenever I got into bed, that's when my mind would start scrolling, reminding me of all the things I had to do and what had to happen tomorrow. It was usually hours before I could drop off. And that's when I was in my bed, in my own century, in a place where everyone knew who Beyoncé was and everyone just accepted the theory of relativity.

So I was sure, as tired as I was, I was not about to get to sleep anytime soon. I was in a fairy tale, sleeping in a house that was half tree, in the same room as an enchanted princess, with three good fairies down the hall. I was sure I'd be up all night, going over everything that had happened, trying to get to the root of *how* it had happened, figuring out a plan. . . .

I looked out the window, at the dust motes floating in a shaft of moonlight, and felt myself yawn.

And the next thing I knew, sunlight was pouring in through the window, and it was morning.

Twelve

blinked as I looked around the room, trying to get my bearings.

I'd just . . . woken up. On my own with no alarm. I couldn't remember the last time that had happened. Elementary school maybe?

Normally, the first thing I did when I woke up was to grab my phone. I'd turn off the alarm, then check my texts and emails and messages. I'd look at social media and play Wordle. Allyson and I texted each other our scores every morning, and both of us were determined to keep our streaks going.

I looked over to Rose's bed, but true to what she'd told me last night, she was already gone, her bed neatly made. I stretched and yawned—which was when I realized I wasn't alone.

Sitting on the sill outside the closed window were a whole bunch of animals. Like, *way* too many animals. There was an owl, two other kinds of birds I couldn't identify, a squirrel, and a chipmunk. And they were all staring in the window like they were waiting for something.

I pushed the covers back and got out of bed—the quilt was still blue, and I decided that thinking it had once been pink could be chalked up to my imagination—and walked over to the window. All the animals just looked at me, expectant, giving me the feeling like I was in a play where everyone else knew their lines but me.

I opened the window, not sure what else to do, since they clearly seemed to want something. As I did, I could hear the bells—but a second too late, I realized I wasn't keeping count. It seemed like telling time used to be more high stakes; if you missed the bells, you'd just have to wait an hour or find someone who'd been paying attention.

I looked at the menagerie on the windowsill. Now that the window was open, I was a little worried that they were all going to stream inside, but nobody moved. The owl ruffled his wings in a haughty way, like he was getting impatient. "She's, um, not here," I said even though this sounded ridiculous. I was telling a bunch of forest creatures Rose's whereabouts? But, like they'd understood me, the squirrel and chipmunk scampered off, jumping easily to the closest tree, and the birds flew away until only the owl was left, blinking at me implacably. What did owls want? Lollipops? Monuments to Athena? I didn't have any of those. "Okay, bye now," I said as I closed the window again, and it finally flew away.

I got dressed, then looked around, at a loss for what to do.

I reached for my phone out of habit, only remembering a moment too late that it was useless here. But my phone was where my schedule was, and normally by this point in the morning, I'd planned out my whole day in my notes app—usually hour by hour, but sometimes even minute by minute.

And now I just had . . . the whole day stretching out in front of me with no structure? I didn't even know what time it was! Yesterday, this hadn't been as pressing, but there had been *a lot* going on yesterday. Now, I needed to get things back on track, which meant I needed a plan. I wanted to see if the fairies had had any thoughts about how we might get home again and what our timeline here might be looking like.

I grabbed the snack bags and headed downstairs. I stepped off the bottom step, walking into the kitchen—and also into chaos.

I couldn't see Rose anywhere, but I almost couldn't tell that at first, since the three fairies were all in motion. Flora was cleaning, Fauna was pacing around the kitchen, flipping through a book and muttering, and Merryweather was stirring something on the stove. They were all talking, even though they didn't actually seem to be listening to each other.

"Um . . ." I said, trying to raise my voice above the din. "Good morning?"

Everyone stopped what they were doing and looked over at me. "Good morning, dear," Fauna said, giving me a smile. She set her book down—it snapped closed—and her face immediately fell. "Oh no, now I lost my page. What recipe was I supposed to be looking for, again?"

"Good morning," Merryweather said, turning around at the stove to give me a nod, sounding harried. "Sorry about the excitement in here this morning."

"Just like every other day," Flora said with a sigh as she swept.

"Not *quite* like this," Fauna said, as she started flipping through the book again. (Which I could see now was a recipe book.) "This is a *bit* more chaos than usual."

"Our . . . landlords are coming to visit today, instead of later this week. We got a message this morning, so we have to prepare."

I was about to ask her *how*, since I had no idea how communication even happened here, when Flora spoke.

"I don't want to speak ill of our . . . landlords," she said, in the exact tone that always preceded speaking ill of someone, "but they're intruding on our time, and right at the very end . . ."

"They're allowed to do it," Merryweather pointed out. "And we know what these visits mean. We have to be gracious. They're coming for lunch," she explained to me, maybe seeing that I looked confused. Which I was, but *what meal are these people coming for* had not been the question at the top of my mind.

"Ooh!" Fauna said, squinting down at her book. "Was it a whole roast hog? Is that what I was looking for?"

"No," Flora sighed, sounding irritated. "What about a small casual lunch says *whole roast hog* to you?"

"Maybe they're hungry," Fauna said defensively. "I don't know."

"It wasn't that," Flora said. She closed her eyes for a moment and tapped her forehead. "It was the one with the potatoes in it."

"Well, that narrows things right down," Fauna muttered under her breath, surprising me. She shot me a quick smile, then started turning the pages again.

"Will it be okay that I'm here? I don't want you guys to lose your security deposit." They all just stared at me. "Never mind."

"Are you hungry?" Flora asked. "Did you want some breakfast?"

"Sure—" I started, just as Merryweather set down a bowl of oatmeal, a dish of berries, a cup of tea, and a small pitcher of milk in front of me. "This looks delicious," I said honestly. My parents weren't much for cooking, and neither was I, really. We mostly did takeout or meal-delivery services. And we almost never ate sitting around the table, all together like we had last night. It just never seemed like our schedules lined up so that we were all in the same place at the same time. After all, running a logistics company meant you had to always be on call; it wasn't like you could just set an out-of-office message when a container ship was being held up in customs at Bristol or whatever. And if we did somehow manage to end up sitting together, the odds were high that one or both of them would end up leaving halfway through to go deal with work. The fact that we'd all sat around together last night, eating, talking, nobody jumping up, had been really nice.

But this? Trying to get down a few mouthfuls in the eye of the storm while chaos unfolded all around me? *This* felt like home.

"Oh, tell Stella about the thing," Flora said as she placed a spoon and napkin in front of me.

"Thing?" I echoed. "Also, where's Rose?"

"She's doing her chores," Flora explained, patting my hand.

"Oh." I froze, a spoonful of oatmeal halfway to my mouth. Was there something I should be helping with? I probably should have volunteered to help out before now. Was I being a terrible guest, taking their hospitality and dresses and food and giving nothing in return?

"But we *did* want to talk to you alone," Merryweather said, leaving the stove and hopping up onto the bench next to me. Her feet didn't quite touch the floor, and I realized what a comfort it was to not be the shortest person in the room for once. "We think we've figured out a plan."

I took a bite of oatmeal—rich and silky and way better than the oatmeal they had at Starbucks—and swallowed quickly. "A plan?"

"To get you home again. You and that handsome young man."

"Reece?"

"Ooh!" Fauna said, stopping at a recipe. "Got it! Jellied eel?"

"Of course not," Flora snapped. "Do you even *have* any eels?"

"I could get eels."

"Where could you get eels? On such short notice?"

"Yes, of course, Reece," Merryweather said to me, ignoring the other two. She shook her head and laughed. "Is there another handsome young man wandering around the forest?"

"Hahaha!" I laughed loudly. "Nope! Sure isn't." I ducked my head and quickly took another bite of my oatmeal. "So what's the plan?"

Flora glanced over at the door, then came and sat across from us. "If you could get the young man to come by later this afternoon, we'll explain everything."

"You think you can get us back home?" My heart leapt with hope. "Really?"

"I mean, we don't know for sure." Flora's voice was pragmatic. "We're in uncharted waters here, after all. But we think we have a good idea."

"That's awesome," I said. I finished my oatmeal and felt something in my shoulders unclench, like I'd finally been able to put down something heavy. "Thank you so much."

"So just send word," Fauna said, like it was the most natural thing in the world, "and we'll tell you both together."

"But," I started, "how am I supposed to do that?"

"Use a bird," Merryweather said with a shrug. "Rose will show you."

"Show me what—"

"My stew!" Merryweather shrieked as she jumped up and ran over to the stove, where I could see a pot was boiling over.

"And tell Rose to come in, would you?" Flora asked as she picked up my empty bowl and spoon.

"Did you get enough to eat, dear?" Fauna asked as she poured me more tea. I nodded, and she patted my hand with a smile. "I'm so glad."

I picked up my mug of tea, then stepped outside into the sunshine. For just a moment, I stood on the threshold, feeling the warmth on my face as I took another sip of tea. Normally, I was an iced-latte or cold-brew devotee, but I had to admit this was pretty good.

Just as I was about to go looking for her, Rose came around the corner of the house, carrying a basket. "Morning," I said.

"Morning! I hope I didn't wake you earlier."

"Not at all. But when I got up, there were a bunch of . . . animals?"

"Oh, they just come by to say hello." Sure enough, she stretched out her hand and a tiny blue bird fluttered down and landed on her shoulder. The bird looked around for a minute, like it was getting the lay of the land, then flew off again.

"Right," I said, like this was in any way normal or like anything I had ever experienced. I glanced into her basket and saw it was full of eggs. "Do you need help with your chores? Anything I can do? Your aunts asked me to tell you to come inside."

"I've finished all my chores, but thank you." Rose was wearing a white dress this morning, her hair in a low ponytail that somehow looked great. Whenever I tried to wear a low ponytail, I inevitably looked like a Founding Father. And not one of the attractive ones, like Hamilton. "Is it still a madhouse in there?"

I nodded. "I guess they're preparing for your landlords' visit?" I hadn't known this was a thing. We'd rented our apartment when we lived in the

Bay Area, before we moved down to the O.C. And back then, we saw our landlord whenever there was a problem with the plumbing or a noise complaint. We never, like, cooked her a fancy lunch. But maybe it was an old tradition that had passed out of fashion.

"I know," Rose said, and her eyes were shining. "They're coming a bit earlier than usual. Normally, they come after my birthday, and it's just wonderful."

"It . . . is?" I couldn't remember ever being super excited when our landlord was going to come over. Usually the opposite, since it meant my parents would be arguing with her about something that needed to be fixed.

"They're just so lovely," she gushed. "You'll see."

"Um . . . Okay." Maybe people were just a lot closer with their landlords here? Which was nice! Who was I to judge it? "Also, I wanted to send a message to Reece—and Phil—to get them to come by later."

"Is Reece staying with Phil?"

"Hopefully?" I involuntarily glanced in the direction of the castle. "I mean, I think that was the plan, since Phil offered and all. Anyway, your aunts want Reece to come by so they can talk to us." Even just saying it made me feel a little better, remembering the fairies' calm assurance that they'd figured something out, that we'd be able to go home again.

Rose nodded. "Sounds good."

"But um . . . how do I do that? Let him know?" I asked, baffled. Was this the same way Rose had felt when she'd stared at my phone in confusion? Or the way my nana felt whenever we asked her to attach a PDF?

"Oh, we'll just send him a message," Rose said easily.

"*How?*"

She smiled at me, and I could tell she was enjoying this. Just a little. "Well, I might not have your fancy device, but I can show you."

She set her basket of eggs down on the top step, then reached to her waist, where I could see now there was a kind of pouch tied, the same color fabric as her dress. She opened it and pulled a scrap of paper and a small piece of lead from it.

"Wait," I said, taking a step closer. "What is that?"

"What's what?"

"That," I said, pointing at her pouch.

"Oh. I made it. It's really handy."

"You *made* it?" I blinked at her, surprised. Had Rose invented the fanny pack? She nodded. "It's very cool," I said, very impressed that she'd done this.

"Thanks," she said, giving me a smile. "I always love when I can do that—see a problem and then come up with a solution. Like this!" She held out the basket to me and I saw she'd devised little slots for each of the eggs to go in, like a very early version of the egg carton.

"That's amazing," I said, leaning closer to look at it. "So they don't break?"

"Exactly." She nodded down at her pouch. "I can make you one, too, if you'd like. Now." She lifted the piece of lead to the paper and looked at me expectantly. "What should we say?"

I still wasn't sure how this was going to get to Reece, but she seemed so confident that I just decided to go with it. "Maybe . . ." I thought for a moment. "Come by the cottage later this afternoon?" It pained me to say so vague a time, even though I was just repeating what the aunts had said. But what did that even mean? "Aunts want to talk to us. Bring Phil, but leave him in the forest." I looked down and saw that even with a makeshift pencil on a scrap of paper, Rose had the most beautiful handwriting I'd ever seen. Gorgeous, flowery cursive that was nonetheless still completely legible. "Your handwriting!"

"I know," she said, making a face. "I promise it's better when I have ink."

"It's fantastic, are you kidding me? Mine's the worst."

"I'm sure it isn't."

"Um, it really is."

She held out the paper and lead to me, and I wrote—trying my best at cursive, which I could barely do—*See you later, Stella.* I gave it back to her and watched as Rose's eyes widened in shock. "I told you."

"Well," she said, squinting at the paper, clearly trying not to laugh, "um . . . it's not *that* bad?"

I laughed, and she laughed, too. "You're such a bad liar."

"How does this even happen?" she asked, staring at the paper.

"I know. I always wanted to have better handwriting, but . . ." I hesitated, not sure how to explain laptops and computers and texting. "Anyway, I think I'm just out of practice."

"I can help you. You know, if you want."

"Really?"

"Of course."

I was about to tell her that wasn't necessary, but looking at my messy, half-print, half-cursive scrawl next to Rose's beautiful copperplate handwriting, I changed my mind. "Well—thank you. That'd be great."

She clapped her hands together. "This will be fun! I've never gotten to teach anyone anything before." She nodded down at the message. "Are you happy with that?"

I nodded, and handed it back to her. "Now what?"

"We just decide if it should go air or ground." She tapped her fingers on her chin like she was thinking it over.

"I . . . what?" These were the kinds of conversations I had when I was helping my parents at work. How was this possible? Was there a Ye Olde FedEx hiding around here somewhere?

Rose whistled, and a few moments later, a rabbit had hopped up. A second later, he was joined by a small brown bird, the owl, and a squirrel. They all sat in a lopsided semicircle in front of us, looking expectant.

"That's incredible."

"Is it?" she asked, sounding surprised. "I'm just trying to decide what would be fastest. Maybe air until we know exactly how far away Reece is." She held out her arm, and the brown bird hopped up on her shoulder. She extracted, from her pouch, a mini version of it, and put our note inside, then carefully placed the pouch over the bird's head.

The bird, looking very proud that he'd been chosen, was hopping up and down on Rose's shoulder excitedly. "Take this to Reece, okay?"

"Will . . . the bird know how to find him?" I asked, absolutely gobsmacked by this. The bird shot me a look that could only be described as withering, and having never been on the receiving end of a look like this (from a bird), I was honestly a little taken aback. "Um, sorry for doubting you," I said quickly. "He's, um, around my age. Dark hair. Some people might think he's handsome, but only if you're into that super-obvious thing."

The bird looked at Rose, who smiled. "Thanks so much." The bird pecked once at her shoulder, like it was agreeing, and then flew off.

"That really works? The bird can find Reece?"

"Of course," she said easily. "They met yesterday, remember?"

"And it'll give Reece the message?"

"What else would he do with it?" She asked this like it was the most normal thing in the world—which maybe it was here.

"Rose?" one of the aunts called from inside the cottage.

"Coming," Rose called back. She pushed herself to her feet, and the animal gathering broke up, the owl flying away and the rabbit hopping off to nibble at some grass nearby. I got up as well, careful not to spill my tea, trying to get my head around the fairy-tale mail service I'd just witnessed.

We stepped inside the house, and I could see the chaos of the morning seemed to have abated some; all three fairies now had cloaks on, and there were no longer any pots bubbling on the stove.

"Oh good," Flora said crisply. "We're off to the market to get some provisions for today."

"We can go," I suggested. I wanted to try and be helpful, especially after I'd fallen down on chore duty. And plus, I really wanted to talk to the people at the market about how their supply chain worked. Pre-industrial-age logistics! I could learn all about the trade routes! When was I going to get the chance again?

"No!" all three fairies said this at exactly the same time, their voices sharp—even Fauna's.

"That is," Flora said, after a moment, "you girls will have a much better time here. Just stay inside the grounds of the cottage and be sure not to talk to anyone or open the door for strangers. But aside from that, have a nice time!"

"Maybe I should stay behind," Fauna said, glancing at the other two women. "Maybe it's not the best . . . moment for us all to be gone."

"No, it's fine," Rose said quickly. "We'll set the table for lunch and get everything ready while you're gone." She widened her eyes at me and I jumped in immediately.

"Absolutely! We'll hold the fort down here. Nothing to worry about."

The three fairies exchanged a look, and finally Flora nodded. "Well . . . okay."

"Stella," Merryweather said, turning to me. "Can I borrow this? I can't find my basket." She held up my El Arco Iris canvas bag.

"Of course," I said, and Merryweather slung it over her shoulder, looking very pleased with it.

"These straps are nice," she said. "Lovely to have your hands free."

"What does it mean?" Fauna asked, looking at me.

"It's a restaurant from where I'm from," I said, not sure exactly what needed to be explained here. Maybe all of it? "And a taco is like . . . meat or vegetable tucked into a little bread . . . crepe . . . thing."

"And *guac your world*?" Flora asked, raising an eyebrow.

I took a breath, about to try and explain avocados to someone who had never had one. But a second later, decided not to, which was probably the kinder thing to do. Why describe the nectar of the gods to someone who'd never get to try it? "It's just, like, a greeting we say," I finally answered. "That's all."

They all nodded, and then after a few more last-minute preparations and instructions, they hustled out the door. "We'll be back as soon as we can," Flora promised.

"Guac your world!" Merryweather added, looking pleased she'd been able to work this into conversation.

Rose and I waved and then shut the door, locking it behind them. When the three fairies had passed out of sight, she turned to me with a smile. "Now," she said, "we can have some fun."

Thirteen

'm not sure we should do this!" I yelled down to Rose, who was currently balancing on a rock ledge.

"Why?" she called up to me, looking perplexed. "Can't you swim?"

We were standing next to a gorgeous clear-water lake, which, to put it lightly, was not where I'd thought I'd find myself this morning.

Once the fairies had left, Rose had turned to me and told me we were going on an adventure, but she hadn't given me any details about what was going to happen. And since I wasn't often asked on an adventure, it meant I had no idea how to prepare.

"Are we allowed to?" I'd asked her back at the house, following her up the stairs to her room. She grabbed her satchel from where it had been hanging over the doorknob, and hurried over to her wardrobe, flinging open the doors and rummaging around in it. "Didn't we tell your aunts we'd stay here?"

"We did," she said, giving me a quick nod and tossing me my sneakers. "You might need these." I sat down on the floor and started putting them on, but before I could ask the relevant questions—like *why*—Rose was continuing. "I love my aunts," she said as she tucked something into her satchel. "I do. But they can just be a little bit . . . overprotective sometimes. It's gotten worse this last year, too, I don't know why. . . ." She paused, frowning, then shook her head. "I'm nearly sixteen! And sometimes they treat me like I'm still a child. So I just have to make the most of things when they're not around and keeping an eye on me. Which is *rarely*. Ready?"

"No," I said, even as I tied my shoelaces and stood up. "I still don't know what we're doing, so how can I know if I'm ready?"

"If I told you, that would negate this being a *surprise*," she said with a laugh. "Let's go."

I was glad, as we walked through the forest, that I'd listened to Rose and put my sneakers on. She was actually wearing shoes as well, maybe since we were going deeper into the woods, well beyond the clearing we'd been around yesterday.

"You really know your way around here," I said as I pulled my dress closer to me, away from the brambles. Again, walking through the woods in a dress was *not* ideal, and I couldn't help but think of all the work-out clothes neatly folded in my closet back home. I was very tempted to introduce the concept of athleisure to this world. I mean, it had handled sneakers and hoodies and Ruffles, were leggings going to break anything fundamental?

"I should," Rose said as she held a branch aside so I could walk past it. "I grew up running around these woods. I've been exploring here forever."

We'd tromped through the forest, and it was incredibly peaceful—the scent of the pine, the rustle of the leaves, the sunlight dappling through them. Birds were flying overhead, hopefully one of them en route to Reece with our note, and after we'd been walking for a few minutes, I started to notice forest creatures as well. There were deer ducking out of sight and leaping away when they saw us, squirrels in the branches of trees, occasionally curious bunnies hopping forward.

"Here we are," Rose finally said, gesturing in front of her. I stopped short, seeing what was in front of me. It was a gorgeous lake with rock ledges all around it. The water was light blue and clear, and the surface was totally still.

"Here!" she reached into her satchel and handed me a bundle of clothes.

"What is this?" I asked as I shook it out. It was a light mossy green, and looked like a nightgown.

"For swimming," she said like it should have been obvious. She pointed to a nearby tree. "I'm going to change. Meet you down there!"

Which was how I ended up standing next to a lake, wearing an early version of a bathing suit, asking Rose if any of this was actually a good idea. "Yes, I can swim," I assured her. "I just . . ."

"Good!" she yelled, then reached over and pulled a length of rope out from where it had been tacked up behind a tree. I could also see that it was tied to a branch that extended over the lake. "See you in there!" She grabbed the rope, walked back a few steps, then launched herself forward, flying over the water—and then disappearing with a splash. She surfaced a moment later, pushing her hair back and laughing. "Come on in!"

I could see the rope swinging back, so I carefully made my way down to the rock ledge, grabbed for it, and contemplated the situation. It *did* look fun. And I was hot, especially after tromping through the woods in a long dress. . . .

I held on to the rope with both hands and copied what I'd watched Rose do, taking a few steps back before launching myself forward. For just a moment, flying through the air, I panicked. What if I let go too late? And then I crashed onto the rocks and got a cut and it got infected? I knew for a fact that antibiotics had definitely not been invented yet. But when I was right over the center of the lake, I opened my hands and dropped straight down, hitting the cool water with a splash.

I surfaced to find Rose smiling at me. "Nicely done."

"Thanks." I plunged under again, surprised at how well the bathing dress was doing. It wasn't taking on water and getting heavy, like cotton would have done. But it definitely wasn't the bathing suit material I was used to. "This is great," I said, gesturing to my dress. "Thanks for lending it to me."

"Isn't it good?" She looked down at her own, which was a very light purple, almost a periwinkle. "Aunt Flora made them for me. She thought it was important that I learn how to swim. She *doesn't* know that I sometimes come here without her."

"I won't tell," I promised.

Rose ducked under, swam underwater for a few strokes, then surfaced and floated on her back, looking up at the impossibly blue sky.

I tried to do the same, but after a few moments of sky-staring, there was a twitch in my fingers, like they were reaching for a phone that wasn't there. I could practically feel the lack of my phone, like a phantom limb, more notable because of its absence.

"So," I said, switching to treading water. The center of the lake seemed pretty deep, which was a good thing, and probably something I should have checked before I plummeted off a rope swing and down into it. "What's the plan?"

"What do you mean?"

"Like, how long are we going to stay here? And when do we have to leave so we can get back before your aunts, and set up before your landlords arrive?"

She just laughed. "We don't have a plan."

Those words were like a dagger in my heart. "But . . ." I said, shaking my head, sending water droplets flying. "I just . . ."

"We can just enjoy this." She gestured all around her. "There's nowhere we have to be right now."

I took a breath, to try and get Rose to understand that unscheduled time was wasted time. "See, the thing is, back home—"

"But you're not back home," she reminded me. "And we do have to leave before my aunts return. So how about if we stay here until we tire of it, and then go back? Whenever that turns out to be?"

I swam over to the shallower water, where my toes could touch, but just barely. Because I felt like I had to get my feet on solid ground while I processed this; it was a truly revolutionary concept for me. I couldn't remember the last time I'd done something without a clearly structured time frame. What would that even be like?

I ducked my head under for a moment and realized, with startling clarity, that Rose was right. All the things I had to do and places I had to be and meetings I had to chair and assignments to work on and classes to attend—none of them existed here.

I surfaced and remembered the first time Reece and I had come back after seeing the christening, and how no time had passed at all at Disneyland.

Was that what was happening now? Was time passing at all back home? I kind of hoped it wasn't—otherwise, I would bet that my parents currently had a *lot* of questions about just where I'd been for the last sixteen hours or so.

But it would seem to be more logical that the same thing that had happened when we'd been at the castle the very first time was happening again: that we'd found our way into a little bubble, a moment in time where I could just *be* for a while.

That is, if it *was* going to be just a while, and not the rest of my life. I smoothed my hair back, and tried to comfort myself that the fairies had said they'd found a solution, and I was going to put my faith in that. And in the meantime . . . maybe it wouldn't be the worst thing in the world to take things as they came, and without having to plan everything.

"Maybe," I said, my voice coming out hesitant, "I could try and do that. To plan a little less, and just . . . be."

Rose smiled at me. "That sounds good. So," she said, like she was getting down to business, "race you to the side?"

"Oh, I don't know," I said with a sigh, all the while secretly getting myself into position. "I just . . . Go!" I yelled, and started to swim as fast as I could.

"No!" Rose yelled in frustration, but I could hear that she was laughing, too, as she raced after me.

We stayed there, swimming and talking, until our fingers started to prune and Rose squinted up at the sun and said we should probably be getting back if we wanted to beat her aunts home.

We changed back into our dresses behind our respective trees, and I wrung out my bathing dress, surprised by how little water it seemed to retain. I wasn't sure if it was due to magic, or if it was just a fabric we didn't have in California, but either way, I was impressed.

I was just starting to head back to Rose when I heard a *caw* from somewhere above me. I looked around for the bird but couldn't see it. And all at once, I had the unsettling feeling of being . . . watched.

I tried to tell myself that it was normal, that there were lots of birds in the woods, and it probably wasn't anything to worry about. But even so, I hurried away from my tree to go catch up with Rose.

We were out of the clearing and almost back to the cottage when a bird swooped down in front of us. I instinctively ducked, but Rose just held out her arm, and a second later, I realized the bird had a pouch around its neck; it was the same bird we'd sent off earlier.

"Look who's returned!" Rose smiled at the bird and gently rubbed the top of his head. The bird lowered his neck and she slid the little pouch off of it. The bird pecked at her shoulder in an affectionate way, then flew off. Rose opened the bag, pulled out a piece of paper, and smiled when she read it.

"He found them. And they wrote back!" She frowned at the paper. "At least, I think they did. Reece's handwriting is worse than yours, and I didn't think that was possible."

"Let me see that." I was still a little stunned by the fact that a bird could apparently become a GPS device—a Global Positioning Sparrow. But sure enough, on a piece of paper much nicer than ours, there was a reply.

Hey it's Reece what the heck?! A BIRD just delivered this to us?

I was somewhat relieved to see that Reece's handwriting was, in fact, a little worse than mine: It was boy handwriting, a mix of uncertain script and blocky capitals. Following this, though, came a line of ornate cursive, almost like calligraphy, even more beautiful than Rose's had been, and I had thought that was the pinnacle.

Hello, it's Phillip —I mean, Phil. Just Phil and nothing else! Reece seems to think it's strange to get messages via bird!?? Not sure about him. But we will be there! I'll be the one hiding in the forest.

But seriously, you have to explain this. See you this afternoon—R.

Until then! Phillip

I lowered the paper and looked up at Rose. "I'm very impressed."

"It's *not* that good a note. Mostly just informative."

"I meant about the bird."

Two rabbits were suddenly racing up to us, hopping full tilt. They stopped in front of Rose and looked up at her, their eyes intent. "My aunts are on their way."

"Wait, how did you know?"

"I asked them to warn me. Thank you so much," she said to the bunnies, who hopped away again. "We should go—"

Just then, there was a *snap* of a twig and the sound of three people talking all at once, sounding very close now. "The aunts!" we cried at exactly the same time.

We raced toward the cottage, running as fast as we could. We flew through the door and dashed upstairs, taking the steps two at a time. Rose held out her hand, and I tossed her my swimming dress. She tossed them both over the branches of a tree just outside her window, then tossed her satchel to the ground while taking off her shoes. I stepped out of my sneakers, and she gave me a nod.

We raced downstairs again, and she went straight to a cupboard, shook out an embroidered linen tablecloth, and threw it over the kitchen table.

I heard the sound of the voices getting closer and remembered how we'd assured the fairies that we'd have the whole table set and ready by now. "How are we going to explain this?" I asked, while helping to make the tablecloth even. "That we haven't done much?"

Rose's brow furrowed for a second. "We had a fight. A battle over how to best set it up."

"Right. Because you weren't listening to my far superior ideas."

She grinned. "Exactly." The door swung open, and the fairies, laden with food and flowers, stepped in. "Because I think the pink linen is the best choice!" Rose yelled at me, then widened her eyes, and I could tell she was trying not to laugh.

"You would say that," I said, trying to get in character and pretend I was back in the gym, arguing with Avery about decorations. "You're the one who wanted *place cards*."

"What's wrong with, um, place cards?" she bit her lip hard, and I could tell she was on the verge of laughter—which, in turn, was pushing me closer to it.

"They're gauche!" I wasn't sure if Rose even knew what that meant, but she gasped like she did.

"Girls!" We turned around to see the fairies staring at us, open-mouthed.

"Oh," Rose said, trying to make her voice sound surprised, but not really succeeding. "Why, hello. We did not see you there."

"We were just arguing about the best way to set up the table," I said, turning fully to face the fairies. I knew if I kept looking at Rose, and her much too exaggerated "mean" face, I would fully lose it and start laughing. "But now that all seems so silly! Let's not fight."

"We can forget the . . . card places," she said magnanimously. "If you want."

"Why do you both have wet hair?" Flora asked, looking between us.

I looked at Rose, and there was a small beat of silence in which you could practically hear our brains whirring, both of us trying to come up with an excuse.

"It was, um—"

"Rain," I finished quickly. "We got caught in a rainstorm."

"Just a little one."

"It didn't rain at the market," Fauna said, looking confused.

"It must have been a . . . precipitation pocket," I said, trying to recall all the weather-related words I could. "I know that sometimes happens. Meteorologically. Anyway," I added quickly, feeling like the sooner we changed the subject the better, "how can we help?"

"Yes," Rose said, coming forward to take the baskets and bags from the fairies. "Let me get these."

Twenty minutes later, or thereabouts, we were ready. The table had been set. The food was either keeping warm in the oven or keeping cool in dishes that had been placed in the creek that ran right by the side of the cottage. The cottage had been swept and picked up, and all the random assorted ephemera—spare books and sweaters and cups—tucked away.

"Okay," Merryweather said, her hands clasped behind her back like a field general as she surveyed the scene. "Looking good in here."

"I really think—" Rose started, just as there was a knock at the door. "They're here!" she cried. Her face was suddenly alight, and all at once I understood that she was about to see people she'd sorely missed—people who were really important to her.

She ran to the door and flung it open. Standing on the threshold were a tall, dark-haired, mustachioed man and a shorter, golden-haired woman. They were both dressed simply, but something about their clothes seemed to indicate that they were well made and expensive, even though they weren't showy in the least.

They embraced Rose, their eyes shining. She pulled them inside, talking a mile a minute as the fairies bustled around, offering food and beverages. They had come with a small entourage, and they trooped in, looking askance at the cottage. Seeing their expressions, I felt myself bristle. I may have only been staying here for two days, but I was already feeling myself get defensive as I took in their smirks and raised eyebrows. I was on the verge of saying something snarky—because who even *were* all these random people?—when Rose called me over.

"Stella! Come here so I can introduce you!"

I headed over to the other side of the room and got an up-close look at the landlords. My friendly greeting died somewhere in my throat when I realized, with a shock, that I knew these people. I'd seen them before, and pretty recently—when they'd been at Rose's christening, sitting on golden thrones, wearing crowns.

Because I was looking at the king and queen.

Fourteen

blinked at the couple in front of me, my mind going a hundred miles an hour as I tried to get my head around this.

I was looking for any other explanation, but I kept coming back to what my mom always said: *The simplest solution is usually the best.* And the simplest solution here was that this was the king and queen. I'd always been good with faces, they were two very distinctive-looking people, and I had seen them just the day before. True, they looked a little older and more lined than the last time I'd seen them—which, in fairness, had been sixteen years ago their time. But it was them. I was *sure* of it.

As I looked between the king, queen, and Rose, the resemblance was plainly obvious. She had her mother's blond hair, her father's eyes and height. She was their daughter. These weren't random strangers—they were her *parents*.

But what were they *doing* here? And why were they pretending to be landlords?

"You're—" I started to say before I could stop myself.

The queen met my eye, and a quick understanding dawned on her face. Before I was able to say anything else, she had crossed over to me and gave me a hug. "Say nothing," she whispered in my ear, too soft to have been heard by anyone else. Then she straightened up and stepped back. And even though she was smiling, I could see the fear in her eyes. "So lovely to make your acquaintance." She was looking at me closely, like she was trying to figure something out. I glanced behind her to see the king looking at me in the same way, like I was a puzzle to be solved. "We were so surprised when we'd heard you'd turned up suddenly! Out of nowhere!"

"So we wanted to meet you," the king said, stepping forward. Though he had also plastered on a smile, there was a warning rumble in his low voice.

"Oh. Well," I said, looking from the fairies, to Rose, then back to the queen, utterly unsure how to respond to any of this. I was fighting the urge to curtsy now that I knew I was in front of royalty. But I didn't want to do anything to blow up their spot, and I had a feeling curtsying to two people who I thought were just landlords might be seen as pretty strange.

All at once, out of the blue, I wished Reece was there, too, going through this with me. I somehow knew he could have helped me navigate things. Because I was very aware I was totally out of my depth. I'd never even come close to meeting any royalty for my whole life, and in the last two days, I'd met four royals and counting, and I still had *no* idea how to correctly behave around any of them.

"Yes. Hi," I finally said, knowing this was probably the wrong response, but giving up on finding the right one, because what was the *right* response here? What was I supposed to know? What information did I need to keep from whom?

"Maybe Stella can show me the cellar," the queen said. She placed her hand, gently but firmly, on my upper arm. It didn't exactly sound like a request.

"The—cellar?" Rose asked, her smile fading. "But what about lunch?"

"We'll be just a moment!" The queen made it sound like we were doing something fun, but that didn't do anything to stop the feeling of trepidation spreading through me as we headed toward the cellar.

As I walked down the steps, half pulled and half steered by the queen, I couldn't help but notice that I somehow seemed to be spending quite a lot of time in the absolute worst part of this house.

We stepped onto the cellar floor, and after a moment, my eyes adjusted to the space, letting me see that nothing had really gotten better since yesterday. Same spiderwebs, same uncomfortable chairs where Reece and I had been interrogated. I looked at the set of the queen's jaw and wondered if the same thing was about to happen again. If it was, I comforted myself with the knowledge that she at least couldn't turn me into a frog. But then a second later, I remembered that she *did* probably have an army at her disposal. So maybe it wasn't that much of an improvement.

I turned to face her and then dropped into a shaky curtsy. I had never done one before, for obvious reasons, unless you counted acting in *Little Women* in elementary school, which I did not. "Your, um, majesty?"

The queen shook her head, looking pained. "Please."

"Right." I straightened up. "Sorry about that."

"Tell me the truth," she said, her brow furrowed. Even clearly worried, this woman radiated elegance; it was like there was a flashing neon sign that read ROYALTY above her head. I hadn't felt this way around Phil, just that his manners were much better than ours. But I was very aware of it now. She took a shaky breath. "Does Aurora know?"

"No," I said quickly. "I mean, I didn't know until just now. I thought you were just the landlords."

The queen shook her head, but I could see a softening in her eyes, her defenses coming down slightly. "We had to tell her something. It seemed like the best explanation. And there hadn't been any danger of her finding out until we heard you'd suddenly arrived."

"Heard?" I echoed. I suddenly remembered she'd said the same thing upstairs, that they'd heard I arrived. But how? Was there a fairy-tale gossip network where information was spread around? I truly didn't even know what was possible here. "Did . . . the birds tell you?"

"Merryweather sent word. The fairies don't communicate with us very often—we can't risk anything being intercepted—but in this case, she thought we should know. I understand this was before she'd decided that you could be trusted. But nevertheless, we thought we should move up our annual visit and investigate for ourselves."

"I promise I'm not working with . . . you know," I said, then mouthed *Maleficent*. I wasn't sure if this was a name I should avoid saying, like *Beetlejuice*. "I wouldn't do anything to hurt Rose—I mean, Aurora. And as soon as I can, I'm going home. The fairies said they think they have a way." As I said it, I felt a small, unexpected pang, one that I immediately tried to brush off. Why was I feeling tied to this place after only two days? Of *course* I wanted to go back to California, to Nisha and my family and Wi-Fi and tacos. My real life: the place where I actually fit in. "I just want everything to work out . . . the way it's supposed to."

She gave me a small, tentative smile. "Me too," she said softly. "So you won't tell her the truth about who we are?"

"No," I said, then hesitated just a moment before continuing. "But . . . don't you think you should?"

She took a breath to answer, just as I heard footsteps coming down the cellar steps. "Hello?" Rose called. She ducked her head down so she could see us. "Lunch is ready. What are you two doing down here?"

"The, um, landlady . . ." I said, stumbling over my words, starting to speak without any real idea where I was going.

"I just needed to look at the cellar to make sure the insulation was holding up," the queen said smoothly, already walking over to the stairs. "And I thought I'd take the opportunity to get to know your new friend."

"Oh," Rose said, still looking a little bit confused. "Well—all right." She headed up the rest of the stairs, and the queen and I followed.

When we reached the top, she turned to me. "I'm Leah," she said, her voice soft. "And my husband is Stefan."

"Stella. It's nice to meet you." I held out my hand, then a second later, froze, wondering if this was some huge breach of protocol.

But the queen just smiled and shook my hand. "It's a pleasure."

"Lunch is ready!" Flora cried, bustling up to us. And even though she was smiling, her expression was worried, her eyes searching the queen's face. But then Queen Leah nodded, and Flora visibly relaxed. "Excellent," she said, steering us both over to the table. "Let us eat."

Lunch was *delicious*. In addition to all the fairies had cooked, it seemed like part of the entourage's job—in addition to looking askance at the cottage—had been to bring in food, since there was way more than we could possibly eat.

And the entourage made a lot more sense, now that I knew we were hosting the *king and queen*. Everyone around me talked and laughed over lunch, but I mostly listened, drinking in the stories and observing the interactions between Rose and Stefan and Leah: a family, even if all of them didn't realize it just yet.

It was clear after only a few minutes how much all three of them looked forward to these annual visits; they told stories about their meetings in years past, the books and games the king and queen had brought for Rose, the drawings and stories she'd sent off with them. You could tell all three of them were trying to extend their relationship beyond the one day a year, to try and make the memories last as long as they could. There was comfort and easy laughter between them, and I noticed both Stefan and Leah glancing over at their daughter, like they were trying to memorize her while they could.

The three fairies chimed in occasionally, but they were also hanging back a bit; it was the quietest I'd yet seen them. They were watching the interaction as well, all with wistful, slightly bittersweet smiles.

The lunch broke up when one of the royal entourage announced, in no uncertain terms, that it really was time to go.

"I can't believe I won't see you again for another year," Rose said, looking crestfallen as Stefan and Leah put on their traveling cloaks. Both their cloaks had hoods, and I realized now that this was probably expressly for concealing their true identities on their journey.

"Maybe it won't be so long," King Stefan said with a twinkle in his eye.

"Really?" She looked from him to the fairies, who all seemed to suddenly find either the floor or the ceiling very interesting.

"Well, who can say," Queen Leah said smoothly, going to embrace her daughter. "None of us know what the future will bring."

As she said this, I felt all the fairies' eyes slide over to me. But the truth was, I *didn't* know what the future would be—and not only because I wasn't as up on the plot of this story as Reece was. But because I was in the mix of the story now, and I had no idea what that had done to it. Had I pulled it too far off its axis? Messed with something I shouldn't have?

"Stella, you'll walk us out, won't you?" Queen Leah asked, as she tucked her bright hair under her hood.

"I'll come!" Rose immediately volunteered.

"I need your help, dear," Fauna immediately cut in, indicating the dishes on the table and general upheaval of the cottage. "Let our guest, um, see our other guests out."

I walked with the king and queen out of the cottage and to the clearing on the edge of the woods. Their royal attendants were walking past, in the direction that Reece had gone yesterday, all of them looking very happy to be leaving. "Where are they going?"

"It's too wooded here for carriages. The horses and carriages are waiting by the main road."

I nodded, and as I looked around, appreciated just what an ideal spot this was if you were looking for a place to hide a princess from an evil enchantress.

Stefan looked back at the cottage, then took his wife's hand. "With any luck, today was our last visit here. Less than a week now, this terrible curse will be lifted, and our daughter will be back home with us, where she belongs."

"But we're not there yet," the queen said, worry clouding her expression. "And we feel that as the deadline looms closer, Maleficent is getting more desperate, and therefore more dangerous."

"How do you know?" This was similar to something the fairies had said, but they were . . . well, magic. How did the king and queen know what her innermost feelings were? Did she have a kingdom-wide newsletter she distributed or something?

"We can see her stronghold from our castle," the king explained. "And the more upset she gets, the more we can see the manifestations of it. Fog, smoke, storms . . . She's angry, and getting angrier."

"Like Tía Pepa in *Encanto*!" I said excitedly. They stared at me blankly, and I shook my head. "Nothing. Just . . . never mind."

"We're worried," Queen Leah said, her brow furrowed, "so please be on guard."

King Stefan nodded. "Stay vigilant. We're almost at the end of this, and the next few days might be the most crucial."

"I will," I assured both of them. I wasn't sure what I'd really be able to *do*; there were three very powerful magical beings looking after Rose, after all, and I was just a high school junior who had failed my driver's test the first two times. But I *did* have pepper spray. So that might even things out a bit.

"It will all be over soon," the king said, putting his arm around his wife.

"Well—yeah," I said, without even thinking about it first. "The curse part will be over."

"Exactly," the king said, raising an eyebrow. "As I just said."

"No, but . . ." I wasn't sure I should even be going down this road. But I couldn't get the image of Rose's face out of my mind, with her expression so incredibly trusting. "I mean Rose—Aurora—she doesn't know the truth. You're going to have to tell your daughter she has a whole family and a whole role to play that she knows nothing about. And that you've been . . . well, lying to her the whole time about who you really are. That's going to be . . . a lot."

The king and queen exchanged a look. "We hope she will understand," the queen said, "that we did it to protect her. Because we had to keep her safe."

"I just think that when you have one expectation of the way your life is going to go and then someone just pulls the rug out from under you with no warning . . ." I stopped, realizing that I wasn't actually talking about Rose any longer: I'd been thinking back to how I'd felt when Cooper had ended things.

I shook my head, trying to focus. "Sorry. You're right. We should concentrate on keeping her safe for now, and deal with everything else later." I wasn't sure if therapy existed yet, but surely they could all find some kind of safe space to process their feelings? Maybe with a nice apothecary or something.

"We really saw no other way," the queen said quietly. And just like that, I could see it in her face, how painful this had been for her. To have her daughter right here, so close, and only get to see her one afternoon a year. "And at least this way, she got to know us—and we got to know her." She shook her head. "It really was the best we could do."

"Right, absolutely," I said quickly, regretting that I'd even said anything.

"Take care of her," the king said.

I nodded. "I promise."

They gave me a nod, and I gave them a wave that I regretted a moment later, realizing that I probably should have curtsied instead. But it was too late: They were already walking away from me, through the trees, heading back to the road that would take them home to their castle.

I stood there, watching them go until they passed out of sight and it was just me, standing there at the edge of the forest. I ran my hands through my hair; it was still slightly damp. Even though I couldn't see it, I had a feeling I knew what it looked like, because it was the way my hair always looked when I didn't have my serums and hair oil and blow dryer and round brush to tame it. It would be curly and wavy, but not in a consistent way, more like my entire head went rogue, with individual strands resolutely doing their own thing. But since we didn't have electricity here, and I was pretty sure a candle-powered hairdryer didn't exist, I resigned myself to my hair looking like this for the rest of the time that I'd be here.

Which *hopefully* wouldn't be the rest of my life.

I twisted my hair up in a knot, then pulled it down again. I could feel a nervous, agitated energy flooding through me. And even though I knew I should head back to the cottage and help out with the cleanup, another part of me knew I should really calm myself down before I subjected myself to other people right now. I picked up a fallen leaf and started shredding it, just to have something to do with my hands.

What was really bothering me—what I really couldn't shake—was the way Rose had looked at the people she didn't realize were her parents. If everything went well, in the best of circumstances, she was going to find out that the women who'd raised her weren't really her aunts, that she was actually a princess, and by the way, those nice landlords were her *parents*.

And probably it would be fine—or more than fine: a dream come true. After all, I reasoned, wasn't that what we *all* used to dream about? When I was little, all I had wanted was someone to knock on the door and tell me that I was actually a secret princess and whisk me away to a palace where I could have fantastic dresses and hang out with my cute animal sidekicks.

But now that I was in the middle of this exact situation—and no longer seven—nothing seemed quite so clear-cut. Suddenly, there were real people who would be affected by that kind of bombshell revelation, and actual consequences that would follow from it.

And while it was strange to feel protective of someone who was my same age—and who had way better hair than me—the fact was, I *did*. And not just because an evil villain seemed bent on killing her. It was the sense I'd gotten the night before, when we were talking about Phil, and I realized that Rose had never had her heart broken. Just like last night, I felt a fierce desire to keep that from happening as long as possible, even if I could see the expiration date for that state of innocence was right around the corner.

But, I reasoned, tossing what was left of my leaf aside, I could try, for as long as I was here, to make this week *fun*. It was going to be the last one, after all, when Rose would be able to just *be*. When she could run through the woods and go swimming and hang out. Because, best-case scenario, this time next week she'd have gotten true love's kiss, and awoken, and would be back and living in her palace. And worst-case scenario . . .

I shook my head, not even letting myself go there. This story ended with a happily ever after. It all worked out in the end. And it would now, even if there were two people who'd crashed the party.

I let out a long breath and felt my pulse steady. I glanced around, trying to take in everything that was around me: the afternoon light dappling through the leaves of the trees, the deer and her fawn walking past the meadow in the distance, the bunny in the undergrowth nibbling some grass. As I stood there in the peace, the wind blowing through the trees, I realized I'd actually landed somewhere pretty magical. It might not have been *Moana*, but if I had to get stuck in a fairy tale, I could have done a lot worse.

Feeling much more centered, I turned to head back to the cottage. I had just started to walk when I heard thundering hoofbeats behind me.

I turned around and felt my jaw drop open.

Phil and Reece were galloping toward me. On literal white horses.

Fifteen

s I stood there, staring, the horses—braked? Whoa-ed? I didn't know horse lingo—slowed down and came to a stop next to me. "Hi," I said, looking up at them. I glanced from Phil to Reece, feeling like there was far too much to take in at the moment.

Phil looked much the same as he had yesterday, minus the jaunty hat, which I was sad to see. It's not everyone who could pull off a hat with a feather, but Phil had managed it.

But Reece was no longer in his hoodie and jeans. He was wearing black pants, high black boots, and a white shirt. Phil had a black cloak around his shoulders, but Reece didn't. His hair had been combed in a kind of swoop, and the sleeves of his shirt were rolled up, his first two buttons undone....

"Stella?" Phil asked.

I blinked. I shook my head and tried to focus, dragging my eyes away from Reece and what he looked like on the back of the white horse, his hair blowing gently in the wind. . . .

"You okay?" Reece asked, frowning at me, effectively breaking this spell.

"Yes," I said quickly, trying to compose myself. "How's it going?"

Phil dismounted easily from Samson, gracefully swinging down to the ground and giving me a smile. "Wonderful. And you?"

"*Nrg*," Reece said. I looked over and saw that he was wincing as he heaved a leg over his horse's back. He stayed like that for a moment, wobbled, then fell to the ground, one foot still stuck in the stirrup. "Ow," I heard him mutter from somewhere under the horse.

"Are you all right?" Phil called. He took a step closer to me and lowered his voice. "Honestly, Stella, I didn't know that you *could* be bad at horses. But I think Reece . . . is? And Delilah is by far the easiest horse we have in the stables."

"Reece, you need a hand?" I asked, leaning down to look at him.

"I'm fine," he muttered, pushing himself to his feet and wincing. He brushed some of the dirt off his black pants. "Every muscle in my body hurts, but, you know, I'm fine." He straightened up, then looked at me and took a tiny step back. "Oh. Hi."

"Hi?" I glanced at Phil, worried. Hadn't we just done this? Maybe Reece had hit his head harder than I'd thought.

"You just . . . look different," Reece said, staring at me. "The hair, I guess? Or the dress?"

"Oh." I looked down at the dress I was wearing—the yellow one this time—then ran a hand through my now-curly hair, hoping it wasn't a total disaster. "I mean . . . you do, too. Look different, I mean."

He glanced down at himself. "Yeah, Phil lent me some stuff."

"It looks like it, um, fits you okay." I couldn't quite look away, and I couldn't stop myself from wishing that Reece had been just a little bit bigger than Phil so that everything would have been just a tad bit tighter, and more formfitting, the remaining buttons on his shirt would have been threatening to open....

I shook my head firmly, trying to clear it. I *had* to get ahold of myself. I knew this didn't have anything do with *Reece*, after all. You can't have guys walking around dressed like fairy-tale princes—because they've literally been dressed *by* fairy-tale princes—and not expect to have *some* reaction, especially when you used to love fairy tales. It was practically Pavlovian.

"I was happy to!" Phil said cheerfully, walking over. "Well, I mean, at first, I was surprised to see him show up. But Reece explained that he'd recognized me back in the forest, and knew who I really was and where to find me."

Reece shot me a quick glance, and in that moment I understood I needed to go along with the story he'd spun. "Oh yeah?"

"And you did, too, right?" Phil asked me. "I thought you had, when you called me Phil."

"Right," I said quickly. "I did. I'd heard your story—and seen your picture." Reece gave me a tiny, almost imperceptible nod, letting me know I'd kept our story on the right track. "And I'm just happy Reece was able to get into the castle and find you."

"Yes!" Phil said, nodding. "Me too. I mean ... there was a *little* bit of a problem with the guards at the gates. Which I think is actually a positive, since that means security is functioning properly. You don't want potentially dangerous people to be able to simply walk into the castle. But after that, er, misunderstanding, Reece got in eventually. It helped that he had my hat." Phil frowned, like he was reconsidering his words. "Well—perhaps *helped* isn't the right word, since for a moment there they thought you'd kidnapped me."

"That was not a fun moment," Reece agreed.

"We decided it would raise less alarm if we told everyone that he's a friend from my kingdom, come to visit me," Phil explained. "It seems to be going okay so far." Reece caught my eye and made the *so-so* gesture with his hand, and I bit my lip to keep from laughing. "But we were so happy to get your note!"

"Well, I wasn't," Reece interjected. "Since a *bird* somehow knew where we were and tapped on the window with his beak until we opened it and took the message."

"It's quite standard," Phil said, shaking his head at Reece. "Who delivers *your* mail?"

"Rose said the same thing," I told Reece, widening my eyes at him. "I guess it's normal in this, um, kingdom."

"Speaking of Rose," Phil said. His whole face had lit up, and he carefully removed a bouquet of flowers from his saddlebag. "Is she inside?"

"No!" Reece and I said together, and I glanced automatically back at the house. "It's probably better that you don't introduce yourself to her family *just* yet," Reece continued.

"This is why I told you to wait in the forest," I pointed out. "But I can tell her you're here, and she can come meet you." Just as I said this, though, a whole new array of questions presented themselves and I shook my head. "Wait, first we all have to get on the same page, here. So, Reece and I know you're a prince. But you're still . . . in disguise?"

Phil ran his hand forward and backward through his hair. "I am," he said with a sigh, and looked down at his flowers. "It's . . . a bit hard to explain. I've always known I have a duty to fulfill. And it means my future has already been decided for me. And I understand that, and I don't shirk it. But it's why I was out riding in the woods yesterday, and why I didn't want to reveal who I was. I only wanted a little bit of time where I could put all of that aside. And to forget about my duty . . . for just a little bit."

I nodded, turning Phil's words over in my head. "I can see that."

"And while I'm happy for you and Reece to know the truth . . . I'd prefer Rose not know."

"But why?" It seemed like *Oh, by the way, I'm a prince* was something you might like to drop into conversation frequently, especially if you had a crush on someone, which Phil very clearly did. I was about to blurt out that it really might not be an issue, because Rose was actually royalty, too, but I held back before saying anything. After all, it didn't seem right to tell Phil before Rose herself knew.

"I just . . ." Phil hesitated. "I've never been able to know if anyone liked me for *me*. Not because of who I was, or what I would be someday. And this feels like a chance to find out if someone I like"—he stopped suddenly, a faint blush creeping into his cheeks—"actually likes *me*. The real me."

"I won't say anything," I promised.

"Me neither," Reece agreed.

"Okay, so we'll keep mum on the prince thing. And we'll just say Reece is staying with Phil, but without going into details?" They both nodded, and I turned to Phil. "So, what's your deal?"

"Pardon?" Phil asked. He glanced at Reece, like he could help translate.

"Like, if you're not a prince, what's your story? What do you want to be?"

Phil's face brightened. "Can I be a wood-carver? I've always wanted to be a wood-carver!"

"I mean, it's okay with me."

"Oh good!" Phil went back to his saddlebag, pulled something out, and held it toward us. "What do you think?"

I squinted at the carved wooden lump in Phil's hand and tried to think of something to say about it. I was suddenly glad that Phil already had his future career locked down, because I didn't think he was going to go very far as a craftsperson. I picked it up like that might give me more of a clue. "Is it a bird?"

"Totally a bird," Reece chimed in, looking relieved to have something to hold on to. "Great bird, buddy."

"It's a bear," Phil said, looking crestfallen.

"Oh." I stared at it, trying to work *bear* out, but then gave up. "Well, maybe your story can be that you're a wood-carving *apprentice*. Still learning your trade. How about that?"

"All right," Phil said as he took back the bird/bear hybrid monstrosity, looking like he was disappointed but trying not to show it.

"Cool. So you're Phil the apprentice wood-carver. Who has"—my gaze drifted over to Samson and Delilah—"really nice horses, for some reason."

"Of course, I will tell Rose the truth at some point," Phil said quickly. "And it's not as though I'm enjoying this deception. I just . . ."

"Maybe you can just wait on the whole telling-her thing," Reece interjected hurriedly. "And hey, why not clear it with me before you do? That could be fun, right?"

"Uh . . . absolutely," Phil said, his ever-present manners coming through, even though he shot me a puzzled glance.

"Okay," I said with a nod. "I'll go tell Rose that you're here? If you want to wait in the forest?"

"Yes," Phil said, his face lighting up again. "That's perfect." Then he looked down at the unsuccessful art in his hand. "So you think I shouldn't give her this?"

"I think the flowers are great," I said, trying to focus on the positive aspect of things.

"Who doesn't love flowers?" Reece chimed in, clearly thinking along the same lines.

"Right you are," Phil said, pocketing the carving. He and Reece tied the horses up, out of sight of the cottage, then Phil headed to the meadow in the woods with a spring in his step.

As Reece and I walked toward the cottage, I snuck a glance over at him. I was trying to reconcile the guy from the day before with *this* Reece, who looked like he'd just stepped off the cover of a romance novel, or the poster of a movie about pirates.

"So," I finally said, "how's the palace life?"

"I think it's technically a castle."

"What's the difference?"

He paused, like he was trying to find the answer. "I'm not sure, actually."

"But seriously. How is it going?"

"Well, I hurt everywhere. Like muscles I didn't even know I *had* are hurting. Apparently when you ride a horse for the first time, it's the most painful thing imaginable?" I laughed at that, but with a tiny pit in my stomach. Because since I hadn't ridden a horse in any meaningful way—one lap around the ring during a pony ride at a carnival hardly counted—I had a premonition that at some point, this feeling might be coming to me as well. "But aside from that . . ." He glanced over at me. "It's *great*," he finished, grinning widely.

"I'm really glad," I said, meaning it. His whole face was alight, and it was making me realize how much I wasn't used to seeing him like this.

"Stella, it's so much better than the reproduction at Disneyland. Because it's *real*." There was a note of wonder in his voice. "It's like waking up inside a story you thought you knew by heart and then getting to find there's so much more to it than you could have ever imagined. Getting to be a part of that world, actually live inside it . . ." He shook his head. "I only wish my sister could see it, too. She'd love it. It would be like a dream come true."

"How old is she?"

Reece glanced over at me and smiled. "She's eight. She's the best."

"I'm an only child."

"I couldn't have guessed," Reece said in a meant-to-be-heard undertone, giving me a quick smile.

Choosing to ignore this, I continued, "But I've always been jealous of people with siblings. Nisha is the closest thing I have to a sister. But it's nice you're so close with yours."

Reece nodded as he looked around. "She'd never believe that I actually got to . . . be here. Right in the middle of it all."

"You can take pictures, I guess?"

"My phone's dead." Reece stopped walking and looked at me sharply. "Is yours not?"

"No, mine is, too. I have a charging cord, but it's useless right now."

He nodded. "Good. Just make sure nobody sees it—"

"Rose saw it," I said with a shrug, and then remembered how all the contents of my canvas bag had been laid out on the bed. "And at least one of the fairies, too." Reece took a breath, like he was about to tell me how this would rattle the fundamentals of this civilization, and I jumped in to cut him off at the pass. "I told her it was a communication device, and they're really normal where we come from. It's dead, so she didn't see anything."

"Just . . . be careful. We don't want to show anyone anything that could mess things up irreparably or push things too far in the wrong direction. This next week, leading up to Rose's birthday, is going to be crucial."

"That's just what the king and queen said."

Reece stared at me. "The— *What* king and queen?"

"Rose's parents," I explained. "They came for lunch before you guys got here." Reece just opened his mouth and then closed it again, so I jumped in to explain how they'd come to investigate when they heard we were here. About the landlord thing, and the fact that they'd had a relationship with Rose this whole time.

"I had no idea," Reece said when I'd finished. We started walking again, crossing the little footbridge that led to the cottage. "But that's also . . . really nice? That she actually likes and knows her parents? It's such a weird concept."

I laughed. "I know, right?"

"They do seem nice, though. The little I've seen of them. Phil's dad, on the other hand . . ." Reece made a face.

"The apple falls far from the tree?"

"The apple falls in a whole other time zone. But are you doing okay here with Rose and the fairies? Even though it's not a castle?"

"Who cares about castles?"

"Well . . . you did. Yesterday. Remember?"

I waved this off. "It's *so* much better than a castle. We're having fun." I smiled when I thought about it: being able to run off into the woods and explore, go swimming, hang out, stay up late laughing . . . It suddenly seemed a lot better than being stuck in some dusty old castle. "And Rose . . ."

"Talking about me?" Rose swung the top half of the door forward and leaned out, smiling. She raised an eyebrow at Reece. "Nice clothes."

"Phil lent them to me," he explained, coloring slightly and tugging on one of his cuffs.

Rose pulled the top half of the door closed, and then a second later, opened the whole thing and came out, her cheeks slightly pink. "Is he . . . here?" she asked, lowering her voice slightly. It seemed like she was trying to appear nonchalant, but wasn't quite pulling it off.

"In the meadow by the woods," I told her, tipping my head toward it. "Where we were yesterday."

She grinned, then called, "I'm going to pick berries!"

"But, dear, don't you . . ." Fauna appeared in the doorway, wiping her hands on her apron, but stopped when she saw Reece. "Yes, good," she said as she handed Rose a basket. "Take your time, now!"

Rose gave me a smile and then hurried toward the forest. She would break into a run every few steps, then slow herself down, then break into a run again.

"Now," Fauna said, clapping her hands together and looking between the two of us. "Let's get started."

Sixteen

s anyone hungry?" Fauna asked, looking around the kitchen table at us. "Tea?" I shook my head.

"I'm fine," Reece said. "Thank you though."

"Let's begin," Flora said, looking toward the closed door. "Obviously, we want to get through this before Rose comes home and hears any of it."

I shrugged. "She might take her time." Reece shot me a look, and I saw all the fairies look over at me in confusion. "I mean . . . you know how it is with . . . berries."

"Anyway," Reece said quickly, "Stella told me that you might have some information about our . . . situation?"

"Right," Merryweather said. She adjusted her kerchief with the air of someone who was getting down to business. "We hit upon something quite ingenious, if I do say so myself."

Flora nodded. "So. You said you two know the events that are to come."

"Yes," I said, nodding. Reece raised an eyebrow at me, and I bit back a smile. "Well, Reece knows it better than me. But I am *somewhat* familiar."

"Now, we don't want to know too much," Fauna said, giving Merryweather a stern look. "But. In the version of events you know, do things"—she lowered her voice to a whisper, even though it was just us at the table—"work out?"

"Yes," Reece said. He paused for a moment, and it was like I could tell he was weighing all his words carefully. "I don't think I should tell you how it all comes together, exactly." Flora and Fauna nodded, and Merryweather sighed. "But the spell is broken, and there's a happily ever after for Rose. I mean, Aurora. And all of you."

"The spell is broken," Fauna echoed, her eyes shining. "That's *wonderful*."

"We did it!" Merryweather clapped her hands. "I knew we could do it."

"Calm down, Merry," Flora admonished.

"But aren't you proud of us?"

"We haven't done anything yet!"

"But we will! We *do*. They said so."

"We do in the version of events where these two don't show up," Flora pointed out, gesturing to me and Reece, and Merryweather deflated a little bit.

"Oh. Right."

"But assuming that's still going to be the outcome," Fauna said, "we devised a plan that revolves around the spell being broken."

"You see, we can only use our powers for good," Flora explained. "And while this ordinarily is a good thing, we're going to need more help to get you back home."

"But!" Merryweather interjected. "A spell being broken creates a powerful burst of magic. There are few things stronger than that. Especially because this spell isn't only good magic or evil. It's Maleficent's curse, but with Merryweather's amendment mixed in."

Merryweather cleared her throat. "It was nigh these sixteen years ago, at the christening of the princess—"

"They *know*," Flora cut her off.

"Fine," Merryweather huffed. "I never get to tell that story, but *fine*."

"At any rate, once the spell is broken, and that magic is released, we can contain it and harness it to build a door to send you back again."

"That sounds amazing," I said. I could feel my fingers itching for a pen and paper—or better yet, my phone, so I could make a spreadsheet and organize my thoughts. I looked around at all three of them and felt a swell of gratitude. "Thank you so much for doing all this work to help us."

"But it will have to happen shortly after the spell breaks," Fauna cautioned us. "Magic starts to lose its potency."

"And it means that this might be our only window," Flora added, her face serious. "Our one chance to get you back."

"Of course, we don't *know* that," Merryweather pointed out. "But it's our best guess."

"It doesn't seem likely we could do it without the additional magic," Flora said, shooting her a long-suffering look. "So we're only going to have one chance to pull this off."

"And the spell breaks on Rose's birthday," Reece said. "So . . . a little less than a week from now."

"A week," I echoed. A week felt very manageable. A week was so much better than an unknown timeline, stretching on with no end in sight. I could handle a *week*. "That sounds good."

"But this means," Flora explained, "that for the spell to be broken—and for you two to get back home again—things will have to unfold as close as possible to the events that you remember. Because if the spell isn't broken . . . well, there will be consequences." I noticed Fauna give a tiny shudder, and I saw Merryweather quietly knock twice under the table. "Among them . . . you won't be able to get home."

I nodded, feeling my stomach drop, as I pictured this outcome. It meant Rose would be stuck in some kind of forever sleep, and Maleficent would win, and I wouldn't ever have boba again or watch the new Spider-Man . . . or see Nisha.

But I couldn't focus on that right now. I felt myself reverting to my logistics brain, which had always been my most comfortable place. You couldn't think about the worst-case scenarios—this had also been drummed into me over the years. If you really thought about all the things that could go wrong, nobody would ever send anything by boat. Or plane or truck, for that matter. You just had to prepare the very best you could, make a backup plan—and then a backup backup plan—and hope for the best.

"Right," I said, nodding, trying to focus on the bright side, which was actually quite bright. We had a viable path home, and that wasn't nothing. "So to sum up, we'll just do our best to keep things on track."

"Without giving too much information about what exactly that looks like," Reece added.

Merryweather sighed deeply. "I *guess*."

"And then," I continued, trying not to smile, "on Saturday, the spell will be broken, you three will capture the magic and use that to send us home again."

"And don't forget," Flora said, glancing at the door, "we have to do this without letting Rose know anything that's coming."

"Absolutely," Reece agreed.

I nodded, even as I felt a guilty pull in my stomach. "It is her destiny, though. Shouldn't she . . ."

Fauna shook her head. "Oh, no, dear. If we were all given peeks into our destinies, the whole world would fall apart. For example, if you had told me that this would be my future—living in the woods for sixteen years with no magic . . ." Merryweather let out a very deliberate, fake-sounding cough. "With *nearly* no magic," she amended, her cheeks coloring slightly. "I would not have been happy about it. But actually living through it, getting to be here, and raise our Rosie . . ."

I noticed that her eyes were glistening, and Merryweather, surprising me, reached over and patted her hand. "It's been wonderful," she confirmed.

"But only because we lived through it," Flora pointed out. "If you skip ahead to the ending, you miss the best part."

"You mean, it's the journey, not the destination?" Reece asked, shooting me a look that could only be described as *smug*. Before I could respond, he turned to the fairies. "We won't tell Rose anything," he promised. "And we'll do all we can to make sure we get to Saturday with all the pieces lined up for the spell to be broken."

That seemed to end the meeting, because the fairies nodded and got up from the table. Merryweather still looked pleased with herself, Flora deep in thought, and Fauna smiling at both of us. "Tea?"

"I'm still good," I assured her, smiling back. "But thanks."

"We should go and see what's keeping Rose," Flora said, opening the top part of the door and peering out of it.

"I can go get her," I volunteered.

"And come right back," Flora added.

Merryweather shook her head. "Let the young people enjoy themselves," she said. "It's a nice change for Rose, getting to spend time with friends her own age and not just two old ladies."

Flora and Fauna blinked, and it was like I could practically see them doing the mental arithmetic. "There are three of us," Fauna pointed out.

"Two of *you*," Merryweather said, straightening her kerchief. "I'd like to remind you that I'm the youngest one here. And by far the most fun."

"Well, I never . . ." Flora huffed. She and Merryweather started bickering, and Fauna turned to us, shaking her head.

"Go," she said. "Just be careful."

"We will," Reece assured her. "We know what's at stake."

"I think it's good for her to have some fun," Fauna mused as she walked with us to the door. "Before . . ." Her voice trailed off. "Well. Before life changes."

"Oh—I believe this is yours, dear," Flora said as she handed me my cell phone—the one I thought I'd left upstairs. "Merryweather was using it as a paperweight, and I thought you might need . . . whatever this is."

"Right," I said, taking it back from her. "Thanks."

Reece and I stepped out the front door, and a second later, he plucked the phone from my hands. "Hey!" I exclaimed.

"What is this?" he asked, turning it over in his hands.

"Um, my *phone*?"

"No. This." I saw what he was pointing to: the I ♥ HCH WP sticker attached to the case.

"Oh." I said, feeling my cheeks start to get hot. "That just means I love Harbor Cove High Water Polo."

He just stared at me, and then we started walking again. "Um . . . do you?"

"Of course not! But Cooper—my ex—"

"We've met," Reece assured me.

"He used to play, and I guess I just never took it off. But I really don't," I said, edging my nail under the sticker. I pulled it off and crumpled it up. "Water polo is stupid."

"It really is," Reece agreed as we crossed the footbridge together.

"On the other hand," I pointed out, "if it was played with actual horses, it would be way more interesting."

He smiled, and we walked toward the forest in silence for a moment before he said, "Sorry. I didn't mean to bring him up."

"It's okay." It really was okay, I realized a beat later. It's not like Cooper had been occupying my thoughts lately. He suddenly seemed really far away. Well, he *was*. But even the feelings I'd had for him felt far away. I had thought of our situation when I'd been talking to the king and queen. But I could see now that my feelings about our breakup, and how unmoored by it I felt, really weren't about Cooper at all. They were about how I'd felt so thrown for a loop when my plans had been upended—when something happened that I couldn't control.

"I'm not sure we were actually the best fit," I said slowly. I couldn't help thinking about all those bored Saturdays pretending to watch Cooper play water polo while I actually read or did homework, all our fights about restaurants, the way we never seemed to laugh as much as Nisha and Allyson did. "I see now that I liked the idea of us more than the reality of . . . him." It seemed that Cooper had been right about this, after all. "So

I promise I'm okay." Reece nodded and I let out a breath, feeling somehow a little bit lighter.

"Well, I'm glad." He gave me a small smile, and returned my phone. "But now that the sticker is gone, you're going to have to explain the case."

I looked down at it: my Band of Brothers case, with anime versions of the Powell Brothers (and their cousin Doug). "It was a gift from Nisha. Ironic, but also very much sincere." Reece snorted, and I raised an eyebrow at him. "What's wrong with Band of Brothers?"

"Well, my *sister* likes them."

"She's got good taste."

"She's eight." Something passed over his face for a second—some expression I couldn't quite identify—and then it was gone.

"Nisha and I loved them when we were young, but lately I've come to appreciate them on a whole new level. I really think they never quite got their due."

"I'm pretty sure they did."

"Come on. 'HeartPower'? 'Staring @ the Ceiling'? 'Blame It on the Brain Freeze'? Classics!"

"You can keep saying that. It's not going to make it true."

"See, if my phone was charged, I could play you some songs and prove it to you. The power of their lyrics is unmistakable."

"I think I'm really okay without it."

I shook my head at his narrow-mindedness and started walking again. I could hear low laughter coming from the clearing and knew we were probably getting close to Rose and Phil.

"Wait!" Reece caught my arm. He dropped it a second later, but I could still feel my skin tingling where he'd touched me, the warmth of his fingers. . . .

"Um . . ." I said, trying to act like everything was fine. Because it *was*. "What?"

"We just have to get on the same page," he said, tilting his head toward the direction of the clearing. "With them."

"What do you mean?"

"I mean we have to keep everything on track."

"I think it's pretty on track. They clearly like each other."

"I know that. But breaking the spell is the only way for us to get home. And in order for the spell to break, true love's kiss needs to happen. Which means they need to be in love by this time on Saturday."

"So what's the problem? It seems like they're on the way toward that."

He nodded, even though he still looked apprehensive. "We'll just have to make sure things stay good." He ran a hand through his hair, and a lock of it fell forward on his forehead. I suddenly had the strongest impulse to brush it back, but I immediately squashed it. "In the real version of the story, they meet and fall in love all in one day. That's . . . easier."

I shook my head, scoffing at this. "It's also patently unrealistic."

"It is a story with fairies and curses," he reminded me.

"Okay. But, frankly, even those feel more realistic than falling in love—in *true* love—in an afternoon."

"Whether you believe in it or not, it's what happens. And—"

"Do you believe in it?" I interrupted.

"What?"

"That you can love someone after only a day?"

"Why are we talking about me?" Reece asked, glancing off toward the forest. "I'm not in this story."

"Well, you kind of are now," I pointed out. "That's the whole issue, right?"

Reece gave me a smile. It was quick and bright, like sunlight on water. But then it was gone, and he shook his head. "I don't know. I mean, back home, I'd say no. But we're *not* back home. We're in a place where things like that can happen. And isn't that why we like these stories to begin with?"

I took a breath to dispute this, tell him that I *didn't* like these stories, and how I'd strenuously opposed the prom theme. But I realized a moment later that at one point, I'd *loved* these stories. I'd loved the idea that things could be so clear when so little else in the world was. "I guess so," I finally said.

"I'm just worried because the more time they have together, the more things can go wrong."

"But it also means that they have a chance to actually get to know each other," I pointed out. "Which is something that's normally seen as a good thing before you decide you're in love with someone."

Reece shook his head, but he was smiling. "Let's just do what we can to make things work out, okay? We can be the men behind the curtain. The *people* behind the curtain," he amended.

"We can be like Rosencrantz and Guildenstern," I agreed, remembering them from my Shakespeare class. A second later, though, I recalled what actually happened to Rosencrantz and Guildenstern. "Um, just without the murders."

Reece laughed. "Yeah, I'd prefer that."

"You really think this can work?" I hadn't wanted to ask the fairies or seem anything but grateful for the plan they'd come up with. And it had seemed really convincing in the moment. But now that it was just the two of us responsible for keeping this on track, I was feeling the seeds of doubt start to grow.

"I think that it's our best chance," Reece said. "And I believe in the fairies. If anyone can help us get home, it's them."

"We're going to be able to pull it off." I wasn't sure if I was trying to convince Reece or myself. But the fact was, it was our best—not to mention only—option. If we didn't want to be stuck here forever, we were going to have to make sure things continued as close to the events of the story as possible. I felt a tiny twinge of guilt—would doing this mean I was keeping something from Rose that I shouldn't? Going behind her back?

But a second later, I reasoned that what Flora had said was correct: that none of us should know our destiny ahead of time. I wasn't going to go so far and admit that it was the journey, not the destination—that was *patently* nonsense—but I could at least appreciate that, sometimes, it wasn't a good idea to know how things ended up before you got there for yourself.

And also, it wasn't like I was tricking Rose into falling for someone random. She *liked* Phil and had from the first moment she'd seen him. Reece and I were just going to do our best to help keep things on that course.

"We can do it," Reece agreed, no question at all in his voice.

I nodded and gave him a smile. After a moment, he gave me one back, and I couldn't help but notice that the silence between us felt . . . easy. Not frustrated or angry or charged, like it had in so many of our interactions. More than anything, it was comfortable. Like we were finally on the same side.

"Hi!" I looked over to see Rose and Phil walking out of the clearing together. "We were wondering what was keeping you," Rose said. She showed me her basket, full of berries. "Because I picked all the berries, and Phil has to go."

"Council meeting," Phil said, looking regretful. Reece widened his eyes at him, and a second later, Phil seemed to realize what he'd said. "The ... wood-carver's council. It's quite serious. We're deciding if we're going to invade the, um, trees. To get more wood. For our ... carvings."

"Great," Reece said quickly, clearly trying to prevent Phil from continuing to talk. "That sounds like something very real that you need to be getting back for."

"But come back tomorrow. We can hang out," I said. Phil and Rose just looked at me quizzically. "Spend time together," I quickly amended. "Sorry. That's how we say it in our, you know, kingdom."

We walked Phil and Reece back to their horses. Delilah seemed happy to see Reece again, but Samson appeared annoyed—as much as a horse could be, at any rate—at having been left alone this long. He turned his head whenever Phil tried to talk to him, not relenting until he was offered a carrot, which he gobbled up immediately.

"See you tomorrow!" Rose called as the two of them turned to ride away, Phil sitting easily in his saddle, Reece hanging on for dear life and wincing. And a second later, they disappeared from view.

The two of us headed back toward the cottage, and I reached over and grabbed a handful of berries from Rose's basket. "Hey!" she said, pulling her basket back a moment too late.

"I'm just testing them," I pointed out. "Making sure none of these are poisoned. Or have gone bad. I'm *helping*."

"If you eat them all, I won't be able to make a pie," she pointed out, then glanced back toward the clearing. "Though I really don't know what I'm going to say tomorrow to get away. I can't say I'm picking berries. There are quite literally no more to pick."

"I think it might be okay," I said slowly, thinking about Fauna wanting Rose to have some fun before everything changed. "I don't think your aunts would mind you hanging out with me and Reece."

"But you still don't think we should tell them about Phil? I don't want to keep lying to them. It's not like they've kept any secrets from me." I choked on one of the berries I was eating and she looked over in concern. "You okay?"

"Fine," I managed in between coughs. "Just . . . wrong pipe. Sorry." I stopped walking and shook my head, trying to focus. I couldn't remember why, exactly, we had to keep this under wraps, but I knew that Reece had been insistent on it. And if that's what it took to keep things humming along until the spell broke, that's what we needed to do. I wasn't going to admit Reece knew better than me about many things, but when it came to *Sleeping Beauty*, he really did. "I don't think you'd exactly be *lying* to them by not mentioning Phil. It's just . . . not saying something. Lying by omission."

She laughed. "Lying is right there in that phrase!"

"But it's not like you wouldn't tell them the truth if asked a direct question," I pointed out. I tried to remember back to the one semester I'd participated in a mock trial. "If you came in, and they were like, *Hey, did you happen to meet a cute wood-carver in the forest lately,* you could absolutely tell them the truth. Or you could say, *Define* lately."

"I somehow don't see them doing that."

I grinned at her. "See? Problem solved!" I glanced over, but Rose wasn't smiling; her brow was furrowed, her shoulders hunched. I took a breath, trying to think of the best way to explain. "I think . . . maybe just wait until you're really sure how you feel. One time, when I was like twelve, I made the mistake of telling my mom I liked this boy, and then three days later, I saw him picking his nose on the playground and realized he was the worst. But then I had to endure months of her asking me about him." I shook my head. "And if I'd just waited, and seen his nose-picking for myself, all of that could have been avoided."

"What was that like?"

I let out a huffy sigh. "Really annoying, because even though I *told* her—"

"No," Rose said. She shook her head, her expression wistful. "I meant . . . having a mother."

"Oh." I blinked, suddenly finding myself in a land I wasn't sure how to navigate.

"It's not that I don't love my aunts dearly," she said quickly. "I truly do. But I've just always wondered."

"It . . . Well . . ." As I cast around for what to say, I suddenly flashed to the fairies, and how they'd light up whenever Rose came into the room. The way she never seemed far from their thoughts, the way they'd talked about spending these years with her as the most wonderful gift. The way it was clear to see just how much they loved her. "I kind of think," I finally said, feeling like I was choosing each word carefully, "that a mother isn't someone who needs to be so strictly defined. I think it's anyone who loves you and looks after you and wants the best for you, even if that means sacrifices. So it seems to me that you have one. Or even like you have three."

Rose nodded slowly, clearly taking this in. Then she smiled at me. "Maybe you're right."

"I'm always right," I replied immediately. "Don't listen to Reece if he says otherwise."

She laughed at that, and we started walking again, two bunnies falling into step with her. I realized, as I watched them hopping along, just how quickly it had become normal, our rabbit honor guard, just part of the routine.

"What did my aunts want to talk to you and Reece about anyway?" she asked as we crossed over the footbridge.

"Oh," I said, realizing Reece and I hadn't thought of a good answer for this. I willed my brain to work faster and come up with something plausible. "They . . . um . . . had an update about the, you know, plague. In the kingdom of Anaheim. It's getting better, but they still think we should stay here, just to be safe, until Saturday." I glanced over at her, hoping this wouldn't be an issue. After all, she was *not* used to having a roommate. Maybe she wanted her alone time back?

But Rose just smiled at me. "That's wonderful! I mean, not about the plague," she added quickly. "But this means you'll be here for my birthday!"

"I will," I said, relieved that I hadn't worn out my welcome, and that she wanted me to stay. I crossed my fingers, just hoping that by Saturday—six days from now—things would be on their way to working out.

"Race you back?" She raised an eyebrow at me. And before I could even reply, she'd taken off running toward the cottage. I hesitated for only a second before racing after her, trying to catch up, both of us running as fast as we could toward home.

Seventeen

HEY PHIL AND REECE! IT'S STELLA

Which you can tell because of the handwriting

HEY!

But we're going to work on it!

WE ARE. ☺

What is that? It's so cute!

THE SMILEY FACE?

Yes! I love it. 😊 😊 😊

ANYWAY, MEADOW? THIS AFTERNOON AROUND 2?

Good morning! How are you both—

You can't send the owl to bring us messages anymore. He practically cracked the window, he was pecking at it so hard.

No, it's fine! Send whatever bird you like. That's why we have the ~~royal glaziers~~ regular glaziers that wood-carvers use. 😊 Did I do it right? The smile portrait?

This afternoon is great. I'm hurrying!! Gah this bird is going to peck me to death.

Until then! ~~Phillip~~ just Phil

After only three days, we began to fall into a routine. Rose and I would get up early; she still somehow always managed to beat me, telling me more than once that she thought sleep was nothing but a waste of time.

Once I was up, I would get a mug of tea, since as I'd feared, oat-milk lattes weren't really a thing here. Once I was caffeinated, I'd help Rose out with her chores. Most of these were fine—I could gather firewood and sweep with the best of them—but the one thing I couldn't seem to do was get eggs from the chicken coop. I don't know why, but the whole group of them seemed to have agreed ahead of time that they hated me, and every time I tried to get some eggs, my hand got pecked within an inch of its life.

After we were done with the chores, we'd join the fairies in the kitchen, and the five of us would have breakfast together. And following breakfast (unless there was something to be done around the house), the rest of the day was ours for the taking.

At some point, we would usually send a bird over to Reece and Phil and make plans for the day. And I couldn't help but notice that, for the first time ever, my days were wide open. Even when I was little, it seemed like there had always been lessons and appointments and playdates that were meticulously timed. But now, when I woke up in the morning, usually to Rose's bed neatly made and a forest creature or two peering in the window, there was a kind of peacefulness as I thought about the day ahead of me. No structure. No plan. Which, I was finally starting to understand, meant that anything could happen.

"I don't know about this," Reece said as he looked down into the lake where Rose and Phil were already swimming.

Rose had sent them a note via sparrow that morning telling them to meet us at the lake, and to bring something to swim in. But while we had our swimming dresses, Reece and Phil were wearing, for reasons passing understanding, long pants and tank tops.

We'd all been taking turns flying off the rope and into the water, but

Reece had just stood on the side of the lake, resolutely dry, not jumping in (in any sense of the word), and I'd finally gotten out of the water to see what was wrong.

"Why not?" I asked, squeezing the excess water out of my swimming dress, and then out of my hair. "Is it because you're about to go swimming fully dressed?"

"I'm sorry I didn't bring a *bathing suit* with me to a fairy tale."

"I have one."

"Well, I don't have fairies making me sportswear."

"It's a fair point."

"But I might actually be able to see if I could get something that would work. Did I tell you Phil took me to see the royal tailor? He's making me a suit, and . . ." Reece went on, his eyes shining, telling me all about the tailor's studio, with its rolls of silk and velvet, and the giant Great Dane who served as the tailor's assistant.

I would sometimes complain to Reece about the modern amenities that I missed, but apart from the initial horseback-riding muscle soreness, Reece had never mentioned even disliking anything about our current situation; he clearly loved it here.

Each day seemed to bring new stories of what he'd discovered, more excitement about the world we'd found ourselves living in. He'd tell me about the rides he and Phil would take through the woods, racing each other across as birds swooped overhead. He'd talk about the book he'd found about dragons—*actual* dragons, he made sure to point out to me—in the library. The only time I really got jealous that he was in the castle and I wasn't was when he mentioned the map room, filled with illustrations of whole cities and countries that were specific to this world, which was something I would have *very* much liked to have seen. Reece promised to look at the maps again for me, and I'd told him to come back with as much detail as possible.

But more than any of what he was discovering, Reece just seemed *lighter* here. He smiled more now, and joked more, and the closed-off, anxious expression that I'd occasionally clocked back in California was nowhere to be seen.

"Here I go!" Phil yelled. Reece stopped talking about the suit he'd been promised, and I looked down to see that Phil had swung from the rope over the lake—but hadn't let go and was just now dangling from one hand over the water. Below him, Rose was treading water and laughing, her glorious hair floating behind her.

"Dude," I yelled down to Phil, even though, as usual, Reece winced slightly at this, "what's your plan?"

"I think I missed my chance," Phil called. "I always do this! I hestitate and then the moment passes me by."

"This is fixable," Reece called down to him, maybe since Rose seemed like she was laughing too hard to speak. "Just drop!" After a moment, he did, landing with a splash and emerging a second later, pushing his dark-red hair back.

"So the fairies were okay with this?" Reece asked, gesturing around us. "With you leaving?"

I nodded. "I told you, as long as we're keeping an eye on Rose, they seem fine with it. I think they want her to have some fun. Now." I turned to face him more fully, raising a hand to block the glare. "Are you swimming, or what?"

He nodded at my hand, which was, admittedly, red and swollen. "What happened here?"

"Oh, that. I got into an argument with some chickens."

"Chickens?"

"Apparently they don't like it when strange people try and take their eggs from them? Who knew."

He took my hand in his, turning it over, brushing his fingers softly over the back of my hand. "Does it hurt?"

I shook my head, my mouth suddenly dry. We both seemed to realize we were holding hands at the same moment, and we stepped away quickly.

"Phil!" I called, mostly just to break the tension. "Send the rope back!" Phil threw it up to me, and I missed the first time but managed to catch it on the second attempt. I grabbed it in both hands, pushed myself off, and went flying over the lake, then dropped with what I thought was a fairly impressive cannonball. "Come on in," I yelled up to Reece when I surfaced. "The water's fine!"

I started to throw the rope up to him, but he just shook his head and walked up to the edge. And rather than jumping, he executed a perfect dive, landing with almost no splash.

"Not bad," I said, as he swam over, trying not to show how impressed I was. Rose and Phil, however, were not following my lead at all, and were both clapping.

"Well," Reece said with a nonchalant shrug. "I heard a rumor that the water was fine. Just wanted to check it out for myself."

Hey Stella— meadow this afternoon? Also, Phil is very proud of his newest carving, so if he shows it to you, just know it's supposed to be a cat. (Even though it looks like a dinosaur.) ☺ Reece

"Thanks," I said to the sparrow who'd brought the message. It had only taken a few times for this—getting literal airmail and thanking the winged creatures who sent and returned what were basically texts—to seem totally normal.

I was sitting on the front steps of the house trying to get up the courage to go face the chickens. Rose and the fairies were inside finishing up breakfast and talking over their empty plates, reminiscing about something that had happened when Rose was seven. I had snuck out the kitchen door to give them some privacy. It wasn't that anyone in the cottage was making me feel like I was in the way. But I was just becoming more aware, with every passing day, that the time they would all have together was ticking down.

I would sometimes catch one of the fairies looking lost in thought or watching Rose with expressions already slightly wistful. So I just wanted to make sure that the four of them were getting some time together without me interrupting their last days. They'd been a family for a long time now, after all. And even though Rose may not have known it, it had an expiration date.

It was an overcast day, the first of its kind I'd experienced since I'd been there. It gave everything a kind of charged, unsettled feeling, like it was threatening rain, but rain wasn't coming. I'd found my gaze drifting over to where I knew Maleficent's castle was, wondering if she was somehow causing this. If her frustration was growing as the time ticked down to Rose's birthday.

An uneasy feeling swept over me as I thought about it. Was she getting desperate to get her revenge before the time ran out?

I was about to head inside and (subtly) show Rose the note we'd gotten, when the sparrow hopped a little closer to me, and I noticed that one of his wings was bent strangely, his feathers ruffled. "Hey," I said, sitting up and looking closer. "You okay?"

I was no expert, but it didn't look like he was okay, so I carefully picked him up and headed into the house. Rose smiled when she saw me, but then her expression faltered. "What's wrong?"

I held my hands forward. "I think something's wrong with this bird."

"With Arthur?" She hurried closer and leaned down to look. "I think you're right. Poor thing. Let's show him to Aunt Flora. She'll be able to fix him up."

She scooped the bird—Arthur, apparently?—into her hands and took him over to the table where the three fairies were.

"How did you do with the chickens today, Stella?" Fauna asked me.

"I didn't get there yet." Merryweather gave me a skeptical look, and I felt my cheeks heat up. "I will! We just got waylaid by this bird."

"Can you help him, Aunt Flora?" Rose asked, holding the bird out to her.

Flora frowned. "What's wrong with him?"

Rose shook her head. "I'm not sure. Something with his wing."

"Let's see." Flora gently took the bird and held him up to the light. "It looks like maybe another bird attacked him. Maybe . . . a raven." I saw her exchange a look with the other two fairies that I didn't understand. "But I can get him fixed up in no time." I wasn't sure if she used magic, but it seemed like she must have, because a second later, she was handing the bird back to Rose with a smile. "Good as new."

Rose gave Flora a hug, then took the bird back from her. "Thank you so much."

Rose hurried outside with the bird, and I followed. She walked a little ways away from the house and set Arthur the bird down on the grass. He took a few tentative hops, and then rose up and started flying, all better.

But even though Rose smiled widely at this, I couldn't help my gaze from turning toward Maleficent's castle. And for no reason I could explain, I felt myself shiver.

"The name of the game is *gameball*," I declared from the water.

"I never agreed to that," Reece protested.

I pointed to Phil. "He suggested it."

"But this isn't gameball," Phil said, looking confused. "Because you don't play it in the water."

"Gameball is an actual sport?" I asked, stunned, as I tossed the ball from hand to hand. We were in the lake. The day had dawned bright and hot and sunny, and perfect for swimming. Reece and Phil had both arrived today with slightly shorter pants, but nothing that could actually be considered shorts. But I didn't think that there was any way to ask the fairies if they could make us two dudes' bathing suits without raising questions we'd prefer not to answer. "I thought it was just like calling something sportsball."

"Ooh, I like that," Rose said. "I think we should call it sportsball."

"Wait, what are the rules?" Phil asked, frowning. "I haven't played this before."

"None of us have," I assured him.

"So we get to make up our own rules?" Rose asked me, pulling her hair into a knot on top of her head. She grinned. "That sounds fun."

"Or we could just play something we already know the rules to. Like water polo," Reece suggested. But a second later, he shook his head. "No, forget that. Water polo is the worst."

"It really is," I agreed.

"So we just . . . decide for ourselves?" Phil asked, starting to smile.

"Well, the four of us should probably agree," I pointed out. "Just so we're all on the same page. It'll be a democracy." I suddenly remembered who I was talking to. "Um, that means we all get to decide together."

Reece ducked under the water for a moment and emerged, pushing his hair back. "So . . ." He pointed to a nearby tree. "Maybe that's the goal? You have to hit it?"

Rose shook her head. "That doesn't seem nearly challenging enough."

"You have to hit it from under the water?" Phil proposed.

"I like it," I said, then looked around. "Should we be writing these down?"

"Fold," Flora said.

"Fold," Merryweather said.

"Fold," Fauna said with a sigh as she set her cards down.

I'd taught the fairies poker my second night there, and we'd played most nights after dinner, sitting around the table, candles burning. The fairies had taken to it right away, and Rose had, too. She was a veritable whiz at the mathematical side of poker, calculating odds and best possible moves in seconds. But she wasn't great at figuring out when people were bluffing. Which I thought was actually a good thing: It meant that she was more unfamiliar with lying than the rest of us. But it also meant that it gave me an advantage I wasn't hesitating to use.

She looked at me over her cards, her eyes searching my face, and I concentrated on keeping my expression as blank as possible. "Fold," she finally said, and I smiled and pulled the small pile of matchsticks—what we were using in lieu of poker chips—toward me.

"What did you have?" Rose asked, turning over my cards, which were *terrible*. "What!" she said in outrage as I tried not to laugh.

"That's the thing about poker," I explained as Merryweather gathered up the cards and started shuffling, clearly eager for the next game. "People aren't always telling you the truth."

She huffed, shaking her head. "Well, I really don't like that."

"I don't like it either in, like, the world," I said, and Rose laughed. "But it's good to know for card games."

"Okay, rematch," she said, narrowing her eyes at me. But there was such a funny expression on her face that I burst out laughing, and a second later, so did she.

"Are we playing?" Flora asked, rapping on the table.

"Yes," I said as I flexed my hands, trying to get my head back in the game. "Let's do it."

"How was that out?" I demanded, as I pointed to the goal, treading water in the lake. Phil and Reece had shown up that afternoon with a giant metal circle, and we'd threaded some rope through the center and hung it from a nearby tree—it was about the size of a giant tire swing, and this was our new goal in sportsball (the name had ended up sticking).

The rules had also gotten much more complicated, really for no reason except that it was actually a lot of fun to create your own sport. So it had morphed into a combination of water polo, swimming, basketball, and

Phil's favorite, gameball. Phil kept trying to explain the rules of it to me, but I couldn't seem to grasp them no matter how many times he went through it.

The basic objective was to get as many goals as possible. You got extra points the deeper in the water you were, if your back was turned, or if you were able to lob it from *under* the water.

There weren't teams—it was every person for themselves.

Basically, every time we played, a few new rules got added, and though I hadn't told anyone, I was secretly keeping track of all the addendums and amendments on a piece of paper back in the cottage.

"It bounced off the ground and then went in," Reece said, folding his hands and shaking his head at me. "Doesn't count."

"I think it should count for something," Rose protested. "Maybe she gets an extra try?"

"I've got it," Phil said, scrambling out of the lake and tossing the ball back to me.

"Okay," I said, concentrating hard. "Three pointer!" I yelled, and arced the ball through the goal perfectly, and I celebrated with a brief underwater victory dance.

"Nice shot," Reece said when I surfaced, having recovered the ball.

"What's *three pointer*?" Rose asked.

Reece and I looked at each other and I contemplated trying to explain what basketball was, before giving up. "It's . . . what you say when you need to make an important shot," I finally said. "When you really want it to count."

"Ooh, should we make that a challenge?" Rose added. "If you call *three pointer* but miss the shot, you immediately lose?"

"High stakes," Phil said, smiling at her. "I like it."

I nodded. "I'll add it to the rules." Then I quickly amended, "Not that I'm writing them down or anything. Never mind. Whose turn is it?"

"What do you think?" I asked, showing my pouch to Rose. I'd gotten jealous that she was the only one with pockets around here, so she'd offered to show me how to make one. I'd never really sewn before, so mine wasn't nearly as good as hers, but I was secretly really pleased with it.

She leaned over, looked, and gave me an approving nod. "Amazing!"

Phil, Rose, Reece, and I were sprawled in the meadow. Rose and I had originally had more ambitious plans for this afternoon—more swimming, or walking in the woods, or maybe finally teaching me to ride a horse (this one hadn't been my idea). But the day had dawned hazy and hot, and as a result we'd found ourselves here, feeling that doing anything else—or even moving very fast—would be far too ambitious.

Rose turned away from me and back to trying to coax a shy squirrel out of the undergrowth so it could say hello. Reece was leaning up against a tree trunk, his long, booted legs stretched out in front of him, and Phil, to my surprise, was reading. It wasn't that he didn't seem like a book guy, it was just that he was usually much more engaged with us and never seemed to like to pass up an opportunity to look at Rose.

"So what are you reading?" I asked Phil.

"Oh," Phil said, turning red. "Forgive me. I've been so rude. It's just so *good*." He held it up and I saw that it was *Wings of Destiny*—the book Reece had brought with him to Disneyland.

"Is that Reece's?"

"Uh-huh." Reece shot me a smug look.

"So clever to have it bound like this," Phil marveled as he turned the paperback over in his hands. "It's portable! All our manuscripts are so large."

"What's it about?" Rose asked, leaning closer to look.

"It's about a kingdom torn asunder, menaced by a vengeful dragon." He flipped through it. "I just can't put it down. And normally, I don't even like realistic fiction."

I met Reece's eye and had to bite my lip hard to keep from smiling.

"When you return to Anaheim," Rose asked as she held out her hand to a rabbit who was hopping up to her, "will there be another ball? Or did the plague put the kibosh on that?" She frowned and glanced at me. "Did I use it right?"

"Perfect." She'd heard me say it to the fairies the night before, loved the sound of it, and was now trying to use it as much as possible.

Rose raised her eyebrows, and I remembered a beat too late that she'd asked me a question, and one I wasn't sure how to answer. "Oh. Um . . ." I glanced across the clearing to where Reece was clearly trying to read over Phil's shoulder. "Reece?" I prompted.

"Hm?" he asked, looking up.

"Rose was asking about the ball. And if we can go when we get back home." I truly wasn't sure what to say to this. Based on what had happened to us before, I was operating under the assumption that very little time would have passed when we got back. I had no proof for this, but it was what I was hoping would happen. I didn't want people back in Orange County to have been looking for us the whole time. So assuming we would show up back at Disneyland, with nearly no time elapsed, that *would* mean that we were still going to be able to attend the ball. Or, you know, prom.

Reece made a face. "I don't even want to think about back home. Who would want to when you could be here? Nothing we have can compare to this." He looked around and smiled, then shook his head. "I wasn't even planning on going in the first place."

"Not *go*?" Rose asked, looking baffled. "Not go to a ball?"

"Seriously," Phil chimed in, looking equally shocked. "You get to *dance* at a ball. Why wouldn't you want to go?"

"I'm not much of a dancer," Reece said.

"I can help with that," Phil said, setting the book aside and jumping to his feet. "I had to take dance lessons for years."

"You did?" Rose asked, and Phil's eyes got wide.

"It's really . . . important for wood-carvers to know how to dance."

"I've heard that," I said quickly. "That's what everyone says. Anyway. You can help Reece?"

"I'm really okay," Reece said, but Phil was already holding out a hand to him and pulling him up to his feet.

"What's your weak spot? Farandole? Quadrille? Pavane?"

"Yeah, Reece," I said. I had a feeling I was going to enjoy this. "Show us your waltz."

"We can teach you," Rose said, also standing up. Her voice was sympathetic. "There's no need to avoid a ball just because you can't dance. I mean, I'd love to go to one."

"You will," Reece said confidently. We all glanced over at him, and he seemed to realize his mistake a moment later. "I mean, most likely. Dances are happening all over, right? They're a common . . . occurrence." I raised an eyebrow at him, trying not to laugh. "Hey," he said, clearly trying to change the subject, "anyone else hungry?"

"So," Phil said, clapping his hands together. "Everyone ready?"

Today, Phil had an authority to him I wasn't used to. And it was like I could see, in flashes, the king he would be someday. Though I *did* think it was funny that this side of him was coming out when he was trying to teach us to dance.

It was the following day, and we were back in the meadow—but we weren't just hanging out, which I would have preferred. Instead, Phil and Rose were going to teach us to dance. And even though I'd offered to sing—I was all ready to share Band of Brothers with two people who'd never heard them and one person who didn't appreciate them as he should—Reece had flatly turned this down, so the dance lesson was happening without music.

"Start by taking your partner's hand," Phil said.

I extended my hand toward Reece, who blinked at it in horror.

"They did it again?"

"Yeah," I said. For the first time, I understood where the phase *henpecked* came from. My hand was red and swollen, covered with tiny cuts. "I think they were getting their revenge for last time. I swear, they coordinated their attacks."

"You *could* just let Rose collect the eggs."

"And let the chickens *win*?"

"Can you even hear yourself right now?"

"You weren't there. The chickens, they mocked me."

"Are you two paying attention?" Phil called to us.

"Yes," we said in unison.

Rose shot me a look that clearly indicated she didn't believe me, and then turned back to Phil. She extended her hand to him, a bit shyly. Phil smiled down at her and took it, then carefully placed his hand on her waist.

"Okay," Phil said, ostensibly talking to me and Reece but not taking his eyes from Rose. "Are you watching? It's *one* two three, *one* two three . . ." As we watched, they started to move in time together, Phil carefully spinning Rose under his arm.

"See?" Rose called to us. "It's simple."

"Uh-huh," I called back.

"Got it," Reece added.

"I can't actually do that," I said to Reece in a low voice.

"Of course not," he responded immediately, like it was obvious. "But I don't think they've noticed."

I looked to Rose and Phil and saw what he was talking about. They were starting to turn in large circles around the meadow, moving faster and more fluidly. And it was clear, from the way that they were looking at each other, that everything else except the two of them had utterly disappeared.

Eighteen

Hey, it's Reece.

They can tell. They can read—or not, in the case of your handwriting. (My apologies, that was rude.)

No, it's great! Phil's got insults!

☺

Anyway, Phil had an idea —

I had an idea! Could you meet later tonight? At midnight? Sneak out after everyone has gone to bed and head to the meadow? We'll have a surprise.

I turned over the paper in my hand, then folded it up and stuck it in the pouch I now always kept tied around my waist.

This kind of invitation was definitely new: For the last five days, whenever we'd hung out with Reece and Phil, it was always during the day. I wasn't sure what the plans for the midnight meet-up could be, to say nothing of the surprise, but just thinking about it was making my heart beat a little faster in happy anticipation.

I was sitting on the front step of the cottage again, where I'd taken to coming in the mornings with my tea, so that the fairies and Rose could have some time and I could have a moment to myself before I had to face the day—and the chickens.

I took another sip of my tea, and stretched my legs out in front of me, just listening to the sound of the wind in the trees and the chirping of the birds in the trees. I closed my eyes for a moment and felt the sun on my face. It seemed like my fingers hadn't been itching for my cell phone in a while now. I'd left it in the wardrobe in Rose's room, since there was absolutely no point in carrying around a dead cell phone. The mornings when I'd wake up with my phone in my hand, already scrolling through my schedule, were starting to feel very far away.

A second later, the door opened and Rose stepped out. "Ready to do this?" she asked, nodding toward the coop. "Or are you too . . . chicken?"

"I regret teaching you that phrase. Also." I held up the note. "Phil and Reece want to know if we want to meet them in the meadow at midnight."

"At *midnight*?" Her eyes widened. "For what?"

"No idea," I said. "They just said for a surprise."

"Hmm." She glanced back toward the house and lowered her voice. "We'd have to . . . steal away, I guess?"

I nodded. "I somehow don't think your aunts would be okay with it."

"Merryweather might be. But then she'd also want to come."

"You're probably right."

"I've never done anything like that before. Not that I would have had anyone to sneak out to meet before now."

"I've never done anything like that either," I assured her. Sure, there had been the occasional time I would tell my parents I was sleeping over at Nisha's, and we would go to a party we would probably not have been allowed to go to if we'd asked permission. But for the most part, I hadn't strayed too far out of the boundaries of my curfew. I was about to explain this to her when I realized that we weren't at all in the same boat—Rose had never had a best friend, or parties to sneak out to.

And so even though it was going against what I'd promised her parents—and the fairies—I couldn't help thinking that this might be the kind of thing that Rose needed to do while she still could. Because if she wasn't going to go to a meadow at midnight to meet a fairy-tale prince and his temporary roommate, when was it going to happen?

"I think we should say yes," I said with a nod.

"It could be fun," Rose agreed, starting to smile. "And I really want to know what the surprise is! So we're going to do it?"

I set my teacup down, pushed myself to standing, and nodded. "Let's do it." I glanced over at the chicken coop. "Assuming I'm still alive by tonight, that is."

"I believe in you," Rose called as I started to walk toward it. "Remember your training!"

I let out a breath and tried to empty my mind of all fear as I approached the chicken coop. I pulled open the door, and the birds all stared back at me. "Okay," I said, inclining my head. It was always best to show your

enemies respect. "Henrietta. Louise. Josephine. Bonnie. Margaret. Carla."
I flexed my hands and cracked my knuckles. "Let's dance."

"Ready?" Rose called up to me in a half-whisper.

"Um . . ." I called down, trying not to make too much noise. I had not climbed a *ton* of trees in my life, and now I was being asked to climb down one, in the dark, and what's more—do it silently.

Rose and I had decided that our best bet for sneaking out without getting caught was to go via the tree outside her bedroom window. We'd acted like everything was normal all evening, and when we were sure everyone else in the house had fallen asleep, we'd changed out of our nightgowns and back into our regular dresses, sitting near the window and straining to hear the far-off bells that would tell us when the hour was striking. (I'd explained to her that back in the kingdom of Anaheim, we all knew what time it was, down to the second, but upon hearing this, Rose had shuddered. "Why would you need to know that?" And while I'd put up a defense, I had to admit she kind of had a point. After nearly a week of living in a place where everyone knew the hour but not necessarily the minute, I couldn't help but notice it was a lot more restful.)

We'd stayed up late, talking in whispers, and were deep in conversation when we heard the twelve bells sound. We hurried over to the window and made our break for it. Rose went first. It had seemed simple when she did it, so it wasn't until I was leaning halfway out a window, looking at a drop that suddenly seemed *very* far down, that I hesitated.

"You can do this!" Rose whisper-shouted up to me. She gave me a thumbs-up, which she'd picked up from me and Reece. I gave her a half-hearted one in return and reached out for the trunk.

"Okay, okay, okay, okay," I muttered to myself as I tried not to think about the fact that I was climbing down a tree, in a dress, in the dark, in a world where there was no ER if you broke your leg. When it seemed like I was close enough to the ground, I closed my eyes and dropped. I accidentally stepped on a twig when I landed, and the *snap* sounded like a firecracker in the quiet of the night.

I froze, looking up at the windows for any sign of movement—candles being lit, fairies stalking out and demanding to know what we were doing. As nice as they'd been to me, it was never *super* far from my thoughts that they could probably very easily have turned me into a toad if they wanted. As we stood there, I could feel a little flash of guilt. Because what *would* the fairies say if they found out about this? Especially after I'd promised all of them—and the king and queen—that I'd do everything I could to keep Rose safe. I somehow had a feeling none of them would think that this fell under that category.

Flora had even pulled me aside the day before and explained her theory about the hurt sparrow. She told me she had no way of knowing, but she thought maybe the sparrow had been attacked by one of Maleficent's ravens. She might have sent her bird after the sparrow to try to find where it was going.

"Obviously, she didn't succeed," Flora had said, looking relieved. "The bird made it here, safe and sound, having managed to shake the raven off. But as we get closer to Rose's birthday, I am pretty sure she's going to be stepping up her efforts."

"Maleficent has *ravens*?" I asked. "Like, attack ravens?"

Flora nodded, her expression grim. "All of which is to say that things are getting more precarious. So *be careful.*"

"Think we're okay?" Rose asked, shaking me out of these thoughts.

I stared up at the cottage—no light, no noise—and nodded. "I think we're in the clear." We hurried toward the meadow, running every few steps, then trying to slow ourselves down ... and then running again.

But the closer we got, the more I knew in my bones that the fairies wouldn't have been happy with what we were doing. This was certainly not being *careful.* I was starting to have second thoughts as I looked around, fully taking in the situation. I'd brought Rose away from the fairies who could protect her, to the middle of the woods, in the pitch dark. Had this been a huge mistake? Was I putting us both—but especially her—in danger?

But before I could say anything to Rose, we reached the clearing. And as I saw what was in front of me, I felt all my worries and concerns melt away. Because this was worth it.

Standing in front of us were Phil and Reece, and behind them was a moonlight picnic.

It truly was impressive. Blankets had been laid out on the ground, and candles in holders flickered, giving everything a soft glow. The moon was shining huge above us, lighting up the truly impressive amount of food the guys had brought with them: cakes and tarts and dishes of treats spread out everywhere.

"This is amazing," Rose said, her eyes shining as she looked around.

"Surprise." Phil met her eye and he smiled the widest I'd ever seen him smile. I was secretly glad to see it—because as cheerful and polite as Phil invariably was, every now and then, I'd see something pass over his face, like he was somewhere else and wasn't happy about it. And when that happened, I would remember what he'd said the first day he'd met us all—that he had to do some duty and didn't want to, but didn't know any way out of it—and would wonder if that's what was going on with him.

But seeing him now, and his unfettered happiness just because of how happy Rose was, I felt my heart lift. "This is great," I said, looking around at the picnic, trying to take everything in. "I've never had a midnight feast before." It was the kind of thing I'd read about in stories—which was, I realized a moment later, just where we were. "It all looks amazing."

"It's cool, right?" Reece asked, smiling at me.

"Very."

For the first few minutes, we were all running around, trying every single dish, laughing and comparing and trying not to knock the candlesticks over. Everything was delicious, which maybe shouldn't have been such a surprise, since I was pretty sure this feast had been cooked by royal chefs in a castle. And while I thought about pointing that out to Reece, just to needle him about the fact that he was staying in a castle and I wasn't . . . I decided to let it go. I didn't want to fight right now. I just wanted to enjoy this.

After we'd eaten all we could and I felt like I was going to burst—but in a good way—I lay back on the blanket and looked up at the sky. It was dense with stars, more than I'd ever seen before—certainly way more than you ever got to see in California. Sometimes, in the mountains or on camping trips, you could see lots of stars, but I'd still never experienced what I was looking at. Was this what the sky had looked like for everyone before lights and electricity and planes crossing the sky? This huge, inky canvas, dotted with diamonds? It was breathtaking.

And as I took it all in—the stars, the meadow, the half a piece of cake I still had left, my friends all around me—I realized just how peaceful I felt. I was calm in a way I never was back home with my mind always going over schedules and spreadsheets and plans. Before I'd come here, I'd never just let myself *be*. And I found, to my shock, that I liked it. That it felt like I could really breathe for the first time in a long time.

"Hey."

I looked over and saw that Reece was lying next to me on the blanket, just an arm's length away, close enough to touch.

I was looking at him by candlelight, moonlight, and starlight. But nonetheless, I could still see him perfectly: his long lashes, his slightly crooked nose, his mouth curling up on one side. Or maybe I couldn't actually see him so clearly. Maybe I'd just, without even realizing it, committed him to memory.

"Hi," I replied, giving him a smile. I had a sudden urge to reach out and run my hand through his hair, pushing it back from his forehead, but I stopped myself before I did this, and decided to blame the impulse on the moonlight. "This was really great," I said, gesturing toward the feast. "I loved it. Thanks so much."

Reece smiled back at me, his eyes not leaving mine. "I'm glad." After a moment, he looked up at the sky again, and when he spoke, it was like he was choosing each word carefully. "I still don't know how it happened, but I'm really happy I ended up here." He took a breath and looked back at me. "With you."

I blinked, my heart pounding hard—and I didn't think I could blame it on the sugar in my cake. I knew I could have brushed it off, or made a joke, but I suddenly found that I didn't want to. "Me too," I finally said, my eyes searching his.

He took a breath, like he was going to say something, and my heart started pounding triple time. I wasn't sure what he was going to say—or what I even wanted him to say. I mean, this was Reece. But also . . . this was *Reece*. Suddenly, it felt like I was seeing him in a new light. Not as my waiter-nemesis, or as my sparring partner, or as my friend.

For the first time, it was like I could really see something . . . *more*. But was he thinking along the same lines? Was this all in my head?

A flash of light streaked across the sky, interrupting these thoughts. I sat up to get a better look at it: a shooting star. I looked around to point it out to Rose . . . which was when I saw she was on her own blanket, sitting close to Phil. Her head was on his shoulder, and his arm was around her.

I decided that privacy was probably what they would want most right now and not me pointing out celestial activity. I lay back down again, feeling happy and content. Not only was I thrilled for Rose, but it also meant that Reece and I had done what we needed to. Tomorrow was the day before her birthday, and things were clearly good with them. We'd done it. Well—they had. But we hadn't messed anything up along the way, and that felt like something.

"What was it?" Reece asked, looking over at me.

"Shooting star," I said, pointing up and tracing its arc across the sky.

"Cool," he said, folding his arms behind his head as he looked up. "Did you make a wish?"

"Didn't think of it in time."

"Maybe there will be another one."

I laughed and looked up, too. "Maybe they come in threes. Like sneezes?"

Somehow, without even looking at him I could tell he was smiling. I could hear it in his voice, coloring it. "Well, if you see another one, tell me?"

"I will," I promised. I looked up at the sky, searching for any more streaks of light traveling across it. Even though, in that moment, I couldn't think of a single thing I wanted to wish for.

Nineteen

A re you all set?" Merryweather asked me.

I nodded and pulled my tote over my head. I'd finally taken it back from her, though it wasn't easy; she seemed to have developed a real fondness for it, in addition to making *Guac your world!* her new preferred farewell phrase. "I am. And promise I'll be careful. After all," I added, dropping my voice, even though Rose wasn't in the kitchen with us, "Maleficent isn't looking for me. I'll be safe."

It was Friday, the morning after our meadow picnic, and the day before Rose's birthday. Which also meant it was the day before Reece and I would leave, if all went well. And so I'd basically begged the fairies to let me go to the market instead of them, all too aware that this was probably my last opportunity to do it. After all, the three of them went frequently. Surely I'd be safe to go for an hour, maximum. And I knew I wouldn't be able to tell anyone back home about it, but the chance to go to an *actual market* in this world, to find out about the supply chains and trade routes—I could think of few things that would make me happier.

I'd explained it all to Rose this morning as we were getting ready in her room. I hadn't done anything on my own in a while, and I was feeling a bit rusty as I tied my sneakers and grabbed my empty tote. Out of habit, I tossed in all the things I usually took with me on errands: keys, phone, lip gloss.

"The *trade routes?*" Rose had echoed incredulously, not quite able to disguise the laugh in her voice. She did seem interested, at first, when I explained how vital they were, and how the placement of rivers deter-mined the placement of cities, how empires could rise and fall because of access to water. But as I started to get into more detail, she'd just laughed and told me to have fun. Then she looked out the window with a dreamy, half-formed smile on her face. It had been there ever since the midnight feast the night before. As we'd walked back to the cottage together, Rose had been practically humming with happiness, like a tuning fork when it's found the right pitch.

"Okay, you and Phil," I'd said, turning to her when we had gone far enough to be out of earshot of the guys. "Oh my god!"

In the moonlight, I could see that her eyes were shining. "I know!"

"Did you guys kiss?"

"No." But even in the moonlight, I could see she was blushing. "But . . . hopefully soon?" She did a happy little spin, and she was now *actually* humming, a tune that sounded familiar to me even though I couldn't quite place it. She stopped spinning, took a few wobbly steps, and grabbed onto my arm to steady herself. Then she raised an eyebrow at me. "So, what about you and Reece?"

Only hours ago, I would have dismissed this out of hand. But now, after that moment we'd shared . . . that couldn't have been nothing, right? "I . . . don't know," I said slowly. "Maybe?"

But even this nonanswer was enough for Rose, who clapped her hands together, jumping up and down with excitement until we were both laughing and couldn't quite remember why.

So when I'd seen her go all fuzzy again this morning, I knew exactly what—or should I say *who*—she was thinking about.

"Are we sure this is wise?" Fauna asked now, joining Merryweather and me by the door, wringing her hands.

"The girl is going to the market, not Spain," Flora said crisply from the kitchen table, even though I could see worry in her expression. She raised an eyebrow at me. "And you have our . . . special list?"

I nodded, and patted my canvas bag. The fairies had some surprises planned tomorrow for Rose's birthday—which was something I *did* have a vague memory of—and I had been tasked with picking up the things they'd need, like bolts of cloth and extra baking supplies. "I'm all set," I assured them.

"Going out?" Rose asked as she practically leapt down the steps. "I'll come, too!"

"Not to the market," Merryweather said at once.

Rose shook her head and grabbed her satchel from its hook near the door. "No, I'm going to pick some berries. I won't be long!"

I waved at the fairies and we hustled out together, Merryweather leaving us with a cheery *Guac your world!* "I take it we got a message?" I asked Rose when we were out of the house.

She nodded, her face aglow with happiness. Even her hair seemed bouncier, which was not something I would have believed possible without seeing the proof. "They're meeting us in the meadow. Should I tell them you'll be there after the market?"

I nodded. As much as I wanted to see Reece again, I was also nervous to, which was ridiculous, since nothing had really even *happened*. "I'll come by when I'm done," I promised. Rose nodded, then pulled me into a quick, tight hug. "What's that for?" I asked, even as I hugged her back.

"I don't know!" But she was beaming, and I could see that she was practically on the verge of spinning again. "It just feels like . . . everything is working out. Doesn't it?"

I smiled back at her, even as I fought a sudden urge to knock on wood. "I hope so," I said honestly. She waved goodbye to me, then practically ran toward the meadow. I watched her go until she passed out of sight, and then I took the opposite path: the one that would take me to the road and after that, to the next village, and the market.

As I walked, I adjusted the canvas bag on my shoulder, wondering why it was so heavy—and one glance was enough to tell me why, and also that it was all my fault. It was heavy because I'd swept my phone and keys into the bag, just because it was what I always did whenever I was leaving the house back home.

I rolled my eyes at myself as I pulled it over my shoulder again. What use were a dead cell phone and keys for a car that was centuries in the future and possibly several dimensions away? Also weighing things down was the pepper spray attached to my keys, but I doubted I'd have any use for that, since it had been on my keys for years and I'd never yet needed it.

But because I didn't want to turn back, I'd just have to deal with having a slightly heavier bag than usual. It really was amazing how quickly you could get used to being unencumbered. Having been without it for almost a week, my cell phone felt like it weighed several pounds inside my bag. Had I just hauled this around with me wherever I went, never thinking about how much weight it added?

I picked up my pace again, heading for the market, keeping my eyes open, just taking in what was around me, making sure I was clocking it all, but there was nobody around, just a bird flying overhead.

Flora had given me the directions to the market, and she'd offered to write them down for me, but I told her I'd be fine. One thing I knew I could do was get from place to place and remember directions once they'd verbally been given to me. If I couldn't pull this off, my parents would disown me.

As I walked down the road, I tried to picture what was ahead of me: the stalls, the traders, the people who would hopefully tell me how things got transported in a world with no internet, or airplanes, or cars, or tracking numbers. But they always did, one way or another—that was what my mom had told me one night.

I'd been at the office, doing my homework while she worked late sorting out an issue for a client. To put off having to write my essay about the Stamp Act, I'd pointed to the large framed map that had always been on the wall, the one showing the shipping lanes in Sweden circa 1619.

"How did that even work?" I'd asked, staring at it. "How did they figure things out without being able to communicate?"

My mom gave me a look that let me know she was onto the fact I was avoiding my homework, but then smiled as she looked at the map.

"They communicated," she said. "Just not in the way that we do. Every generation always thinks they have the most advanced technology, after all. And people and things have always needed to get from place to place. All throughout time. When the need is great enough, no matter what the obstacles, you somehow find a way."

Then she'd sighed and gotten back on the phone to try and find out what had happened to a shipping container in the South China Sea, and I went back to writing my essay. But now, the thought of actually getting to find out about how this worked from people currently living it—it was so exciting, I found myself picking up my pace, just wanting to get there sooner.

After I'd been walking for a while, and starting to wonder if maybe I should have packed a snack, I was suddenly aware of a large black bird circling overhead. Was it the same bird I'd seen before? I couldn't tell. But it wasn't acting like a normal bird. It would swoop down closer to me, then back up above the tree line once again, but it wasn't letting me out of its sights.

I made myself keep walking, even though I could feel all the hairs on the back of my neck rising, letting me know that something was *off*. I told myself it was just a bird, and not even a bird of prey that I might need to be worried about, like an owl or a hawk or something. But while this bird was acting strangely, it didn't seem like it was big enough to cause me any harm. It looked like it was just a crow, or a raven.

A *raven*.

The realization was enough to stop me in my tracks. Because Maleficent had a raven—that was what Flora had said. Was *this* that bird? Or was it just a random crow acting weirdly?

I hesitated, frozen in place, not sure what to do now. All my instincts were telling me to turn around, go back, get out of there. But if this bird had something to do with Maleficent, what if I led it right back to the cottage, revealing where Rose and the fairies were? I couldn't take that risk. I couldn't go back—which meant I had to keep going forward.

I stared straight ahead, making myself keep walking like everything was fine, even as the bird was dipping lower and lower now, coming closer to me, close enough that I could see its individual black feathers, its yellow beak, the pink rings around its eye.

The bird let out a *caw* and then flew right at me, coming fast. I stumbled back, tried to run, and then my feet tangled beneath me and I fell backward, hitting the ground hard.

And then everything went black. Again.

I opened my eyes and blinked as I looked around. The first word that came to my mind was *gray*. Because that was all I could see—cold, gray stone. I frowned as I tried to make sense of where I was. I was in a huge room with giant carved statues along the walls and torches flickering in holders. The room seemed to be round, and I was up on a kind of raised platform with staircases going down on either side. Below, there was a large, circular space, currently empty. But there was an *ax* just lying in the middle of the space, which really didn't add to my feelings of well-being. It was all very cold, very scary, and just immediately a place where you *know* bad things happen. I'd never stumbled into a deserted cabin during a rainstorm with a killer on the loose, but I had to imagine it gave you the same feeling. Just a pervasive sense of *wrongness*, the knowledge that things are dangerous, that you're in a place you shouldn't be.

The second word that came to mind was *ow*. My head was throbbing, and I carefully reached up and patted it and found a slightly raised lump. Well, that would explain why I didn't remember anything after I'd fallen—and why I now had a splitting headache.

"And what are *you* supposed to be?" a cold, musical voice asked.

Just like that, it felt like ice had been injected into my veins. I sat up and turned around, and that was when the third word came into my head: *scared*.

Because, I realized as I pushed myself to my feet on legs that felt shaky, I was pretty sure that I was in the castle of Maleficent.

And that the person in front of me, the one who'd spoken . . . was the villain herself.

Reece may have been giving me (possibly somewhat deserved) grief for not being as up on the story as him, but I recognized her right away. It would have been hard not to; this was not a forgettable person. She was sitting on a throne carved of the same gray stone as the rest of the room. She had her horned headdress on, the one that came to a sharp widow's peak in the center of her forehead.

She was wearing a long black gown with a black cape over it. The collar of it stood up on either side of her face, and the inside was lined with purple. Her lips were perfectly outlined in red. She had purple eyeshadow and seriously impressive brow game. And she was looking at me like I was a slug she'd just found in her dinner.

I felt a cold rush of fear go through me, sharper than I'd ever felt before in my life. Even when the fairies had tied us up in the cellar and I'd been slightly concerned about being turned into an amphibian, I hadn't felt *this*. The absence of any goodness, or kindness, or warmth. This was real fear—because for the first time, I was truly in danger. I could feel it down in my bones.

This wasn't just a nice story anymore. All at once, I was remembering just how *dark* fairy tales got—the actual moments of peril and danger and . . . death. And just like that, I was flashing back to the christening. Even when I'd still thought we were in an immersive experience, I had been scared by Maleficent. Remembering the way she'd looked at the baby—my friend Rose—with nothing but bad intentions made my stomach drop. And now I was here, alone, on her turf, without any backup—no fairies, no Reece.

So, in all, I was getting the general impression that things were *not good*.

"I said . . ." Maleficent intoned. Her voice rose only slightly, but seemed to lower the temperature in the room—which hadn't been super balmy to begin with—another ten degrees. "What are *you* supposed to be?"

"Me?" My voice came out as a squeak. I cleared my throat. I may have found myself in an evil villain's lair, but I could at least *pretend* I wasn't going to pieces.

"Of course, *you*." She arched an already-arched brow at me. And even though I knew there was other stuff to be focusing on, I couldn't help but notice again how amazing her eyebrows were. I was tempted to ask her what she did, but I had the feeling the answer was probably something along the lines of *steal children's happiness*. I suddenly saw that she was carrying a staff with a yellow ball at the top of it. I'd seen enough movies to know that staffs like that, in the hands of a story's villain, are never just decorative. They're not there for *show*. They electrocute people, or open wormholes, or melt people into goo while Thor looks on in horror. I didn't want to be anywhere near one, I knew that much.

"I'm Stella," I said, not sure exactly what she wanted from me, or why

I was even there in the first place. Had what the fairies worried about come to pass? Was she going to try and get information about Rose from me? Had she somehow found out I'd been staying at the cottage, that we were friends? I waited for a reply, but Maleficent just stared at me. "Stella . . . Griffin?"

"Stella. Griffin." She said each word like it was somehow distasteful and far beneath her notice.

"Y-yes," I replied, my voice shaky. She was still looking at me like I hadn't provided the answer she wanted, and I tried to think of what else I could give her. My rising sign? Locker combination? Social security number?

The raven—the one who'd flown right at me—fluttered down to her outstretched fingers and started preening his feathers. "Hello, my pet," she said, her voice much warmer now that she was talking to the bird. "Go get them." The raven lifted off again with a squawk and went flying away.

She turned her gaze on me again. I tried to keep my breathing steady as I lifted my chin. I had the feeling that she could somehow see right through me, could read every tell. I was trying to keep my face as blank as possible, and not let her see that I had information she wanted, or how scared I was. . . .

"Here!" I heard a commotion behind me. I turned around to see what it was, and gasped.

Standing in the area below the raised throne level and filing in on the staircases on either side of us were . . . creatures. I just stared at them for a moment, not really sure what other word to use to describe what I was looking at. They were all standing on two legs, but they weren't—and I cannot stress this enough—*people*.

There were pigs and giant birds and what looked like a crocodile and something I couldn't even identify, with big round eyes and huge ears, like a bat gone wonky. They were all wearing battle armor, including helmets, and they were all carrying weapons. One had a quiver of arrows and a bow, another a huge meat cleaver, others with axes and swords. . . . It was horrifying, and yet I couldn't tear my eyes away. It was like my subconscious was loading up images for any future nightmares I might have.

"Now," Maleficent said to the creatures as the raven flew down and alighted on the shoulder of her cape. She gestured to me. "Tell me about what you've brought, would you please?" Her voice was sweet in a way that immediately put me on edge.

A pig-creature stepped forward, looking proud of himself. He snorted a few times and then began to *speak*. I don't know why this should have been such a surprise. After all, there was an upright alligator brandishing a meat cleaver just to my left. But somehow, this was as shocking as anything that had happened since I'd gotten here, and *a lot* had happened.

"Brought maiden," the pig said proudly, pointing at me. "Like you said."

I relaxed a tiny bit at these words. So maybe Maleficent *didn't* know anything about me—didn't know that I had a connection to Rose. All of which was good news. But the bad news was, I was still in the lair of a villain, and now she was angry. I could see it even if her minions couldn't.

"A *maiden*," she echoed, giving them a smile, which they should have known better than to trust. I'd only been here five minutes, and that smile was enough to make me want to run for the exits.

"Yes!" the pig said smugly, pointing at me. "Older girl. *Not* baby." He added this last part proudly, and I frowned, trying to figure that out.

"And what *exactly* did I tell you," she said, the sweetness in her voice slowly getting replaced with steel, "when I told you to go look? I said to bring me a maid with golden hair." She pointed at my head with her staff, and I immediately wished that she wouldn't. "Does *that* look like golden hair to you?" I tucked it behind my ears self-consciously.

"Um . . ." The pig suddenly looked a lot less confident. His eyes darted nervously around. "I'm . . . colorblind?"

"No you are not," she snapped. "And I said she would have lips to shame the red, red rose. *Those* lips? Please."

"Okay," I said, quite certain I was being insulted, and feeling like I had to say something to defend myself. "I don't think—"

"I never said you could speak," Maleficent interrupted, her voice suddenly loud, echoing in the room.

I swallowed hard and fell silent. I looked at her staff and saw that the ball on the end had started to glow ever so slightly. I clasped my hands together; I could feel they were beginning to shake.

Maleficent turned back to the pig, who was now attempting to hide, not at all successfully, behind the bat creature. "You just grabbed a random girl! *Not* the right one."

"But . . . you said . . ." the pig whimpered, gesturing to me as Maleficent raised her staff. She brought it down, and purple lightning erupted from it. I felt its heat as it rushed past me with force, blowing my hair back and making my eyes water. It streaked past me and landed, full force, on the pig who had displeased her.

I clapped my hand over my mouth in horror as he shrieked, lifted up in a beam of light and held aloft for a moment before he crashed to the ground again. But it didn't seem like he was dead—just shocked, and now desperately trying to run away. All the creatures went running as she sent lightning raining down on all of them, zapping again and again, making me flinch every time. As I watched them scatter and flee, as she pointed her staff at a group running for the exit, I spotted something on an iron hook next to the vaulted doorway—something familiar. A canvas bag with *El Arco Iris* written across it in graffiti-style font. And as her lightning hit the group scurrying for the exit, I saw my bag get caught in the cross fire.

I closed my eyes so I didn't have to witness it. When I opened them, I fully expected to see my bag in flames or reduced to a pile of ashes. But it was still hanging there, apparently unhurt. And from the depths of my bag, I could hear a faint *ding*—the sound an iPhone makes when it gets powered back on. I frowned, trying to make this make sense. . . . Had Maleficent's magical lightning just charged my phone?

I started to edge toward it. I hadn't gotten as far as devising a clear escape plan, but everything in me was screaming *go go go*. It was probably how antelope felt around an apex predator, with the threat of mortal danger all around, practically shimmering in the air. But I'd only taken a few steps when Maleficent said, quietly but commandingly, "No."

She pointed her staff at the staircase I'd been edging toward, and a pile of rocks fell at my feet, blocking my way.

"Cool," I said, taking a step back, trying to act like this was a normal thing I could definitely handle. "That's fine. I wasn't going anywhere or anything."

"Who *are* you?" she said as she looked at me, tapping her fingers on her chin.

"Stella," I started, but she shook her head, cutting me off with a look.

"Do you know, I'm extraordinarily good at reading people?" She asked this almost conversationally, like we were having a nice chat over some matcha lattes. She fluttered her fingers and the raven came to rest on them, right above what was actually a stunning black cocktail ring. She fixed me with a piercing gaze and I swallowed hard. "I can always tell when someone is *lying* to me."

"What a nice quality to have!" I said brightly. "Must make it really easy when you play poker. Oh—it's a game? With cards." She just stared at me, unamused, and I took a breath, trying to regroup. "I'm not lying. I'm Stella Griffin—"

"Yes. So you've told me." She frowned, then got up from her throne and walked toward me, her dark eyes boring into me like X-rays. She turned in a full circle around me, the raven studying me as well, as I stood as still as possible and just hoped she couldn't hear the pounding of my heart, or somehow sense how wobbly my legs had gotten. "There is something . . . off about you," Maleficent finally said. And for the first time, she didn't sound totally in control, like there was something happening that she didn't understand. "As though you're not . . . from here."

"I'm not," I said, thinking about what she'd just told me—that she was essentially a human polygraph machine. If I didn't want to raise her suspicions, I needed to tell her versions of the truth. "I'm . . . visiting."

"Visiting."

"Yes."

She regarded me for a moment longer, then swept a few steps away. "Do you happen to know anyone named . . . Aurora?" Her voice was casual, like she couldn't have cared about my answer either way.

"I have never met anyone named Aurora," I said, concentrating on the truth of these words. Because I *hadn't*. Even Rose didn't know that was her name, which was actually kind of bananas, when you thought about it.

"You're *sure*?" She leaned a little closer to me, her eyes narrowing.

"I am."

She met my gaze, and I forced myself to stay calm and keep my thoughts far away from anything that had happened here. Instead, I concentrated on going through the state capitals, and I'd gotten all the way to Tallahassee before she broke her gaze. "Fine," she said, her voice irritated. "Then you're useless, just like everyone around me."

"So," I said, looking toward the other staircase, the one that wasn't blocked by a mini avalanche of rocks, "I can go?"

But Maleficent didn't seem to have heard me as she flung herself into the stone chair, and despite everything, I winced. *Stone* did not seem like it would be a particularly comfortable thing to sit on. It was the same question I'd always had about the Iron Throne. If you were important enough to have a throne, wouldn't you make it the most comfortable seat in all the land?

"Sixteen years," Maleficent said, turning the staff in her hands. Her voice was tired, with a streak of bitterness running through it. "Sixteen years and the closest I've gotten is . . . *you*."

"Totally," I agreed, edging another step toward the staircase. "So if there's nothing else—"

"Do you know what that's like?" she snapped, stopping me in my tracks again.

"No," I replied honestly.

"It wasn't supposed to *be* like this!" she hissed. She smacked her hand down on the side of the throne. The raven flew away, looking frightened. "It should have worked. It would have. I know it. It was very nearly there . . . and then those fools had to intervene. The good fairies." She spat out the words, like they tasted foul. "Those simpering *idiots*."

I felt my hands clench into fists. I was on the verge of jumping in and defending them, but I stopped myself just in time. Letting Maleficent know I knew them would not be helpful for anyone right now. I needed to think about the big picture here, no matter how much I wanted to yell at her.

"Something wrong?" she asked, looking at me with renewed interest.

"No." I was fighting to keep my mind as calm as possible. "I just . . . What you were saying about your plan—"

"Hmm." She looked at me a moment longer, like she was trying to work something out, then shook her head. She pushed herself up out of her chair and started stalking around the platform, circling me.

"Do you know," she said, her voice low, "how long it's been since I've slept through the night? Since I've enjoyed that simple pleasure afforded to the satisfied?" Her robe whipped around her with a *snap* each time she turned, and every time it happened, I jumped.

"I . . . don't," I said after a moment, tracking her with my eyes as she paced around me, the way lions do—deliberately, not spending more energy than they have to, secure in their power.

"Sixteen years," she said, her voice low. "That's how long it's been. I stay up at night, and I go over it. Trying to figure out how things went this wrong. Because it was perfect. My *plan*. I was going to get my revenge, and it was going to be so satisfying. . . ."

Her face lit up when she said this, a smile forming as she imagined what could have—in her mind, what should have—been. And seeing it, seeing Maleficent *happy*, was the scariest thing that had yet happened since I'd gotten here.

But a moment later, her smile faded, and she looked around at the reality of where she was. As she did, her expression curdled into anger and disappointment. "But then it failed. And everything I'd planned for was dashed. Everything I'd expected . . ." Her voice was shaking with anger.

I swallowed hard, starting to get a sinking feeling in my stomach. There's probably never a good moment to realize that you have something in common with a famously evil person, but having that revelation while standing in front of them somehow makes it hit even harder. And the way Maleficent was talking about her plans—and her need to hold on to them at all costs—it was like looking in a really scary mirror.

Because this was exactly what I'd been doing with Cooper. Not cursing innocent babies and trying to wreck their lives, but clinging on to something that wasn't working. So focused on how something *seemed* perfect—and ignoring the reality of what it actually was.

And for the first time, I realized that I was actually grateful to Cooper for breaking things off. He'd seen things weren't good and had been brave enough to do something about it—unlike me. I'd just insisted on clinging tightly to someone I really didn't even get along with, and all because I didn't want to back down, admit any failure, be human. Which I wasn't actually certain Maleficent *was*, but the point was the same.

She'd been holed up here, clinging to her rage and her plans for over a decade now, and it certainly didn't seem like it had made her any happier.

Memories were flashing past, but I was seeing them in a new light now. The way I hadn't even enjoyed my sixteenth birthday party because I was so focused on following my schedule. All those weekends I'd wasted, sitting on the bleachers pretending I cared about water polo, since I had told myself I was happy in this relationship and hadn't wanted to question it. Telling Avery that the decorations were wrong just because it wasn't how I would have done them. Even today, insisting on setting off to the market so I could talk to people about shipping lanes and brushing aside any objections. Why had I been so stubborn? Where had it gotten me?

Well—here. Facing off against one of the most formidable villains ever. So . . . nowhere good, at any rate.

"Maybe your plan isn't so perfect," I said. Maleficent glanced over at me sharply, like she'd forgotten I was there. "If it's not working," I clarified. "So maybe this thing, whatever it is—since I don't know anything about it!—isn't going that well, and you could just let it go. Do, I don't know, a spa day or something instead?"

"You dare to question *me*?" Her voice was low, but her eyes were blazing. "Such impertinence. As though I need advice from *you*." She turned the staff between her long fingers, and tilted her head as she looked at me. "You're of no use to me."

As I watched in horror, the staff started to glow. "Um . . ."

"And since you're just . . . visiting . . . I'm sure it will be a while before anyone realizes that you've gone."

"Listen," I said, my heart pounding hard as I watched the light at the end of the staff get brighter and brighter. "We can talk about this! We don't need to do anything rash, right?"

She laughed and lifted her staff, which was glowing brighter than ever. "How sweet that you think so." She took a breath, like she was seconds away from cursing me. I flinched but made myself keep standing, not wanting to give her the satisfaction of seeing me cower.

"Mistress!" The pig-creature was back, hurrying into the throne room. Even from a distance, I could see that his ears and his curly tail looked singed.

She looked away from me, her expression irritated. "What?" she snapped. "I am in the middle of something!"

"We think we found one," the creature snorted as he ran up to her, his expression equally excited and fearful.

Maleficent lowered her staff, looking intrigued. I let out a shaky breath, feeling like I'd just gotten a reprieve, even though I knew it might be temporary. "One . . . what?" she asked.

"A . . . machine," he said in a loud whisper, glancing over at me.

She dropped the staff farther, her eyes lighting up. "Really."

"We can show you." He backed away a few steps, eyes on her staff. "Or we don't have to, if you're busy."

She looked over at me, eyes slightly narrowed, like she was considering it.

"Well, um, good luck with your whole project," I said, starting to edge off again, just wanting to put some distance between us. My bag was by the doorway, and if I could just grab it—

"Begone," she said, pointing her staff at me.

I gasped and closed my eyes. What did that mean? Was this the end? Was I about to be purple lightning-ed?

But a second later, I hit the ground hard. I looked around and saw I was back in the spot where I'd first seen the raven. And Reece, a panicked expression on his face, was running toward me.

Twenty

blinked at him. "Reece?"

"Stella!" His face was ashen, and I could see the worry on it.

As I watched him get closer, I tried to figure out what was happening. Why was Reece even here? Last I'd heard, he was meeting up with Rose and Phil back in the meadow. I started to push myself up to standing, but Reece had closed the distance between us. He reached out his hand to help me up—and then, to my surprise, pulled me into a hug.

"You're okay," he said, relief palpable in his voice.

After a second of shock that this was happening—because Reece and I weren't in the habit of doing this—it hit me just how nice it felt. Reece's arms were strong around me, holding me tightly. It was like I could breathe him in; he somehow smelled like woodsmoke and sugar and early mornings. And it occurred to me that I could just lean my head against his shoulder and rest it—he was right there. But a moment after this cascade of revelations, Reece stepped back suddenly, like he'd just remembered that we hadn't, until this moment, ever hugged.

"I'm sorry," he said, shaking his head. "I shouldn't have just . . . without asking . . ."

"No, it's fine," I said quickly. "It's more than fine. But, um . . ." I gestured to him and looked around. "What are you doing here? I thought you were back by the cottage with the others."

"I was." I could see now that the stricken look on his face was fading, and he was starting to look like himself again. "But I got worried when they told me you were going to the market alone."

"I'm perfectly capable of going to the market by myself!" I retorted automatically. But then a second later, I realized that since I'd been spied on by an evil bird and kidnapped by an evil sorceress, maybe this wasn't *strictly* true.

"It wasn't just that," Reece said. "I saw a raven circling the palace this morning, and it gave me a bad feeling."

"Oh yeah, he's the worst," I said, shaking my head. "So you came here looking for me?"

"How do you know that he's— No, I went to the market first," he explained, still looking baffled. "I looked there for you, but nobody reported a girl demanding to hear all about the spice road, so I started to retrace my steps, and that's when I saw you." He stopped and took a breath. "What happened?"

I gave him the bullet-point version of what had just happened: Maleficent, her weird animal army, and the fact that she wasn't giving up on looking for Rose. That she seemed more determined than ever. I explained it all but decided to leave out the revelation I'd had—that I had more in common with Maleficent than I was comfortable with—and my subsequent resolve to do something about it. To be better. But I figured Reece didn't necessarily need to know this, so I just skipped over that part and took him to the end of the story, Maleficent sending me back here.

"But the most important part of this all is . . . my phone is now charged."

Reece stared at me. "*That's* what you've taken from this encounter?"

"But it *is* still trapped in her evil lair. Along with my keys. So that's not great."

"I can't believe you met Maleficent—and escaped unscathed." I couldn't help but notice that Reece was looking at me differently—with a little bit of awe. And I found that I really didn't mind it.

"I was just glad she didn't know about my connection with Rose. I thought that's why I was there, but it turns out, it was just a random kidnapping!"

Reece laughed, but I could hear he still sounded a little shaken. "That's not normally a good thing," he pointed out. "But in this specific case, I am also very glad that it was just a random kidnapping." He smiled, but it faded almost immediately as he looked around. "But it might not be over yet. Her raven found you here, after all. He might still be somewhere nearby. We have to get you home to the cottage—without him or any of her minions seeing you."

"They were so weird," I said with a shudder, remembering their dull expressions and their very sharp-looking weapons—never a good combination. "And they could all talk. Did you know they could *talk*?"

"Luckily, they're not that bright," he said. "Which may have been your saving grace as well as Rose's." He nodded down the road, where I could see Delilah was tied up to a tree. "I'm parked over there."

I laughed as we started walking toward the horse together. Somehow, seeing Delilah there really brought home for me what Reece had done. "I can't believe you rode off looking for me."

"Not that I needed to, clearly."

"I know, but . . ." I hesitated, not sure what I was even really trying to say. "Um . . . thank you."

"Of course. It really wasn't even a question." He met my eye, then looked away quickly. "I mean," he said, his tone suddenly more formal, "we're so close to the birthday deadline, right? We just need to hang on until then and we can go home. I didn't want anything to derail that."

I nodded, even though I could feel something in me start to deflate. Like a balloon, slowly losing hope and happiness. I suddenly realized that maybe I'd read all of this wrong. "So you just came because you were worried I was going to get in the way. You thought I might mess things up."

"No," he said quickly. "Of course not. But I *was* worried . . ." His voice trailed off and he looked down at the ground.

"But you would have done the same for Phil or Rose," I clarified. "It wasn't anything . . . else." I was trying to make my voice sound upbeat, which was the exact opposite of what I was currently feeling. And it wasn't like this was a bad thing! It was *good* that Reece was a considerate friend. I had just thought for a moment that it meant something more.

But really, if Reece didn't want me to think that, should he really go around giving people amazing hugs and smelling like woodsmoke and smiling at them during midnight picnics? This was *not* my fault.

"Of course I would have," Reece said, still sounding a little lost as to what we were talking about. "But . . ."

"Oh, look, the horse," I said, trying to change the subject and hide my disappointment. "Hiya," I said to Delilah, putting my hand flat under her nose, like Phil had showed me, for her to snuffle. She nudged my hand, clearly looking for an apple or a sugar lump. But when she didn't find one, she seemed to forgive me, giving me a gentle headbutt that I knew was affectionate.

"So," I said, running my hand along the horse's silky mane. "Should we get going?"

Reece took a breath, like he was going to say something, but then just nodded. "Let's." He swung onto Delilah's back easily, like he'd always been doing this, even though I could remember not very many days ago when he was wincing with every step after his introduction to horseback riding. But, I reasoned, he was getting practice as he rode with Phil every day, and he'd clearly taken to it like a natural.

Once he was on the horse's back, I just stood there for a second, contemplating my next move—and how exactly I was supposed to get up there. Horses were high, after all. And I was wearing a dress. "Um . . ."

"How about this?" Reece moved forward on the saddle and took his foot out of the stirrup. "Can you get your foot in there? And I'll help you up."

"I can also just walk," I suggested. The reality of riding on a horse with Reece was hitting me—and the fact that we would have to sit *very* close together. It wasn't that I was opposed to this—quite the opposite—but since he'd just told me that he only saw me as a friend, I wasn't sure that riding together on a horse was the best idea. It was practically a staple in rom-com movie montages, after all. "I mean," I explained, as Reece looked down at me, his expression skeptical. "I walked here and it was fine."

"Except for when you were captured by an evil sorceress."

"That was *one time*."

"I want to get you out of here faster than that." His voice was serious, and his expression grave. "Any moment now, she could show up here. She's the one who sent you here, after all."

"Good point. Okay." I wiped my hands on my dress, and took a breath. Then I heaved my leg up as I high as I could get it—and even then, barely got it into the stirrup.

"You okay?"

"I'm fine!" I said through gritted teeth, even as I was hopping on one leg, trying to get my foot farther into the stirrup. "This horse is really tall," I said, out of breath. "And I'm short, okay?"

Reece looked like he wanted to smile, but instead, just held out his hand to me. I took it and heaved my leg over the horse's back, with Reece helping to lift me over. "Good?"

"More or less." I took my foot out of the stirrup and moved as far back on the saddle as I could, which really wasn't that far. It didn't seem like this saddle was really meant for tandem riding; it was definitely a one-person saddle.

Reece put his feet back in the stirrups and picked up the reins, then turned to look at me. As he did, I drew back a little; I hadn't realized that when he turned around our heads would be so close. I mean, he was right there, like I could just lean forward and . . .

"Stella?"

"Right." I blinked, telling myself that I needed to focus on the matter at hand. Horseback riding. Guy who just wants to be friends. Evil sorceress who wants to kill Rose. Priorities.

"You all right?"

"Uh-huh." I gave him a nod, trying to act like I did this all the time, and it was just no big deal.

"Um . . . you might want to hold on to me. If you're comfortable with that," he added quickly, turning back around. "No worries if not. I just don't want you to fall off."

"Me neither," I said honestly. I moved forward a little bit on the saddle, and I couldn't help noticing just how close together our legs were, mine fitting in right behind his, like we were the big and little spoons. I hesitantly extended one arm, then the other, and put them around Reece's waist. But there was still space between Reece's torso and mine. My arms were extended almost their full length, like we were slow dancing at a middle-school dance.

"Good to go?"

I nodded, then realized he couldn't see me and this was useless. "Uh, yeah."

"Here we go." He made a kind of clicking sound, tapped the reins on Delilah's neck, and she jolted forward. As she did, I found myself gripping Reece more tightly, as I had to lean forward to avoid tumbling off the back of the horse, which was something I really didn't want. I'd already fallen down once today, after all, and didn't think I needed to double my head-injury quotient.

So I moved forward on the saddle and tightened my arms around Reece's waist as the horse galloped forward. For the first few moments, I was bouncing and jolting along, like I was on a bumpy carnival ride. But after a few minutes, it was like the horse found her rhythm, and I was able to settle into it as well. It wasn't a bad way to travel, I had to admit, as I watched the scenery flying by around me. It was slower than when you were in a car. You were able to take in more, enjoy it before it passed out of sight.

And I couldn't help but notice just how *good* Reece was at this—how easily he was sitting in the saddle, how Delilah seemed to respond to all his commands. It was like watching someone who'd grown up doing this, not someone who'd done it for the first time a week ago.

Reece and I both ducked in unison to avoid getting clotheslined by a low branch, and when we straightened up again, he was leaning back a little more against me, and I tightened my arms around him, even as I told myself it was just to make sure I could keep my balance. I leaned forward and let my cheek rest, for just a second, against the soft fabric of his white shirt.

"Almost there," he said, turning his head slightly to look back at me.

"Right." I glanced around, realizing that things were starting to look more familiar. I straightened up and let go a little bit so we weren't quite as close together. Reece pulled back on the reins, and Delilah slowed to a trot, then a walk. "Thanks for the ride."

"Just rate me five stars," he said, and I could hear the smile in his voice. He steered Delilah over to where Samson was tied up.

"Four stars," I countered. "Could have used more horsepower."

Reece turned around to look at me, a smile tugging at one corner of his mouth. "You did *not* just say that."

I laughed. "What?"

Samson had been munching on some grass, but he quickly straightened up and tried to pretend he hadn't been doing anything so uncouth. Phil's horse, I'd come to realize, took great pride in being a royal stallion, and rarely allowed himself to be seen doing anything foolish or even, frankly, horse-like. That was, until you gave him an apple—then all dignity went out the window.

Reece pulled Delilah to a stop, then swung himself down to the ground. I swung one leg over, and Reece held out his arm to half catch, half lift me down. "Thanks," I said as soon as I was on solid ground again, shaking out my dress.

Reece tied Delilah up next to Samson, then walked back over to me. He took a breath, and when he spoke, it was fast, like he wanted to get his words out before he could stop himself. "Listen, I don't want you to think that . . ." He hesitated, shook his head and tried again. "It's not that I don't . . ." He let out a frustrated breath. "What you said before. About me going to help Phil or Rose—it's not true."

I felt a little flare of hope somewhere in my chest, like an ember from a campfire I'd thought was totally out.

"Not that I wouldn't want to help them," he amended quickly. "Of course I would. They're my friends. But when I thought that *you* might be in trouble . . ." He shook his head. "It was different. It *is* different." He took a step closer to me, and my heart started to beat faster. "And when we were at the picnic, I thought maybe . . ."

I nodded, trying very hard not to let a smile take over my face entirely. I took a step closer to him, and Reece reached down and took my hand in his. And just like all the other times we'd touched, this sent a spark all the way through me. "I was thinking the same thing," I assured him, giving his hand a squeeze. I could hardly believe that this was happening, but it really seemed like it *was*.

"Yeah?" A quick, bright smile passed over his face, lighting all his features up. He took my other hand in his and I moved a step closer, my heart beating a symphony in my chest.

Reece looked down at me. We were close enough to kiss, and felt like we were on the precipice of it. He drew in a breath, his head starting to tilt down toward mine. . . .

I heard a twig *snap* and jumped. I whirled around, expecting the worst—Maleficent had tracked us, she was here with her hench-creatures, the jig was up . . .

But when I saw it was just Rose and Phil running toward us, I relaxed—but only for a second. Because I could see that Rose's face was tearstained and blotchy, and Phil was pale as he ran after her.

"But if you'll just—" Phil was saying, his voice anguished.

"No," Rose said, her voice breaking. She stopped short when she saw us, and I saw her eyes widen for just a second as she clocked that Reece and I were holding hands. We glanced at each other, immediately dropped hands, and stepped away. I hurried over to Rose.

"What's going on?" I looked from her to Phil. My heart had started to pound again, but in a totally different way than it had been doing just moments before, when I'd thought Reece and I were on the verge of kissing. This increased heartbeat wasn't because of happy nervous excitement. This was that ominous drumbeat of *something is wrong.*

Rose's bottom lip was shaking, and her voice came out cracked and halting. "Phil," she started. "He . . ." She shook her head.

Now that I was closer to her, I could see that she'd been crying—*really* crying. Not just one delicate tear-down-your-cheek crying, but the kind you do when your heart has just been broken. And all at once, I started to get a very bad feeling about things.

"Phil told me . . ." she said, then paused to take a halting breath. "That he's engaged."

I turned to him, feeling my anger flare to the surface. "*What?!* Is this a new thing?" I felt myself get angrier with every word I spoke. "Or has this been going on the whole time you were hanging out with us and you just, I don't know, forgot to mention it?"

"I kind of tried," Phil said. To his credit, he looked absolutely miserable, his face pale and drawn. "That first day, when I met you all. And I was saying that there was something my parents wanted me to do, but I didn't want to—"

"Oh, of course!" I smacked my forehead theatrically. "How could we not understand that very clear information you gave us." I glared at him.

"Listen—" Phil started.

"Let me explain," Reece jumped in.

Rose and I both turned to him. "Wait," I said. My stomach dropped, like I'd somehow gotten on a roller coaster without realizing it. I just stared at him, wanting it not to be true. "What do you mean *explain*, Reece? You—you *knew* about this?"

"Reece," Rose said, looking crushed. Her eyes filled with tears. "How could you keep it from me? I thought we were friends."

"It's just that—" Phil started, but Rose was already talking over him.

"Were the two of you laughing at me? For being foolish enough to think . . ." She glanced at Phil, then looked away, folding her arms over her chest.

"Wow. Okay," I said, shaking my head at Reece. "Real nice."

"Stella—"

Rose turned to go, heading toward the cottage, but then spun back around, reached into her pocket, and took out a small wooden object. "You can keep this," she said, flinging it toward Phil. The object hit his chest and he caught it. "Three pointer," she said, her voice cracking.

Phil turned it over in his hands and I could see it was a rabbit—I noted, in the small remaining part of my brain that wasn't currently furious or heartbroken, that he really had gotten better with his carving. Rose turned and ran for the cottage.

"Stella," Reece said, his voice low and pleading. "Just listen to me."

"Yeah," I said with a short sarcastic laugh. "Right. I don't think I'm going to be doing *that* ever again." I glared at him, then ran to catch up with Rose.

When I reached her, she had stopped running—she was walking fast, wiping away the tears that were spilling over her cheeks. "I'm so sorry." I tried to put my arm around her shoulders in a comforting way, but she was too tall and it was impossible, so I just threaded my arm through hers.

"Stella," she managed, but then her lip started quivering again.

I let out a shaky sigh. "I know. It's awful. But I've been here before, and I know what we need."

She blinked at me. "You do?"

I nodded. "Yep. We're going to need chocolate. A *lot* of it."

Twenty-One

The three fairies were at the kitchen table playing Texas Hold 'Em when we came in. Rose didn't say hello, just ran straight up the stairs to her room. Luckily, Flora had just laid down her cards, so they only caught a glimpse of her when she was already halfway up the stairs.

"Where did Rose go?" Fauna asked, glancing after her. "Was she . . . crying?"

"Allergies," I said quickly. "Lots of, um, ragweed blooming today. Hey, do you know where my sweet-snack bag went?" The first morning I'd been at the cottage, I'd gifted the fairies all my snacks. I figured it was the least I could do, since I literally had no other way to repay them for all they were doing, for the meals and dresses and hospitality. As I'd predicted,

Merryweather got really into the extreme flavors of chips, and the Flamin' Hot Cheetos had all disappeared by the third day. Flora had been partial to the trail mix, and Fauna had gone crazy for anything sweet.

"Read 'em and weep," Merryweather said, setting her cards down with a flourish. She glanced at me. "Did I get that right?"

"Perfect," I assured her, then looked around the kitchen. "Is there *any* chocolate left? I thought we had some Snickers, at least."

Fauna tossed her cards down, a disgruntled expression on her face, then looked up at me. "Wait, where are our things? The pink cloth—"

"Blue," Merryweather corrected.

"The ingredients for my cake?" Flora asked, looking around.

"Oh. Right." Truly, too many things had happened already today and I hadn't even had lunch yet. "I never even made it to the market, because I was kidnapped by . . ." I glanced upstairs, and tried to mime horns on my head. The three fairies just stared at me blankly, and I was relieved I'd never tried to introduce them to charades. "Maleficent," I whispered, and they all gasped. I pulled up a chair and sat down at the table, wanting to get through this as quickly as possible so I could go up to my friend. In a voice just above a whisper, I gave them the abridged version of what had happened.

When I had finished, the fairies were all staring at me, grim looks on their faces. "So we were right about the raven," Flora said with a heavy sigh.

"But to snatch an innocent girl and bring her to that wretched place," Fauna said, shuddering.

"Wasn't it awful?" Merryweather asked, a tiny gleam in her eye. "That tacky stonework, and all those terrible torches . . ."

Flora shot her a stern look. "Merryweather."

"What? I'm just saying the décor reflects her personality. Both horrible."

"But it is what we were afraid of," Flora said, glancing upstairs. "That with the approaching deadline, she's doing everything she can to entrap Rose."

Fauna nodded. "We'll just have to stay vigilant. We're almost there."

"Yeah," I said, glancing upstairs. "I should go see how she's doing. With the . . . allergies and all." All the fairies nodded, and I fixed my gaze on Fauna. "*Is* there any chocolate left?"

Fauna sighed and pointed to the cupboard. "Upper left cabinet."

"Thanks," I said, crossing over to it. I grabbed a Snickers and a Kit Kat, leaving her the Reese's Pieces. I started to head up the stairs when Merryweather caught my hand.

"Are *you* okay, dear?" she gave me a worried look. "I know Maleficent can be a lot. Even I don't like facing her. And we have powers to defend ourselves."

I thought about it and involuntarily shivered as I remembered the look on Maleficent's face as she pointed her staff at me. How close I'd felt to something truly awful happening. But as scary as it had been, it was over. And mostly, it had left me with the conviction that I needed to do whatever I could to make sure Rose never fell into her clutches. "I'm okay," I finally said.

"You handled it very well," Fauna said, giving me a smile. I smiled back, and stood up a little bit straighter. I had survived it, after all. Which actually made me feel a little better about upcoming life events—how bad could college admissions be if I'd already faced down an evil sorceress and an alligator with a meat cleaver?

I gave the fairies a nod, and they all smiled at me. As I started to head up the stairs, it hit me just how much I'd miss them when—if things worked out—I'd be home tomorrow. As I took the stairs up to our room, I tried to wrestle with this dichotomy of simultaneously wanting to leave and to stay. Feeling the push and pull in equal measure.

The door was closed, and I knocked on it with the secret knock Rose had taught me: three quick raps, three seconds pause, two heavy knocks. "Come in," I heard from inside and pushed the door open. Rose was sitting on the floor by her bed, her face blotchier than ever.

I closed the door behind me and held up the candy. "I brought reinforcements."

"I just feel so foolish." Rose shook her head. It was an hour later; we'd finished most of the chocolate, and she'd moved from sadness to anger.

I had encouraged her to let it all out, everything that she was feeling. But while she'd been crying, I couldn't help but think about what I'd realized at the beginning of the week: that Rose was someone who'd never had her heart broken, had no experience with this. And as of today, that was no longer true. And seeing the pain and hurt in her eyes now—pain that hadn't been there before—made me even angrier at Phil. *He* had done this. "I know," I said. "But you have no reason to feel foolish. It's all Phil's fault. You didn't do anything wrong. You were putting yourself out there. It's good. It's *brave*. He's the coward here."

"And Reece, too," she said with a sigh. She started to reach for the last bit of the Snickers, then hesitated.

I pushed it closer to her. "All you." I was suddenly hit with an intense craving for pizza. This was normally the moment that carbs were called for to help manage the heartbreak. Maybe I could explain to Flora and Merryweather how to make one? It was very possible they'd have all the ingredients, after all: just bread and tomatoes and cheese . . .

"Are you okay?" Rose asked.

I snapped out of my pizza reverie. "Me? I'm fine."

"I meant . . . about Reece."

"Oh." At just the mention of his name, my anger flared up again. "Ugh. I can't believe him. Especially—"

"Since you were holding hands?" Rose gave me a tiny, knowing smile. "Sorry if I wrecked your moment."

"Of course you didn't. I just can't believe that Phil has been lying this whole time—and that Reece has been helping him."

Rose shrugged. "I guess we should have paid more attention to what Phil said that first day? He said he did try and tell us. . . ."

I rolled my eyes. "No way. It's not on us to figure out cryptic things boys say. This isn't a mystery! We're not Sherlock Holmes." She just stared at me, and I added quickly, "He's a . . . really smart person. Always figures things out. But anyway, the truth is that Phil could have just told us from the beginning, and then you wouldn't have—"

"Fallen in love with him?" she finished, her voice sad.

"Well, yeah." The weight of these words seemed to hang in the air between us for just a moment, heavy and true.

Rose pushed herself to standing but didn't go very far, just climbed onto her bed and hugged her pillow. "Does it always hurt like this?"

"In the beginning." I thought about my first unrequited crush in sixth grade; of my tenth-grade boyfriend who dumped me mid-party; of Cooper walking away from our table at the Mermaid Café. I thought about Nisha's first girlfriend, who'd shattered her heart into a million pieces, and of sitting with her while she sobbed. "But it does fade," I promised. "It just . . . takes time."

Rose raised her head slightly. "I've just . . ." She looked down at her hands, twisting them together. "I've just had a dream of someone like him my whole life. I've been alone so much, and I used to think about it all the time—about finding someone who understood me, who liked the same things I did, someone I could . . . see a future with. And then I met Phil, and it seemed so real, like my dream was finally coming true." She gave me a watery smile. "But I guess not."

I took a breath to answer, just as a rock struck the window.

"What was that?" she asked, rolling over to look.

I got up and crossed to the window. "I'll check. Maybe the owl wants to come in?"

"Tell Orville to come back tomorrow," she said with a sigh.

"You *know* he doesn't listen to me." I reached the window and opened it just as another rock flew toward me. I ducked out of the way just in time and leaned out the window to see Reece standing below. He gestured for me to come down, and I gave him a very different kind of gesture in return.

"Was that a *rock*?" Rose asked, sitting up now, looking across her room where it had landed.

"Um, yeah," I said, glancing between her and Reece. Reece's gestures were getting bigger, like he was doing charades for a partner who just wasn't getting it. "Maybe it was a . . . mini-tornado?"

"A mini *what*?"

I glanced back out; Reece was planted under the window, still gesturing, and I had a feeling he wasn't going away—and might just start throwing more rocks—unless I went down there. I crossed over to the door. "I'll go investigate. You get some rest, okay?"

Rose nodded, hugging her pillow tighter. "And maybe see if there's any more chocolate?"

"You might have to fight Fauna for it," I replied, heading out, and was rewarded by a faint ghost of a smile. And that, more than anything else, let me know she was going to be okay.

I thought I was going to find Reece outside, but as I walked down the stairs, there he was sitting at the kitchen table, surrounded by the fairies, who were all fussing over him.

"Hi." I kept my voice friendly while simultaneously staring daggers at him. No need to worry the fairies about anything else at the moment.

"We haven't seen you in ages," Fauna cooed, pinching his cheeks. "Have you been keeping well?"

"Just fine, ma'am."

"And so polite," Flora said approvingly. I rolled my eyes.

"They were telling me that you taught them . . . Texas Hold 'Em?" Reece asked, raising an eyebrow at me.

I crossed my arms over my chest. "So?"

"Want to play?" Merryweather asked. She picked up the deck and did the bridge shuffle like a pro. "Where's Rose? She wouldn't want to miss a game."

"She's . . . um . . . resting," I said quickly. "Big birthday tomorrow and all. But I *was* thinking about dinner and wondering if you'd ever made a kind of . . . bread-tomato-cheese thing. And then baked it in the oven?"

Reece stared at me. "Are you trying to get them to make you a pizza?"

"I've had a stressful day, okay? No thanks to *you*." I muttered this last part under my breath, but loud enough so that he could still hear it.

"Pizza?" Fauna echoed, looking puzzled.

274

Reece shot me a look. "It's a . . . delicacy. From, um, southern Anaheim."

"Well, I guess we could try it," Merryweather said as she crossed to her cookbooks. She pulled one off the shelf and started flipping through it. "Like a quiche?"

"Not that deep," Reece and I said at the same time.

Merryweather nodded, and continued flipping pages. Flora picked up the cards and gestured toward Reece. "Deal you in, Reece?"

"I actually have to talk to Stella," he said, giving her a smile.

"Well, I don't want to talk to you."

"Five minutes," he said, his voice low. "Be right back," he said to the fairies, heading outside.

I stood stock-still, realizing a moment too late that he'd outmaneuvered me. I couldn't just stay here, knowing he was outside, with the fairies all looking at me and wondering why I was being so rude and keeping him waiting. "Fine," I muttered to nobody in particular. I walked through the door he'd left open and slammed it shut behind me.

I found Reece around the corner of the house, pacing back and forth. I folded my arms and prepared to listen in stony silence. But a second later, my annoyance took precedence and threw my stony silence out the window. "How *could* you!"

"Stella," Reece said, shaking his head. "Just listen—"

"Nope. Shan't."

"But—"

"You kept telling me all about how we have to make things work with Phil and Rose, and that there's going to be a happily ever after—"

"If you'll just—"

"When all this time, you've been lying, and he's been engaged—"

"He's engaged to *her!*"

I was on the verge of continuing, but this brought me up short. "He . . . What?"

"He's betrothed to Princess Aurora!" Reece took a breath and lowered his voice. "They have been since they were little. You know—a royal alliance."

I shook my head, trying to get things straight. "So, wait. He fell in love with the girl he's engaged to. But doesn't realize it's actually her?" Reece nodded, looking relieved that I was getting this. "And she loves him—well, did—and doesn't realize he's actually her fiancé?"

"Exactly."

"This has some real Shakespearean vibes."

"He's not born yet."

"Even so. You get what I mean." I felt my heart rate start to slow down as I saw the first glimmers of hope for the whole situation. "Well . . . okay. But then why did Phil even say anything?"

Reece grimaced. "This is what comes of having us here a week too early. He was apparently trying to tell her that while he has a fiancée, he's going to tell his dad he wants to break it off. Because he wants to be with Rose."

"Who's actually the fiancée he's going to break things off with."

"Right."

I shook my head. "This is giving me a headache."

"But the problem was, he only got through the first part of that sentence before Rose got upset and ran away."

"I mean, understandably," I pointed out, getting annoyed on Rose's behalf all over again.

"I get it," Reece agreed. "But it still means we're in a bad situation. Things need to be good with them tomorrow if this is going to work out so we can get home again. I'm not sure what the future looks like if they're in a fight and not speaking. I know for *sure* that true love's kiss doesn't happen, which means the spell doesn't break." He let out a sigh. "I just wish he would have talked to me about it first. . . ."

"I still don't like that Phil's been cheating on his fiancée with Rose this whole week."

"Phil doesn't know her! As far as he's concerned, he just knows he's been engaged to Aurora his whole life and is expected to marry her when she comes of age. But he's realized that he doesn't want to marry Aurora, since he loves Rose. Who's actually Aurora, the fiancée he's prepared to break it off with." He ran a hand over his forehead. "Okay, now *I'm* getting a headache."

"But the upshot is, Phil was trying to tell Rose that he wanted to be with her, right?" Reece nodded. "Was he going to tell her about the prince thing?"

"I don't think yet. But I know he wants to tell his father that he's not going to marry this princess because he's fallen in love with a commoner. Well, who he *thinks* is a commoner. Anyway, he's been wrestling with it all week. He's been struggling to weigh his duty with actually getting to know someone without any of the royal stuff getting in the way. . . ."

"Okay. So we need to get them in the same place, right? So Phil can explain." A moment later, I frowned. "Wait—*can* he explain? Will that wreck things if she knows too much?"

Reece shook his head. "I feel like he's going to hold off on the prince reveal for the moment, so hopefully it will be okay? We just need to clear things up, or there's no chance of this succeeding."

I glanced back toward the house, thinking of Rose curled up in bed with a broken heart. "I'm not sure she's going to want to hear anything he has to say right now."

"We have to try, though, right?" Reece's brow was furrowed, and he spread his hands. "Otherwise . . ."

"Yeah." I sat down on the grass, and after a moment he sat next to me. I was half hoping that a bunny would hop over and settle into my lap, but I was not Rose. So the most I got was a passing squirrel, who gave me a mistrustful look before continuing on. "Um . . ." I said, after a moment's silence, in which I'd realized I was in the wrong. "I'm sorry about before."

"It's okay," Reece said, giving me a half smile. "You didn't know. You were just being a good friend."

"Yeah, but you're my friend, too." As I said it, I felt the truth of those words. My feelings for Reece might have recently gotten scrambled—from liking him as more than a friend to being furious at him—but over the course of this week, we *had* become friends. And I'd repaid that friendship by turning my back on him and not giving him the benefit of the doubt. "I shouldn't have believed you'd do something like that."

Reece nodded, and he gave me a small smile. "Well, thanks. But it's understandable. I mean, especially after what's-his-face."

"Cooper."

"If you say so." I laughed at that. "So of course you're not going to be feeling so trusting. I get it."

"It's more than that, I think." I leaned back on my hands, trying to think how to put this into words. "Rose had never had her heart broken . . . and I think I was feeling extra protective because of that."

"We all get our hearts broken eventually," he said, and I could hear the resigned sadness in his voice. "One way or another."

"Oh?" I attempted to keep my tone light, like I was just casually asking. "When did— I mean, did you?"

He hesitated, then nodded. "Before we moved here. Well, there. Harbor Cove, I mean. But that's a story for another time."

There was a note of finality in his voice, and I nodded, even though all I really wanted was to ask a bunch of follow-ups. I met his eye and gave him a small smile. And after a second, he gave me one back.

The moment we'd been on the verge of before—when we'd been holding hands, and I was so sure that kissing was *just* around the corner—was gone now. Maybe not forever, but it really no longer felt like that vibe was still happening. For one thing, we had stuff to figure out. "Okay," I said, feeling myself shift into logistics mode. "First things first—we need a plan."

"Exactly. We have to figure out how to get them back together again."

"And you really think we can?"

"Whatever it takes. We'll fix the heartbreak." Reece made a face, like he'd just bitten into a lemon. "Where's that from?"

"That's a Band of Brothers lyric!" I laughed. "I *knew* you were a fan. And this is proof."

"I told you, my sister likes them. I've just absorbed it through osmosis."

"Don't deny you love them."

"Um, I believe I will."

"There is power in their poetry," I insisted with a laugh—but then a moment later, thought about what I'd just said. "Actually . . . that's not bad."

"What's not bad? Also, can you even say that about yourself? Isn't it an incoming phrase?"

I waved this away. "Of course I can say it. Especially when it's a good idea. And this one is. Listen." I leaned a little closer, and Reece leaned in, too. "Here's what I'm thinking."

Twenty-Two

"What are we doing, again?" Rose whispered to me as I dropped from the tree and hit the ground, a little more easily than I'd done the first time. We'd climbed out her window, once we were sure the three fairies were all asleep. Which had actually happened a little earlier than normal; Merryweather's pizza had been a huge success, and we'd all fallen into carb comas.

"It's a surprise," I whispered, gesturing for her to follow me. We crossed the lawn quietly, and when we were over the footbridge, I felt like we were far enough away that I could talk at a normal volume again. "To cheer you up."

"But I'm not sure I do want to be cheered up," Rose said as we fell into step together, heading toward the meadow. "I kind of just want to be sad and see if we can find any more chocolate."

"I know," I said sympathetically. And for just a second, I was seized with a flash of guilt. If it didn't work, would Rose think I'd betrayed her? That I was no better than Reece, keeping things from her and plotting behind her back? I swallowed hard, but then tried to keep focusing on the bigger picture. It wasn't like I'd taken Phil's side for no reason. There was an actual misunderstanding we needed to clear up here. And it *would* work, no matter what Reece thought.

"This isn't going to work," he'd said after I'd told him my idea.

"Of course it is," I'd replied with more confidence than I'd actually felt.

"I feel like we're putting a lot of stock in some very badly written songs."

"How dare you. It *will* work."

"How can you be so sure?"

I'd taken a breath to reply, realizing I didn't even need to think about my answer—it was right there. "Because they both want to move past it. They want a reason for it to be okay. They love each other."

"You really think so?" I'd nodded, and Reece had given me a long look, like he was trying to figure something out. "I thought you said . . . that it wasn't possible. To fall in love that fast."

"I think," I said, no longer entirely sure I was still talking only about Phil and Rose, "that sometimes it's not. But . . . with the right person, you can know. You can know in a moment, or an hour. Or, you know. A week."

Reece held my gaze for a moment, then nodded and folded up the paper I'd given him, with the lyrics carefully written out. "This better work."

"It will!"

And now, as we were nearly to the clearing, I was trying to convince myself of that as well. Now that the moment was here, the first slivers of doubt were creeping in.

"Maybe we should just turn back," Rose said, stopping short.

"But we're almost there! For my, um, surprise!"

"And I appreciate it," she said, giving me a tired smile. "I really do. I just . . ."

"Hello." Phil stepped forward, carrying a candle.

"Agh!" I yelped at the sight of him.

Maybe it was meant to be atmospheric or romantic, but it actually just looked really spooky, like evil-zombie-ghost Phil had just shown up. Even I was startled by the sight, and I'd known to expect him.

"What!" Rose yelled, jumping backward.

"Gah!" Phil yelled, upsetting his candle and spattering himself with wax. "Ow! That's hot."

"Phil?" Rose looked from him to me, understanding—and betrayal—dawning in her eyes. "What is this?"

"I just think you should talk to him," I said quickly, moving to block Rose's way. God knows I'd never be able to catch up to her if she made a run back to the cottage, not with her mile-long legs and my fifty-yard ones.

"Please," Phil said. "It won't take long." He was looking at Rose beseechingly, but he was still holding the candle under his chin like we were around a campfire and he was about to tell us the story of the hook-handed man. It really wasn't helping his case.

"Let me get that," I said, taking the candle in its holder from him. I glanced around and saw Reece standing a few steps away, leaning against a tree with a skeptical expression on his face. He raised an eyebrow at me. *It'll work!* I mouthed to him.

"So," Phil said, looking a little bit unsure what to do with his hands now that he no longer had his candle. He glanced back at Reece, who nodded. He faced Rose, cleared his throat, and began. *"Oh baby, baby,"* he said haltingly. *"You drive my car like you drive my heart . . . wild,"* he recited, speaking the words to one of Band of Brothers' greatest hits, "HeartPower."

"What's a car?" Rose asked. "And why are you calling me an infant?"

"Um . . ." Phil faltered. "I . . . well." I gave him an encouraging look, and he nodded and kept going. *"Whatever it takes, we'll fix this heartbreak, child."*

"What?" Rose asked, sounding baffled—and angrier than ever. "What *is* this?"

Phil deflated. "It was Reece's idea."

"It was Stella's idea," Reece said immediately, and I glowered at him.

"They thought that I should recite some of the finest poetry from Anaheim. To try and win you back?"

"*This* is their finest poetry?"

"It sounds better when it's put to music," I said. "I promise."

"Just—forget about them." Phil took a small step closer to her. "Forget about the poetry. I just had to talk to you. From the heart."

Rose shook her head. "I don't want to hear anything you have to say," she said, but I noticed she wasn't actually leaving.

"Please, Rose," Phil said, his voice breaking. "I just need to explain. Yes, I'm engaged, but it's been that way since I was young. I don't know this woman. We have no relationship. And I don't want to marry her." He stopped and took a breath. "That's what I was trying to tell you."

"Oh," Rose said. And like I was watching a time-lapse picture, I could see happiness and hope slowly starting to bloom on her face. *"Oh."*

"My parents want me to marry her. It would preserve an important, um, wood-carving alliance—but I can't do it. Not when I feel the way I do about you."

Rose's eyes were glistening with tears, but they were the happy kind. Even with only one candle for light, I could see that much. "I see."

"In addition," Phil went on, starting to smile as he looked at Rose, "I hear she's quite mean. And not attractive. And she hates animals, apparently. So . . ."

Rose laughed, and took a step closer to Phil. "So it doesn't sound like she'd be a good match for you."

"Absolutely not," Phil said firmly. "Yuck." Rose smiled at that, and Phil took a step closer still. "But I am sorry," he said softly, carefully reaching out and tucking a lock of her hair behind her ear. "That I ever made you feel that I didn't care . . . That's the last thing I wanted."

I was watching, riveted, when I felt a gentle hand on my back. I turned and there was Reece. "Maybe we give them a moment?"

"Oh," I said, nodding. "Right." The way Phil and Rose were looking at each other, it seemed like they'd completely forgotten there was anyone else in the meadow, but it was a good point. "Wow, look, the moon," I said loudly. "Let's go look at it over there, far away." Rose caught my eye and she gave me a smile as Reece and I walked out of the meadow, leaving them alone. "It worked!" I said triumphantly, once we were (hopefully) out of earshot, holding my hand up for a high five.

Reece gave me five, even as he was shaking his head. "It did *not* work."

"They're talking, aren't they? They've gotten past their mis-communication."

"But the *lyrics* didn't work." He sounded like he was trying very hard not to laugh. "Things worked out despite the lyrics. I think they actually set the situation back."

I shrugged. "Maybe." I honestly couldn't seem to get too upset about it, considering the result that had occurred. "I guess I never realized how much the music helps. And the fog machine. And the tight pants. And the choreography . . ."

"See, if I'd had time to teach it to Phil, I would have."

I laughed at that. "So we did it?"

"It seems like it's back on track, at any rate. No thanks to Band of Brothers."

"Excuse me, *all* thanks to Band of Brothers." Reece just shook his head, and I let out a breath, feeling a little bit lighter. "Things are okay now, right? Everything's going to work out?" The second I said it, there was a clap of thunder, loud enough to make me jump. "That's not a sign," I said immediately.

"Listen," Reece said, his brows drawing together. "About tomorrow . . ."

"Oh, right," I said, shaking my head, trying not to wince as thunder sounded again, closer this time. "Tomorrow's when the movie syncs up, so you know what's going to happen. So weird."

"I know." He hesitated, taking a breath before speaking again. "Maybe let's just . . . stay out of the way. Rose is going to pick berries in the morning. She'll meet Phil here. Then she'll be back at the cottage, and then she and the fairies will go to the castle."

"Ooh, fun!" I said, brightening. "That's when they're going to tell her she's a princess?" Reece nodded, not meeting my eye. "Should I go with them?"

"No. When they leave, just come meet me here, okay? And we'll figure out next steps."

"Okay." I paused, studying him. There was something about his expression that I couldn't quite read. "Is there . . . something you're not telling me?"

Thunder sounded again, the loudest yet. It was followed swiftly by a flash of lightning illuminating everything so brightly for a second, it was like someone had just turned on the lights. And then, a second later, the heavens opened up, and it started to pour.

"Just meet me here tomorrow after they go. Okay?"

I nodded, brushing water off my face, trying to concentrate despite the fact that his white shirt was getting steadily soaked and more translucent. "It'll be okay, right?"

"In the end," he said, "it will."

I was about to ask him what he meant by this when Phil and Rose ran up to us, Phil trying to shield Rose from the rain and not succeeding at all. "We should get home before we're soaked," Rose said to me. She turned to Phil. "I'll see you tomorrow?"

He nodded. Gone was the glum guy with bad candle placement; he seemed utterly transformed, practically glowing with happiness despite the rain.

"So—" I said to Reece, just as thunder boomed again and it started to rain even harder. "Yeah, okay, let's go."

We waved at the guys, then ran for it, gripping onto each other and giggling as we slid in the rain-soaked grass. It wasn't until we were halfway to the house that I stopped short, struck by a terrible thought. "Wait. Now we have to climb back up in the *rain*?"

Rose's eyes widened, as I could practically see this realization hit her. I started laughing as I looked at her expression, and then she started laughing because I was laughing, and we stumbled back the rest of the way home like that.

"So?" I whispered. We'd made it back into the house—much louder than normal, because as we both soon found out, it's really hard, not to mention messy, to climb trees in the rain. But luckily, it seemed like the persistent thunderclaps had masked both the twigs snapping and my stream of profanity as I bumped my arm tumbling back through ungracefully. And now we were in our nightgowns, hair still wet, Rose on her bed and me on mine. The time hadn't seemed right as we were running through the rain or getting ready for bed, but now, I was ready for my debrief. I wanted to hear everything. "What happened?"

Rose rolled over so she was lying on her stomach, and beamed at me. She was in the same spot she'd been this afternoon, but that felt ages ago now. Her sadness was gone, replaced by a steady, hopeful happiness that I felt like I could have seen even without the benefit of the candle that was guttering between us.

"We figured things out," she said with a smile. "No thanks to your poetry."

"It's supposed to be *sung*," I explained. "You're not getting the full—" I stopped short, and leaned forward, my eyes going wide. "Wait. Did you guys kiss?"

"No," she said with a groan. "We were *just* about to, and then the rain started."

"But kissing in the rain is romantic," I protested. I had never been able to test this out myself, since it only rained in Southern California in December and sometimes in January, and I'd never been dating or crushing on anyone during those months. "At least, that's what Taylor Swift says."

"Who's he?"

"She's kind of like our queen," I said, after thinking about it for a moment. "Or a benevolent deity. Unofficially. But gah! Phil!"

Rose laughed. "I know. As we were walking back, he apologized once more. He said he did what he always does—hesitates and misses his moment." I nodded, remembering him dangling from the rope swing by one arm. She raised an eyebrow at me. "So then *I* said—"

"What?" I hugged my pillow and leaned closer.

"Next time there's an opportunity . . . don't hesitate."

"Omg!" I shrieked, and she did, too, and then we were both laughing. "I can't believe you said that. That's so awesome." I leaned back against my headboard. The whole night had taken on a punch-drunk, midnight-at-a-sleepover feeling. I was a heartbeat away from suggesting that we prank-bird Phil and Reece.

"So, tomorrow," Rose said, her smile starting to fade. "You leave?"

I nodded. "Yes. I wish I didn't have to, but—"

"Your life is back home," she finished.

"Well—yeah." And that was the truth of the matter. There was just no way around it.

Rose got under her covers and I got under mine. I looked around the room, trying to memorize it all—every inch of it. The furniture, the rain pattering the windows, the flickering shadows from the candle. I knew I could technically see it again once I went home, but it wouldn't be the same. I wouldn't be there, with my friend.

"It's been . . . really fun, Stella," Rose said as she turned to face me. "I'm so glad you came to stay."

"Me too," I said, feeling the words hit me deep. This time tomorrow, I'd just be . . . back in Orange County? With no friend to talk with all day, nobody to make fun of how much chickens hated me? "It's been the best."

"We'll see each other again," she said, rolling onto her back. "We're not so far away."

"Right," I said, swallowing hard. "Of course we will."

"Would you get the light?" she asked around a yawn.

I looked around for one moment more, trying to commit it all to memory. Not just how it looked, but how it *felt*. So that when I was back in my own world, centuries and miles away from this one, I could call it up and remember what this had been like.

I breathed it all in until I was sure I had it.

And then I leaned over and blew out the candle.

Twenty-Three

I sat on my bed surrounded by all the things I'd brought with me, trying to shake off the last-day-of-school feeling that was weighing me down.

I'd awoken to find Rose up before me, as usual. But after I'd gotten ready, I'd hesitated and hadn't immediately run downstairs after her. I was very aware that starting today, a different plot was kicking into gear, and it was one that I really had no place in—*especially* if we wanted to get this right. For the first time, I was feeling like a background player in a story I probably shouldn't have had a part in to begin with.

And even though I wanted to go downstairs and see everyone, I found myself dragging my feet, taking much more time than was necessary to gather up my things. It was irrational, but I somehow knew that once I went downstairs, the ending would begin, and I would start walking down a path that only went one direction.

After I'd gotten everything together, I looked around and realized I'd have to borrow a basket or something to carry it. My bag was still presumably hanging in Maleficent's throne room, and I was just hoping it hadn't been co-opted by some terrible bat creature. I wouldn't need anything big; it wasn't like I had that many things to pack up. There was my toiletry bag, my Forget Me Not sweatshirt, my useless phone charger . . . and my prom dress. I hesitated for just a moment before adding it to the pile. The last time I'd worn it—at Disneyland, a week earlier—felt like a lifetime ago. I tried to picture myself wearing it tonight, back in the Harbor Cove High gym, back in my real life . . . but found that I couldn't. There were too many steps and too many unknowns in between here and there, now and then.

I opened the door and poked my head out. "But I picked berries yesterday!" I heard Rose say, and then the sound of the front door closing as the three fairies hustled her out. I walked out and settled down on the top step where I had a view of what I was pretty sure happened in the movie as well: the three fairies bustling around, preparing for Rose's birthday. Fauna had decided she wanted to make a cake, and I immediately shook my head, silently agreeing with Merryweather and Flora, knowing that this was *not* a good idea. And then Flora deciding she wanted to make Rose a dress—I had to cover my mouth to keep from laughing. I knew them well enough by now to be totally sure that this was going to be a disaster.

And from my perch at the top of the steps, I could see that was exactly what was happening. The whole kitchen was soon filled with pink and blue lights as Merryweather and Flora fought over the color of Rose's dress. And it wasn't until there seemed to be a break in the hostilities that I decided it was safe to venture downstairs.

"Morning," I said, dodging around a mop that was mopping by itself. Only a week ago, this would have stopped me in my tracks—and made me question the nature of reality—but now, I just moved out of its way as I continued into the kitchen. Flora and Merryweather were aiming pink and blue beams of light at each other from their wands, both trying to take charge of the (very beautiful) dress in the middle of the kitchen. I looked at it, then down for a second at my gray dress, trying not to compare them. It had been a free dress, after all, and a lovely gesture, and it kept me from having to wear my prom dress for a week. But really, this other dress was a *lot* better. It was just undeniable.

"Good morning, Stella," Flora said, glaring at Merryweather as she pointed her wand at the dress. "Did you sleep okay?"

"Morning," Merryweather said, looking over at me with a nod. In that second, Flora changed the dress back to pink, and Merryweather, seeing this, gasped in frustration. "Why . . . you . . ."

I decided being in the middle of this was not the best idea and joined Fauna at the kitchen table where she was putting candles on a delicious-looking cake.

"Looks great," I said, smiling at her.

"Oh, why, thank you, dear," she said, patting my hand. "Did you get breakfast?"

"Porridge on the stove!" Merryweather yelled, diving and rolling like a champion laser-tag player as she shot her blue blast of light toward Flora and then ducked for cover behind a chair. "Don't let Fauna cook for you. You should have *seen* the first cake she made."

"She's not wrong," Fauna admitted as she fussed with the candles.

I went over to the stove and was getting myself breakfast, when I felt a spark—like the kind you get from static electricity discharging. "Ow!" I looked down at myself and saw that my dress, which had been gray just moments ago, was now bright pink.

"Oops! Sorry, Stella. That wasn't meant for you," Flora said. She aimed her wand at me and closed one eye. "I can fix it."

"No," I said, giving a little bit of a spin as I took it in. "I like it this way."

"See?" Flora said, gesturing to me, then at Merryweather. "She likes it."

"There's no accounting for taste," Merryweather huffed, as she raised her wand, and the light battle continued.

"I hope you'll have some cake and celebrate with us," Fauna said as she stopped fussing with the candles and stepped back to admire her handiwork. She looked at me, and her brow furrowed. "How is everything going? Are we . . . on track?"

"I think it'll be okay," I said, silently crossing my fingers behind the back of my now-pink dress. I wasn't entirely sure we'd done enough to keep everything on track. And I was all too aware that we could easily, and without even meaning to, knock the story off its axis.

But Reece seemed to think we could get this to work, and I was putting all my faith in that. In *him*, I realized a second later. In Reece. I might not know the story, but I knew him. And that was enough for me.

"Reece knows what's supposed to happen," I told Fauna. "And he's going to do everything he can to make sure we get home." I finished my oatmeal and went to wash the bowl out at the sink. I'd just arrived there when Merryweather pointed her wand at me, and suddenly my bowl was sparkling clean.

"Wow," I said, blinking as the bowl and spoon lifted up from my hands and slotted themselves in the cupboard. "So—we could have been doing that this whole time?"

Merryweather shrugged. "It's the last day. So, in for a penny . . ." She aimed her wand at me, and then I felt a series of the same little shocks from when my dress changed color. I looked down and saw my dress was now blue and my sneakers were sparkling clean. My head was tingling, too, and I rushed over to the mirror by the door. My hair was pulled back with a blue bow that matched my dress, and it looked better than it ever had before in my life, like I'd just gotten a professional blowout.

"Wow," I said, staring at my reflection. My hair wasn't quite at Rose level of bounciness, but I supposed there was only so much that magic could do. "Thanks so much."

"Of course," Merryweather said. She pointed her wand at Rose's dress at the exact same moment that Flora pointed hers, and a second later, it was a splotchy mess, both blue and pink, and covered with spatters.

"Now look what you did!" Flora and Merryweather said at the exact same time.

Fauna paused in lighting the candles. "I think I hear Rose coming."

"I'll give you some space," I said as I hurried toward the stairs. Fauna gave me a smile as they all ducked behind the table, clearly eager for their surprise (the dress was now solidly pink again, but I had a feeling that wasn't going to last long). I grabbed a basket on my way upstairs, and back in our room, started packing all my things up.

Occasionally, I could hear raised voices from downstairs, but I just assumed it was Rose exclaiming over the dress or cake. I heard footsteps running up the stairs, and I turned around to see Rose coming into the room. "Hi!" I said, smiling at her. "Happy birthday!"

A second later, though, I realized she didn't look like someone who'd just gotten a new pink (or blue) dress and a cake. She was leaning back against the closed door, her face pale.

"Are you okay?" I asked, hurrying over to her. "Was it the cake? We probably should have been careful. Fauna made it, after all."

"I . . ." Rose shook her head, closing her eyes for just a second, then taking a shaky breath. "I'm . . . a princess."

I blinked, suddenly aware I had no idea how to play this, despite the fact that Reece had given me the heads-up last night that this would be happening. "Um. Wow. I mean, what?"

"My aunts just told me." She walked over to her bed and sat down, still looking like she was in shock. "Apparently, my real name is Aurora. And I have to leave and go live in the castle. And it seems I have parents after all—and they're the king and queen?" She rubbed her head, like it hurt, and let out a short laugh. "I'm just waiting to wake up from what I'm sure is just a dream."

"Wow," I said, feeling overwhelmed on her behalf. "Okay. So . . . that's a lot." I suddenly thought of something, then dropped into an awkward curtsy. "Um, milady?"

"No, please don't do that," Rose said. Although maybe she was technically Aurora now? This was making *my* head hurt.

"Sorry," I said, straightening up. I sat next to her on the bed, trying to think of what to say. I'd found out, when I was twelve, that my dad was a Dodgers fan, but I somehow didn't think that came close to what Rose was dealing with at the moment. I'd known, of course, that Rose was secretly a princess and would find it out on her birthday. It was something I'd been aware of, intellectually. But until right now, looking at her stunned face, I hadn't actually understood how seismic getting this information would feel. "That is all . . . so much."

"And that's not even the worst part," she said, her voice hollow.

"There's a *worse* part?"

She nodded and looked down at her hands, letting out a shaky breath. "It's Phil," she said, her voice cracking. "I finally told my aunts that I met someone I really like. When I saw him in the woods this morning, we even arranged for him to come by later and meet them. I thought it was going to be . . . just the best birthday present ever." Her breath hitched, and she shook her head. "But apparently that can't happen. Apparently I'm already betrothed to someone—a prince I've never met—and I have to marry *him*." She let out a short laugh. "It's . . . What did you call it? Ironic? Since this was just what happened to Phil. With his engagement, and the wood-carvers' council . . ."

"But—" It was on the tip of my tongue to just blurt it out. That this random prince she thought she didn't want to marry was actually Phil! But at the last moment, I stopped myself. After all, Reece seemed to think we needed to let things play out. And since he understood this story better than I did, I held back. "But . . . like you said, Phil was engaged, too. And he was going to get out of it, so maybe you can, too. I mean, you're a modern woman. It's the . . ." I hesitated.

"Fourteenth century," she supplied, raising an eyebrow at me.

"Fourteenth century," I said quickly, trying to cover. "Just what I was going to say."

"I don't know," Rose said, running a hand over her face. "My aunts say I'm not supposed to see him ever again, and that we're going to . . . the castle"—she let out a slightly hysterical laugh—"tonight so that my new life can start. And I'm just not sure how he would fit into that, or if he'd even be allowed to be a part of it. . . ." Her voice trailed off, and my heart clenched when I saw how utterly lost she looked.

I bit my tongue, even as I was silently raging at the Reece inside my head. This could all be solved with *one* conversation! Why were we taking the most circuitous route to the end point? I took a breath and tried to keep my voice measured. "I wouldn't count Phil out yet."

"It's really some birthday, huh?"

I laughed in spite of myself. "Maybe you shouldn't have asked for a surprise party."

Rose laughed, too, but it only lasted for a moment. "And you're leaving, as well." Her eyes got wide as this realization seemed to hit her. "I wish you could stay and join me at the castle."

"Same," I said, meaning it. But if we were reliant on the spell breaking to give us the magic we'd need to get back home again, I didn't know how that was possible.

Tears spilled over Rose's cheeks, and she brushed them away, but they just kept coming. I crossed to the wardrobe, found a handkerchief, and handed it to her. I so wanted to be able to tell her everything would turn out all right in the end, but I was also aware that simply by telling her this, I might cause that not to be the case. I had never really understood Schrödinger's cat when we'd studied it in Physics this year, but now I felt like I finally did, because I was in that situation myself. Schrödinger's fairy tale.

"Are you excited about the princess thing at all?" I asked, trying to find a silver lining in all of this.

Rose shook her head. "I ... don't even know what I'm feeling right now. It's like the earth just got pulled out from under me, and everything I thought I knew was a lie." She let out a shaky breath. "Also, I'm not going to be *good* at it. I'm not fancy, or cultured, or well educated. . . ."

"Stop that," I said firmly. "You're going to be great. You're kind and smart and brave. And whether it's people or animals, you *care*. That's the most important thing in a leader, right? Or it should be."

She nodded slowly. "That makes sense."

"And you might be able to do some good, right? Really help people. It's probably an advantage that you didn't grow up in a castle—you'll have a better perspective. You can really make changes. See the things that could be better run and made more efficient."

She gave me a look, tilting her head slightly to the side. "You're thinking about the trade routes, aren't you?"

"Maybe a little," I confessed. "Listen—as soon as you get to the castle, you need to get a topographical map and look at the waterways. . . ."

"Right," Rose said, shaking her head. "That will be the first thing I do."

"It should be!"

"I'll just go into a *castle*, meet my parents for the first time, and then say . . . what?" She was laughing now. "Before we get to know each other, I'd really love to see a *topographical map*?"

"I mean," I said, even though I was laughing now, too, "maybe it could be the *second* thing you do—"

"Girls?" I looked over to see the fairies standing in the doorway. "We need to get going soon," Fauna said, her voice gentle.

"Right." My smiled faded as I realized I was not included in that *we*. Rose and the fairies would be going to the castle, and Reece and I would stay behind to try and figure this out. I looked at them and realized that they were dressed a lot more nicely than I had yet seen them. Their aprons were gone, and they were wearing hats instead of kerchiefs. And, in the biggest change of all, semitranslucent gossamer wings were now sprouting out of the backs of their dresses.

"Aunt Fauna," Rose said, her eyes wide. "What . . . is that on your back?"

The fairies all looked at each other, and then Flora stepped forward, clearing her throat. "Okay. So about that . . ."

I sat on the front step of the cottage, my possessions in a basket next to me, my heart heavy. The cottage was dark, the curtains pulled shut. The fairies and Rose—Aurora?—had gone, walking to the castle. Any moment now, I'd go to meet Reece in the meadow. But before that, I needed to take a breath, just to try to sort out my own swirling thoughts.

The fairies had been eager to leave once they'd told Rose/Aurora—Rorora? No, that was terrible—the truth about who she was and what her future was going to look like, bustling Rose out the door so they could begin their journey. She was wearing her new dress, but it didn't seem like it was making her particularly happy. Any laughter we had shared was totally gone as we stood together in the doorway while the fairies flitted around, making sure everything was closed up.

"I sent Phil a note," Rose told me as she scanned the sky, like she was hoping a response might come flying down to her. "But in case he doesn't get it and shows up here, you'll let him know? That I can't meet him?"

"Of course I will. Did you tell him . . . everything?" That seemed like a *lot* to get down on paper and expect a bird to carry without injuring its neck. Unless she used, like, a giant hawk or something. I glanced up at the sky, suddenly a little worried.

Rose shook her head. "I just said that . . . I couldn't keep our meeting. But that maybe, in the future, when things are a little clearer . . ." She shrugged helplessly. "I didn't know what else to say. I don't even know if that'll be possible."

"It'll all work out," I said, trying to inject this with all the confidence I could. I'd *seen* the pictures of the happily ever after in the castle, after all. It was going to happen—as long as Reece and I didn't wreck things.

"You can't know that," she said sadly. "Nobody knows the future." I had to bite my lip to keep from replying, and just nodded.

"Stella, dear," Fauna said, giving my hands a squeeze. "We'll see you . . . at some point soon?"

"Absolutely," I said, nodding. The fairies were the ones who were going to get us back home again once the spell had broken, so I certainly was planning on seeing them, and hopefully sooner rather than later. I just wasn't sure where or exactly when, which I really didn't love.

"I'll see you again," Rose (Aurora) said to me, looking like she was holding to this like a lifeline. "Right?"

I hesitated for a moment, because I wasn't sure I *was* ever going to see her again, which was making my heart hurt. As far as Rose knew, I lived in the (now hopefully plague-free) kingdom of Anaheim, not in a completely different reality. But I wasn't sure that telling her that would do any good. "I hope so," I finally said, meaning it.

"Me too," Rose said, her eyes still sad and haunted. She took a shaky breath. "You'll tell Phil? That I couldn't be here and . . . I'm sorry?" Her bottom lip started to quiver again, and I gave her a quick, tight hug.

"Of course," I said as she hugged me back.

We stepped apart and she nodded, clearly trying to pull herself together even though her lip was still trembling. "Here you go, dear," Flora said. She placed a blue traveling cloak over Rose's shoulders and pulled the hood up over her head.

"Good luck, Stella," Flora said, giving me a smile.

"Tell me what happens!" Merryweather whispered to me, but I shook my head.

"I don't know," I said, honestly. "You'd have to ask Reece."

"Okay. Where is he?"

"Merryweather," Flora said sharply. "Enough of that. We have to get going. We want to be there well before sunset."

"Fine," Merryweather sighed. She reached up to adjust the bow in my hair and gave me a smile. "Guac your world."

"Um, you too. Get there safe," I called after them as they headed away from the cottage. Rose stopped and turned back to me, and I raised a hand in a wave.

"Come along dear," Fauna said, and then they passed over the footbridge and out of sight . . . and I was alone.

Now, I hugged my knees to my chest, looking around at the view that had become so familiar to me. I could hear the bells faintly start to chime the hour. It seemed impossible that soon, I'd be back in a world where I'd always know what time it was, down to the millisecond. Where I could reach anyone instantly and without the help of birds. Back to a world where people were much more connected—but one where, paradoxically, everyone felt farther apart.

I sat there for a moment longer until the sound of the bells faded away. Then I pushed myself to my feet, picked up my basket, and glanced back at the house behind me. It was dark and quiet now, this place that had been my home for the last week. Where Rose and I had become friends, where I'd been interrogated in the cellar (twice). The place we'd snuck out of and back into, the place we'd stayed up talking and laughing into the night. Where we'd all played cards and eaten meals and been together. And now, all of that was gone.

I gave the cottage one last look, then turned and walked forward.

Twenty-Four

By the time I reached the meadow, Reece and Phil were riding up on Samson and Delilah. Reece's backpack was tied onto his saddle, and Phil was resplendent in the clothes he'd worn the first day I'd met him, complete with his jaunty red hat.

"Stella!" Phil beamed at me. He looked like he was thrilled with life—happiness was practically coming off him in waves. "You look lovely this afternoon."

"Yeah," Reece said, blinking at me. He gave me a quick look, then glanced away. "New dress?"

"Uh—kind of." My stomach sank as I realized that Phil's happy expression meant that he must not have gotten Rose's letter. Which, in turn, meant it would be up to me to tell him she wasn't at home. "I got caught in some dress-dyeing cross fire."

"And you wound up with blue, not pink?" Reece asked, giving me a smile.

"Exactly." It was still off-putting that he knew what had happened. But of course he did—it was like he had CliffsNotes on my day. I turned to Phil and took a breath, trying to make my voice sound casual. "So, I take it you didn't get a letter?"

"From Rose?" he asked as he dismounted easily. "No, I just saw her this morning."

"Okay." I took a deep breath, wishing that I had some chocolate or something to give him to soften this blow. "So—"

"Good luck," Reece interrupted, clapping Phil on the back, giving him a big smile. "You'll do great."

"You think?" Phil sounded nervous as he adjusted his red hat, moving it forward and backward, so that it ended up in exactly the same place where it started.

"They'll love you," Reece said confidently. "And we'll be here, and you can both tell us about how it went."

I frowned at Reece; did he not remember what he'd told me just the night before? "No," I said slowly. "That's not going to happen. Because—" Reece let out a short, fake cough, his expression clearly telling me to stop talking. I gave him a *What the heck?* look.

"Because?" Phil prompted, looking between us. His smile was guileless and open, totally trusting—basically, the most Phil expression I could imagine. "Is something wrong?"

I glanced at Reece, who gave me a tiny head shake, probably

imperceptible to anyone else. "Oh . . . never mind," I finally said, no longer sure what was happening. "Um, good luck?"

"Thanks," Phil said. He gave me a quick hug, and surprised, but pleased, I hugged him back. "I can't thank you enough for everything you've done, Stella."

"Me?"

He nodded, setting his feather bobbing. "I feel like you were just so crucial in getting Rose and me back together, helping with communication issues. . . . You're a good friend." I tried to give him a smile back, even though it felt like something was squeezing my heart.

Phil started to tie up Samson, then paused. "I can go right up to the house," he said, a note of wonder in his voice. "We don't need to hide anymore."

"That's right, bud," Reece said.

Phil grinned, got back on Samson's back, and gave us a wave. "See you later!" he called before galloping off toward the cottage, humming a tune as he rode.

The second Phil had disappeared from view, I turned to Reece. "Okay, what the heck is going on? I mean, hi," I said, flashing back to the last time I'd seen him, when he'd been standing in the rain with his wet white shirt and a furrowed brow like something out of a Jane Austen–movie dream. I tried to focus. "But why did you tell Phil to go to the cottage? Rose—Aurora—whoever she is, she's gone. She and the fairies left for the castle, like you told me they would. She sent Phil a note—"

"I know." Reece pulled a piece of paper out of his pocket. "I took it before Phil could see it."

"You intercepted his letter?" I asked, stunned by this. "Why would you do that? What's going on?" Reece wasn't meeting my eye, and instead seemed to be taking a long time making sure Delilah was tied up. "You know, Rose was heartbroken this morning when the fairies told her the truth. About who she was. She thinks she can't be with Phil. And I couldn't tell her otherwise. . . ."

"This is the way it has to be, Stella," Reece said, as he finally stepped away from the horse, who immediately lowered her head to nibble on some grass. "If we want to get home, this is the way it has to happen."

All at once, for the first time in my life, I wished that I remembered the plot of a story. I'd thought that it would never matter, that this was information that would never be helpful, but I was totally wrong about that. Because I could see now that it was putting me at a real disadvantage: that Reece knew things about what was going to happen, and I didn't. I was dependent on him to tell me what happened next—or *not* tell me, which was what I suddenly realized was going on now.

"Why did you send Phil to the cottage if you know nobody's there?" I asked slowly, starting to put things together. "What's going to happen to him?" I was getting a really bad feeling about things. Reece didn't answer me, just stared down at the ground, his hands in his pockets. "Reece!"

He finally looked up at me, and I could see the pain in his eyes. When he spoke, his voice was flat. "Maleficent and her goons are in the cottage waiting for him. It was why I had to get you out of there. It's a trap."

I took a step backward and ran into a tree stump. I put my hand on it to steady myself. The thought of gentle Phil, who I'd honestly never even seen angry, not even when we were changing the rules of sportsball on him constantly, walking into a nest of those horrible beasts with their clubs and cleavers—and knowing *we* were the ones who'd sent him there—was almost more than I could take. I took a breath and tried to keep my voice from shaking. "Do they hurt him?"

Reece winced and looked away, but it was all the answer I needed.

"We have to help him!" I started to move toward the cottage, but Reece caught my arm.

"We *can't*. Listen. We have to let the story unfold now, okay? And I didn't tell you what happens because I know you. And I knew you would try and fix it. Nothing good happens for a while, okay?" His voice was rising now. "Maleficent tricks Rose—Aurora—into touching a spinning wheel, and she falls into her dreamless sleep. Phil gets taken to Maleficent's compound and thrown in the dungeon. The fairies break him out, and he battles Maleficent, eventually slaying the dragon."

"An *actual* dragon?"

"I told you this!"

"I thought you were using a metaphor! I thought it was like your stupid book."

"But it all works out." Reece looked down, and it was like we both realized at the same time that he was still holding my arm, that we were still touching. He didn't let go, but looked up at me, his eyes searching mine. "If we just keep to ourselves, and stay out of the way, it works."

Even though it was really hard to do so, I pulled my arm free. "No. It doesn't have to be that way. We can help our friends and stop them from getting hurt, and still have the same outcome—"

"No!" Reece practically yelled this, his voice reverberating in the meadow, echoing all around us and causing some birds in a nearby tree to lift off in startled flight. "No," he said again, quieter now, raking a hand through his hair. "You can't stop people from things that hurt and are hard, Stella. You can't reroute to avoid pain at all costs. You can't plan your way around everything. Sometimes, you just have to go through it. Sometimes there's no other way, okay?" His voice broke on the last word.

"Okay," I said slowly. Not in the *I agree with you* way, more in the *I'm listening* way. I sat down on the tree stump and waited. Reece's back was to me, and he was breathing hard, like he was engaged in a battle I couldn't see. But I could tell that he was on the verge of something. And if I was patient, and gave him space, he would tell me what it was when he was ready.

After a moment, he let out a long sigh, and his shoulders dropped. He walked toward me and sat on the grass near my stump. When he finally spoke, he addressed his hands. "I know something about this." A quiet, resigned sadness was shading his voice. "When we moved to California . . . it was just me and my dad."

I frowned at that, searching my memory banks for records of our previous conversations, trying to make it make sense. "But . . . your sister . . ."

"She stayed in Connecticut with my mom. Part of the divorce agreement." Reece let out a long, shaky breath. "I haven't seen her in months."

I felt this like a punch in the gut. "Reece, I'm so sorry."

"We usually FaceTime on Sundays. We watch a movie together, always her pick. And for a while, now, every week, it's been—"

"*Sleeping Beauty*," I finished.

He nodded. "But it's not enough. She used to be in my life, and I used to be in hers, and now the most we get to talk is two hours, once a week. I don't know what's really going on with her in school, or with her friends. . . . I feel like I'm missing so much. And she's so young. . . . I know it won't be long until she forgets—forgets how things used to be."

"But maybe not," I said, desperately searching for a silver lining even though I couldn't seem to find one. "Maybe . . ."

But Reece just shook his head. "There's nothing I can change about it. And so this is how I know that it doesn't matter what kind of *plan* I had, or if I wanted to make it easier or less painful. There was nothing to be done. Just like there's nothing to be done now." He shook his head sadly. "I'm sorry, but sometimes people you love get hurt. Things are out of our control. And the best plan in the world won't change that."

I nodded. I didn't *like* it, but I could feel the truth of this hitting me deep in my chest. "Thank you for telling me about your sister."

He gave me a small smile and a nod. "Her name's Gabi."

I nodded back, and then we sat in silence for a moment—nothing but the sound of the birds, the whistle of the wind, and the echo of all that we'd just said reverberating around us.

"So then," I said, after a minute, trying to get my head around this, "we're just going to sit here, out of the way, and let the events of the story unfold without us."

"We're not in the original story," he reminded me. "We did all we could to get things to where they were supposed to be. And if we were to get involved now, we might mess this up in a way that can't be undone. We don't have a week to fix things anymore. This is a now-or-never thing, if we want a chance to get back again."

"So what, we just wait?"

"For a while," Reece confirmed.

"We couldn't, I don't know, wait *in a castle*?" I shook my head. "Do you have something against me ever going into this castle? It's starting to get weird."

"Everyone in the castle is going to be put to sleep by the fairies, once Aurora—Rose—" He let out a frustrated sigh and shook his head.

"Our blond friend?" I supplied, and he smiled.

"Exactly. Everyone who's there gets put to sleep, and I thought we'd want to avoid that if at all possible."

"Fine. Good call," I said, a little grudgingly.

"So we'll just stay here until it looks like the spell is going to be broken, and then we'll ride to the palace."

"How will we know?"

He pushed himself to his feet and climbed up on a nearby rock. He held out his hand, and I stepped up next to him. He pointed, and I could see what I'd been able to glimpse from Rose's bedroom window: there, in the distance, the castle.

"Soon, there will be a huge forest of nettles and thorns popping up around the castle. That's Maleficent trying to keep Phil out. But when Phil slays the dragon Maleficent turns into, all her dark magic disappears. So the thorns all vanish. And when that happens, that'll be our cue to head over."

"If she can turn into a dragon, you wouldn't think she'd need to go around cursing babies to get what she wants, right? She could just show up with her dragon powers and threaten to barbecue anyone who stood in her way."

Reece gave me a look that clearly indicated he wasn't about to engage with me on that point. "Anyway, like I said, then we'll ride to the castle, Phil will give Rose—or Aurora—true love's kiss, and the spell will break. She'll wake up, the fairies will collect the magic, and they can—what did they say?"

"Create a door," I supplied, glad that I could finally contribute to this. "What do you think they'll trap the magic in? Maybe there's something we can use in the castle. I wouldn't know, since I've never *been there.*"

"I was actually thinking we could use this," Reece said, as he crossed over to Delilah, patting her lightly on the neck before he unzipped his backpack. He pulled out a blue plastic bag. It had the Disneyland castle on it, with fireworks above. Seeing it here was a little disarming, like a relic from another time—which, I supposed, it was. He raised an eyebrow at me, and then drew out a *Sleeping Beauty* wand with pictures of Aurora and the fairies along the handle.

"So *that's* what you bought back at the park."

"Yeah. It's for Gabi." I smiled as I looked at it, knowing now just what this meant to him. "Sorry to be so mysterious about it. I just didn't want you to make fun of it."

"I wouldn't have!" I protested. But he gave me a look, and I shrugged, remembering how spiky we'd both been with each other that first day. "Okay, maybe I would have a *little*. But now I wouldn't."

"I mean," Reece said, his voice faux-serious, "what is there even to make fun of? This thing is awesome. And . . ." He pressed a button and bubbles flowed out from the top of the wand.

I laughed. "Very impressive. Can I try it? I'll be careful."

"I wasn't worried." He handed the wand to me, and I waved it in large arcs, pressing the button to release the bubbles into the late-afternoon sunlight.

"Gabi will love it," I assured Reece. I went to hand it back to him, but he was staring at the line of gently popping bubbles, his brow furrowed. "What?"

"Never mind," he said quickly, shaking his head. "Just . . . bubbles."

"Yeah," I agreed, wondering what I was missing. "They sure are."

"It's nothing." He took the wand back from me, sounding a little like he was trying to convince himself. "Just a coincidence, that's all."

"Okay," I said, raising an eyebrow at him. I sat back down on the stump, but a second later, got up again and started pacing around the meadow. "I can't believe that we're just supposed to sit here while our friend is being menaced by an evil sorceress."

Reece sighed dramatically. "If I have to hear that *once more* today . . ."

I laughed at that just as a cold wind—with a threat of rain—blew through the meadow. I shivered and walked over to where I'd left my basket, rummaging in it until I found my sweatshirt. I pulled it over my dress and saw that Reece was staring at me. "What?" I asked, as I smoothed my hair down, hoping that I hadn't totally wrecked my magical blowout.

"It's just . . . your sweatshirt."

"What about it?" It was just an ordinary gray sweatshirt: little blue flowers on the front, FORGET ME NOT written underneath, ALASKA! on the back.

"It . . . Those flowers just look familiar," he said, then shook his head. "Don't listen to me. I'm just stressed, I guess."

"Are you okay?" I asked, genuinely concerned. Maybe the strain of knowingly sending our friend into mortal peril was starting to wear on him.

"Fine," he said, even though he was starting to look freaked out. "I'm . . . fine. Just seeing connections that aren't there, that's all."

We settled into comfortable silence after that, and I found myself wishing that I'd grabbed the deck of cards before we left—anything to pass the time and keep our minds off what was going on with our friends. "Hey," I said after a bit, breaking the silence, glancing over at Reece. "Think we can send a bird to Phil in the dungeon? See if he can grab my bag before he leaves?"

Reece shook his head, but he was smiling. "While he's racing out and fighting for his life, you want to see if he can snag your tote for you?"

"It *does* have my phone in it," I pointed out. "*And* my keys. Maybe that would change things?" Reece just laughed. "And Merryweather has become really attached to the bag itself. I was planning on giving it to her as a thank-you."

"Why does she like the bag so much?"

I shrugged. "Who knows? Maybe totes are just more comfortable than carrying around baskets? But it *is* a nice tote. It's from El Arco Iris Tacos, have you been yet? It's so good. And it says *guac your world* on it, which I *might* have told her is a common farewell phrase where we come from—"

"El Arco Iris?" Reece echoed. He was looking truly freaked out now.

"Yes," I said slowly, wondering what was going on with him. "It means rainbow."

"I know it means rainbow!" he said, sounding exasperated. "So this bag . . . it was the one you had at Disneyland, right?"

"Yeah."

Reece furrowed his brow like he was trying to remember. "Does it have a rainbow on it?"

"Yeah, also a taco. And a smiling pineapple. Why?"

Reece shook his head and sank down onto the grass, looking like he was on the verge of throwing up. He closed his eyes for a long moment, and when he opened them and looked up at me, he looked shell-shocked. "I think I just realized something." He gestured to the ground, his expression grim. "You might need to sit down."

"Okay," I said, really starting to get worried. I sat down across from Reece in the grass and pulled my hands into my sweatshirt sleeves. "What's going on?"

He took a deep breath. "I think I may have been wrong."

"I believe it," I said immediately.

"Don't you even want to know the context?"

"I'll still believe it," I said, mostly just trying to get him to laugh. "Wrong about what?"

Reece looked down at the wand in his hands and turned it over. "I thought we needed to stay here, out of the way," he said slowly. "And I don't know how it's possible . . . but I think we might have more of a role to play in the story."

"What do you mean?"

"At one point in the battle with Maleficent, the fairies transform the weapons used against them and Phil into more innocuous things that won't hurt anyone." He took a breath. "They turn them into bubbles, flowers, and rainbows."

I just blinked at him, trying to understand what he was saying. "But that's just a coincidence, right? It has to be."

"Or maybe it's *not*. Maybe we're supposed to be there with them, telling them what to do or giving them the ideas. . . ."

"But that would mean," I said, not even wanting to speak this idea aloud since it was so ludicrous, "that we're in the story?"

"It would."

"That we've *always* been in the story?"

"Right."

"But . . ." I shook my head. "This movie was made back in the fifties, right? How is that possible?"

"Because we dropped into the story a week early. So if we're here now, it would be before the story we know started. So we would have always been in the later version that we know, influencing the events."

I closed my eyes for just a second. "This is giving me a headache."

"Me too. But . . ." Reece leaned closer to me. "Rose told the fairies she was going berry picking yesterday, right? When she came to meet us?" I nodded. "And what did she say this morning? When the fairies were trying to get her out of the house?"

"She said, *I picked berries yesterday*," I said slowly. "But I'm not sure . . ."

"I'm not sure either," Reece admitted. "But on the off chance that this *is* what we're supposed to do . . ."

"We can't just sit around," I finished, and Reece nodded.

"I think maybe we have a part to play in this fight," he said. "And if that's the case, we need to make sure it comes out well so we can get home."

"And help our friends." I wasn't thinking of myself in that moment. I was thinking about Rose, falling into a fairy-tale coma, and Phil having to battle terrible creatures and dragons and Maleficent.

But if we were going to make this work, we would have to plot out all our next steps carefully. I'd have to get all the information from Reece about this battle and work out where we could slot into it. We'd need a *plan*.

"I know that expression," Reece said, starting to smile. "Is your logistics brain kicking in?"

I grinned back at him. "I think," I said, flexing my fingers, "it's time to make a spreadsheet."

PART

Three

Twenty-Five

We were about fifty feet from Maleficent's castle, riding fast on Delilah, when I felt myself shiver. Which was understandable—we were heading toward the stronghold of a canonically evil villain, whose castle was located in a place that was literally called the Forbidden Mountain. And it was appropriately named; we'd had to follow a series of hairpin turns to get up there, and once we'd arrived, it really wasn't a very comforting sight. The castle was perched on top of the mountain, and half of it seemed to be falling apart. The other half of it was decorated in a way that seemed specifically designed to deter people. There were stone gargoyles everywhere, and even the entrance to the castle was a giant, angry-looking bat, its wings raised and fangs bared.

The whole thing was shrouded in a muddy, mustard-colored fog. There was a scent, too, one that got stronger the closer we got: a kind of sulfurous, fetid rotten-egg smell that meant I was trying not to take deep breaths if I could avoid it. But even more than the building itself . . . there was just a *feeling* about it. A sense of dread that only seemed to be increasing, like everything inside was telling me to leave, get out, that nothing good would happen here. Kind of like going to the DMV, but on a *much* larger scale.

"You okay?" Reece asked, turning his head to look at me. He was riding in front of me, and my arms were around his waist, his backpack tied behind me. I'd put my stuff in his bag, since I wouldn't be able to take my basket on the horse.

"Kind of?" I said, even as I clasped my hands more tightly around him. "It's just . . . really creepy."

"It really is, isn't it? But you've been here before."

"But I didn't have to go through the front door. Not that I can remember, anyway. It's just all seeming . . . really real now." It was not escaping me that we were two teenagers from California, armed with not much more than moxie and movie trivia, and we were preparing to face off against a legendary villain who, I had a feeling, would not hesitate to dispatch either of us without a second thought.

Reece pulled on the reins to bring Delilah to a stop, then turned more fully to look at me, giving me a smile. "Hi."

"Hi," I replied. My arms were still around him, but loosely, and sitting together on the back of the horse, we were close enough to kiss. I knew we had *much* bigger things to think about at the moment, but it didn't change the fact that he was just there, only a breath away.

"Are you ready for this?" His eyes were searching mine.

I wasn't sure that I was, but Phil was in there, and he needed us. And plus . . . we had a plan. And it was a *good* one. And whatever doubts I was feeling seemed to melt away as I looked into his eyes and saw nothing but confidence. Reece knew I could do this. And that gave me the boost I needed to nod and sit up straighter. "Let's do it."

He reached out and carefully brushed a lock of hair back from my forehead, his hand lingering on my cheek for just a second. "Together."

I reached up and covered his hand with mine, and nodded. "Together."

"Got the spreadsheet?"

I grinned and pulled it out of the pouch Rose had designed for me, holding it up. "You know it."

It had been more fun than I'd realized it would be, to plan things out in the notebook that had been in Reece's backpack, using his ballpoint pen. After a week of scraps of paper and lead, it felt like a real luxury. And after about thirty minutes, I'd looked up from our planning, feeling satisfied. Between Reece's knowledge of the situation and my ability to time out sequences of events, this document was truly a thing of beauty.

"Phil is in the dungeon," I'd said, wanting to be clear before we headed off.

Reece had nodded. "Yes, chained up. Eventually, the fairies break him out, but before that, Maleficent goes down there and tells him the truth—that Rose is actually Aurora, and that she's cursed her. That Phil is the only one who can wake her up and break the spell, and she's going to keep him locked up so he can't."

"But he's already going to know that," I pointed out. "Because *we're* going to tell him first."

"We just have to get there before the fairies," Reece had reminded me, tapping the timeline on the spreadsheet. "Because if we show up and Phil is already gone, then we'll just be . . . trapped in a dungeon."

"That won't happen," I said, with more confidence than I felt. I looked over the rest of the plan—the sections marked *Dungeon Escape*, *The Power of Song*, and *Magic X 3*. It seemed like we had things under control, if all went well.

"Ready?" I asked as I folded the paper and tucked it in my pouch.

Reece nodded, giving me a smile. "Let's do it."

When we reached the drawbridge, Delilah stopped, glanced back, and gave us a look.

"I know," I said sympathetically. "It's okay." I wasn't sure that it was, but I was trying to be comforting. It didn't seem like Maleficent had spent any of her free time in the last sixteen years on home repairs. The drawbridge was made of mostly rotting wood with big gaps everywhere, and Delilah clearly wasn't a fan.

The horse started walking again, stepping carefully. We were halfway across when one of Maleficent's goons, who'd been guarding the entrance, ran up toward us. He looked like a giant warthog but was walking upright on two legs, carrying a gigantic battle-ax. And all these facts taken together produced a very unsettling sight—one I was fairly sure I'd be having nightmares about for the foreseeable future.

"Hi there!" Reece yelled, waving at him.

"Who're you?" the goon grunted at us, swinging the ax around forebodingly.

I could feel Delilah tense beneath us, and I saw Reece reach down and stroke her neck. "It's okay," he whispered, his voice soothing.

"We're bad people!" I called to the goon. "Clearly."

"Up to no good," Reece confirmed. "Just the worst."

He squinted at us. "You fairies?"

Reece looked back at me for a second, but that one glance was enough to let me know he was also trying to figure out how to answer. "No?" I finally said.

"Supposed to be on the lookout for fairies," the goon snorted, swinging the ax again. He stopped and looked up at me, his eyes narrowing. "You look familiar."

"Right," I said, seizing on this. "I was here before, remember? Getting you in trouble. I'm bad news."

"We both are," Reece agreed. "I really think the only place for us would be the dungeons."

"No!" I gasped, finding I was actually getting into this. "Not the dungeons! That would make me really sad, but probably make Maleficent really happy."

The goon smiled, which was actually the most frightening expression of all. "Yeah . . . dungeon! Dungeon for both of you!"

Reece turned his head and gave me a tiny smile.

Ten minutes later, just as I'd planned, we were being shoved into a darkened dungeon, and the goon was throwing my bag in after me.

"Not that bag," I cried. "Please! Have a heart!" Even though I could practically feel Reece telling me to tone it down, I'd spent the whole walk into the castle telling the minion how much I needed him to keep the bag away from me: the one that was hanging on the iron hook, right by the entrance to the throne room. And much to my delight, the reverse psychology seemed to have worked. All the goons had been celebrating, dancing and leaping around a bonfire below Maleficent's throne, and it seemed like enough had been going on that she hadn't seen us and, hopefully, had no idea she now had two unexpected captives.

"No," the goon chuckled, clearly enjoying this. I waited for him to chain us up, but he wasn't making any move to. And I certainly wasn't about to give him the idea if he hadn't gotten there on his own.

"Please stay here with us," Reece pleaded. I could tell he was *also* getting into this, even if he'd never admit it. When we were both back home, it seemed like we should both consider auditioning for the school plays. But there were probably better times to broach the topic. "Don't leave us alone in the dark and go back to enjoy yourself at the celebration!"

"Now I go and enjoy the celebration," he said, sounding very pleased with himself. "Mistress will be so happy with what I've done. I bet I get promotion!" He grunted happily at the thought, then left, slamming the door behind him and leaving us in the pitch dark.

"You okay?" Reece asked.

"Yeah." I blinked, willing my eyes to adjust faster. Reece reached down and grasped my hand, helping to pull me to my feet and off the (supergross) floor. I reached into my bag and fumbled around for my phone. "Please, please," I whispered as I pulled it up. I touched the screen, and a second later, it lit up. I let out a sigh of relief. Part of this plan had hinged on my phone, even if Reece hadn't been on board with The Power of Song. I squinted at the screen and saw, to my shock, that my battery was at 150 percent. Apparently, getting hit with a bolt of lightning was like using a super charger. I just hoped that it would actually work when I was back in a place with Wi-Fi and cell towers, and not immediately get overloaded. But that was a problem for Future Stella to deal with.

"How is that the first thing you're focused on?" Reece hissed at me.

"Look," I said, as I pressed the button on the front of the screen to turn the flashlight on. I aimed the light around the dungeon, which frankly showed me more than I wanted to see: puddles on the stone floors, rats scurrying in the shadows, cobwebs, and a pile of bones I really didn't want to look at too closely. And there, huddled in a corner, was someone who looked familiar.

"Stella?" Phil asked, squinting in the light. Both his arms and legs were shackled, chained to the wall behind him. He was disheveled, with cuts and bruises and bloodstains on his face. He stood up to try and get to us, but the chains pulled him back. "Reece? What are you guys doing here?" His eyes landed on the iPhone in my hand. "Uh . . . what's that?"

"Are you okay?" Reece asked, hurrying over to him. Even in the iPhone light, I could see he looked pale as he took in what had happened to Phil. "Are you hurt?"

"I'm all right," Phil said, even as he winced, like his ribs were bruised. "But how did you get here? Where are we? What's going on?" He stopped and shook his head. "Sorry, I'm being so rude. How are you both doing?"

I bit back a smile as it hit me just how much I'd miss Phil, if—*when* we were able to pull this off.

"Okay, so it's kind of a good-news-bad-news situation," Reece said, coming to sit next to Phil on the little bench he was chained to. "The bad news is that you're being held prisoner by a, frankly, unhinged woman who's determined to keep you here for a hundred years."

Phil blinked. "I'm— What?"

"Also," I pointed out, "another hundred years seems like a wildly optimistic prediction for how long you'll live." Reece shot me a look that clearly said I wasn't helping. "What? I'm not an actuary, but come on. Anyway, the good news is that we're here to rescue you!"

"But why am I even here in the first place? Is it a ransom thing?"

"No," Reece said. He glanced at me, then took a breath. "It's actually about your fiancée, Aurora."

Phil sat up straighter, his expression growing grim. "Maleficent," he said, and Reece and I nodded. "It's one of my first memories when I was a kid, when she showed up at the christening. You could just feel it in the air how terrible she was."

"We were there," I assured him.

"You— What?"

"Nothing," Reece said quickly.

"But what does she have to do with me now? I thought the curse on the princess Aurora was breaking today. That's what everyone was saying back at the palace."

I shook my head. "Maleficent got to her first and put a spell on her. She's in a dreamless sleep, and only true love's kiss can wake her. That's why she captured you and brought you here: so that you can't."

"But how does that accomplish anything? I'm not going to marry this girl. I told my father this afternoon that I wasn't. And since I don't love her—I don't even know her—how could I possibly break the spell?" Phil shook his head. "I'm truly sorry to hear about it, but I just want to be with Rose." He turned to me, his brow furrowing. "Is she all right, do you know? When I got to her cottage, she wasn't there, and I'm worried something happened to her."

"Well, back to the good-news-and-bad-news thing," Reece said. "So, Rose *is* Aurora. She was raised in that cottage for her own protection. She doesn't know she's a princess."

"Wait," Phil said, looking from me to Reece. A kaleidoscope of emotions was passing over his face. "Really?" We nodded. *"Really?"* We nodded harder.

"Wild, right?" I asked. "I wanted to tell you both from the beginning, but I was outvoted." I tipped my head in Reece's direction.

"But," Phil said slowly, looking like he was trying to put this all together. "But that means . . . that we actually found each other ourselves. We fell for each other without any pressure, or encouragement. . . ." He looked up at me, a smile lighting up his face.

"You wanted to know if someone liked you for you," I said, remembering one of the first conversations we'd had. "And now you know. And she does, too."

Phil's smile widened, but then a second later, faltered. "But that means my Rose is the one who is cursed! I have to get to her! She needs me!" He jumped to his feet and strained against his chains. "I have to get out of here!"

"Rose's aunts will be coming by to help bust you out," Reece said.

"Oh, one thing," I added, feeling like this was pertinent information. "They're not *technically* her aunts; they're magical fairies." It was maybe a testament to how much Phil had been through today that he just nodded at that. Maybe once you've been attacked by a bat holding a kitchen knife, not much else will faze you.

"It's going to be a fight to get out of here and get to her," Reece said, looking steadily at Phil. "But you can do it. And we'll help."

Phil smiled at him. "Thank you, my friend." He glanced over at me and nodded down at my hand. "But again—what is that, Stella?"

I glanced down at my iPhone. "Oh . . . this?" I wasn't sure what to say here. It was one thing to tell Rose it was a communication device when it was just a darkened brick. But when it was charged, lighting up and making noise? I wasn't sure I'd be able to get away with being so vague. I took a breath to say something—I hadn't gotten as far as what yet—then paused. "Do you guys hear that?"

We all got quiet to listen, and sure enough, I could hear footsteps coming down the hall outside, and a second later, the rasp of a key in the door.

I hit the button to turn the flashlight on my phone off, and Reece grabbed my hand and pulled me into a darkened corner of the dungeon, behind a wall that stuck out, just as the door opened and Maleficent strode in.

She must have lit the torches, because a second later, the dungeon was flooded with light. I took another step back, pressing my back against the wall, pulling Reece in closer to me, hoping she couldn't see our shadows.

My heart was thumping in my chest as I heard Maleficent croon, "Oh come now, Prince Phillip. Why so *melancholy?*"

I was all too aware that one breath, one sound from us and we'd be discovered before we could help get Phil out of here, before we could see this through. The very idea that we might have a role to play in this seemed to mean that victory was anything but assured.

Maleficent launched into a monologue, basically telling Phil everything we'd just told him—about how the peasant girl he'd met was actually Aurora—and you could hear in her voice how much she was enjoying telling him about all the horrible things she'd done. And as she did, I was glad that we'd gotten there first, and that he knew everything all already. Phil could maintain a stony silence—not give her the satisfaction of seeing him falter as he took this in.

But after only a few moments, it was like her voice got fuzzy and started fading out, because I was suddenly aware that Reece and I were closer than we'd ever been before.

I was pressed back against the stone wall, and Reece had one hand resting on the wall above me, his feet in between mine. We weren't touching, but there was only a whisper between us. I could see his pulse beating at the base of his throat as he turned his head toward me, a fraction of an inch at a time, until we were right there, just a moment, just a breath away from each other. All at once, the idea of kissing Reece changed from a *what if* to a *when* to a *now, please.*

I could practically hear the more logical voice inside my head, asking if now was *really* the moment for this. But a second later, another voice—one that sounded a lot like Rose's—chimed in, saying that of *course* it was the moment. That there wasn't a better time to realize how much you felt for someone than when everything was on the line and the question of if you'll get home again was far from settled. That moments like this can clarify things like nothing else.

And as I looked up at him, his lips just a tiny bit of courage away from mine, I realized, all at once, just how *much* I liked him. What I was feeling, right now, put what I thought I'd felt for Cooper to shame. It was like comparing a guttering candle to a meteor shower. And it wasn't just thinking Reece was cute, or wanting to kiss him in a moonlit meadow while shooting stars flew by above.

If you liked someone, I realized in one incandescent flash, you liked them in a disgusting dungeon next to a literal pile of bones. You liked them everywhere. Because it wasn't about the setting—it was about *them.*

I reached up, every centimeter feeling like it was a mile, and touched his face. He leaned his forehead down until it was pressed against mine, and took a step nearer to me. His hand slid around my waist, closing the distance between us. "Stella," Reece said in a voice just above a whisper.

"Reece," I whispered back. I leaned toward him, my eyes already starting to close—just as the door slammed shut again.

We both froze. And though we didn't move away from each other, it was like I could feel the moment hovering between us for a moment longer . . . and then it passed us by.

"I guess she's gone," I whispered, still not daring to speak at top volume.

"Yeah," Reece whispered back. And then, all at once, I heard three very familiar voices fill the dungeon.

"Prince Phillip," I heard Flora say. "No time to explain." Reece looked down at me, and I nodded. We stepped out from our little corner, Reece's hand on my back for just a moment.

"We could take a *little* time to explain," I said, very much enjoying the shocked look on all three of the fairies' faces as they saw us.

"What are you doing here?" Fauna asked, picking up her wand from where she'd dropped it in surprise.

"Helping," I said.

"We're trying to, at least," Reece added.

"This is part of the plan, then?" Merryweather asked. She nodded, looking smug. "I knew it would be."

"Come on," Flora said, holding out her wand. "We don't have much time. Let's get out of here." She pointed her wand at Phil's wrist manacles, and Fauna did the same with his leg irons. Sparks started to fly as they broke the chains, and Merryweather focused on opening the door.

While Flora was warning Phil all about the dangers that could lie ahead, and giving him a (very shiny) sword and shield, I was digging in my El Arco Iris bag for my keys. I handed them to Reece, who shook his head.

"I'm still not sure this is going to work."

"It'll work," I insisted, even as I crossed my fingers. "They'll be mesmerized. It's time for Operation Power of Song."

Reece groaned, but before he could reply, Merryweather got the door open and gestured for us to leave. We rushed out of the dungeon together, the six of us shoulder to shoulder. But then the three fairies suddenly disappeared. A second later, I saw that they had shrunk down into the size of Funko Pops and were currently floating around our shoulders. "Okay," I said, blinking at these new mini-fairies. "So that happened."

We started to head for the exit, but then, just like Reece had warned me, there was Maleficent's raven. He spotted us and started squawking loudly, raising the alarm.

Phil ran the other direction, the mini-fairies keeping pace with him. I started running as fast as I could, trying to catch up with him. "Excuse me," I said, breathing hard as I tried to get in front of him.

"Stella, what are you doing?" Phil asked, sounding baffled. "I have the sword."

"I know," Reece said, his voice resigned. "But Stella has the Powell brothers."

I brandished my phone in triumph. "And their cousin, Doug!"

Phil frowned. *"What?"*

Reece pointed. "Look out!"

Even though I knew it was coming, it was still terrifying when a horde of goons came rushing down the stairs toward us, all yelling and waving very shiny and dangerous and sharp weapons. "Get out the other way," I yelled back to the others in a voice I hoped was braver than what I was feeling. "We'll hold them off!"

"With what?" the Flora floating by my ear demanded.

"Art!" I yelled.

"Also, poison," Reece added, coming to stand next to me.

"But first, art!" They were getting closer, and I pressed play on my phone with trembling hands. Then I turned the volume up, and thrust the phone out toward them—the phone that was playing Band of Brothers' hit "Don't Fight (This Feeling, Baby Baby)."

It was one of my favorite Band of Brothers songs, the one that got everyone grooving as one at dances and weddings. And I just prayed that it would work here, too.

The goons slowed, and then stopped, causing a mini pileup as they stared at my phone, where the music, with its persistent beat, was coming from. They looked at each other, just confused at first. But then I noticed one alligator-goon start to sway side to side, and a pig-like creature shimmying his shoulders (did pigs have shoulders?). And as I watched, heart in my throat, their weapons lowered and hung limply by their sides, forgotten.

"Is it working?" Reece asked.

"I think so," I whispered back. I turned around and gestured to Phil and the fairies. "Go!" They started running the other way, as fast as they could. All the goons were still grooving to the music as the Powell brothers (and Doug) built to the big chorus. I said a silent thanks for them, the pride of Tampa. I reached for the button to turn the volume up more—but accidentally hit the button to lock the screen instead. The music shut off, and the goons glared at me, the spell broken. They all raised their weapons again, seeming angrier now because I'd taken their newfound love of pop music away from them. "Uh-oh."

"Time for poison?" Reece asked.

"I think so."

"Run!" Reece yelled to me as he lifted my keys and started spraying the pepper spray that was attached there. I heard angry minion yelps and hurried to catch up with Phil and the fairies. I glanced back to make sure

Reece was okay. He lowered the pepper spray and started to run just as one of them tackled him.

"Reece!" I yelled, my heart jumping into my throat.

"I'm fine," he called, wincing as he struggled to get to his feet, then falling again. "Get out of here!"

"Not without you!" I changed direction and hurried toward him. He'd managed to push himself up to standing. I grabbed his hand, and together we ran, following behind Phil as he made his way to the courtyard below, where I could see Samson and Delilah were chained up next to each other.

"Are you okay?" Reece asked, turning to me, taking my face in his hands, his expression scared. "Did you get hurt?"

"I'm okay!"

"Is everyone all right?" Merryweather asked, flitting in the air from me to Phil to Reece, checking in on us.

Before I could answer, Samson neighed in alarm, and I looked up to see that above the west parapet, a group of the goons were about to drop rocks over the top onto us. Not small rocks—*huge, giant boulders*, right on our heads. "Look!" I yelled, just as Reece took the wand out of his backpack and let loose a stream of bubbles.

"Flora!" I yelled, pointing at the bubbles, then the rocks.

Flora looked, and I could see understanding dawning on her face. "Watch out!" she yelled. She pointed her wand at the rocks, which immediately transformed into giant bubbles, before they could land on us.

"That's one," Reece said, stowing his wand. "Two more to go."

I heard the sound of archers preparing to shoot and turned to the other parapet to see a second goon squad all about to let loose a volley of very sharp-looking arrows on us. "How did you all get here so fast?" I muttered angrily.

"Sweatshirt!" Reece yelled.

"Fauna!" I called, looking around. She was flying around Phil's head, and I caught her eye and pointed to my sweatshirt, then the arrows. "Flowers!"

"Flowers," she said, nodding. "Yes!" She leveled her wand at the arrows, and they all transformed into a shower of forget-me-nots.

"That's two!" Reece yelled, pumping his fist in triumph.

Merryweather unchained the horses with her wand, and Phil jumped on Samson's back. Reece vaulted onto Delilah, then held out his hand. I took it, and he swung me onto the horse behind him. Phil raced Samson toward the one exit—the drawbridge—and a second later, Reece patted Delilah's neck and she took off at full speed. It didn't seem like the horse needed any more encouragement; she clearly wanted to get out as fast as possible.

I held on as tightly as I could as the horses raced for the exit. The fairies were fluttering around us, yelling at us to hurry up, which frankly didn't seem all that helpful right now.

"There!" Reece yelled, pointing above the final castle wall. A group of Maleficent's minions were on top of it with two huge cauldrons of boiling liquid—water? Oil? Either way, I didn't want to find out—about to tip over on us. I wasn't clear on the logistics of this; did they just have it ready to go? But having met Maleficent, it wouldn't have surprised me if she kept boiling oil on hand at all times.

"Merryweather!" I yelled, looking around for her. I held up my tote with the one hand that wasn't desperately clinging to Reece. She met my eye, and I waved the bag at her, then pointed toward the cauldrons. "Guac your world!"

She nodded, closed one eye, and aimed her wand at the cauldrons. A second later, a huge, glorious rainbow appeared above us, and we galloped under it, heading toward safety.

"That's three!" Reece yelled, triumph in his voice.

"Did we do it?" I was holding on to Reece for dear life as we raced away from the castle at speeds I really wasn't comfortable with. I looked around: Flora and Fauna were flying next to Phil, keeping up with him. "Where's Merryweather?"

"Here," she said, appearing by my right ear. "I was always here. I wasn't getting my revenge on a bird or anything."

"Um . . . Okay."

We thundered through the last archway just a second before the spiked metal gate slammed down behind us. Merryweather and the other fairies were keeping up as we raced away from the castle. I could hear, from somewhere behind us, Maleficent shouting. And sure enough, soon the road was being blasted away from under the horses' hooves with her purple lightning. The fairies were trying to fix it as fast as they could so that the horses could keep going and we could be done with all of this.

I turned around to see if anyone was chasing after us, just in time to see a portion of the road collapse just inches from where we'd just been, close enough to send a shower of dust and pebbles toward me. I turned away, deciding I didn't need to look back any longer, brushing the dirt out of my eyes. "Are we almost there?"

"Almost," Reece said, sounding out of breath. He patted the side of Delilah's neck. "Just a little farther."

I could barely believe it, but a few moments later, it was like the fog cleared along with the feeling of dread that had been buzzing in a low-level way ever since we'd been near her castle. Suddenly, everything seemed brighter and more hopeful. We were away from the Forbidden Mountain, there was an actual road before us, and best of all, I could see the castle in the distance. "We did it," I said, letting myself breathe for what felt like the first time in hours.

"Well . . ." Reece said. And just as he did, a forest of thorns started to grow all around us.

Twenty-Six

stared at the branches that were appearing all around us, trapping us, blotting out the sky. I didn't have to touch one of them to know for sure that the thorns were razor-sharp; you could tell just by looking at them.

"Maleficent?" I asked, looking at the insta-forest that now surrounded us.

"Maleficent," Reece confirmed, his voice grim. He turned to Phil, who was trying to quiet Samson, who—quite rightly—was *not* happy about this new situation. "She's doing whatever she can to stop you from getting to the castle."

"Well, she didn't count on my having a sword," Phil said, extracting it and waving it around. "Thanks for these, by the way," he said to Flora, glancing down at his sword and shield. He urged Samson forward and started chopping his way through the thorns.

"Keep going," she encouraged him, as she and the fairies flew around him, zapping away the thorns that were catching on his cloak and pulling him back.

"So is this like a metaphor?" I asked as we inched forward on Delilah, picking our way behind Phil and the path he was carving out for us. "Phil has to get through the briars before he can get to Briar Rose?"

"I don't think Maleficent is capable of anything so elegant," Merryweather sniffed as she pointed her wand at some thorns to blast them away. "I think she's just being a mean jerk, as usual." She flew off to help Phil, and Reece looked back at me.

"Mean jerk?"

"I may have let a few anachronisms slip," I confessed with a shrug. "I think everyone will live."

As Phil fought his way through the thicket, I could see that dawn was starting to appear, a faint ribbon of light on the horizon. I ran my hand over my face, feeling just what a long night it had been, compounded by the knowledge that it wasn't over yet. Reece turned his head slightly to the side, and I could see that he had a gash across his cheek and a smudge of dirt down his neck. He looked a little worse for wear, and I was sure I did as well.

I was on the verge of asking the fairies if maybe they could rustle up a machete or two to hurry things along, when all of a sudden, I saw the castle. It had looked great from a distance, but it looked even better now. Because now, seeing it meant that we were almost done, that this was almost over. But before I got the chance to say anything about this, Reece pulled back sharply on the reins, bringing Delilah to a stop. "What?"

He nodded ahead, where Maleficent was appearing in front of the castle entrance, blocking our path—and she did *not* look happy. "Now shall you deal with me, O prince," she fumed.

I shook my head, feeling like I now understood Avery's need to throw her hands into the air. Sometimes there's just no other response. "Seriously? Haven't we *been* dealing with her? How is this a change?"

"Stella, *shh*," Reece said in a quiet voice, clearly not wanting to draw attention to ourselves, but I could tell that he was trying not to laugh.

"So what happens now?"

"Enter the dragon." Reece turned to look at me, clearly pleased with himself, and I just shook my head.

"You did *not* just say that."

"When else was I going to get the chance?"

Before I could respond, Maleficent was suddenly flying upward into what looked like a giant purple mushroom cloud—never a sight I was going to be super psyched to see. She passed out of view in the cloud, and then a *gigantic dragon* emerged from it.

Very strange things had happened today already—weird sentient animal creatures had tried to pour boiling substances on me not all that long ago. And Reece had told me there was a dragon, so I had thought I was prepared.

But it turns out? You're never *actually* prepared to see a dragon.

I just stared at it, my mouth hanging open, as I struggled to understand what I was looking at. It was purple and black, with foot-long teeth, massive wings, and claws that were each probably the size of a minivan. In short, it was truly terrifying in a way I'd never really experienced.

And as if all that wasn't bad enough, as I watched, it took a breath and then aimed a blast of green-and-yellow fire right at Phil. Thankfully, he was able to block it with his shield, but when he lowered it, he looked shaken, and I didn't blame him; I could feel the heat on my face from feet away. I held on to Reece more tightly as I watched Phil, undaunted by this, charge forward on Samson *toward a dragon*, waving his sword that honestly seemed like a toy now—cute but ultimately useless. But if Phil had any doubts, you wouldn't know from looking at him as he raced forward, his face brave and determined, looking every inch the storybook prince that he was.

Delilah started to whine and buck nervously, and Reece slid off her back. He held out his arms and helped me off as well. "It's okay," he said to the horse, stroking her neck. "It's okay."

"Is it?" I whispered as I watched Phil—our friend—fight a dragon that could breathe fire, whereas he only had a sword and shield. "Will it be okay, Reece?" I kept my voice low, not wanting Phil to somehow hear I was doubting him. "Will he—" But before I could finish speaking, the dragon let out a blast of fire so strong, it knocked Phil off Samson's back, sending him tumbling hard to the ground. Samson whinnied, terrified, and raced back toward us.

Reece caught his bridle, trying to do his best to calm him down. But it wasn't working; both the horses seemed to feel exactly the same as I did, jumpy and scared. As I watched a fight that seemed to be increasingly lopsided, my heart in my throat, I wasn't sure that this was going to work out. I wasn't sure Phil was going to survive this.

Because now he was down a horse, bloody and bruised as he staggered backward, and the gigantic dragon snapped at him with her gigantic jaws, spewing fire in his direction. Phil was swinging with his sword, but it didn't seem like it was doing all that much good.

I watched in horror as Phil retreated—stumbled back—and fell.

"We have to help, right?" I looked at Reece, who was tracking all of this, his expression grim.

"I don't know how we can."

"Maybe now is the moment we tell the fairies about rocket launchers? And get them to make one for us?"

Before Reece could answer, Maleficent sent out a huge jet of fire. But it wasn't at Phil—it was all around him. Soon he was surrounded by flames so hot that I could feel them even from where we were standing.

"Reece," I whispered, reaching for him. He pulled me close, wrapping his arm around my shoulders. "Is he . . . ?" I couldn't even make myself finish the sentence.

Because it didn't look good. Phil was trapped at the base of a sheer rock face, the flames getting ever closer, boxing him in. He coughed, covering his mouth with his sleeve, looking around for a way out.

"Up this way!" Flora yelled as she helped him free-solo his way up to the top of the cliff, away from the fire that was, frankly, getting a little too close to us for comfort.

"Um . . ." I said, looking between Phil fighting the dragon atop a cliff and the green flames that were getting ever closer to us and our horses. "Merryweather?"

"Fauna?" Reece called, a note of real alarm in his voice. She looked over, then zoomed toward us. She pointed her wand at the flames and water spouted out of it, dousing the flames around us and sending acrid smoke up into the air.

"Thank you!" I called as she flew back to the cliff, where the dragon was now forcing Phil to the very edge.

I was tempted to close my eyes, but I couldn't do that to Phil, so I made myself watch, and witness, just hoping he could somehow turn things around. A blast of fire sent his shield tumbling over the edge, and I gripped on to Reece harder, because this was *not* looking good. "Oh my god," I murmured. The three fairies were hovering around Phil, but all he had left was a sword.

For just a second, I flashed back to all of us in the lake playing sportsball, Phil drawing his arm back to make an impossible shot. "He needs to throw it," I said, realizing this all at once.

Reece nodded. "He does."

"Three pointer!" we both screamed at the same time. Phil glanced over at us. I saw understanding dawn on his face—and he launched his sword. It flew, straight and true, and lodged deep in the dragon's belly.

Maleficent screamed in pain, writhing, her claws swiping angrily but only getting air, and then falling off the cliff and out of view.

And she was gone.

Relief flooded through me, as cool and sweet as an iced coffee on a sweltering day. I let out a long shaky breath, and my legs suddenly got wobbly beneath me.

But the battle had ended—and we'd won.

"We did it," Reece said, sighing with relief. "It's over."

"Not quite," I said.

And then I gathered all the courage that I possessed, stretched up, and kissed him.

Twenty-Seven

Reece kissed me back.

Like it was that easy. Like we'd always been doing it. He kissed me back.

And then I was pulling him close, and he was cupping my jaw with his hands and stroking my hair back, and we were kissing and kissing, like we couldn't get enough of it, like we'd been drowning and this was our oxygen—that necessary, that life sustaining.

We broke apart for just a moment and looked at each other, both of us breathing hard. "Wow," Reece murmured, turning a lock of my hair around his fingers, then tucking it behind one ear.

"Same," I said, smiling up at him.

And then he bent down and kissed me again, sweeping me up in his arms, lifting me off my feet for just a second. "Stella," he whispered in my ear, saying my name like an incantation, an answered prayer. The thing you've been looking for all along and have finally found.

"Reece," I whispered back, not able to stop a smile from taking over my whole face.

"Uh . . . Guys?"

We broke apart and I blinked as I looked around. The forest of thorns and all the terrible things Maleficent had conjured must have died along with her. It was all gone now, and the rising sun was showing us a castle sparkling in the new morning light, untouched by an evil woman who only wanted to cause harm.

I looked over and saw Phil, soot-stained and battle-scarred, but nonetheless giving me and Reece a very knowing smile. "About time."

"Phil!" I yelled. Reece and I ran up and hugged him, a three-person hug that caused him to stagger back slightly. "Are you okay?"

He nodded. "I'm all right."

"You did it," Reece said, clapping him on the back. And even as Phil winced, he gave Reece a smile. "It was a nice shot."

"I had a lot of practice," he said with a laugh. Then he turned to the castle, and I did as well. There was nothing blocking our way now; it was a clear path to Rose and the end of the story.

"You ready?" I asked Phil.

He gave me a smile, but it wasn't wide and goofy. Phil suddenly seemed older, more serious, somehow. Probably facing off against a murderous dragon will do that. But I couldn't help but clock the change. He nodded. "I'm ready." He swung onto Samson's back, and Reece climbed onto Delilah's, then pulled me up behind him.

We cantered toward the palace, the fairies flanking us like an honor guard. I held on tight to Reece, knowing that it was okay for me to do this, knowing that he liked me, too, that this thing between us was just beginning. And we had lots and lots of time to figure out just what it was.

"I finally get to go inside the castle!" I exclaimed as we passed into the courtyard. But right away, I could see that things were probably different than they normally were. For one thing, everyone in the castle was currently unconscious. Reece had told me that the fairies had put everyone to sleep, so I knew it intellectually. But it was quite another thing to see the reality of it: people sleeping on the ground or standing up, leaning back against walls or stairs or fountains.

We got off the horses and tied them up in the courtyard, then rushed inside.

The fairies were leading the way up twisting stone steps. As I hurried behind them, I tried to take in as much as I could see: the tapestries and sigils on the walls, the art and suits of armor in the hallways. We made it to the top of the staircase, and when the fairies stopped in front of a closed door, Phil squared his shoulders, took a deep breath, and pulled it open.

The room was very grand, with a black-and-white checkerboard marble floor and a towering canopy bed—but I could barely register any of that, because in the bed, looking small and still, was Rose.

My breath caught in my throat as I looked at her. She was lying on the bed, a crown on her glorious hair, her hands clasped around a single red rose. But her skin had a greenish tint and looked waxy and cold. It hurt me to see her like this. This was not someone taking a peaceful nap or getting a well-deserved night's sleep.

And it just didn't seem right. Rose had always been the first one up.

She'd hated sleeping in, had always declared sleeping late the loss of a day. The fact that she was trapped in this state was just *wrong*. I needed it to be fixed—needed to get my friend back—and as soon as possible.

All the fairies turned back into the life-size versions of themselves, and Merryweather gave us an appraising look. "You all look awful."

I glanced at a gilded mirror on the wall and saw what she was talking about. We were bloodied and bruised and dirt stained, our clothes singed and smudged.

"Poor dears," Fauna said, clucking at us. "You've been through so much."

"Not in a fit state to be presented to a princess," Flora agreed.

"It's fine," Phil said. His eyes were on Rose. They hadn't left her since he'd walked in.

"It's not," Merryweather insisted. She nodded at Flora and Fauna, and they all raised their wands as one. They pointed them at Phil, and a second later, he was transformed. His wood-carver's outfit was gone; he now looked like the prince he was. His cuts and bruises had vanished, his hair was shiny and perfectly coiffed, and he was wearing a dark suit with high black boots, a red cape over his shoulders.

They turned to Reece next, who took a worried step back. "I'm really okay," he protested. But they just pointed their wands at him, and a second later, the dirt was off his face, the gash had healed, and he was wearing an outfit similar to Phil's, but the suit was a pale gray with navy accents.

"And Stella." Merryweather looked at me and lifted her wand.

"Wait!" I yelled. I dropped my tote on the ground, pulled off my sweatshirt, and placed it on top. I wasn't sure how this magic worked, but in case it wasn't possible to get articles of clothing back once they'd been transmogrified, I didn't want to find out the hard way. I made myself stand up straight and nodded at them. "Okay." Fauna gave me a smile, and all three fairies raised their wands. I closed my eyes and felt a series of small sparks, the same way I had back in the kitchen of the cottage.

I opened my eyes, looked down at myself, and gasped happily. I was now wearing a *stunning* long gown: pale gray with navy accents, half off the shoulder, cinched in at the waist. I glanced in the mirror and saw my hair was now softly curled. I turned to Reece and realized that they'd matched our outfits—his gray and mine were perfectly coordinated.

"You look beautiful," Reece said, taking my hand in his.

"You two are so sweet!" Fauna gushed.

"Very nice," Flora said crisply, even as she gave me a smile and a tiny wink. "Now. Reece. You have the container?"

"Yes," Reece said as he dropped to one knee and pulled the plastic wand out of his backpack. He held it out, and Merryweather took it from him.

"This will do nicely," she said, smiling as she saw the picture of herself on the handle. "When the spell breaks, we'll contain as much of the magic as we can."

I nodded, just hoping that it would work. "Sounds good." I turned to Phil, who was still looking at Rose, twisting his hands together nervously. "You've got this," I said, patting him on the back.

He gave me a worried look. "I don't know. Is it okay to just . . . kiss someone when they're asleep?" He shook his head. "I'm not sure, Stella."

"Okay," I said, secretly glad that Phil had such good instinctual boundaries about consent. "First of all, this has to happen to wake her up—there's just no other way. Second, I know for a fact that she wanted to kiss you. She told me. And third, what did she tell you the last time you guys almost kissed but didn't?"

"What did she say?" Reece asked, looking interested.

"Oh," Phil said, blushing. "She, um, told you about that?" I nodded. Phil cleared his throat. "Well . . . she said . . ." Just like that, I could see the meaning sink in for him. "She told me the next time the opportunity came along . . . don't hesitate."

"Exactly."

"Okay," Phil said. He nodded, took a deep breath, then walked slowly over to the bed.

Reece reached down for my hand, threading his fingers through mine. He lifted it up to his lips and kissed it, and I squeezed his hand back, feeling my heart swell.

Phil carefully sat down at the edge of the bed. I could see it all on his face as he looked at Rose. It was like he was seeing all that had been and all that could be; his past and their future, all on the other side of one kiss.

He leaned forward, inch by inch, until he was hovering, in that in-between moment I'd seen on the castle wall back at the park. And now, witnessing it in real time, I understood why this was the image that had been chosen. I could see the power of it: getting to witness the moment someone's destiny changes forever.

And then Phil leaned forward a bit more and closed the distance between them, giving Rose a kiss.

There was a pulse, and light flooded the room. The fairies all pointed their wands at it and guided the light into a ball. They transferred it into what, moments ago, had been a fake magic wand but now was the real thing. It glowed and shimmered so brightly it was almost hard to look at. "We got it?" I asked.

"Got it," Flora confirmed.

I turned to look at Rose, who was starting to get her color back. Her eyelids fluttered, and then she opened up her eyes. Seeing who was in front of her, she smiled wide. "Phil?" she said, sitting up. "Hi! Oh my good-ness, you're here—" She threw herself toward him, kissing him fiercely and wrapping her arms around his neck.

Reece averted his eyes and looked at me. "Maybe we should go?"

"Shh," I shushed him.

Phil and Rose broke apart, both looking dazed and happy. She reached up, her eyes shining as she touched Phil's cheek. "But . . . what are you doing here?" She looked around the rest of the room, and her eyes widened as she clocked all of us. "Oh—hello. What's going on?"

I took a breath, ready to explain everything. "*Well* . . ."

But before I could get further than that, Reece squeezed my shoulders. "Maybe we let them sort this out," he murmured.

"I mean, I'm glad to see you here," Rose said to Phil. "You have *no* idea. I'm so happy you decided to ignore my letter."

Phil frowned. "Letter?"

"We should just keep moving on," Reece said, laughing nervously. "Why dwell on the past, you know?"

"I didn't know how to tell you," Rose said, the happiness slowly fading out of her face. "But . . . I'm engaged."

Phil took one of her hands in his. "See, that's the thing. I am too."

Rose's face fell. "You are? Still?"

Phil nodded. "Yes. And she's really nice, and incredibly beautiful, and she loves animals."

"So—what are you saying? I don't . . ." Then her eyebrows flew up. "No," she said softly, looking like she was afraid to believe it.

Phil smiled at her, and nodded. "Yes."

"So," she said, sitting up straighter, a smile pulling at her lips. "I'm engaged to some prince."

"How about that," Phil said, his eyes shining. "I'm engaged to a girl named Princess Aurora."

She held out her hand to him. "Princess Aurora."

Phil smiled so wide, it was like it was going to split his face open. He took her hand in his and shook. "Prince Phillip." Then Phil swept her into his arms, and it didn't seem like they were going to be breaking apart anytime soon.

I looked at Reece, who'd already averted his eyes. "Okay, *now* maybe we should go."

Twenty-Eight

The throne room hadn't really changed very much since the last time we'd seen it, back at the christening that kicked this whole thing off. The one difference now was that lots of people were getting off the floor and looking around sleepily, like they were trying to figure out what had just happened.

Reece and I walked in with the fairies, our hands linked and swinging between us. I was still getting used to the fact that we could do this, that it felt so comfortable.

"We need to speak to the king and queen," Flora said, nodding over to the thrones at the front of the room, where I could see King Stefan and Queen Leah were both yawning and blinking as they looked around. "And then we're going to have to move quickly."

"Yes," Merryweather said as she looked down at the wand in her hand. I could see that the glow inside was already a little less bright than it had been only a few minutes ago. "We don't have long."

"But it's going to take us a moment to figure this out," Flora said, giving us a smile. "So you can say your goodbyes." I nodded at that, feeling a lump in my throat as I thought about it.

"Isn't it wonderful?" Fauna asked, her eyes shining. "We did it!"

"*You* did it," I corrected. "The three of you. You're the real heroes of the story."

"I've always thought that," Reece agreed, smiling at them.

The fairies hurried to the thrones, managing not to bicker as they did so. By the entrance, I saw a high-back chair decorated with ornate curlicues. I hung my tote on one of them, and Reece laughed and did the same with his backpack.

"So this is the castle," Reece said as we walked farther in, adopting a real-estate-agent voice.

"I can't believe I'm here," I said, smiling, "Despite all your futile attempts to keep me away."

"How's it measure up?"

"That depends. Can we see the room where the maps are?"

"Now?"

"Of course now! It's—" The rest of my sentence flew out of my head as a guy hurried past me. He was wearing blue leggings and a short gray hooded tunic, the hood pushed back. I turned to Reece. "Wait . . ."

"Oh, right. I meant to tell you. That's one of the stable hands."

I shook my head as understanding dawned, and I thought back to what Reece had been wearing that first day—essentially, an identical outfit. "So you were accidentally copying their uniform?"

Reece laughed. "I was."

"No wonder everyone was trying to tell you to get to the stables." I could see that the king and queen looked more or less awake now, talking to a man sitting next to King Stefan. He was wearing red and had a crown of his own. "Who is that?"

"That's Phil's dad," Reece said.

I met Queen Leah's eye and smiled at her. She gave me a startled look of recognition, followed by a hopeful smile. I nodded and gave her a thumbs-up, just hoping she'd understand the meaning of this and that it wasn't some kind of terrible, obscene gesture here. "So what happens next?" I asked, turning to Reece. "Assuming that everything's on track now."

Reece nodded to the grand staircase in the center of the throne room. "They'll come down that," he said. "And everyone cheers, and then they dance. And that's basically the end of the story."

I nodded. I could feel a kind of peaceful contentment spreading through me. It was the feeling you get when you're approaching the last essay question on a test, or seeing the sign for your exit on the freeway. It was knowing you were almost there, almost home. It was the light at the end of the tunnel.

"Speaking of dancing." I reached up and ran my hands through his hair—not for any real reason, just that I'd been wanting to do that for a while now, and now felt like I could. "When we get back, you could . . . come to the prom with me? If you want," I added quickly. "You're already dressed for it and all." My heart pounded as I asked this, as I suddenly realized that soon, we'd be back in our world together, and I had no idea what things would look like with us when we were home. But we'd survived dragons and mutant bat creatures and Fauna's cooking. I was pretty sure we could get through anything.

Reece smiled at me, then dropped a kiss on the top of my head. He took a breath to speak, but before he could continue, musicians appeared in the upper balconies around the throne room and started playing a fanfare. And a second later, I realized why. Phil and Aurora were walking down the staircase.

As I looked at her, resplendent in her dress, a gold crown on her head, I realized she really was Princess Aurora now. The Rose I'd known was gone. Phil, though, I realized after a second, was still Phil.

They descended the staircase together, and a hush fell over everyone in the throne room. It was impossible to look at them and not see the happiness that seemed to be suffusing both of them. And it was all the more palpable and poignant because these were two people who had each thought they'd lost the other, only to find their way back together in the end. And as they walked down the stairs, you could see it in both their faces: the gratitude and joy in equal measure.

Queen Leah and King Stefan stood up to greet them, both looking nervous. I saw Aurora stop short. She was frowning as she looked at the people she'd only known as her landlords, who were now standing in front of her wearing golden crowns.

Then happiness broke across her face and she ran toward them. And as her parents embraced her, everyone crying, I felt a lump form in my throat.

"That's nice," Reece whispered, and I nodded, squeezing his hand in mine.

"It really is," I said, my voice breaking. I glanced up to see the three fairies watching from an upper balcony, smiling and wiping away happy tears.

After everyone pulled themselves together, the queen had commanded the musicians to play, and the throne room was quickly taken over by waltzing couples.

I looked over and saw, just outside the throne room in the entry hall, the three fairies standing in front of a stretch of wall. They were pointing their wands at it and passing the magic bubble wand between them—and even from a distance, I could tell they were bickering. So clearly, they hadn't solved the issue of how to build us a doorway. I just hoped they'd get there before the magic dissipated.

I was about to point this out to Reece when I was tackle-hugged by a princess. I looked over Aurora's shoulder to see Phil, smiling from ear to ear, giving Reece a more sedate hug.

"Hi!" I yelled, hugging Aurora back.

"Agh!" she yelled, breaking away and grinning at me. "Can you believe any of this?"

"I really can't," I admitted, as I looked at my friend who was now beyond regal and elegant in her gown. I dropped into a curtsy. "Milady."

"Oh, stop that."

"You're going to have to get used to it! You're *literally* wearing a crown."

Aurora gasped as she looked at my outfit. "I love your dress."

"I love *yours*! And the crown. Mind if I borrow it? I'll return it. Eventually. I promise."

Aurora laughed, then looked over at Phil and Reece, who seemed deep in some kind of discussion. "Okay, you and Reece?!" Her voice rose in excitement. "Tell me *everything*."

"I know." I shook my head, not able to keep myself from smiling wide. "I really like him," I whispered.

Aurora waved this away. "I could have told you that a week ago."

"And you and Phil! It's just . . ."

"I know." She nodded toward the king and queen, who were dancing an elegant, swooping dance in the center of the room. "And can you believe that they're my parents? When I was little, I used to wish that they were, and now . . ." She shook her head and smiled at me, happiness practically radiating off her.

"I'm so happy for you."

"Listen," she said, taking my hands in hers. "I know you're planning on going home soon. But . . . what if you didn't?"

I just blinked at her. "What?"

She looked at me beseechingly. "Stay, Stella. I need someone like you here—someone who knows me. Someone I can trust. You can be on my council! My most trusted advisor. We'll have *so* much fun. And you can re-design all the trade routes! What do you say?"

I laughed at that, but then felt my smile falter. "I wish I could," I said, meaning it. As I looked at her, I really felt what our goodbye would mean. It meant I would never see this person—my friend—again. "I really would love it. And you know I could fix all the trade routes! It'd be efficiency city around here."

Aurora laughed. "See? I need you."

I shook my head. "You don't, though. You already have everything you need to be a great princess. Just be yourself. You'll be amazing."

She smiled at me, even as I could see she was disappointed. "You're sure?"

I nodded. As tempting as this was, I knew what I had to do. "I have to get home."

Aurora nodded and gave my arm a squeeze. Her parents waltzed by, smiling at us, and Reece said something that made Phil throw his head back in laughter. "I can understand that you need to go home. Especially because I've just found mine." She shook her head in happy wonderment. "I just don't understand how so many of my dreams are all coming true today."

"Well, it *is* your birthday." That suddenly stopped me. "Wait—I never got you a present."

"You helped Phil fight a dragon. I really don't need anything else."

"No, no," I said, looking around—and just like that, I knew what to do. "Hold on. I'll be right back."

I ran over to the chair where I'd stashed my tote. Through the doorway, I could see the fairies, sparks flying from wands and voices raised. "You guys okay?"

"Nearly there!" Fauna yelled. Merryweather shot me a look that clearly said *no* as she shook her head gravely.

"Well, ready when you are," I called to them as I shouldered my bag.

I waited a moment longer, to see if they would tell me we were on the verge of going, but when it seemed like that wasn't happening, I returned to the throne room and pulled the sweatshirt out of my tote. "Here," I said, holding it out to Aurora. "Happy birthday."

She lifted it up and smiled. "Forget me not."

I nodded, feeling tears prickle the inside of my eyes. "So that you can remember me."

"Always." Aurora gave me a smile that turned wobbly halfway through. "Oh, Stella," she said, her voice cracking.

"I know. Me too." I hugged her tightly, swallowing hard to keep from crying. We stepped apart, Aurora wiping her tears away. Phil and Reece walked over to join us, Phil looking from me to Aurora.

"I guess my fiancée didn't convince you to stay?" He turned to her. "Did you mention the trade routes?"

"I *led* with the trade routes," Aurora said with a sigh. "No luck."

"So I guess this is goodbye?" Phil asked. Over his shoulder, I could see Reece and Aurora hugging.

"Phil," I said, giving him a watery smile. I gave him a hug, and he hugged me back. "Keep up with your wood carving, okay?"

We stepped back, and Phil grinned at me. "Of course I will."

"Come on," Aurora said, taking Phil's hand, "we should dance, otherwise I'm going to have the gates barred so they can't actually leave." Phil took Aurora's hand and spun her away. She raised her hand in a wave to me, her eyes shining with tears, as she and Phil danced away.

"Okay," I said, turning to Reece and wiping under my eyes. "We should go. Are they ready?"

We walked a few steps over to the entrance of the throne room; I could see the fairies clustered around a faintly glowing arch—still bickering, of course. "We're working on it!" Flora yelled, sounding harried.

Reece took my hand and twirled me under his arm. "Dance with me."

I glanced once more at the fairies; they still seemed occupied. Then I smiled at him and let him lead me to the dance floor, and we took our place among the royalty and courtiers all twirling around the floor.

Reece placed his hand on my waist and entwined his fingers with mine. We swayed like that for a moment. I was regretting that we hadn't paid more attention to the dance lessons in the meadow. They would have come in handy right about now—but nobody really seemed to notice we didn't know the steps.

Reece leaned back slightly to look at me. "Stella."

"Reece?"

"Isn't this great?" He spun me out, and then back in again, his face alight with joy. "Usually this is where the story ends, so you don't know what happens afterward. But it turns out ..." He spun me again, and I laughed. "That it just means everyone is happy, and things are working out, and there's a party."

I looked around: at Phil and Aurora, who only had eyes for each other; at the king and queen, waltzing together, looking happy and content; and at Phil's dad, pulling some very impressive dance moves. "It's not bad."

He shook his head. "I don't think I've ever been this happy." I smiled at that, but as I watched, Reece's face went from joyful to serious. "And if that's true ..." His voice trailed off, his expression troubled.

"What?" I asked, as we stopped dancing. "What's wrong?"

"We're ready!" Merryweather was suddenly standing next to us, tugging on my sleeve. She spun herself into tiny-fairy form and zoomed forward, leaving Reece and me to hurry in her wake.

"What is it?" I asked Reece as we crossed out of the throne room and into the entry hall, where I could see an arched doorway had been constructed from what looked like glowing gold thread.

The three fairies were standing in front of it, Fauna holding the bubble wand, and I could see how faint the light was now. "It's time to go," she said.

As I glanced around at the three fairies, I felt my heart squeeze. I wasn't up for this many goodbyes in a row. "Thank you so much for everything. I owe you all so much—"

"It was a joy." It was Fauna who spoke, her voice firm, surprising me. "We loved it."

I took my phone and keys out of my tote and handed the empty bag to Merryweather. "This is for you."

"Really?" Merryweather asked, grinning.

"Take care, dear," Fauna said, dabbing at her eyes.

"We'll miss you," Flora said, her voice shaky.

"Guac your world," Merryweather told me gravely.

"Okay, here we go." I stepped forward—and then realized Reece hadn't moved. "Ready?" I asked him.

He glanced back at the throne room, then looked at me, shaking his head. "I—think I'm going to stay."

I stared at him, trying to make these words make sense. "You— What?"

"Stella, dear," Flora said, her voice worried. "We're running out of time."

"You can't— What do you mean, stay?" I asked Reece, feeling my stomach plunge down to my sneakers.

"This is the happiest I've ever been," he said, shaking his head. "I'm finally getting what I always wanted—to live in a story. There's nothing for me back home. I can have an actual life here."

"But what about your sister? What about your future? What about . . ." I hesitated. *What about me*, I really wanted to say.

"You could stay," he said, taking my other hand in his. "Stay here, with me and Aurora and Phil. It would be so great—a continuation of this whole week. Aurora would probably make you a countess or something if you stayed. And just think . . ." He leaned a little closer to me. "We're in a world where a happily ever after is promised. Everything could go according to plan, for once. What do you say?"

For just a second, I thought about it all—Aurora and Phil and how much fun I'd had, the quiet peace of the mornings here, how this was a really nice castle. And Reece. Getting to stay here, be with him, see everything that this could be . . . but I shook my head.

"I can't," I said. "Because the thing is, you were right. If there are no detours, you don't get the fun surprises. And I'd rather live a life not knowing what's going to happen, not being able to plan for it—because that's when the really great stuff happens. Like . . ." I swallowed hard and made myself go on. "Like you," I said, my voice breaking. "Like us."

Reece looked down at me, his brow furrowed, his eyes wet.

"It's time," Merryweather said, and I saw the glow in the bubble wand was almost gone. "Now or never."

She tugged me forward, but I turned back to Reece, my heart pounding hard. "Please don't do this—or this is it. You can't change your mind. And I'll . . . never see you again."

"I know," he said, his voice cracking. "I'm sorry. But I'm staying."

I pulled him into a hug, and he hugged me back tightly. The kind of hug you give when you know it's the last time you'll get to touch someone.

"We have to do this *now*," Flora said, ushering me toward the doorway they'd built.

Knowing there was nothing else to do, I made myself look away from Reece. I took a shaky breath and stepped forward.

The fairies all raised their wands as one. "Concentrate, Stella," Flora said. "Think about where you came from and want to go back to. . . ."

I closed my eyes, thinking as hard as I could about Nisha, Allyson, Disneyland, Reece—not Reece—and home. . . .

There was a pulse, then a bright flash of light.

And once again, everything went black.

Twenty-Nine

I hit the ground hard, bracing myself with my hands. I turned to see I'd just come through what now just looked like solid wall. I could still see a few tiny lines of glowing gold on it . . . the faint outline of a doorway . . . and then it was gone.

I looked around, trying to orient myself. I could see people everywhere. People with sneakers and strollers and Starbucks cups. People talking self-ies, and eating popcorn, and talking on the phone.

People wearing mouse ears, groups in matching T-shirts. There was music playing, and the faint sound of delighted screams, and the *whoosh* of a roller coaster.

I was in Disneyland. It was now again.

I was back.

I pushed myself up to standing, brushed off my hands, and walked back a step so I was out of the way. I was in the castle passageway, and just seeing this many other people all at once was jarring. I realized, as I took it all in, how used to long dresses and pointy hats and men in boots I'd gotten. Being back to reality—even if it was *my* reality—was throwing me for a loop.

I looked down at the phone in my hand and saw that the date and time were back, along with the bars showing that cell phone networks were now a thing that had been invented. I stared down at the time: 7:26.

I'd just lived a week of my life. I'd experienced highs and lows, love and loss—but not even a minute had passed here. It just didn't seem like it should have been possible.

"Stella?" I looked over to see Nisha and Allyson, both with Starbucks cups and annoyed expressions, walking toward me. "Where have you been? We were waiting—"

"Oh my god, Nisha!" I pulled her into a tight hug. "I missed you so much!"

"Um . . . Okay," she said, extricating herself. "I saw you, like, forty-five minutes ago."

"Allyson!" I gave her a hug as well and then stepped back to look at them. "Oh man, it's *so* good to see you guys!"

"Are you okay?" Allyson raised an eyebrow at me. "Did you get too much sun or something?"

"Wait, what is this dress?" Nisha asked, her eyes going wide. "It's amazing. Where did it come from?"

"Did you get it at the Bibbidi Bobbidi Boutique?" Allyson asked.

"I'm sorry, *what*?" Nisha asked, turning to her girlfriend, looking like she was about to crack up.

"The Bibbidi Bobbidi Boutique," Allyson repeated.

"You can keep saying it, but that doesn't make it make any more sense."

"It's a real place! I took my niece."

Nisha shook her head, then looked at me. "Anyway, now that we've tracked you down, we should get going to the prom, or we're going to miss it. I want to hear all about this dress in the car."

Allyson frowned as she looked around. "Where's Reece?"

"He's not here," I said, trying—and failing—to keep my voice steady. "He . . . he left." I tried but found I couldn't go beyond that, and broke down into sobs. Now that I was here, so thoroughly back, with a solid wall where my doorway had been, I was feeling the truth in a visceral way.

I'd never see Reece again. And all that we had been starting, all that could have been—it was over. Full stop. I took a hitching breath and tried to pull myself together, but the tears were coming faster now, and it felt like someone was squeezing my heart in a vise.

I saw Nisha and Allyson exchange a concerned glance. "Well, it sounds like he just got an Uber or something. It's really okay."

"It's *not*," I sobbed. "It's not okay. He just left me, and—and—"

"Stells," Nisha said, bending down to look at me, her brow furrowed. "Is this about Cooper?"

I stared at her blankly. "Who?"

"Okay," Allyson said, shifting into caring-but-competent-counselor mode. "Let's head to the car, and maybe get something for Stella's blood sugar. We might be having a little bit of a dip, hmm?"

"Here," Nisha said, handing me her iced latte and giving my shoulders a squeeze. "All yours."

I took a shaky breath and wiped my hand across my face, struggling to pull myself together. Though I wasn't sure I needed to; there were at least three other people I could see currently sobbing. True, none of them were over five, but still, I was in good company. "My blood sugar is fine. It's . . . I just . . ." I took a sip of the iced latte; Nisha and I liked them exactly the same way, with oat milk and one pump of vanilla. My eyes widened as I drank it. "Oh wow," I breathed, looking at the cup, at the mermaid I hadn't seen in far too long. "I forgot how good that is!"

"You had one this morning," Nisha said, reminded me. "I was there, remember?"

"Coffee is *so* good!" I enthused, taking another sip. "They don't know what they're missing in the fourteenth century."

"I'm lost," Allyson said.

"Come on, let's get to the prom," Nisha said, starting to steer me through the castle passage and toward Main Street. We'd almost walked all the way through it before I stopped.

"You okay?" Allyson asked, sounding a little bit like she was afraid of my answer.

"I just . . . wanted to give it a last look," I said. Somewhere, in another world, in another time, were Flora, Fauna, Merryweather, Aurora, Phil . . . and Reece. They'd go on, live their lives—and I'd live mine. And they'd never overlap again.

"We'll come back soon," Nisha promised. "Maybe after school gets out? To celebrate being done with finals?"

"I'm going to be here for grad night," Allyson said, sounding smug.

"I'm well aware you get to go to the all-night Disney party," Nisha sighed. "You know I'm still a year away from it, you don't need to rub it in."

"No, I think I really do," Allyson said, as they started to walk away together. "Did I mention that we get to ride the rides all night?"

"I think juniors should be able to do it, too," Nisha grumbled. "Everyone knows junior year is actually harder."

I started to walk after them, but gave the castle one last look. I took in the sight of it in the inky darkness, aglow with magic and possibilities.

"Bye," I whispered softly to it. And then I hurried to catch up with my friends.

The ride to Harbor Cove High was jarring; nothing seemed quite right anymore. The lights were too bright, the cars were going too fast, and my phone kept buzzing and lighting up with notifications. I couldn't see the stars, and I held on to my seat belt tightly the whole ride, wishing Allyson would drive slower, squinting against the headlights that seemed to be blinding me.

I knew that, soon, this would just be my new normal again. I wouldn't think anything of it. But until that happened, I wanted to hang on to the differences. I didn't want to forget. I needed to remember what the last week had been like, and all that had happened.

Allyson parked in the lot behind Harbor Cove High, and while I considered changing into my prom heels, I'd gotten pretty attached to these sneakers. So I left them in the car and just grabbed my prom clutch, wrestling my phone and keys inside it.

We walked inside, Allyson and Nisha holding hands, both of them looking thrilled. Every time Nisha turned back to look at me, I gave her the biggest smile I could muster, but all the while, I was aware of how hollow it was. How much my heart was hurting.

I stepped into the gym. It was crowded, and the dance floor was packed, most of my classmates screaming along to the words of a pop song as they danced under the changing colored lights. I looked around, taking in the decorations—and then stopped short. All around me was the world that I'd just left behind.

There were castles, and dragons, and fairies. Princes on white horses. Golden crowns and princesses dreaming big dreams. I felt my breath catch as I looked at all of it.

"We're going to dance!" Nisha said. She grabbed my hand. "Come join?"

"In a second," I said, giving her a quick smile. She grinned back at me, then ran to join Allyson on the dance floor.

"Well?" I turned and saw Avery standing behind me, her arms folded over her prom dress, looking defensive. "You hate it, right? You can tell me."

"Are you *kidding*?" I threw my hands up for emphasis. It really was a useful gesture, I had to give her that. "It's wonderful!"

"It's— What?" Avery frowned at me. "Is this a trick? Are you being mean?"

"I love it," I assured her. "You were right—it is magical. Really great job."

She narrowed her eyes at me. "What happened to *fairy tales aren't real?*"

I shook my head. "That was a long time ago, Avery."

"It was this afternoon!"

"Well, this afternoon was a long time ago." I shook my head as I looked around at it all. "There's nothing more real than this, I can tell you. I do have one tiny note about the color of the fairies' dresses, but aside from that, it's great. Congratulations." I walked away, leaving the stunned

Avery in my wake as I walked across the dance floor to join Allyson and Nisha.

But when I reached them, I couldn't help from flashing back to another dance floor—everyone whirling around me, Reece spinning me out and then in again, his face aglow with happiness.

And just like that, I knew I wasn't going to be able to stay there and pretend like my heart wasn't breaking. I gestured for Nisha to bend down so that she could hear me above the music. "I'm going to go!"

Nisha's face fell. "No! They haven't even played Band of Brothers yet."

"I know, but I'm just not in the mood. You guys have the best time, okay? I'll call an Uber."

Nisha gave me a look, her face changing from pink to green to purple under the lights. "Okay," she said, finally, nodding. "But promise you'll text me when you get home?"

"Promise," I said. I held out my pinky to her and she smiled and held out hers, and we shook.

"Love you," she said.

"Love you, too. Have fun, okay?"

"I'll try my best!" She grinned at me, then danced back to Allyson.

I walked out of the gym, sure with every step I was taking that I was making the right call. I hadn't even begun to process everything that had happened, and I certainly wasn't going to be able to do that while power ballads played and my classmates broke out their best dance moves.

I pushed out of the front doors of the school and took a deep breath of the cool night air as I walked down the front steps. There weren't a ton of people still arriving; it seemed like most everyone was inside already, just the occasional straggler hurrying up the stairs.

There was a line of limos parked in front of the school. The drivers, clearly waiting for the prom to be over, were standing around or leaning against the hoods of their cars.

Now that I was outside, I felt like I could finally breathe again. As I walked down the steps, I thought about what Avery had said. And whatever I might have believed a week ago, the fact was, I *did* believe in fairy tales now. How could I not, having lived inside one for a week? But it was more than that.

Because the stories were more than I'd known. It wasn't just that Aurora had gotten her prince; she'd also found her family. Phil had found someone who loved him for who he really was, flaws and bad carvings and all.

And even though things had worked out the way that had been promised, all according to plan—from all I had seen, it looked like they *did*, in fact, live happily ever after—it wasn't the ending that mattered. It was what it had taken us all to get there: the fun and hanging out and crushes and fights and misunderstandings and, at last, joy. It really had been the friends we'd made along the way. Even though I never thought I would believe it, the evidence was clear—it *had* actually been about the journey, not the destination.

And just because it hadn't worked out with Reece didn't mean I was going to shut myself off again. I might not have had the happy ending, everything wrapped up in a bow, the handsome guy riding up on the white horse.

But I'd tried. I'd kissed Reece and told him how I felt and had fought for my friends—and also *literally* fought for my friends. I'd faced down dragons, and my own fears.

I'd risked, which meant I'd won. And I wouldn't ever shut myself off again—from life, or love, or believing in what could be.

And I somehow knew, deep down, that I would be fine.

I had just pulled out my phone to call the Uber when I heard the thundering of hoofbeats.

Thirty

looked around, trying to figure out where the sound was coming from. It was a welcoming, familiar sound, even though I didn't understand why I was hearing it here and now.

But then a second later, I had my answer.

Reece was riding through the night, galloping toward me on a white horse.

He was wearing his gray suit, his hair blowing in the wind, and Delilah was looking as regal as she ever had.

I stared, my heart pounding hard, half convinced I was hallucinating—just seeing what I wanted to see. Because this wasn't real. It *couldn't* be. . . .

"Stella!" Reece yelled.

"Is that a horse?" a limo driver asked, sounding freaked out. "Like a real one?"

"Reece!" I ran down to him as he jumped off Delilah's back and handed the reins to a very startled-looking limo driver. We reached each other at the bottom step, both of us talking at the same time, overlapping with each other. "How did you get here? I don't—"

"I'm so sorry," he said. "I can't believe I was going to stay without you. I don't know what I was thinking—"

"But how is this possible?" I asked. "I thought . . . the fairies said . . ."

"I know," he said. "But when I told them that I needed to get to you—needed it more than anything—they were able to make it happen."

For just a moment, I flashed back to what my mother had said, all those years ago—that when the need to get from place to place is great enough, no matter what obstacles are there . . . you find a way. I hadn't realized that would cover things like magic and interdimensional travel, but I was thrilled to find that it did.

"You're really here," I said, touching his arm, his cheek, just to be sure.

"I am. And I'm not going anywhere." He shook his head. "It was after you left that I realized I'd gotten it all wrong. It's not the story you're in, it's who you're in the story *with* that matters."

I smiled up at him, feeling my heart beat a happy, excited rhythm. "But we don't know what happens now," I pointed out, feeling a little thrill in the words as I said them. "The fairy tale is over."

"No," Reece said, his voice soft. He took a step closer to me, holding my eyes with his. "I think it's just beginning."

He touched my cheek gently, and I smiled at him. And as the power ballads played back in the gym, and Delilah whinnied happily, I took a step closer to him and felt my heart swell with happiness—for everything that we'd been through. And for everything that was coming. No plans in sight, the wonderful, messy, unknown future of it all.

With this thought in my mind, and Reece smiling down at me, I stretched up and he swept me into his arms, and we kissed.

And it was *magical*.

The End

. . . *or is it?*

The troubadour took in the size of the assembled crowd and plucked at one of his strings, making sure that it was in tune. He was pleased as he noted just how many people had gathered in the castle courtyard to hear him play. He knew for certain that it was because of the new song, the one that the bards had been singing all over the city. It was filled with nonsense words and strange syllables, but that had only seemed to increase its popularity. And he had been the first one to sing it, and he had the best rendition—hence, the crowd.

He looked up and smiled. Then he took a breath, and began to sing.

"Oh baby, baby. You drive my car like you drive my heart: wild . . ."

The crowd cheered, and by the time the second verse started, everyone was singing along.

One month after the prom

Hi!" I said, leaning over to look at the screen of Reece's phone. "Hey, Gabi!"

The purple-haired third-grader grinned back at me. "Hey, Stella," she said. "Can you please ask my brother to show me something interesting?"

"What!" Reece said, moving his phone away from me, looking insulted. "How was Main Street not interesting? I thought you'd like talking to the Dapper Dans and hearing about the history of barbershop quartets!"

"I've got this." I took Reece's phone from him and changed the focus to Sleeping Beauty Castle. "Better?"

Gabi nodded, her eyes wide. "So cool," she breathed.

I raised an eyebrow at Reece, who just shook his head. It was our first time back at Disneyland, and since Reece couldn't bring his sister along in person, he wanted to make sure to bring her virtually.

"You'll see it for yourself when you come in August," Reece promised her, putting his arm around my shoulders and leaning over to talk into his phone.

"And I want to see your horse," Gabi said. "Even though I still don't understand how you have a *horse*."

"We can go to the barn and visit her," Reece assured his sister.

"Why does she live at the barn?"

"Well, she's not going to fit into the apartment," Reece said with a laugh, and I handed him back his phone. "And I told you, the owners let me keep her there in exchange for giving riding lessons."

"But how are *you* qualified to give riding lessons?" Gabi sputtered.

Reece glanced at me and smiled. "Oh you know," he said with a shrug. "You move to one of these fancy California towns, you pick things up."

Reece talked to Gabi for a few more minutes before she had to go, then hung up and put the phone in his back pocket. "Hey," he said, taking my hand in his.

"Hi," I said, stretching up to give him a kiss. When we broke apart, I squeezed his hand. "So what's the plan?"

He gave me a look. "Don't pretend you're asking *me* the plan. I know you have a spreadsheet."

I laughed, busted. "Not an actual one," I protested. "Just, like, a mental idea of potential things we might want to do, but it's flexible. Ish." Reece shook his head and we started walking through the castle passageway together, our hands swinging between us. "So I was thinking we might want to hit the Avengers compound before it gets too hot—"

Before I could finish my sentence, the ground trembled underneath my feet. I stumbled, and fell. Reece reached down for me. "You okay?"

I nodded, getting up to my feet. "Yeah. I just . . ."

I tried to see what had happened but could only see a cloud of dust—and a shimmering golden outline in what had, seconds ago, been a solid wall. A moment later, the outline disappeared, and it was back to being a wall again. I coughed as I squinted through the dust that was settling—and then felt my eyes widen.

I couldn't see clearly who was in front of me, but I'd seen enough—a jaunty hat, a flash of blond hair—to be pretty sure.

I squeezed Reece's hand as I waited for the dust to settle . . . and for a new story to begin.

Acknowledgments

First of all, I must gratefully acknowledge my wonderful editor, Brittany Rubiano. Thanks so much for being such a joy to work with and making the process so fun. Here's to more Disneyland brainstorm sessions! Thank you to Emily Van Beek and the whole team at Folio. Thanks to Kieran Viola, Christine Collins, Sara Liebling, Guy Cunningham, David Jaffe, Dan Kaufman, Matt Schweitzer, Holly Nagel, Danielle DiMartino, Dina Sherman, Bekka Mills, Maddie Hughes, Ann Day, Crystal McCoy, Andrea Rosen, Monique Diman, Michael Freeman, Amanda Marie Schlesier, Mili Nguyen, Kim Knueppel, Vicki Korlishin, Meredith Lisbin, Loren Godfrey, Jerry Gonzalez, and everyone at Disney-Hyperion. Thank you to art director Marci Senders and artist Isadora Zeferino for the amazing cover.

Thanks to Diya for the spark that lit the idea that fanned the flame that led to the book. Thanks to Sarah and Derick, my cul-de-sac buds. I'm so grateful to the whole Wednesday Writing crew—Anna, Jen, Julie, Lauren, Maux, Rebecca, Robin, Sarah, Siobhan—and especially Adele. Finally, thank you to Mom, Jason, Katie—and, of course, thanks to Murphy.